DESERT CITY DIVA

DESERT CITY DIVA

Corey Lynn Fayman

Severn House Large Print
London & New York

This first large print edition published 2017
in Great Britain and the USA by
SEVERN HOUSE PUBLISHERS LTD of
19 Cedar Road, Sutton, Surrey, England, SM2 5DA.
First world regular print edition published 2015 by
Severn House Publishers Ltd.

British Library Cataloguing in Publication Data
A CIP catalogue record for this title is available from the British Library.

ISBN-13: 9780727895523

Severn House Publishers support the Forest Stewardship Council™
[FSC™], the leading international forest certification organisation. All
our titles that are printed on FSC certified paper carry the FSC logo.

MIX
Paper from
responsible sources
FSC
www.fsc.org   FSC® C013056

Typeset by Palimpsest Book Production Ltd.,
Falkirk, Stirlingshire, Scotland.
Printed and bound in Great Britain by
T J International, Padstow, Cornwall.

*To Maria, for the roads we've travelled,
and the solitudes shared.*

One
The Bite

It was a bad idea to go out for Mexican food at 2:30 in the morning, but that hadn't prevented Rolly Waters from stopping by the Villa Cantina for a plate of machaca after his gig. It wasn't the machaca that was going to kill him, though. It was the bite on his leg. It was a whole string of bad ideas that had brought him to this wretched state, on the nauseous edge of mortality. Bad ideas, bad decisions, bad choices – whatever you wanted to call them – each one had inexorably led to the next. And each had led to this moment, as he barfed his guts out in the emergency room at the hospital. He didn't even know the name of the hospital. He didn't know the name of the town it was in. He only knew that he'd never felt this sick. He knew he was going to die.

Medical personnel dressed in grubby green scrubs gathered around him, thwarting his passage into oblivion, perhaps hastening it. One of them jabbed his left arm with a needle. Another wrapped his right arm in a blood pressure cuff. They pulled his pants off and inspected his ankle as the vital signs monitor beeped in his ear. His left leg felt like burning coals had been inserted under his skin. A woman made him swallow two pills. She gave him a shot glass

1

of liquid that smelled like rotten eggs. Stomach acid swirled up in his throat. The doctors and nurses floated on a bilious green cloud. He lifted his head and leaned over the bucket. His stomach heaved but nothing came up. He closed his eyes and lay back on the bed. The air smelled like old fish. He surrendered to the vivid manifestations of an unsettled sleep.

Poisson. It was the French word for fish. One letter different from poison. There were no fish in the desert. There was no water. The aliens drank gold in their water. The people drank poison. The people couldn't breathe. They gasped for air like fish in the living room.

He opened his eyes. The harsh light of the emergency room glowed with a creeping softness. A nurse came by and gave him two more pills. He laughed. Valium always made him loopy like this. If he was going to die, he would be defiant in death, laughing his way into the great darkness. There were worse ways to go. He would die laughing, with a smile on his face. Out of his mind. Definitely Valium. Over and out.

The man had a gift for him. The man was a bird. The bird sang a song. The song had gold notes. The girl had gold eyes.

He awoke. There was no one around. He watched with dull fascination as the blood pressure cuff on his right arm inflated again. It was going to blow up in his face. As it was about to crush his arm into fractured bits of bone gravel, the cuff exhaled and collapsed. He turned his head on the pillow and looked up at the ceiling.

2

The tiles in the ceiling were damaged. Crumpled and stained. His left leg still burned, but less so than before. His stomach seemed steadier.

A nurse appeared next to him, acting like she wanted to take his temperature. He opened his mouth and took the plastic tip under his tongue. She checked the number, nodded and removed the thermometer.

'Coming down,' she said. She looked at the display on the blood pressure monitor. 'Blood pressure's down too.'

'I'm not gun' die?' Rolly said, nodding his head in affirmation.

'No. Doesn't look like you're going to die today,' the nurse said. She smiled at him. 'Of course, we'll need the doctor to confirm that. He's the one that gets to decide.'

The nurse was cute. Real cute. Macy Starr was cute, too. In a different way.

'How's your leg feeling?' the nurse asked.

'Bedder,' said Rolly. His mouth felt like it had been blasted with fine sand.

'Good. I'll check back in a little bit. It's going to be a couple more hours, to make sure you get down to normal.'

'Where am I?'

'Brawley General Hospital. Do you remember checking in?'

'I remember driving in a rocket ship. There were some blue lights. It smelled like fish.'

'That's Brawley, all right. It's the fertilizer that smells. I don't know what the rocket ship part's about.'

'Something bit me.'

3

'A black widow spider. Probably not a good idea to go tramping around barefoot in Slab City like your friends said you were doing.'

'My friends? Are they here?'

'I can check if you want. Do you feel ready to see people?'

'In a little while,' Rolly said, feeling sleepy again. The nurse closed the curtains and left. He lay back on the pillow.

He was sitting in a rowboat on a sandy hill. His father was there. They were in the same boat. His father shouted at him, giving orders. His father handed him a ukulele. He said there was a bomb in the boat. His father saluted, then jumped out of the boat and swam away.

Rolly opened his eyes. He remembered where he was. The Brawley General emergency ward was quieter now, last night's hubbub reduced to a muted hum. He wondered if the staff had forgotten about him and closed the place down, gone to lunch, or breakfast, or whatever meal it was time for.

The monitoring equipment they'd hooked him up to continued to beep at regular intervals, but it seemed less alarming now. The swelling in his leg had gone down, along with the pain. He felt almost normal. He felt ready to check out. That didn't count for much. He knew how it went in the emergency ward. Like Zeno's arrow, each minute got longer the closer you got to being discharged. He lay back on the bed, stared at the crumpled, stained tiles in the ceiling.

Three days ago, he'd gone out for Mexican food at 2:30 in the morning. That's when he'd

4

met Macy Starr, at the Villa Cantina. If he'd gone home right after his gig, or just gone to the grocery store, he would never have taken her case. He wouldn't be lying in the hospital in the rotten fish city of Brawley with a black widow spider bite on his ankle. Things would get complicated with Macy now, accounting his hours, parsing them into the personal and the professional. Last night they'd had sex in the Tioga. The spider bite was a message. The message said he was an idiot.

Macy Starr had golden eyes.

Two
The DJ

Macy Starr had golden eyes. She had strawberry-blonde hair. It hung down in dreadlocks that surrounded her tan, freckled face like a halo of soggy breadsticks. At this moment, she was drenched in sweat, the kind of sweat that pours off your body when you work a room with bright spotlights and poor ventilation. It was nightclub sweat, an affidavit of her vocation, and Rolly's, the sweat that blooms off the bodies of musicians, strippers and stand-up comedians. No amount of antiperspirant or hygienic preparation would hold it back.

Macy was a dance club DJ, cranking out beats until the early hours of morning. She'd just

5

finished her gig at the club adjoining the Villa Cantina restaurant in downtown San Diego. Rolly had stopped in at the cantina after his own gig that night, bending guitar strings at Patrick's Pub six blocks away. Under normal conditions, an old-school guitar player like himself and a young beatmaker like Macy would have little to say to each other. They would not have crossed paths. Vera, the hostess, had introduced them. Macy needed help. She needed advice, the kind only a guitar-playing private detective could provide.

Macy had tattoos all over her thin muscular arms – geometric marks and mythical creatures, symbols of something. Rolly had no idea what. She was a small woman with the nervous energy of a flycatcher. Her eyes were amazing. They sparkled with bright flecks of gold that seemed to illuminate the dim light of the back corner booth. A bead of sweat dripped down Macy's neck and fell into her lovely jugular notch. She was at least twenty years younger than Rolly.

'Not much to look at down there,' she said, interrupting his gaze.

'Your shirt is, uh . . . kind of unusual,' said Rolly, raising his eyes from Macy's chest.

'You like Stoner Mickey?' she said, looking down at the front of her tank top, a rainbow-eyed Mickey Mouse wearing headphones and smoking a king-sized joint.

'I assume that's not officially licensed?' said Rolly.

'It's a one-off. I made it myself. Disney's

lawyers would tear this off my body in copyright-induced rage if they ever saw it. They're hardcore about branding. That's what I heard anyway. What do you think?'

'About Disney?'

'No, dumbass. About that guitar thing. You ever seen anything like it?'

The guitar thing in question wasn't really a guitar. It was a one-stringed instrument propped up on the booth in between them. It was well made, with a finely finished wood body, a gold-plated tuning peg and a vintage single-coil pickup. You could make some noise with it, but it lacked the refinements and playability of a real guitar.

'I'd call it a diddley bow,' said Rolly.

'Diddley what?'

'Diddley bow. They started in the South. Sharecroppers would attach a piece of wood to their house, drive in a couple of nails and stretch a wire between them so they could thump on it. Kind of a poor man's guitar. Homemade. Not usually this nice.'

'What about on the back?' said Macy.

Rolly grabbed the diddley bow and inspected the back. A photograph had been laminated on to it, a black-and-white photograph of a teenage girl and a young man in a baseball uniform. The man had his arm around the girl. Both of them were smiling. There were palm trees in the background. Their smiles looked genuine.

'You think this is your aunt?' Rolly said.

'I guess so. Daddy Joe called her Aunt Betty.'

'Who's Daddy Joe?'

'I'll get to that.'

7

'You don't know Aunt Betty's last name?'

'Not unless it was Harper. That's Daddy Joe's name.'

'And you think it was Daddy Joe that left this here for you?'

'Vera said the guy who left it was a big Indian.'

'The woman in this photo doesn't look Indian.'

'Because she's black?'

'Well, she does look more African-American than Indian, don't you think?'

'You're an expert on racial distinctions?'

'No. I just . . . Are you . . . Native American?'

'No. Not now that there's money on the line.'

'What's that?'

'Nothing. I don't care. I got out of that damn place. I don't need their money.'

'What money?'

'They built a casino. If you're part of the tribe, you get a share of the money. I ain't on that list.'

'Oh.'

'Yeah. DNA.'

'You mean your genes? They check your DNA?'

Macy pointed at three letters tattooed between her jugular notch and her left breast.

'This DNA stands for Do Not Ask,' she said. 'Get used to me saying it.'

Rolly nodded. 'OK,' he said. 'But I'm an investigator. I have to ask questions.'

'It's my personal credo,' said Macy. 'Do not ask. DNA. Just do what you want to do. But if I say DNA to you, that means I want you to shut up.'

'What about Daddy Joe?' Rolly said. 'Can I ask you about him?'

Macy stared at Rolly for a moment. He stared back. She broke first.

'OK, just give me a second,' she said, looking away. 'You can fantasize about what my little tits might look like or whatever else you want to think about this crazy bitch you just met. But don't ask me anything else until I say it's OK.'

Rolly nodded. He tried not to picture what enticements lay under Macy's shirt, but it was like trying not to think about pink elephants once somebody had mentioned them. He scraped at his plate, but there was nothing left worth eating. The refried beans had gone cold. He looked around the room. The cantina was busy. Staying open after last call had been good for business. At three in the morning, it became a refuge for the after-hours crowd with no place to go, for the leftovers who needed sustenance, a greasy ballast to diminish the hangovers they'd be nursing the next day.

'OK,' said Macy. 'I'm ready.'

Rolly nodded. He liked Macy. He liked her directness.

'So here's the deal,' she began. 'I was adopted. I think. Nobody ever explained a damn thing to me and I never cared much, I guess. You could say I've got some parental issues, if you wanna go all Doctor Phil on me. Anyway, I grew up on the Jincona Indian reservation. It's out east, in BF Egypt.'

'My band's playing at their casino tomorrow.'

'Yeah, great, whatever. Daddy Joe Harper and

9

his wife were the ones that took care of me, until Mama Joe died. Then Kinnie took care of me. She's Daddy Joe's real daughter. Kinnie never liked me much. I don't blame her. Aunt Betty was there, for a little while, when I was a baby. To tell you the truth, I'm not sure I'd remember her if it wasn't for that picture there. Daddy Joe kept that diddley bow thing in his closet. He'd bring it out sometimes and tell me about Aunt Betty.'

'What'd he say?' said Rolly.

'DNA.'

'Sorry.'

'No questions right now. Not while I'm trying to get through this.'

Rolly nodded. Macy fingered the gold charm that hung from her neck. The charm was shaped like a tube. There was some sort of inscription on it.

'Anyway,' Macy continued, 'Daddy Joe always used to show me that photograph. He'd say "This is your Aunt Betty. She brought you to our house. She brought you here. We never want to forget her." He'd tell me that, and then one day I asked him, you know, "What happened to Aunt Betty? Where did she go?"'

Macy paused. Rolly waited. DNA.

'He said she went to be with her friends,' Macy said. 'That her friends had all gone away, so she felt lonely and sad. He said she took a walk in the stars.'

Rolly nodded again. 'Is it OK if I ask another question now?' he said.

'Yeah. I guess. If you can make anything out of all that.'

10

'Do you know who your birth mother was?'

'I knew you were going to ask me that. Seems like the obvious thing, doesn't it?'

'That Aunt Betty's your mother?'

'Yeah.'

'You think this baseball player might be your father?'

'That makes as much sense as you being my father. Less, even.'

'What do you mean?'

'Look at me. I've got lighter skin than either of them, and freckles. This blonde, kinky hair? There's no coloring. It's my natural hair. I mean, it wouldn't make sense, heredity-wise, if they were both my parents, right?'

'Yeah. I guess. I don't really know how that stuff works.'

'I did some reading. I'm a mutt, not a purebreed.'

'We're all mutts, in one way or the other.'

'What's your background?'

'Norwegian on my mom's side. My dad's more Scotch Irish.'

'Yeah, well, some of us are more mutty than others,' said Macy. She lifted her eyelids and stared at Rolly again. 'You ever seen anybody with eyes like these?'

'No,' said Rolly. 'I can't say I have.'

'Wolf Girl,' she said. 'That's what the kids on the rez used to call me. Because of my eyes. That and because I ran around in the hills by myself all the time.'

Rolly considered several things he could say about Macy's eyes but none of them seemed

11

appropriate; nothing a portly, fortyish man could say to a woman her age without sounding desperate or foolish. He resisted the temptation. The reservation kids had it right, though. There was something like wolf light in Macy's eyes, a fierceness in her that stirred something inside him. He needed to stop it from stirring. He needed to keep his professional pants on.

'When was the last time you saw Daddy Joe?'

'Five years ago.'

'Have you talked to him?'

'Not since I left. There were some issues. We weren't really on speaking terms when I left.'

'What happened?'

'Just the usual teenager stuff. I had to get out of that place. DNA.'

'OK. You're sure it was him, though, that brought the diddley bow tonight?'

'I'm just going on what Vera said. A big guy. Older. Looked Indian. Daddy Joe's big, enough that you notice it. He used to be chief of tribal police.'

'Your Daddy Joe was a cop?'

'I wouldn't call the tribals real cops.'

'You don't get along with them, either?'

'DNA,' said Macy. 'Anyway, it must be something important, this diddley bow thing. I don't see Daddy Joe driving all the way down from the rez to give it to me otherwise.'

'Maybe you should call him tomorrow.'

'Can't go there. Too complicated. How is it with your dad?'

'My dad?'

'Yeah. How well do you get along with your dad?'

Rolly smiled. 'DNA,' he said.

Macy laughed. 'That bad, huh, Waters?'

Rolly nodded.

'Yeah, I get it,' said Macy. 'Thing is, I can't figure out how Daddy Joe found me here. He's retired. He just sits up there on the rez all the time, in his house, going over his old files.'

'Maybe he saw your name in the paper or something.'

Macy reached in her back pocket, pulled out a postcard-sized piece of paper and passed it to Rolly. 'That's my flyer,' she said. 'I post those around town.'

'DJ Crazy Macy?' said Rolly, reading the flyer. It had a photo of Macy, her dirty-blonde dread-locks spread around her head, backlit into a luminescent corona.

'That's my stage name,' she said. 'One of 'em. Dubstep Blonde, Dizzy Gold Negra. It depends on what kind of mixes I'm playing. This weekend I'm Crazy Macy.'

Rolly resisted the impulse to make a smart remark. Macy looked like she expected one.

'You want to know about my necklace?' she said.

'Hmm?'

'You didn't notice it, did you?'

'Sure I noticed. It's gold, right?'

'Uh, yeah. And?'

'It's a tube. Looks like there's an engraving.'

'You know, Vera told me you were this hot shit detective guy, but I'm starting to wonder if she's smoked too many jalapeños.'

13

'It's late and I'm tired. I'll give you my card. We can talk tomorrow.'

'You still haven't noticed? Look at the damn picture again.'

Rolly looked at the photo on the back of the diddley bow. He noticed this time. He looked back at Macy. 'Aunt Betty's got the same necklace, hasn't she?'

'That's what it looks like to me.'

Macy undid her choker. She passed it to Rolly. 'Read it,' she said.

Rolly squinted his eyes. 'Eight, three . . .'

'Eight, three, six, eight, nine, two, nine, five, four,' said Macy, completing the number for him.

'What does that mean?'

'No idea,' said Macy.

Rolly flipped the gold tube around to look at the other side.

'The same numbers are on both sides,' said Macy. 'That's all there is.'

'Maybe it's a date?' he said.

'I thought that at first,' said Macy. 'But it doesn't make any sense as a date.'

Rolly tried several permutations of the number. He had to admit the date idea made no sense at all. It wasn't a phone number either; it was missing a digit.

'How long have you had this?' he asked.

'A little more than five years,' Macy said. 'Daddy Joe said it was mine.'

'He gave this to you?'

'He said he was going to. When I was of age.'

'Does he know what the number means?'

'I guess he might.'

'Don't you think you should ask him?'

'Like I said, me and Daddy Joe have some issues. He said he was going to give the necklace to me when I turned legal. Eighteen. He would have, I guess.'

'What's that mean? You guess?'

'I left the rez before I turned eighteen. I ran away. I took the necklace.'

'You mean you stole it?'

'Yeah, that's right, Waters. I stole it. I lived in the police chief's house and I stole his twenty-four-karat gold necklace.'

Three
The Hospital

Alicia Waters sat in the waiting room at Mercy Hospital wearing a rumpled green sweatsuit. Her blonde wig was askew. Long streaks of black mascara ran from her eyes. Her pretty pink face looked puffy and red. It was the first time Rolly had seen his stepmom looking less than impeccable. She was usually a chubby bundle of smiling enthusiasm and spotless cosmetics, always tidy, bright-eyed and more than presentable for a night out at the officer's club. But Alicia hadn't had time to pick out an outfit or touch up her makeup after her husband, Rolly's father, had collapsed in their driveway, turning blue and clutching his chest.

'It's that damn Tioga,' she said, wiping her eyes.

'What's a Tioga?' said Rolly.

'He bought a mobile home. I never really liked the idea, but he got so excited about it. He even stopped drinking. Well, he was drinking less – you know, not like he does sometimes.'

'I'm sure that was nice,' said Rolly's real mother, Judith, who sat next to Alicia, providing Kleenex and sympathy. 'Did you have a trip planned?'

'Oh, I couldn't keep up with it. He kept coming up with new places,' said Alicia. 'First it was a week, then a month.' She shuddered. 'I mean, can you imagine me spending a whole month cooped up in that hideous thing?'

'You were leaving soon?'

'Next week,' said Alicia, dabbing at her eyes with the tissue Rolly's mother had provided.

'I guess that trip's off,' said Rolly. His mother glared at him.

'I went along with it,' said Alicia. 'I mean, I thought it would be nice to go somewhere – perhaps a long weekend to try out the whole thing. One of those nice campgrounds where there's lots of people to meet. I thought that would be enough, that maybe he'd get over it. He kept saying he wanted to see the country, like it used to be. To get out in nature or something.'

Alicia shuddered and blew her nose.

'Ugh,' she said, though it was unclear if she was referring to nature in general or the soggy tissue she clutched in her hand. Rolly's mother handed her another Kleenex.

16

'What happened?' said Rolly.

'He was working on the damn thing this morning. Early. Changing the oil or something, I don't know. He had these big wrenches. I went out to bring him some coffee. I knew something was wrong. His face was all purple. I made him sit down. I feel so guilty.'

'It's not your fault,' said Rolly.

'He was trying to fix it up nice for me so I'd be happy. He knew I didn't like it, the whole idea. We bought it used, you see. It needed some work. He spent a lot of time out there. It was too much for someone his age. I wish they'd tell us something.'

Rolly's mother looked over at him. 'Why don't you check again, dear,' she said. 'See if they've got any news.'

Rolly nodded. He turned and walked to the check-in station.

'Yes, sir,' said the clerk, without looking up. 'Can I help you?'

'I wanted to know if there's any news on my father. Dean Waters.'

'A doctor or nurse will come out to see you when he's ready.'

'He had a heart attack.'

The clerk nodded. 'Let me check his status,' she said. She tapped a few times on the computer then looked up at Rolly.

'He's still listed in resuscitation,' she said.

'What does that mean?'

'That's the most recent entry. He may have been moved by now, but there's no update.'

'When will we know something?'

17

'I'm sorry. I'm not able tell you that, sir. A doctor or nurse will speak to you when they're able to provide an update.'

'Thank you.' Rolly nodded. He walked back to his mother and Alicia.

'No news is good news, I guess,' he said. Alicia began crying again. Rolly's mother shot him an exasperated glance.

'Rolly,' she said, 'why don't you see if you can find the cafeteria, maybe bring something back for the rest of us?'

'I couldn't eat a thing,' said Alicia.

'Maybe some juice,' said Rolly's mother. 'You need to have something.'

Rolly's mother shot another glance at him. He didn't argue. He doubted they would know anything soon. An emergency room nurse he had dated told him the secret once. Take any time estimate given by the ER staff and multiply it by four. If someone said you'd be out in thirty minutes, it would be two hours. If they told you an hour, it would probably take four. It was the painstaking sluggishness at the heart of the beast. He'd been in enough emergency rooms to confirm it. He walked back to the check-in station. The clerk gave him directions to the cafeteria.

He went through the swinging doors and out of the ward, spotted an empty chair and slumped into it. His body felt heavy, weighed down with conflicted feelings. He hated his father for having a heart attack. He hated his father for being a drunk, for the way his father had treated his mother, but mostly he hated his father for being

18

an arrogant son-of-a-bitch who was going to die without apologies. His father was an alcoholic bastard who'd never given Rolly anything, beyond a predilection for bottled spirits.

Rolly knew it was stupid to feel this way, like he'd been cheated. He was partly to blame. He'd kept his distance, never speaking his mind, reluctant to face his father straight on. Dean Waters had captained two naval warships, a wife and a son. He'd always been the man who gave orders, until the U.S. Navy demoted him and took away his command, until his wife and son abandoned their home. The old sailor had always worked too hard, too intensely. He'd always drunk too much, too, but he'd never learned to listen to anyone. He never cared what anyone said. Now he'd pressed his second wife into first-mate status for a landlocked cruise she never wanted to take, a low-rent re-enactment of his glory days on the high seas. Except this time they'd be making ports of call in a crummy old Tioga, docking in trailer parks.

Rolly rubbed his chest, confounded by the pain. His own heart would get him someday if he didn't start eating better. Other vices hadn't managed to do him in yet. Alcohol. Drugs. Angry husbands of women who didn't wear wedding rings. Car accidents. All had come close. He stood up and stretched. He wasn't dead yet. And neither was his father, as far as he knew. He walked down the hall and followed the signs.

The cafeteria was quiet when he arrived. The lunch hour had passed. He picked up an apple and a banana for his mother and a bottle of orange

19

juice for Alicia. He paid the cashier, walked into the dining room and placed the tray with the large blueberry muffin and a cup of coffee he'd bought for himself on a table in the corner. He sat down and tried the muffin. It tasted like lemonized chemicals. The coffee hit his gut like pure acid. He finished both items anyway. He didn't want to go back to the emergency room.

He thought about Macy Starr, the woman he'd met the night before at the cantina. She'd agreed to let him borrow the diddley bow, the one-string guitar, so he could do some research. The diddley bow intrigued him – the quality of the work that had been put into something that was usually a rustic homemade instrument. He wanted to take it by Norwood's guitar shop if he got a chance, find out if Rob had seen one like it, if he could tell him anything about it.

He hadn't mentioned it to Macy, but he'd recognized the baseball player in the photograph laminated onto the back. He'd never seen the player in a minor-league uniform before, so he needed to be sure. He pulled his phone out of his pocket, searched through the directory and tapped on a name. There was a picture on the wall, drawn with crayons, of a hospital building with flowers and stick-figure children dancing around it.

'Hey,' said Max Gemeinhardt, answering the phone.

'Hey,' said Rolly. 'I've got a trivia question for you. Baseball. The hometown team.'

'Shoot,' said Max. Max was a baseball encyclopedia. You couldn't stump him.

'Eric Ozzie,' said Rolly. 'Did he play in the minors?'

'Of course he did. Wenfield's the only local guy who skipped the minors. Well, there was Naly and the first Dale Roberts, but neither of them stayed around long. And they both got sent down at some point.'

'Where'd he play? Ozzie, I mean. Did he ever suit up for a team called the Coconuts?'

'Sure. Hawaii. That was our Triple-A team back then. They're gone now. Why'd you want to know?'

'I've got a photo of him, in his Coconuts uniform. I think it's him, anyway.'

'Well, if it looks like him it probably is.'

'He looks pretty young.'

'Just out of high school, I imagine. He got called up halfway through his second year.'

'How long ago was that?'

'Geez, let me think. Not so good with dates anymore. I guess it'd be about twenty years ago, give or take.'

'The Sneaker.'

'He hates that nickname, you know.'

'Yeah. I'm sure that's why he based his whole business model around it.'

'The man's not stupid. The branding was there. So what's this photo you've got?'

'A client gave it to me. She's trying to identify a girl who's standing next to him. Ozzie's in his baseball uniform with his arm around the girl. It looks like it's after a game or something. My client doesn't know that it's him.'

'How old is the girl in the photograph?'

'I don't know. Fourteen, fifteen, sixteen.'

'You didn't tell your client it was Ozzie?'

'No.'

'You want to talk to him?'

'Well, it seems like that might be the easiest way to find out who the girl is.'

'If he remembers.'

'Yeah. If he remembers.'

'That's a long time ago.'

'My client says she was adopted.'

'This isn't some kind of paternity thing, is it?'

'My client's about the right age, but I don't think so. She seems more interested in the girl who's with Ozzie. She says it's her aunt but it might be her mother. That's what she's trying to find out.'

'Sounds a little squeegee to me.'

'That's why I didn't tell her who he was. I wanted to be sure.'

'You did the right thing. You want me to call him?'

'Hmm?'

'I did some legal work for Ozzie a few years back. It was a medical thing. That quack doctor who prescribed the painkillers for him. We settled with the insurance guys, out of court.'

'So Ozzie owes you one?'

'Not really. I got my share of the money. It was a pretty good settlement, though. Helped him finance that first restaurant. He'll take a call from me.'

'Well,' said Rolly, 'if I try to call him I'll have to go through the front office and leave a dozen messages before he calls me back. You know how that is.'

'Let me call him. I'll get back to you.'

'Thanks.'

'Glad to do it. How's your mom?'

'She's OK.'

'Something wrong?'

Rolly looked at the picture on the wall again. Children and flowers – simple shapes drawn in crayon colors.

'I'm at the hospital. My dad had a heart attack.'

'Oh, man, sorry to hear that.'

'We're all here. At Mercy. Mom and Alicia and me. In the ER.'

Max didn't say anything for a moment. Neither did Rolly.

'Well,' said Max, 'I'd offer to come down, but it sounds like you got enough on your hands.'

'Yeah. Alicia's a mess. Mom's getting agitated.'

'And you're in the middle. As usual. You gonna be OK?'

'I don't know. It's mostly just weird right now. I guess I'm OK.'

'Well, I hope your dad pulls through. Give me a call if you need anything. I can find a way to distract your mother if you need some time to yourself.'

'Yeah. Call me if you hear something from Ozzie.'

'I will. Talk to you later.'

Rolly hung up. He checked the time on his phone. Moogus was picking him up around five. They were carpooling to tonight's gig, at the casino on the Jincona Reservation where Macy grew up. It was a longer drive than usual, through the winding roads of the East County mountains.

23

He put the phone back in his pocket. He had hoped to get down to Norwood's today with the diddley bow. Depending on how things went with his father, he might still have a couple of hours. He picked up the apple, the banana and the bottle of orange juice, and headed back to the emergency ward.

Four
The Shop

Rob Norwood stood hunched over the back counter, looking at his laptop computer when Rolly entered the store on Tenth Avenue, a few blocks from the Villa Cantina. Rolly referred to the shop as Norwood's Mostly, as did most of his guitar-playing associates, but the official name for the place was Mostly Guitars. It was a miracle the shop still existed in its present location. Most of the neighborhood had been overtaken by high-rise condominiums and fancy coffee shops. Norwood's worn-down one-story anachronism blighted the block, but Rob remained stubborn in his devotion to staying there. He didn't pay rent. His moneyed wife had purchased the building for him years ago, before the present mania for urban living had revitalized the city center.

'You need something?' said Norwood, without looking up from his computer. 'Or is this just a social call?'

24

'Much as I enjoy our little heart-to-hearts on the issues affecting today's music industry, I can't dilly-dally,' said Rolly, pulling up to the counter.

'This won't be one of your "lemme try that one" marathons?'

'I'm in a hurry,' said Rolly. He pulled the diddley bow out of its case and placed it on the counter. 'What can you tell me about this?'

Norwood looked at the diddley bow, then over at Rolly. 'You want to sell it?' he said.

'Can't. It's not mine.'

'So why do you want to know about it?'

'I told a friend I'd look into it.'

'Does he want to sell it?'

'No. She doesn't. I don't think so.'

'I can get her good money for it.'

'How much?'

'A thousand bucks.'

'Really?'

'Well, it just so happens I had a guy in here yesterday looking for one.'

'Really?'

'Yeah. If it's what I think it is. This guy yesterday was looking for one just like it.'

'Really?'

Norwood sighed and rolled his eyes. 'That's three reallys in a row,' he said. 'Am I so . . . mistrusted?'

'No. I believe you. I'm just surprised.'

'Who's this chick you're asking for?'

'She's a client, that's all.'

'Uh huh.'

'She's more interested in the picture on the back.'

25

'Can I look?'

Rolly nodded. Norwood lifted the diddley bow, flipped it over and inspected the back.

'This is a fortuitous moment,' he said.

'What?'

'It's exactly the one he was looking for – the guy who came in.'

Norwood pointed at two small letters engraved just below the bottom right corner of the photograph. 'B-M,' he said. 'Buddy Meeks.'

'That name sounds familiar.'

'You should remember better than anybody. He worked in the Guitar Trader shop.'

'You mean the nerdy guy, right, with the big glasses? That Buddy?'

'That's the one,' said Norwood. 'I got to know him a little bit when I did commission sales up there. Strange dude. Awesome guitar tech, though.'

'I remember him now,' said Rolly. 'I wouldn't let anybody else work on my guitars.'

'Yeah, I remember that too. You used to piss off the other guys in the shop – the snotty teenage punk who insisted that he had to have Buddy work on his guitars, acting like the rest of them were incompetent peons.'

'I had very high standards.'

'Admit it. You were snotty.'

'Maybe. A little. That Buddy guy did great work, though, you gotta admit. You really think he made this thing?'

'That's what the guy told me. He was looking for a one-string guitar with Buddy's mark on the back. I was kind of thinking "good luck with

26

that" and now here you are walking in with the very thing.'

'You think I could talk to this guy?'

'So you can go around me and sell it to him directly?'

'It's not for sale. Like I told you.'

'Maybe you should check with your girlfriend, see if she wants to sell it, now that you know it's worth something.'

'My client's not interested in how much it's worth. She wants to know about the photo on the back. Did the guy say anything about that?'

'No,' said Norwood, continuing his examination of the instrument. He looked at the photo. 'Who's it supposed to be, anyway?'

'That's what I'm trying to find out.'

'This baseball guy looks like he might be somebody.'

Rolly shrugged. Norwood would have to figure that out for himself.

'It's nice work,' said Norwood. 'But I don't see how the thing's worth a thousand bucks.'

'Surprised the hell out of me,' Rolly replied.

'Well, the guy said he was willing to pay if I could find it for him,' said Norwood. 'Maybe it's got sentimental value for him, too.'

'Are you going to tell me his name?'

'Only if your girlfriend's willing to give me a cut.'

'How much do you want?'

'Thirty percent.'

'Ten.'

'Twenty.'

'All right. She won't want to sell it, though. Now can you tell me the name?'

Norwood extended his hand. Rolly shook on the deal. Norwood placed the diddley bow back on the counter, peeked under his laptop and pulled out a business card.

'Randy Parker,' he said, handing the card to Rolly. 'That's the guy's name. He has a shop called Alien Artifacts over in City Heights. I looked it up on the Web.'

Rolly reviewed the information on the card. Gold stars and planets were embossed on a purple background.

'What does he sell?' he asked.

'Looked to me like it was UFO memorabilia. Science-fiction collectibles.'

'There's a market for that?'

'Apparently.' Norwood shrugged his shoulders.

'You think this has something to do with UFOs?' said Rolly, indicating the diddley bow.

'Your guess is as good as mine,' said Norwood. 'I remember Buddy was into some unusual stuff – theories about aliens, like that Chariots of the Gods stuff. I remember one time he was talking to me about how there were these unique musical frequencies, tunings, with special properties that resonated in our DNA. Too weird for me.'

'You know where I can find him?'

'Buddy? No idea. You could ask up at Guitar Trader. That was a long time ago, though. I doubt anybody up there remembers him. I think he started his own shop, somewhere in East County.'

Rolly pointed at the dots along the neck. 'What

do you make of those inlays?' he said. 'They don't look correctly spaced for fret marks.'

'Yeah, I noticed that, too. I guess they're just decorative. You try plugging it in yet?'

'Nope. Too busy.'

'You want to try it now?'

'I gotta get going,' said Rolly.

'You might ask your girlfriend if she knows anything about an amplifier or something that's supposed to go with it. He wrote the name of the thing on the back of the card there.'

Rolly flipped the business card over, read the scrawled words. 'Astral Vibrator?'

Norwood laughed. 'Yeah, that's it. Maybe your girlfriend wants to keep that for herself too.'

'It's an amplifier?'

'I guess. This Randy guy said you plugged the diddley bow into it. He said it was a box, 'bout so high and so wide.' Norwood indicated the approximate dimensions of the Astral Vibrator with his hands.

'I'll ask her about it,' said Rolly. 'Let me know if you remember anything about Buddy.'

'OK. You need anything else?'

'I could use some guitar strings.'

'How many?'

'Two packs. You got any eights?'

'For your delicate little fingers?'

'I read somewhere that B.B. King plays eights.'

'Using eights won't make you sound like B.B. King,' said Norwood. He squatted down then opened the cabinet on the floor behind him. He pulled out two packs of guitar strings and returned to the counter.

'Ten dollars,' he said, tossing them on the countertop. Rolly pulled a twenty from his pocket. Norwood opened the register, tossed in the twenty and pulled out two fives.

'How's that Telecaster working for you?' he said, handing Rolly his change.

'All cleaned up and ready to go,' said Rolly. 'First public appearance tonight.'

'Where you playing?'

'At one of the reservations. Jincona.'

'You play there before?'

Rolly shook his head. 'First time at this one. I've played at all the others.'

'Kinda soul-sucking, isn't it?' said Norwood. 'All those people sitting there punching one-arm bandits and none of 'em paying any attention to you.'

'Money's good,' said Rolly. He slipped the guitar strings into his back pocket and wrapped the diddley bow up in its cloth. 'Once a month I guess it won't suck up too much of my soul.' His phone buzzed in his front pocket. He pulled it out and answered.

'Hey,' said Max. 'You at home?'

'I'm downtown.'

'Even better. You close to the ballpark?'

'Eight blocks or so.'

'I talked to Ozzie. He's down there, at the ballpark. Some kind of kids' event. Said you could stop by.'

'Great.'

'Just go to administrative office. Give 'em your name. How soon can you make it?'

'I don't know. Twenty minutes?'

30

'That'll work. I'll let him know.'

'Thanks.'

'You bet. Anything new on your dad?'

'They moved him out of emergency. Into intensive.'

'Well, I guess that's some kind of progress. Let me know if you need anything.'

'Thanks. I will.'

Rolly slipped his phone into his pocket.

'Who's in the hospital?' said Norwood.

'My dad had a heart attack.'

'The Captain?' said Norwood.

Rolly nodded. 'It's nothing,' he said.

'It's not negligible,' said Norwood.

'It doesn't mean he's not an asshole,' Rolly said. 'What were we talking about?'

'Well,' said Norwood. 'I gave you that guy's card. Randy Parker. I'm assuming you'll talk to him. You're going to tell him you talked to me and that you've got the guitar he was looking for. You get whatever information you need from the guy and then you talk to your girlfriend about selling the thing. Owes me twenty percent finder's fee if she does.'

'Right, right,' said Rolly. 'Except for one thing.'

'What's that?'

'She's not my girlfriend.'

Five
The Ballpark

Rolly sat in the reception area of the downtown ballpark's business office, waiting for an administrative assistant to locate an employee who could usher him in to see Eric Ozzie. A poster-sized photograph of Ozzie in his baseball uniform hung on the wall, along with those of other well-known players. Ozzie's professional career had been cut short by injuries and a nagging addiction to pain pills, but he'd once come close to setting the team record for stolen bases in a single season. His down-home demeanor and occasional malapropisms had made him a fan favorite, but three straight years battling the Mendoza line had finally ended Eric Ozzie's summers in the big leagues. Within a few years of his retirement, he parlayed his personality and ambitions into a fast-food concession called Sneakers, a variation on the nickname given to him by the team's broadcast announcer. The Sneaker had always been quick on his feet, able to capitalize on opportunities.

The inner door opened. An earnest-looking young man stepped into the office, holding a clipboard and a cell phone.

'Mr Waters?' he said, approaching Rolly. They

shook hands. 'I'm Jerry Kirby. I can escort you out to the field to meet Mr Ozzie now.'

'Thank you,' said Rolly.

'What's that you've got there?' the man asked, indicating the cloth case in Rolly's hand.

'It's a guitar,' said Rolly, 'A one-string guitar. It's got Mr Ozzie's picture on it.'

'It's a gift?'

'Not exactly. I'm a private investigator.'

'Oh. I see,' said Jerry. 'Well, follow me.'

Rolly followed Jerry through the door and down a long hallway.

'Eric's out on the field with the kids,' said Jerry as they walked down the hall. 'Big day today for them. We've got more than five hundred here from the various organizations.'

'What kind of organizations?'

'Oh, you know, representing our underserved population. Boys and Girls Clubs. St Vincent's. Eric loves doing these events. He's got his own foundation, you know. Free sneakers for all the kids.'

They passed through two additional doors and entered the clubhouse. Rolly had been in the locker room once, with Max, on a tour. During the off-season it was just a bunch of empty lockers in a big circle. He followed Jerry through the clubhouse and out to the field.

'Have a seat,' said Jerry, indicating the dugout bench. 'I'll let Eric know that you're here.'

Rolly took a seat and looked out at the baseball diamond. There were kids everywhere, organized into small groups around the various bases. There were more kids in the outfield,

33

getting coached on the fundamentals. Tables had been set up near the visitor dugout. Adults stood behind the tables, handing out box lunches. Rolly recognized the look of the packaging. The boxes contained Ozzie's titular product, Sneakers, which were deepfried balls of cornmeal mush wrapped around various fillings: jalapeño cheese, Italian meatballs and pineapple cream. More than one person had joked that the product's name described its effect on one's digestive system.

Jerry waved to catch someone's attention. Eric Ozzie stepped out from behind the food service tables, wearing a white apron on top of black pants and a purple dress shirt. He still looked in playing shape. Rolly stood up as Ozzie walked into the dugout.

'Mr Waters?' said Ozzie, extending his hand. His grip was solid, just shy of crushing, a well-calibrated professional's grip.

'Thanks for seeing me,' said Rolly.

'No problem,' said Ozzie. 'Any friend of Mr Gemeinhardt is a friend of mine. He said you were a musician?'

'Yeah. I play guitar.'

'You were in that band The Creatures, right? Max told me. I remember when you guys used to play around town. Didn't you sing the anthem at one of the games?'

'Yeah. We did once,' Rolly said. He had a vague memory of standing with Matt, out near home plate, strumming chords while Matt belted out the melody. 'Did Max explain why I wanted to talk to you?'

'He said you're a private investigator now, something like that?'

Rolly nodded. He took a business card from his wallet and handed it to Ozzie.

'Quite a change from playing guitar, I imagine,' said Ozzie, inspecting the card.

'Less so than you might think. I still play guitar some.'

'That's good. Gotta keep up your skills. So what'd you wanna see me about?'

'It's this,' said Rolly, undoing the cloth wrapper from the diddley bow.

'What's that?' Ozzie asked.

'It's called a diddley bow.'

Ozzie grinned. 'Well, I heard of Bo Diddley, but not a diddley bow.'

'There's a photograph, on the back. I think it's you.'

Rolly flipped the diddley bow over and presented the back.

Ozzie squinted. 'Jerry?' he said. 'Can you get me my glasses? I think they're on one of the tables.'

Jerry scurried out of the dugout.

'Can I take a closer look?' said Ozzie, indicating the diddley bow. Rolly nodded and handed it to him.

Ozzie walked to the dugout steps, angled his position to catch the sunlight. 'The Hawaii Coconuts,' he said, reviewing the photograph. 'Man, that was a great place to start your career. Except for the plane flights.'

'How long were you there?'

'A year and a half. Moved up to the majors in August.'

'Do you recognize the girl in that picture?'

Ozzie stared at the picture a moment. 'No. I don't think so,' he said.

'You've never seen her before?'

'Not that I remember. Who is she?'

'That's what I'm trying to find out.'

'It was a long time ago, you know, playing in Hawaii. Look at those palm trees in the background. I think they only had about a thousand seats in that park. Pretty girl. Must've been a fan. Why are you looking for her?'

'My client gave that to me. She's looking for her aunt. That photograph is all she's got to go on. She remembers a woman who looked like that living with the family when she was very young.'

'What about the rest of the family? Wouldn't they know?'

'My client was adopted.'

'Oh.'

'She's estranged from her adopted family. They've got some issues, I guess.'

'Where'd she get this . . . what do you call it, diddley bow?'

'She's not really sure of that either. Someone left it for her. Possibly her adoptive father.'

'Did she say anything about me?'

'As far as I can tell, she doesn't know who you are. She didn't recognize you in the photo, anyway. She never mentioned your name. I didn't tell her – thought I should wait until I'd talked to you first.'

'I appreciate that. How old is this woman, your client?'

'Twenty-one, almost twenty-two. That's what she told me, anyway.'

Ozzie considered the photo for a moment, calculating his past. 'You say this girl in the photo is supposed to be her aunt?' he said.

'Aunt Betty. That's the name she remembers. As I said, she's not sure. She doesn't know her mother and father.'

'I guess I know where you're going with this,' said Ozzie. He looked out towards the field, then back at the photo, then over at Rolly. 'I'd be in a lot of trouble if I'd slept with this girl, don't you think?' he said. There was a slight modulation in Ozzie's voice as he spoke, the barest hint of vibrato. 'How old do you think she is here?'

Rolly shrugged. 'Somewhere between fourteen and eighteen, I'd guess.'

'I don't know about eighteen. She looks younger than that.'

'I hope you don't mind my asking.'

'Well, you haven't really asked yet. But I'll answer anyway. I appreciate you not telling your client about me in case she figures out who I am and gets ideas, but really, I don't remember this girl. I'm damn well sure I never went out with her or nothing.'

Ozzie stepped back into the dugout and handed the diddley bow back to Rolly.

'Thanks for your time,' said Rolly.

'No girls,' said Ozzie.

'What's that?' said Rolly.

'That was the last thing my momma said to me, before I went to Hawaii. No girls.'

Rolly smiled because he couldn't think of anything else to do.

'She made me promise,' said Ozzie. 'Like it was going to ruin my career if I started having sex. She thought those island wahines were gonna lead me into temptation, that I'd end up like my daddy. That first year, in Hawaii, I was good. I was all about baseball. She died around the time I got to the majors, my mom.'

'I'm sorry,' said Rolly.

'Well, she was pretty messed up. She got me as far as she could. I guess maybe I was the only thing she had any hope for in her life.'

'She must've taken pretty good care of you.'

'Not really,' said Ozzie. 'But that's a story for another time. I know you got work to do.'

'I don't mind,' said Rolly.

Jerry returned with the glasses. Ozzie put them on.

'Show me the picture again,' he said. Rolly showed him. Ozzie reviewed it, then took off his glasses. He tapped them against the palm of his hand, looking thoughtful.

'No,' he said. 'I don't remember her.'

'Thanks for taking another look,' Rolly said.

'We're trying new flavors today,' said Ozzie, 'with the kids. I always enjoy this event, having the kids in, giving back something. I spent some time in the shelters growing up. I know what it's like. You really remember days like this. It's something special. You carry it around for a while. It really does help.'

'I'm sure it does.'

'You're welcome to join us.'

'I probably should get going,' Rolly said. 'I've got a gig tonight.'

'Where you playing?'

'Out at one of the casinos.'

Ozzie looked thoughtful again, as if he might say something. But he didn't.

'Well, it was nice meeting you,' said Rolly, extending his hand. 'And getting to sit in the dugout.'

'Yes, nice to met you, too, Mr Waters,' said Ozzie. 'If you need anything else, just give me a call.' He reached in his pocket, pulled out some coupons and handed them to Rolly.

'Two for ones,' he said. 'Use 'em next time you and Max come to the ballpark.'

'Thanks.'

Ozzie stepped out on the field. Jerry led Rolly back towards the clubhouse.

'Hey,' someone called. Rolly turned. Ozzie had ducked his head back into the dugout.

'What is it?' said Rolly.

Ozzie waved Rolly's business card. 'I can call you, right, at this number, if I remember something?'

'Sure. Anytime.'

'I was thinking . . . I just wanted to make it clear. Just so you don't think I'm trying to get evasive or nothing.'

'OK.'

'You were in that band, right? You probably had girls hanging around, chasing after you?'

'Sure.'

'That stuff I said about being good, my first year in Hawaii, that was all true.'

'I believe you.'

'But later, you know, in the majors, that was, well, like they say, that was a whole 'nother ball game.'

'I understand,' said Rolly, not sure if Ozzie was confessing or bragging. He could only imagine how his own behavior might have been in the majors.

'My momma was gone. I had a lot of girlfriends in the majors. And, you probably know this, I guess, but I do have a couple of kids out there. I paid for 'em, though. I mean, I'm supporting them. They're good kids. I'm doing my part, doing right by their mamas, taking responsibility.'

'I appreciate your telling me.'

Ozzie stepped into the dugout and moved closer. 'I just want you to know that I'm not trying to evade anything,' he said. 'I don't remember that girl in the photo. But if you find out something, let me know. If there's a child out there that's mine, I'll take responsibility. That's all I'm trying to say.'

'Understood.'

'This girl, your client, what's her name?'

'I can't tell you, not without her permission.'

'Sure, well, I'd be willing to talk to her if you want, if she remembers anything else. I'd like to help, if there's anything I can do. That's all I'm saying.'

'I'll keep that in mind. Is it OK if I tell her it's you in the photo? I'll let her know I talked to you, that you don't know anything.'

Ozzie nodded. 'Sure. You tell her I hope she finds her aunt or her momma or whoever that girl is.'

'I will,' Rolly said. Ozzie shook his hand again and dashed back on to the field to take care of his kids. Rolly saw something when he shook hands with Ozzie, something he'd never noticed in any photos or on the TV ads. Eric Ozzie had flecks of gold in his eyes.

Six
The Collection

The Alien Artifacts store on El Cajon Boulevard didn't look otherworldly. It looked like any other neighborhood storefront, except that the shades had been drawn, presumably to block the late afternoon sun.

'Looks closed,' said Moogus as he parked his truck in a metered spot half a block down the street. They had carpooled to save gas on their way to the casino engagement. Rolly had talked Moogus into taking a detour. The shop wasn't far from the freeway.

'Give me a minute,' said Rolly. He opened the passenger door. 'I wanta' take a look.'

'OK. Don't take too long.'

'We've got plenty of time.'

'You're the one who's always worrying about being late.'

'We'll be fine.'

'Whatever you say, boss.'

Rolly climbed down from the cab of Moogus'

truck and walked down the sidewalk. The sign in the window of the store said it was closed. There was a light on inside. He tried the door. It opened. A bell tinkled above his head as he walked in. 'Hello?' he called.

'We're closed,' someone answered from in back.

'Yes. I'm sorry. I was looking for Randy Parker.'

A door in the back of the shop opened. A woman appeared. 'Randy's not here,' she said.

'I was hoping to talk to him. He gave me his card.'

The woman walked out towards Rolly. She wore a long purple dress with loose, translucent sleeves. Long white hair fell down past her shoulders. A barrette of gold stars kept the hair out of her face. She stared at Rolly for a moment, attempting to drill into his brain with her eyes. Rolly smiled and deflected her gaze, keeping his eyes impermeable. She turned her head and looked at something on the counter.

'Randy's gone for the weekend,' she said.

'Can I leave a message? I tried calling his phone.'

'That's his phone over there, I'm afraid,' she said, pointing at the counter.

'Is there any other way I can reach him?'

'He went to the desert. I don't know how long he'll be gone. Who are you?'

Rolly pulled one of his own cards from his wallet. 'Roland Waters,' he said. 'Rolly. I'm a private investigator.'

The woman took the card and adjusted her hair

band as she read it. Her white hair made her seem older at first, but Rolly decided she might only be a few years older than he was.

'How did you meet Randy?' the woman said.

'I haven't met him yet. A friend of mine gave me his card. He thought I could help Mr Parker.'

'How so?'

'He was looking for something – Mr Parker was. Do you work here?'

'Yes. I'm Randy's full-time assistant. You can call me Dotty.'

'Nice to meet you, Dotty.'

'What was Randy looking for?' said Dotty.

'I'd like to leave a message, if I can.'

'Is it about that guitar?'

'You know about the guitar?'

'Oh, yes. It's an important artifact. From the Yoovits.'

'I don't know anything about the . . . what's it called?'

'The Yoovits. U-V-T, for Universal Vibration Technologies.'

'You're saying the guitar belonged to them?'

'Randy didn't tell you?'

'I didn't actually speak to Randy,' said Rolly, making a mental note to ask Norwood if Randy Parker had said anything about UVTs. 'Perhaps you could explain it to me.'

'Well, Mr Waters, I'm sure you've heard of the Annunaki theories, about the space travelers who arrived on our Earth from the planet Nubiru in 6000 B.C.?'

'Afraid not,' Rolly said. He pressed his lips together, feeling uneasy about the direction the

43

conversation had taken. Norwood hadn't told him Randy Parker was nuts.

'Well, of course it's not true,' said Dotty. 'It's just one of the early alien theories. I simply use it as an example. The UVTs also believe that aliens are among us. We have interbred over the epochs of time, so we have alien DNA inside us – in varying proportions, of course.'

Rolly remembered the DNA tattoo Macy had inked under her jugular notch. *Do Not Ask*. A coincidental awareness. Perhaps.

'I see,' he said, debating how much longer he felt willing to listen. 'I still don't understand what this has to do with the guitar Mr Parker is looking for.'

'Oh, everything,' said Dotty. 'You see, the Universal Vibration Technologies began as a healing system, combining color vibrations and the ancient musical frequencies. It was discovered that these frequencies could release the alien energy within each human being. It was easier for some, of course – those who already had high levels of cross-pollination.'

'Uh huh,' Rolly said.

'You've heard of the chakras, of course?' said Dotty. 'The Kundalini?'

'Yes,' Rolly said, surprised he'd heard of anything the woman had to tell him. After the car accident, in his first year of recovery, his mother had insisted on teaching him meditation techniques, including the chakra vibrations. He'd gone along with it. He'd chanted the mantras. It hadn't stuck. As far as he knew, his mother still practiced her chants.

44

'There was a young man who lived among them, highly skilled in the craft of instrument making . . .'

'Do you mean Buddy Meeks?'

'Yes, that was the man's name. It was said that he had a strong alien component. He designed the instruments for the Conjoinment.'

'What's the Conjoinment?'

'In the astral year 4017, Saturn and Jupiter aligned. The Ancients approach the Earth at the peak of the alignment. This is known as the Conjoinment. The UVTs gathered together to signal them, so that they might be taken up.'

'You mean like in that movie, *Close Encounters*?'

'The Ancients do not need a physical spaceship. Their approach is more nebulous. There are portents. The Conjoinment occurs approximately every twenty years.'

'You seem to know a lot about this.'

'I am well versed in alien theories. As is Mr Parker. That's why he started this shop.'

Rolly looked around the room, scrutinizing the items on the tables and shelves. There were all sorts of strange things on display, from little green men to ray guns to models of spaceships.

'That's an *X-Files* lunchbox, isn't it?' he said.

'We buy and sell popular culture items, as well as more authentic artifacts of human interaction with the alien existence,' said Dotty.

'Very interesting,' said Rolly. 'Do you have any items related to the UVTs?'

'Oh, yes. Quite a few. Would you like to see them?'

'Definitely,' Rolly said. He wondered if Moogus was getting antsy yet, then decided not to worry. Moogus always got antsy before a gig.

Dotty led Rolly to the back corner of the shop. She stopped in front of two paintings that hung on the wall. In the top corners of the first painting were images of Saturn and Jupiter. Energy beams flowed out from the planets in orange and yellow bands, curving into the foreground where a pyramid shape enclosed a naked, sexless human form holding both palms outward.

'Very nice,' Rolly said, attempting to show his appreciation. The painting was amateurish, bordering on hideous.

'This is a representation of the Ancients,' Dolly said. 'They come from the Oort cloud, as it passes between Saturn and Jupiter.'

'Oh,' said Rolly, fairly confident there weren't any clouds passing between Saturn and Jupiter, but not entirely sure. He wasn't up on his astronomy. 'They look friendly.'

'The human form you see represented is referred to as a Gentling. We are all Gentlings, to one degree or another. The pure form of the Ancients is astronomical and terrifying to human beings. So they must appear to earthlings in Gentling form. The frequency waves you see are more like the Ancients' true nature, but even so, it is just an artistic representation of the forces within them.'

'You mentioned something earlier about vibrations.'

'You are very astute, Mr Waters. This represents the Universal Vibrations.'

46

'Uh huh. And this other painting? Is that the guitar Mr Parker is looking for?'

'Yes,' said Dot. 'That is the one.'

A man stood in the foreground of the second painting playing a one-string guitar, a diddley bow. The diddley bow was plugged into some kind of box. Orange and yellow bands of energy, similar to the ones in the first painting, flowed out from the box.

'What's that?' he asked, pointing at the box.

'It is known as the Astral Vibrator.'

'Is it an amplifier, for the guitar?'

'We have not divined its true use.'

'Isn't Mr Parker looking for one of those, too?'

'Yes. The UVTs were highly musical, you see. They were known for their euphonics. We have some CDs if you'd like to hear.'

Dotty pulled some CD cases off the shelf next to the paintings and handed them to Rolly. He flipped through the covers. *Intuition Modulations. Quantum Perceptions. Codon Transmutation.* The titles reminded him of some of the music his mother listened to, stultifying New Age drivel. He hated it. There were no blues notes, no rock and roll rhythms, no jazz harmonies. He handed the CDs back to Dotty.

'What's that?' he said, noticing something else on the shelf, next to the CDs.

'It is a representation of the Sachem,' said Dotty. She handed the doll to him. It was a baby doll, painted gold, with blonde hair and gold eyes.

'What's the Sachem?' said Rolly.

47

Before Dotty could answer, the bell tinkled on the front door and someone entered the shop. Rolly turned, expecting to see Moogus. The man who'd walked in saw Rolly and stopped. Overdeveloped biceps stretched the sleeves of the man's gray T-shirt. His hair was jet black. It looked unnatural, like a dye job or rug.

Dotty crossed in front of Rolly and walked towards the man. 'Randy,' she said, 'you left your phone here, didn't you?'

The man nodded. He kept his sunglasses on.

'This is Rolly Waters,' said Dotty. 'He's a private investigator. He says he can help us find the guitar.'

The man nodded again. Rolly joined them at the front of the store.

'Hello, Mr Parker,' he said, offering his hand. The man nodded again, then shook his hand. He had a strong, aggressive grip. There was a tattoo of a watch on the man's right wrist. The face on the watch had no hands.

'Rob Norwood gave me your card,' said Rolly.

'Who?' said the man.

'He's got a guitar shop downtown. You were there asking about a one-string guitar?'

'Yeah. That's right. What's his name again?'

'Rob Norwood. His shop's called Mostly Guitars. I think I might be able to locate this guitar you're looking for.'

'You know where it is?'

'I'm a private investigator.'

'You want money?'

'I have some questions about the guitar.'

'Like what?'

'It's not actually a guitar. It's called a diddley bow.'

Randy Parker didn't seem impressed with Rolly's knowledge of stringed instruments.

'What's your questions?' he said.

'Well,' said Rolly, 'I understand a man named Buddy Meeks might have built it. His mark should be on the back.'

'How'd you know that?'

'You told Mr Norwood that. He told me.'

'Yes. That's right.'

'Are there any other identifying marks you might describe to me?'

'Marks?'

'Well, anything unusual or distinctive.'

'No.'

'Nothing about the design or decoration?'

Randy Parker glanced over at Dotty. The sunglasses prevented Rolly from reading his eyes.

'What did you tell him?' Parker said to Dotty.

'We talked about the UVTs,' said Dotty. 'I showed him the paintings.'

Randy Parker returned his attention to Rolly. 'What else do you know?' he said.

The bell rang as the the front door opened. They all turned to see who had entered the store. It was Moogus.

'We're closed,' said Parker.

'I'm with him,' Moogus said, pointing at Rolly. 'We need to get going.'

'Yes,' Rolly said. 'We do.'

Whatever was going on, he didn't want to aggravate Randy Parker any further. He moved towards the door.

49

'Where're you going?' said Randy Parker.

'We've got to be somewhere. In East County.'

'We're rockin' the rez tonight,' said Moogus.

Randy Parker took a step towards them. 'What's that supposed to mean?' he said.

Dotty put a hand on his arm. Parker stopped.

'We've got a gig at one of the Indian casinos,' said Rolly.

'It was very nice to meet you, Mr Waters,' said Dotty. 'Please come back when you have more time to talk.'

'That OK with you, Mr Parker?' said Rolly. 'If I come back to talk sometime?'

Parker glanced over at Dotty. An unspoken agreement passed between them.

'Yeah,' Parker said. 'You come back anytime. Come back and we'll talk.'

'Let's go,' said Moogus.

Rolly followed Moogus out to the sidewalk. As the door closed behind him, he heard a sound like a handclap. His best guess was Dotty had slapped Randy. Or Randy had slapped Dotty. It could have gone either way. They were both telling stories. The stories weren't quite the same. Rolly followed Moogus back to the truck and climbed in.

'Nice rug on that guy, huh?' said Moogus.

'I thought maybe it was a dye job.'

'I'd lay odds he's a cue ball, covering up some head tats. Good thing for you I showed up.'

'He was getting a little agitated.'

'Yeah, well, when a guy like that gets agitated, he's likely to bite off your ear.'

'What?'

'EWMN. The T-shirt covered up part of the tattoo, but I knew what it was.'

'What does EWMN mean?'

'Evil, wicked, mean and nasty. Tattooed on the back of his neck. He's a jumpsuiter for sure.'

'You mean an ex-con? He was in prison?'

Moogus laughed. 'You should hire me, as a consultant or something.'

'Why is that?'

'Well, for a detective, you don't seem too sharp at identifying the criminal element.'

'No, I guess not,' said Rolly. He slumped into his seat. He hated dealing with the criminal element.

Seven
The Tower

'How much longer do you want to wait?' said Moogus.

'Just a couple more minutes,' said Rolly. 'Then we'll give up.'

It was 4:30 in the morning. They'd been sitting for over an hour, parked outside the locked entrance to Desert View Tower, a funky old tourist trap on the eastern edge of the mountains. During regular hours visitors could buy candy, postcards and other knick-knacks inside the tower. They could climb to the top of the circular staircase and gaze from the open balcony into the barren furnace of the Anza Borrego Desert, or explore the rock gardens nearby, where one of the owners had carved animal shapes out of the sandstone boulders. There was a buffalo, a hawk, a crocodile and some other animals Rolly couldn't remember. His mother had brought him here years ago, on one of the countless adventures she'd forced him to endure when he was a teenager.

'Is this what you call a stakeout?' said Moogus.

'I don't know what I'd call this,' said Rolly.

'I always thought it'd be cool to go on a stakeout.'

'This isn't a stakeout. The guy wants us to meet him here.'

'You're sure about that? It's been almost an hour.'

'I'm not sure about anything.'

'Who's this guy s'posed to be, anyway?'

'I don't know.'

'You think it's that ex-con from the shop?'

'I hope not.'

'Could be a trap,' said Moogus. 'He knew we were gonna be at the casino.'

'I expect something would have happened by now if it were a trap.'

'Yeah. I guess. That guy had it in for you, though. I could tell. After my time in the pen, I know an orange peeler with intent when I see one.'

'You were only in jail for two months. You're not allowed to use prison lingo unless you've done at least a full year.'

'Who made up that rule?'

52

'I did. Just now.'

'Hey, hard time is hard time.'

Rolly searched the area outside the car, considering what he should do next, if anything. A field of large boulders stood on either side of the road, casting long shadows as the full moon sank towards the western horizon. Someone had left a postcard of the Desert View Tower in his guitar case, sneaking it in during the band's last set at the casino. A cryptic message had been scrawled on the back of the card.

TEOTWAYKI
Golden Eyes Key
Arrive before sunrise

The first line meant nothing to him. It looked like an Indian word. But he couldn't help feeling the second line referred to his new client. The sender knew something about Macy Starr. The third line he interpreted as a command, that he should go to the place pictured on the postcard by the time indicated. He'd talked Moogus into going along with this stupid idea by promising to pay for a full tank of gas. If no one showed up at the Desert View Tower by sunrise, so be it. He would go home and sleep. He wouldn't charge Macy for the hours.

'You get horizontal with her yet?' said Moogus. 'This chick you're so worked up about?'

'I only met her last night.'

'Since when did that stop you?'

'She's my client. Besides, I'm old enough to be her father.'

'Is she legal age?'

'Yes.'

'I repeat my last query.'

'I'm pretty sure she's not interested in middle-aged guitar players.'

'How about a drummer who likes to think young?'

'Shut up,' said Rolly.

He stared out the window at the dirt road, the rocks and scraggly brush.

'Hey,' said Moogus.

'What?'

'You think the guy who left you the card lives in that tower thing?'

'It's possible, I guess.'

'Maybe we should sneak in, on foot, you know, stealthy-like, and case the joint.'

'Did you really say "case the joint"?'

'Yeah. Isn't that how you detective guys talk? We'll get the drop on him.'

Rolly sighed. His friends assumed his day job was like what they'd seen in the movies – muscle-headed thugs, gin joints and wisecracking dames. In reality, most of the cases he worked on were stupid arguments pitting dumb against dumber. He interviewed accident victims for insurance companies, took photos of deadbeat dads spending money that should go to their kids. He searched for absent wives and runaway teens. He didn't carry a gun. He didn't own one. Even thinking about carrying a gun made him queasy.

Still, he was glad to have Moogus with him. Moogus had actual biceps. He could handle himself in a fight. Moogus had been to prison, after all, if only for two months. He could act like a tough guy. He knew how to intimidate.

Rolly was better at talking his way out of confrontations. Aside from playing guitar, it was the one thing he was good at.

They heard a sound from outside the truck. A bird call. Something clattered against the back window.

'What was that?' Moogus said, turning around.

'I don't know.'

They waited a moment. The bird called again. The rear window clattered.

'Somebody's throwing shit at us,' said Moogus. He reached for the door handle.

'Hold on,' said Rolly.

'For what?'

'I think I see him.'

'Where?'

Rolly pointed to a shadow moving through the scrubby bush. The shadow crouched down behind a scraggly shrub.

'There. You see him?'

As if in response, the figure rose up. They heard the bird call again. The shadow swiveled its right arm. A handful of sand and pebbles rattled the front window.

'I guess he wants to get our attention,' said Rolly.

'He's got mine,' said Moogus, rolling down his window.

'Hey jerkwad!' he shouted. 'Stop throwing crap at my truck.'

The shadow stood its ground. 'Who are you?' it asked.

'It doesn't matter who I am,' Moogus said. 'Don't throw shit at my truck.'

'You're the drummer.'

'Yeah. That's right.'

'I want the guitar player,' said the shadow.

'He's here with me. You the guy who left the postcard?'

'I must query him. The guitar player.'

'Why can't you talk to me?'

'Drummers are nincompoops. They cannot play the proper frequencies.'

Moogus turned to Rolly. 'Can you believe this guy?'

Another handful of dirt and rocks hit the windshield. Moogus opened his door and stepped out. He took a few threatening steps towards the shadow. 'I told you. Stop throwing that shit at my truck.'

The shadow retreated and moved farther up the hill. 'I want the guitar player,' said the shadow. 'I want the Waters.'

Rolly climbed out of the truck, circled around the front and walked up next to Moogus. 'I'm here,' he said. 'What do you want?'

'I will not speak, not with him. I wish to query the Waters.'

'We drove together. He gave me a ride.'

'The questions are for you,' said the shadow. 'Not the skin-beater.'

'What do you want me to do?' Rolly asked. The shadow disappeared. They heard rustling and scraping higher up in the rocks.

'Up here,' said the shadow from a different position. 'The skin-beater must return to the vehicle.'

Rolly and Moogus exchanged glances.

56

'This guy's a wack job,' said Moogus, under his breath.

'I don't think he's dangerous,' said Rolly. 'Go back to the truck.'

Moogus shrugged and retreated. He leaned back against the truck's cabin, folded his arms and stared up at the rocks, channeling his best badass.

'Over here,' said the shadow. 'I will speak from the orifice.'

Rolly stepped off the road and walked up the hill towards the boulder field. As he got closer he noticed a vertical line through the tallest boulder, an open fissure running from top to bottom.

'Hold,' the man said. Rolly halted, three feet from the fissure. The crack was wider at his end of the boulder and narrowed as it went back, amplifying the man's voice.

'Are you a gold drinker?' the man said.

'No,' Rolly said. 'Not that I know of.'

'Are you a Gentling?'

'Same answer, I guess.'

The man made a sound like a bird. 'Teotwayki! Teotwayki!'

'That's what you wrote on the postcard, isn't it?'

The bird call came back for an answer.

'Is it supposed to mean something to me?' Rolly asked. 'I don't understand.'

'Teotwayki. That is what it means.'

'What does the second line mean?' Rolly said. '"Golden eyes key?"'

'Golden Eyes has the key.'

'The key to what?'

'The Astral Vibrator.'

Rolly felt the hairs on the back of his neck stand up. Randy Parker was looking for the Astral Vibrator. It went with the diddley bow.

'Do you know where I can find the Astral Vibrator?' he said.

'It lives with the Gentlings. The Waters must practice the frequencies.'

Rolly had been part of many strange conversations in the early morning hours with drunks and drug addicts, all sorts of chemically impaired nightcrawlers who hung around on the street after closing time. They would stand on the sidewalk ruminating loudly on life's challenges while you packed up your equipment and tried to get away before they decided you were their best friend.

'What are these frequencies you want me to practice?' he said.

'The Waters must learn the Solfeggios.'

'I don't know what that is.'

'Golden Eyes has the key.'

'The diddley bow? The one-string guitar? Is that what you're talking about?'

'I am affirming.'

'I have a question for you, then. There's a photograph on the back, a man and a woman.'

'I am affirming.'

'Who is she, the woman? Do you know?'

'The Waters should ask the big Indian.'

'Daddy Joe? Is that who you mean? Is he the big Indian?'

There was no answer. Rolly cleared his throat. He looked up at the night sky. There were lots of stars but no flying saucers around – at least, none that he could see. Things were weird enough without any aliens.

'He is gone,' said the man in the rock.

'Daddy Joe?' said Rolly. 'Where'd he go?'

'The skin-beater. He's gone.'

'The skin . . . wait.'

Rolly turned and looked back towards the truck. Moogus had disappeared.

Eight
The Shocker

Rolly took two steps down the hill, searching the landscape.

'Moogus!' he called. 'Where are you?'

He heard scuffling sounds behind him. Someone screamed.

'Ayaaah!'

'I got you now!' said a voice. It was Moogus.

'Teotwayki!' the man called. 'Teotwayki!'

'I got him, Rolly!' said Moogus. 'I got . . . Hey! Who . . .?'

Rolly heard a strange sound, like an electric woodpecker tapping on rocks. Someone screamed.

'Aaagh!'

The electric woodpecker rattled again. The screamer screamed.

'Aaagh!'

The screamer sounded like Moogus. Rolly

bolted up the hill and worked his way around the boulders. 'Moog?'

'I'm down here,' said Moogus. 'Shit damn. That smarts.'

Rolly spotted someone lying on the ground behind the big rock. He crept down the incline and squatted down beside Moogus. 'Are you OK?' he said.

'Boo-oof,' said Moogus. 'Just give me a minute, here.'

Moogus sat up and shook his head back and forth like a cartoon character clearing his brainpan. He put his left hand out, touching it against the rock for balance.

'What were you thinking?' said Rolly. 'I told you to stay by the truck.'

'There was somebody else. Up in the rocks. Creeping around.'

'Why didn't you tell me?'

'I don't know. I just had a feeling. I thought I could nab him.'

'What happened?'

'I got up there, where I thought the other guy was. I couldn't find anybody. Then I heard the guy that was talking to you. He was right down below me. So I jumped him.'

'You shouldn't have done that.'

'Next thing I know, someone's zapped my ass and I'm looking up at the stars.'

A cackle of laughter rolled down the hill and bounced off the boulders. 'Teotwayki!'

'I don't like this,' said Moogus.

Rolly stood up. 'Hey,' he called. 'Are you still there?'

'What do you call a drummer with half a brain?' said the voice.

'Seriously, Rolly . . .' said Moogus.

'Gifted,' came the unrequested answer.

'I'm going to kill that guy.'

'Just wait here,' said Rolly. 'I need to talk to him.'

'Be careful,' said Moogus. 'There's somebody else out here. With a taser or something.'

'Sounds to me like his bodyguard's better than mine.'

'Fuck you.'

Rolly turned back to the boulder field. 'Hey!' he shouted. 'Whoever you are. I still want to talk to you.'

No one answered.

'I need some answers,' said Rolly.

'Proceed!' called the voice. 'Find the crocodile.'

'What?'

'Proceed to the crocodile.'

'The crocodile?' said Moogus. 'What's he talking about?'

'There're these statues,' said Rolly. 'Animals somebody carved out of the rocks.'

'To the crocodile!' said the voice.

Rolly stepped forward.

'Don't do it,' said Moogus.

Rolly shushed him. 'Just sit tight,' he said. 'Don't screw things up anymore than you already have.'

Rolly took another step and lifted himself to the top of a small rise. He could see a dirt path curving down the back of the rise and up another hill, where it ran between two large boulders.

61

The first hint of daylight pushed at the darkness. He left Moogus and trudged down the path. The trail rose and twisted. He passed another boulder then stopped in his tracks. A stone crocodile grinned at him in the dim light, baring its bas-relief teeth.

'OK,' Rolly said. 'I'm at the crocodile.'

'The skin-beater is impudent,' said the man. 'Unattuned to the stars.'

'He gets like that sometimes,' said Rolly. 'He won't bother you again.'

'The boogie man stuck him with the bad frequencies.'

'There's someone else out here?'

'I am affirming.'

'Is he a friend of yours?'

'I am denying. Not a friend.'

'He didn't come here with you?'

'I am denying.'

'Who is he then?'

'A villain. He brought the negative frequencies.'

Rolly didn't like the idea of any villain lurking about, let alone one with a stungun bringing negative frequencies. He needed to get out of here. But he needed to ask the man about Daddy Joe and the photograph first.

'The photograph, on the back of the diddley bow – who is it?'

'The big chief must tell you. That is agreed.'

'You mean Daddy Joe, don't you?'

'That is affirmed.'

'Why can't you tell me?'

'The Waters must practice,' said the voice. 'The Waters must read the diagram.'

'What diagram?' said Rolly. 'Does Daddy Joe have the diagram?'

'Daddy Joe is a dead man,' said another voice, from behind him. The electric woodpecker rattled. A negative frequency shot through Rolly's body and his brain exploded into a bright bolt of pain. He twisted away from the stinging wood-pecker and collapsed, almost hitting his head on the crocodile.

'Teotwayki!' the bird called again. Soft foot-steps padded away from him.

'Rolly!'

'Uhnn,' grunted Rolly. He pulled his head up and rested it on the crocodile's neck. A gob of drool fell from his mouth. He heard footsteps approaching, someone walking up from below.

'He got you too, didn't he?' said Moogus.

'Uhnn,' Rolly said.

'Take it easy,' said Moogus. He leaned down and lifted Rolly's head off the stone crocodile, slipped his shoulder in behind Rolly's back for support and helped him sit up. In the distance Rolly heard the sound of a car starting up.

'Someone . . .' said Rolly, '. . . gettin' away.'

'Yeah. I hear it.'

'Uhnn,' said Rolly.

'You'll be OK,' said Moogus. 'Might take a minute or two.'

'Uph,' Rolly said, waving his hand towards the sky.

'What's that?'

'Ged up. Look car.'

Moogus furrowed his brow as the sound of the car's engine floated through the rocks.

'Look, look, lithenth,' Rolly said. Moogus finally seemed to understand. He dropped Rolly against the crocodile and stood up.

'I see it,' he said. 'Over there. What the hell is that thing? It looks like a spaceship or something.'

The sound of the engine faded into the distance.

'He's gone.'

'Lithenth?'

'No license. I could only see the top half. It's a Volkswagen van. I could tell that much. You remember Old Zeke?'

Rolly nodded. 'I remember.'

'Old Zeke sounded just like that,' said Moogus.

'I wrote a song about Zeke.'

'We used to get the whole band in there and a couple of girlfriends sometimes too. What was the song?'

Rolly leaned his head back against the crocodile. He rubbed his temples, trying to access the memory. One verse. That was all he could remember. And the melody. His voice cracked as he sang it.

Old Zeke's got a number, stashed in his
glove box
A number he's waiting to play
She gave him her number, the day that
he met her
A wahine from Hanalei Bay

'Oh, man, that sucks,' said Moogus. 'A wahine from Hanalei Bay? Really?'

Rolly shrugged. 'I was going for a surf-rock kind of thing.'

'Zeke deserved better than that.'

'That's why I never played it for you.'

The fuzziness in Rolly's head began to clear. He stood up and dusted himself off.

'We sure got our asses kicked, didn't we?' said Moogus.

'Yeah.'

'I shouldn't have jumped that guy.'

'You should have stayed by the truck.'

Moogus laughed. 'I guess I'm not much of a bodyguard, am I, buddy?'

'I wouldn't give up your skin-beating job.'

'Let's get the hell out of here.'

'Yeah.'

They walked back down the path. The boulders looked smaller now, less foreboding.

'As I was saying,' Moogus continued as they wound their way down the trail, 'all those Volkswagen vans, they got the same sound. Once you own one, you'll never forget it. That's useful, right? Knowing what kind of car the guy drives.'

'What did you mean, it looked like a spaceship?'

'I only saw it for a couple of seconds. There was this gap in the rocks. It looked like a spaceship to me.'

'How so?'

'It had these little wings on the side, kinda like the space shuttle wings, and some more things jutting out of the top that looked like old TV antennas. There were these round cones, like rocket engines or something, stuck to the back. Just some shapes I could see.'

65

They reached the bottom of the hill and walked to the truck. Moogus pulled out his keys. They opened the doors and climbed into the truck.

'I'd know that sound anywhere,' said Moogus. 'A VW van. That helps, right? You just gotta find a VW van that looks like a spaceship. How hard can that be?'

'It helps,' said Rolly. 'A license plate would be better.'

'Yeah, well, I'm not sure I could have read it anyway, in this light.'

Moogus turned the key in the ignition. Nothing happened. He tried it again. There was a small click but no engine sound.

'What the hell?' Moogus said.

'Did you leave the lights on?' said Rolly.

'No, I turned 'em off,' Moogus replied, looking over the dashboard instruments. He tried the key one more time and got the same result. He reached into the glove box and pulled out a flashlight. He climbed out of the car, popped the hood and inspected the engine.

'Shit dammit,' he said.

Rolly got out of the truck, went to look at the engine with Moogus. 'What is it?' he said.

'Somebody pulled my relay fuse.'

'Can you fix it?'

'Not unless you happen to have one in your pocket.'

As they stood staring at the truck's engine, an old blue Toyota pulled out onto the road a hundred feet down from them.

'Hey,' Moogus called, waving his arms. 'Over here.'

The Toyota turned and drove away.

'Asshole,' said Moogus.

Rolly pulled his phone from his pocket. 'I don't get any signal here,' he said.

Moogus walked to the truck cab, pulled out his phone and tossed it back in the cab.

'Me neither.'

'So what do we do now?'

'Walk back to the freeway, I guess. See if I can get a signal there, find a call box.'

'How far is that?'

'Mile. Mile and a half.'

Moogus turned and pointed back towards the Desert View Tower. 'You think somebody lives in this place?'

'It says they don't open until eight-thirty,' Rolly said, pointing at the gate. 'You want to wait that long?'

'What time is it now?'

Rolly checked his phone. 'A little after five,' he said.

'Sign says it's only a quarter-mile. Let's go wake 'em up.'

They locked the doors of the truck, walked around the gate and headed towards the tower.

'I wish you'd stayed with the truck like I asked you to,' Rolly said.

'Yeah, I do too,' Moogus said. 'This detective stuff is really starting to suck.'

Nine
The Cop

They got home around eight the same morning. Rolly unloaded his gear from the truck. He didn't bother to wave as Moogus pulled out of the driveway. They'd spent longer and more exhausting nights together, but not since their youth.

Rolly's mother opened her back door and stepped onto the stoop. She looked concerned.

'Is everything OK?' Rolly said, walking over to greet her.

'I'm not sure,' she replied. 'Aren't you home rather late?'

'Car troubles. Moogus' truck wouldn't start.'

His mother sighed.

'What's wrong?' he asked. 'Is everything OK at the hospital?'

'Oh, everything's fine there. We talked to the doctors.'

'What'd they say?'

'They expect him to recover, but they'll want to keep him a few more days.'

'He won't be too happy about that. How's Alicia?'

'The police were here. That friend of yours, the blonde woman.'

'Bonnie?'

'Yes. I don't know why I can never remember her name.'

'What'd she want?'

'She wants you to call her.'

'Did she say why?'

'I told her about your father. Just so she'd be aware, if you were acting peculiar.'

Rolly sighed. Those who knew him, like his mother or Bonnie, were always on watch for suspicious behavior, looking for clues that he'd slipped off the wagon. He hadn't been sober long enough to slacken their vigilance. He didn't know how long it would take.

'I just want to say,' his mother continued, 'it's quite disconcerting to come home and find a police car in the driveway. Especially when you've returned from the hospital at seven in the morning and your son is missing.'

'I wasn't missing. I was working.'

Rolly's phone rang. He pulled it out of his pocket and looked at the screen. It was Bonnie. He answered. 'I just got home,' he said. 'What's up?'

'I talked to your mom,' said Bonnie.

'Yeah. She said you'd come by.'

'How's your dad doing?'

'It looks like he's gonna pull through.'

'Glad to hear it. Listen, you got any idea why tribal police might be looking for you?'

'You mean, like Indians?'

'That's usually what tribal means.'

'Um, no. I don't think so.'

'Did you play any of the casinos recently?'

'We were at the Jincona reservation last night.'

69

'Any problems?'

'No. Not that I'm aware of.'

'You usually get home this late?'

'We had some car trouble. Moogus' truck wouldn't start.'

'You were up there with Moogus?'

'He's our drummer, you know. We sound better when we have a drummer.'

'Don't get smart with me.'

'I'm sorry. I'm tired.'

'I'm gonna stop by.'

'I need to sleep.'

'It'll only be ten minutes. I'm still in the area.'

'OK. Fine,' said Rolly. He hung up. Bonnie didn't like Moogus. She had her reasons, besides his ex-con status. Moogus had talked Joan into going to bed with him once. Joan was Bonnie's girlfriend. All these years later, Bonnie still didn't like him.

'Is everything OK?' asked Rolly's mother.

'Hmm, oh, everything's fine. That was Bonnie. She's coming over.'

'Well, at least I'll expect her this time.' His mother crossed her arms and pursed her lips. 'Are you feeling all right?' she said.

'Me? Oh sure. Just thinking about some things.'

'Do we need to talk about your father?'

'I don't think so.'

'I thought perhaps you might want to discuss things. When something happens like this . . .'

'The doctors said he's going to be OK, right?'

'They said he'll be fine. He'll need to make some life changes, I expect.'

'I expect so.'

'I thought maybe you could advise him on that.'

'Me?'

'You've had your own experiences – you could talk to him.'

'What? About his drinking?'

'Well, yes, that, and your brush with . . . mortality.'

'You want me to talk to Dad about dying?'

'I'm just saying it's something you can share now: getting a second chance. You were able to make positive changes in your life.'

'I'm not talking to dad about his drinking unless he apologizes to me first.'

'Apologizes for what?'

'Something, anything.'

'This kind of life event might change him.'

'I think you're too hopeful. We'll see.'

'You don't drink anymore.'

'I kind of wish I had a drink now,' said Rolly, under his breath.

'What's that?'

'Nothing,' said Rolly. 'I'll think about it, but let's wait until he gets settled at home.'

'Don't let this get you upset. You can talk to me if you need to.'

'Thank you. I will. I'm not upset.'

'All right, dear.' His mother gave him a peck on the cheek and turned back into her house. Rolly grabbed his guitar and amplifier from the driveway, opened the door to his house and walked in. He stashed his equipment, plugged in his phone to recharge it then dumped the contents of his pockets on the kitchen table:

71

wallet, guitar picks, keys and a postcard of Desert View Tower.

As Moogus had surmised, the proprietors of the tower lived on the premises. A young married couple, they had been awake by the time Rolly knocked on their door, more than happy to help out and share a cup of their morning coffee with marooned strangers. The woman had been awakened earlier by the sound of something being dropped through the mail slot on the front door. It was a gift for Moogus, a brown paper bag containing his truck's relay fuse. Both she and her husband seemed relieved to have the mysterious incursion explained.

As it turned out, they'd seen a VW van decorated like a spaceship. Many times. It was a regular visitor, at least once a week, in the parking lot and along the service roads. They knew little about the owner. Someone had told them the man lived in Slab City, an unincorporated enclave of hippies and retirees camped out in an old army base near the Salton Sea. The woman gave Rolly a brief history of Slab City, describing its genesis as a training ground for troops during World War II. The army demolished the camp soon after the war, leaving only the concrete foundations of buildings behind. Years later, a vagabond traveler happened on the abandoned slabs and decided they made a perfect place to park a mobile home for the winter. There were no fees or rents to pay, no rules to obey. Word soon got out and others followed. Before long, an offbeat, off-the-grid community of like-minded nomads had bloomed in the desert.

Rolly heard a car pulling into the driveway. A car door opened and shut. Footsteps scrunched across the gravel. Rolly's front door swung open. Bonnie Hammond walked in.

'Aren't you supposed to knock?' Rolly said.

'Door was open,' said Bonnie. 'And you invited me here.'

'Not exactly invited.'

'Is there anything you need to tell me about? Before you get in trouble? You need help with one of your cases?'

'I don't need any help. I just need some sleep.'

Bonnie picked up the postcard from the table. 'Desert View Tower, huh?' she said, reading the back. 'Teotwayki. What's that mean?'

'I don't know.'

'You got any clients you want to tell me about?'

'Not really.'

'No lights going on yet? About why the tribal police want to talk to you?'

'No.'

'Aside from your casino gig last night, have you been in the back country lately, on the reservation?'

'Moogus and I stopped at Desert View Tower this morning after the gig. That's the only other place we've been.'

Bonnie looked at her watch. 'Sounds kind of early for you.'

'Moogus and I wanted to see the sunrise.'

'Uh huh.'

'We're sentimental that way.'

Bonnie put the postcard back on the table. She

picked up Macy's flyer. 'DJ Crazy Macy,' she said, reading the flyer. 'Doesn't sound like your style.'

'I like to keep an open mind.'

Bonnie pulled her phone out of her pocket and tapped on the screen. 'Take down this number,' she said.

'Who is it?'

'Her name's Kinnie Harper. She's chief of police for the Jincona Tribe.'

'You're working with her?'

'No. Luckily for you, this is just a personal call. Kinnie wants to talk to you.'

'Why?'

'Originally she just wanted to find out if I'd ever heard of you. She had your name, for some reason.'

'How'd she get it?'

'She's trying find a woman named Macy,' said Bonnie, waving the flyer. 'Ring any bells?'

'Why didn't this Kinnie woman just call me directly?'

'I said I'd talk to you first, make sure you called back, which you will now.'

'Is this Macy in some kind of trouble?'

'I don't know. Not my business. Not yet, anyway. Kinnie's dad has gone missing. He used to be chief of police up there. Kinnie grew up in the business.'

'Daddy Joe?'

'I see you've heard of him. Kinnie said it's not the first time he's gone missing. He's gone a bit non compos mentis, now that he's retired.'

'She was adopted. Macy, I mean. She told me

74

she grew up on the reservation. Why is Kinnie looking for her?'

'I don't know. Kinnie just mentioned her name. Like I said, she wants to talk to you.'

'How did Kinnie get my name?'

'You'll have to ask her that when you call. Listen, this is not official business on my part. I got no skin in the game. I'm just doing a personal favor for Kinnie. She's part of a professional group I'm in. I thought it'd be easier for both of you if I talked to you first. So you wouldn't start freaking out.'

'Appreciated. Thanks.'

'You ready?' Bonnie said, indicating her phone.

Rolly nodded. Bonnie spelled out Kinnie's name and read him the number. Rolly entered the information into his phone.

'Anything else?' he said.

'That's it,' Bonnie said. She turned to leave, then stopped to look back at him. 'How are you doing?' she said. 'With your dad and all?'

'My mom wants me to talk to him. About his lifestyle. She thinks I could influence him, I guess – get him to stop drinking.'

'I talked to my dad once, when he was in the hospital with cirrhosis. About cutting back, eating better and stuff.'

'How'd that go?'

'He said he wasn't taking nutrition advice from a girl who ate pussy.'

'Your dad was an even bigger asshole than mine.'

'He looked scared to death in that hospital, before he died. I really saw him for who he was then, just a lonely, fucked-up bastard with nothing left in life but getting plastered and calling people names, pushing everyone away so he could crawl into that bottle.'

'I guess we both turned out OK, under the circumstances.'

'Yeah, well, you know what they say: you can't pick your parents. Make sure you call Kinnie. I told her you would. I don't want her telling me you're acting like a jerk.'

'I won't be a jerk,' Rolly said.

Bonnie left. Rolly locked the door. He reached into the back of his amplifier and pulled out the roll of paper he'd stashed there. The woman from the Desert View Tower had found it rolled up in a slot in the shop's map case. She'd been looking for a map to show Rolly the location of Slab City. The shop had all sorts of maps for sale – road maps of California and the Southwest, elevations and trail maps for local parks and wilderness areas. But this map wasn't like any of the others. The proprietors had never seen it before.

It looked like a schematic diagram for some kind of electronic device. There was a nine-digit number printed in the bottom right-hand corner. He couldn't remember the exact number embossed on the gold tube that hung from Macy's necklace, but he had a feeling this one was the same. There was a word printed above the number. *TEOTWAYKI*. There were two more words printed above that. *Astral Vibrator*.

Rolly had realized that the man in the rocks had left it for him, the birdman from Slab City with the VW van that looked like a rocket ship. He'd offered the woman ten dollars for the rolled-up tube of paper. She said he could have it for free. He'd left a ten-spot in the tower's donation box on his way out. The roll of paper was worth at least that much to him.

He walked to the sofa, sat down and took off his shoes. He rolled out the diagram and stared at it for a minute. He had a marginal familiarity with the symbols used in electronic diagrams but this one was too complicated for him to assess, especially in his present condition. He rolled the diagram up, dropped it onto the floor and leaned back on the sofa. Two minutes later, he fell asleep.

Three hours later, his phone rang, waking him. He rolled off the sofa, crawled to the table and checked the number. It was Macy. He answered. 'Hey,' he said. 'We need to talk.'

'Fuck you, Waters,' said Macy. 'Fuck you and that cop you put on my ass.'

Ten
The Plans

'Astral Vibrator, huh?' said Marley Scratch, glancing over the diagram Rolly had handed him. He laughed. 'How come every time you ask me to look at something, it always ends up involving female anatomy?'

'I don't think it's that kind of vibrator,' said Rolly.

'You try Googling it yet? I bet that's what you'll end up with.'

'I imagine I would. I think this is for a guitar, though, like a stomp box or something.'

'Is this a musical or sleuthing endeavor?' said Marley.

'Detective work,' said Rolly.

'Where'd you get a hold of this?'

'Long story,' said Rolly. 'I wouldn't believe it myself if I hadn't been there.'

The two men stood in the kitchen of Marley's loft on Broadway and Seventh, the second floor of the old Apex Music store, which had been replaced many years ago by a Super Discount grocery outlet, an early casualty in the decline of independent music stores brought on by the rise of chain stores and the Internet. It was a dingy old building, spared from its inevitable demolition by the recent economic downturn. The developers would return someday, but Marley could enjoy his twelve-foot ceilings and cheap rent another few years.

Rolly often called Marley when he needed assistance in deciphering computer data that needed to be recovered, analyzed or decrypted. When Marley wasn't working for Rolly, he made a hodgepodge career out of repairing computers and writing for game magazines. He also traded in antique toys and black Americana.

'I need more light to read this,' said Marley. Rolly followed him back to the work area. Marley clipped the schematic to the top of a

78

drafting table, turned on the table lamp and picked up a pair of reading glasses. He studied the document, tracing the signal path with his finger.

'You might be right about the guitar thing,' he said. 'The input impedance is the right level. There's no output, though, just a switch at the end of the signal path. Doesn't make sense for a stomp box. You'd want to feed the signal back out somewhere.'

'Does that number mean anything to you, below the name?'

'It could be a patent ID. Maybe the SKU.'

'There was a guy here in town, a guitar tech, named Buddy Meeks.'

'You think he designed this?'

'I've got this guitar he built. Well, not really a guitar. It's called a diddley bow. There's only one string.'

'Yeah, I know what a diddley bow is,' said Marley. 'Hey, I gotta show you the Molo that I picked up on my trip to the motherland.'

Marley stepped away from the table and returned with a primitive-looking stringed instrument. It had two strings stretched over a hollowed-out gourd and a broomstick for the neck. There was some sort of skin stretched across the gourd opening, like a drum.

'When were you in Africa?' said Rolly. He plucked at the strings. The instrument had a buzzy, lutish sound.

'Took a trip last year.'

'I didn't know that.'

'You've been out of touch, my friend.'

'Yeah. I guess so. How was it?'

'Some beautiful musical expressions. Alternate tunings and stuff. Some beautiful ladies, too.'

Marley hung the Molo back on the wall, next to a movie poster of Amos 'n' Andy.

'Hey, have you ever heard of the term Solfeggio?' said Rolly.

'Don't think so? Why?'

'This guy told me I needed to practice it. I think he's the same guy who left me the diagram.'

'You can Google it on the laptop, if you want.'

'Thanks.'

Marley returned to inspecting the diagram. Rolly moved to the sofa and opened the laptop sitting on the coffee table next to a red Tonka truck. You could count on there being at least a dozen computers scattered about Marley's loft at any given time, in variable states of functionality. There was usually one nearby. Rolly typed 'solfeggio' in the search field. He read through the entry at the top of the results page.

'Do, Re, Mi,' he said. 'That's what it is.'

'Hmm?'

'Solfeggio. It's vocalizing a scale with different sounds, like Do, Re, Mi.'

'Well, there you go.'

Rolly looked down to the list of search results. There was a video link for something called the Solfeggio frequencies. He clicked the link and played the video. A low tone played through the computer's speaker.

'What's that?' said Marley.

'It's one of the Solfeggio frequencies,' said Rolly.

80

'Doesn't sound like no Do, Re, Mi.'

'This is something different.'

'That's all it plays?'

'It says there are nine different frequencies. This one is a hundred and seventy-four hertz.'

'Kind of lacking on the funkiness level.'

'They claim it's for meditating. And entrainment, whatever that is.'

'I know what entrainment is,' said Marley. 'You know it too. Everytime you play with your band.'

'So what is it?'

'It's when people get synced up to music, how we all get hooked into the beat. Rhythmic patterns. People dancing as a group, trancing out together. It's like an evolutionary skill human beings developed.'

'Huh,' said Rolly. He flipped back to the listings on the search page, read through more of the list. There were all sorts of entries for Solfeggio frequencies.

'Each of the frequencies represents a different consciousness level,' he said, reading one of the entries. 'Consciousness Expansion. Awakening Intuition. Transcendence.'

'Sounds kinda woo woo to me.'

'My mom would love this stuff.'

Rolly continued reading. He thought about Dotty, the woman he'd met at the Alien Artifacts store. Universal Vibration Technologies. The paintings of flowing energy fields. The UVTs. She'd talked about frequencies, how they were used to release the alien within. The claims made on the Solfeggio websites were similar.

Some even claimed that listening to the tones could realign your DNA.

Marley muttered something under his breath.

'What's that?' said Rolly.

'What was that number you said earlier, that Solfeggio thing?'

'Umm, let me look: one hundred and seventy-four hertz.'

'Interesting,' said Marley.

'What?'

'That number's written on here. It's on one of the resistors. You say there's nine of them?'

'Yeah.'

'Read me the rest.'

Rolly read the frequency numbers listed on the website.

'They're all here,' said Marley. 'That's gotta mean something.'

'Really?'

'Take a look if you want to.'

Rolly rose from the sofa and joined Marley at the drafting table.

'You see, here,' said Marley, running his finger down the paper, 'above each of these squiggles.'

'Maybe this Astral Vibrator plays those frequencies or something?'

Marley shrugged. 'Maybe. Sure looks like it's got something to do with it.'

Rolly pulled his phone from his pocket and checked the time.

'I have to meet with a client,' he said. 'Can I leave this with you?'

'Sure,' said Marley. 'I'll do some more research. Maybe I can find that number on the bottom somewhere in a patent search. If I can find an abstract, it would help me figure it out faster.'

'I'll be over at the cantina. Give me a call if you find out anything.'

'Will do, Sir Roland.'

Eleven
The Cantina

Rolly sat in a back booth at the Villa Cantina, nursing a mug of Mexican cocoa and coffee. He'd finished his lunch – red enchiladas with an egg over easy. A satisfying meal was all the meditation he needed. It had provided both sustenance and gratification, greasing the wheels of his corroded feelings towards Macy. She had texted him a half hour ago to let him know she'd be late, which he hoped was a sign of appeasement. Neither of them had expressed themselves well on the phone. They were tired and angry, but they'd agreed on a truce and a face-to-face meeting to be held at the cantina. He opened his composition book and jotted down a few lines to keep his mind occupied while he waited.

I'm sitting and eating huevos rancheros.
Drinking black coffee and falling behind.
I'm feeling tired, bewildered and beaten.
Chasing old shadows and losing my mind.

His phone rang. He didn't recognize the number. He answered anyway. A sequence of tones played on the other end of the line, like a fax machine or computer calling. He hung up. The phone rang again, the same number. He muted it, then looked up to see Vera ushering Macy to his table.

'There he is,' said Vera. 'The great detective. You want something to drink?'

'Dos Equis Amber,' said Macy, plopping down on the booth cushion across from Rolly.

Vera wagged a finger at Rolly. 'You be nice to her, Mr Rolly,' she said. 'Macy's my home girl.'

'This is business, Vera,' said Rolly. 'Just business.'

'Yeah, well, I haven't forgotten the nasty business you brought into my place with that little chica a while ago.'

'That was an unexpected situation,' said Rolly.

'What happened?' said Macy.

'No big deal,' said Vera. 'Just some *tunante* who tried to kill me. I shot a hole in the wall upstairs and Hector ended up with some kind of skin condition on his face.'

Macy looked over at Rolly. 'Don't tell me,' she said. 'Your middle name is Trouble?'

'You be careful with this one, girl,' said Vera. 'Don't let those eyes fool you. He can talk you into anything. You gotta be cool.'

'I'm gonna be one chilly bitch,' said Macy.

'Like ice?' said Vera.

'Freezing.'

Vera laughed. Rolly smiled. It was all he had sometimes.

'Could I have a glass of bubbles, Vera?' he asked. 'With a lime? Please?'

'There he goes, Macy,' said Vera, 'With those eyes. You watch yourself.'

Vera walked away.

Macy drummed her fingers on the table. 'Bubbles, huh?' she said.

'Club soda.'

'Yeah, I know what it is. You don't drink alcohol, do you?'

'Not anymore.'

'Why'd you stop?'

'Health reasons. My car tried to kill me.'

'You OK if I drink?'

'No problem.'

'I need a beer. Your lady cop friend really got me riled up.'

'Bonnie can be very . . . focused.'

'I'll say. I thought you weren't allowed to tell people about me? Because I'm your client, right? I'm supposed to have some sort of immunity?'

'Yes. You have client privilege. I didn't give her your name.'

'She told me she'd talked to you.'

'It was that flyer you gave me,' said Rolly. 'It was sitting out on my table when she came by.'

'Damn,' Macy said.

'Sorry. She had your first name already and put two and two together.'

'She asked me where I was two nights ago.'

'Did she say why?'

'Daddy Joe's disappeared. Weird, huh? Same night he was here.'

'You told Bonnie about that?'

'Sure. Why wouldn't I? Daddy Joe gets kind of distracted sometimes. I'm betting he got lost

85

driving home, ran out of gas or something and drove into a ditch.'

Rolly flipped through the names on his phone and found the one Bonnie had given him.

'You know Kinnie Harper, right?'

'Yeah. I told you about her. Kinnie's a bitch.'

'You know she's with the police up there? The tribal police?'

Macy laughed. 'No shit,' she said. 'Kinnie's a cop now?'

'Bonnie told me she's chief of police.'

'Just like her daddy.'

'Bonnie wants me to call her.'

'What about?'

'I assume it's to ask about you.'

'How'd Kinnie get your name?'

'No idea. Did you tell anyone you'd hired me?'

'No. Vera's the only one knows I talked to you. Unless someone else saw us the other night.'

'Someone like who?'

'How would I know? I'm just speculating. Don't get on my case.'

They were silent a moment. Rolly waited, letting Macy cool down.

'Kinnie's like my big sister,' she said after a moment. 'She took care of me after Mama Joe died. Kinnie hated me, but I guess I understand where she was coming from.'

'What do you mean?'

'Daddy Joe put a lot of weight on her shoulders, taking care of the house, watching me. She was eleven or twelve, something like that, when her momma died. Daddy Joe didn't give her much of a break. He's kind of a hard case, real strict about men and women and what he expects. You know what I mean?'

'You think he abused Kinnie?'

'Oh, no, I never saw nothing like that. He just worked her to death.'

'When was the last time you talked to her or Daddy Joe?'

'I don't talk to them. Haven't since I left. I still can't figure how Daddy Joe found me. Your friend, that cop, was asking if I was up there recently, on the rez.'

'Were you?'

'I don't go to the rez. Period. Not since I left. I got too much history there – bad mojo.'

'You want to tell me about it?' said Rolly.

'Just some stupid teenager stuff. DNA.'

'OK. I'll assume it's not relevant.'

'Waters?'

'Yeah?'

'Are you setting me up?'

'What do you mean?'

'I don't know. It feels like I'm in a movie or something. Are you working with the cops to put me in jail?'

'I'm not working with the cops, but if you've done something illegal you need to tell me about it.'

'Hmm, let's see. I smoke weed sometimes. There, I confess. I smoked some weed Friday night. I used to do E when I first started clubbing. I've done a lot of things once. And I totally roll through stop signs.'

'You stole that necklace.'

'Yeah, I did. And I told you about it. That was over five years ago.'

'Here's my scenario. Daddy Joe goes missing. Kinnie Harper, his daughter, looks around the house and notices the diddley bow is missing. Kinnie knows you stole the necklace. Maybe she thinks you came back and stole the diddley bow, too. Took it from Daddy Joe's house.'

'I get what you're saying, Waters, but I didn't steal it. It's just like I told you. Vera gave me that thing Friday night after the guy brought it in.'

'I guess we can ask Vera.'

'Ask me what?' said Vera, arriving with their drinks.

'About the guy that was here the other night,' said Rolly. 'The one that gave you the package for Macy?'

'Oh, yeah. I remember. Big guy. Looked kind of Indian.'

'What'd he say to you?'

'Nothing. He just pointed at Macy's picture and handed me the package. I must've nodded at him or something. Then he left.'

Macy chuckled. 'He's a man of few words, that Daddy Joe.'

'You want anything to eat, Macy?' said Vera.

'I'm not that hungry,' said Macy. 'Maybe bring me some guac.'

Vera left them alone again.

'You satisfied now, Waters?' said Macy. 'I didn't steal the diddley bow.'

Rolly nodded. He felt satisfied, in both stomach and mind. He felt ready to share what he'd found out so far.

'I found someone who will give you a thousand dollars for it,' he said.

'Really?' said Macy. 'That thing is worth money?'

'I was surprised too.'

Rolly told Macy about his visit with Norwood and his confrontation with the man at the Alien Artifacts store.

'What's this guy's name again?' Macy asked when he'd finished.

'Randy Parker.'

'I went out with a guy named Randy once,' she said. 'Randy No Pants.'

'Nopanz?'

'No Pants,' said Macy, separating the words. 'That was his nickname.'

'What'd he look like?'

'Couple years older than me, I think. Even whiter than you. Good hair. Nice ass.'

'Any tattoos?'

'No.'

'The guy I met was a lot older,' said Rolly. 'He had some prison tattoos and a really bad wig.'

'Definitely not the same Randy.'

'Doesn't sound like it,' said Rolly.

Macy took a sip of her beer. Rolly stirred his club soda, watching the slice of lime spin around in his glass.

'What was the name of that weirdo group again?' said Macy. 'The one the lady at the store told you about?'

'She called them Yoovits. U-V-Ts. Universal Vibration Technologies.'

'She said the diddley thing belonged to them?'

'Yes.'

'Damn. That's kinda creepy.'

'What?'

'I think it was them that lived up near the rez. Daddy Joe was there when they found the bodies.'

'What are you talking about?'

'Well, not *there* there. It was after they killed themselves.'

'Wait. Back up. When was this?'

'I don't know. Before I was born. Look it up on Wikipedia or something. They all died. It was one of those suicide cult things, I think. That's how Daddy Joe got involved. He saw the people after they were dead. He arrested one of the guys.'

'How many people were there?'

'That died? It wasn't that many; I mean, compared to Jonestown or something like that. Kinda creepy though, huh?'

Rolly nodded his head and made a mental note to get more information on the UVTs. It was time to creep Macy out even more. He pulled the postcard from his pocket and passed it to her.

'Take a look at that,' he said. 'Tell me what you think.'

'Desert View Tower,' said Macy, looking at the card. 'I remember that place. Daddy Joe used to take Kinnie and me. We'd run around in the rocks.'

'Read the back,' said Rolly. Macy read the back of the card out loud. She stopped after the first line.

'Where'd you get this?' she asked.

Rolly described the ill-fated trip to Desert View Tower and its aftermath.

'Seriously,' Macy said. 'You got tasered?'

Rolly nodded.

'Teotwayki,' said Macy. 'Daddy Joe had that on the dry erase board in his room.'

'Is it an Indian word?'

'Kinnie could tell you what it means. Are you going to call her?'

'Bonnie will kill me if I don't.'

'You got some kind of thing going on with her?'

'Who? Bonnie?'

'Yeah. Are you two swapping fluids?'

'No. We're just friends.'

'I didn't think she'd be your type.'

'You could say that.'

'Yeah, I thought so. I was kinda digging on her, actually. She looks kinda hot in that uniform.'

'Uh huh,' said Rolly. He couldn't figure out Macy at all.

'A woman in uniform gets me hot and bothered. I think it's a sex and authority thing, you know, like a fetish.'

'Thanks for sharing,' said Rolly. 'But can we get back to what's on the card?'

'"Golden eyes key,"' said Macy, reading the card again. 'You think that's got something to do with me?'

'It's the first thought that came to me.'

'OK. I get it, now, Waters. I get why you're giving me a hard time.'

'Do you know anything about a key?'

'No. Do you?'

'Yeah. Maybe.' Rolly pulled out his phone again and tapped into his notes app. 'Read me the number,' he said. 'The one on your necklace.'

Macy read the number to him. It matched the number he had entered in his notes, digit for digit.

'So?' said Macy.

'You know that electronics schematic I told you about, the one I got from the maps display at the tower? It's got that word and that number written on it.'

'What's it mean?'

'I don't know. Could be a serial number or something.'

'Why is it on my necklace?'

'I don't know.'

'This is kind of freaking me out,' said Macy. 'They must be connected, right?'

'It's something simple. We'll figure it out.'

'I got something else freaky for you,' said Macy. 'That guy with the rocket-ship van?'

'Yeah?'

'I know him.'

'You do?'

'Slab City. Me and No Pants were there for a couple of days. After Coachella.'

'You and Randy No Pants were in Slab City together?'

'Yeah. I met that guy with the van. His name's Bob.'

'Does Bob have a last name?'

'I don't know. Everybody calls him Cool Bob.'

'Do you know anyone with a normal name?'

'That's weird about the van. I should go talk to Bob.'

'Maybe I should go with you.'

Macy took another sip of beer. 'Bob might let me stay with him. Don't think he'd go for you being around.'

'We'll just drive out and come back the same day.'

'Folks are kind of tight-lipped out there. I'm not even sure Bob will want to talk to me. We might have to camp out a couple of nights. We'd need a trailer or an RV. You don't want to sleep on the ground. Too many spiders and scorpions and other weird stuff.'

Rolly rubbed his head and sucked the last of his club soda up through the straw. It made a squelching sound. He knew he was going to say something stupid, something he shouldn't. But his tongue and his lips conspired against him. They said the words before he could stop them.

'I know where we can get an RV,' he said.

Twelve
The Rez

Rolly drove the Tioga along Interstate 8, heading up the grade into the mountains of East County on the way to Slab City. Macy rode shotgun, her bare feet propped up on the dash. They would pass the Jincona Reservation soon, then Desert

View Tower, and begin their descent into the desert. The Cuyamacas weren't the loftiest mountains to cross, but it was still slow going in the Tioga. It would take them at least three hours to arrive at their destination.

He'd felt embarrassed asking his stepmom, Alicia, if he could borrow the motorhome, but she been more than happy to lend it to him. She'd seemed relieved to get it out of the driveway, the two-ton elephant that had caused her so much distress. Rolly's father was still in the hospital. His condition had been upgraded to stable, but he wouldn't be taking any trips for a while. The great adventure would have to be rescheduled, put on the back burner for a few months, while he recuperated.

Alicia had primped her makeup and made herself presentable by the time Rolly and Macy arrived at the house. The larder of the Tioga was stocked and the gas tank was full. A great weight seemed to lift from Alicia's shoulders as Rolly backed out of the driveway. He pointed the Tioga in the right direction and set the cruise control. As mobile homes went, the Tioga wasn't that large, but it still felt like he was driving a house.

'You wanna see where I grew up? On the rez?' said Macy.

'I thought you never wanted to see the place again.'

'Now that we're out here, I guess I'm kind of curious. I could show you the place where those people died. The UVTs.'

'It's on the reservation?'

94

'It's next door,' Macy said. 'You can see the house from Daddy Joe's place.'

'You sure about this?'

'C'mon, Waters. I said I wanted to go. DNA.'

Rolly took the casino exit and crossed the bridge back over the freeway. They drove down a narrow country road that twisted through rocks, manzanita and sagebrush.

'Beautiful, isn't it?' Macy said. 'Not.'

'I didn't really get to see the terrain the other night. It seems kind of nice.'

'Not to me.'

'A bit austere, I guess.'

'Desolate is more like it.'

'We can still turn around if you want.'

Macy stared out the window. She'd lost interest in talking to him. Rolly checked his speedometer. The Tioga felt huge on the backcountry road, with the driver's side hanging over the centerline or the passenger side hugging the gravel shoulder. Two cars passed in the opposite direction. Small herds of sheep, horses and cows dotted the landscape.

'That's it, over there, the UVTs place,' said Macy, pointing at a wood sign set close to the ground on the opposite side of the road. Rolly slowed. A dirt road led away from the sign, blocked by a gate.

'Beatrice House for Girls,' he said, reading the sign.

'Yeah, that's the place. Kinnie used to say Daddy Joe was going to send me there. Like all the other bad girls.'

'I don't see any house,' said Rolly.

'It's over that rise, looks out on the mesa. You can see it from Daddy Joe's place.'

Rolly continued down the road. A large, open vista came into view, a mountain peak in the distance. Macy pulled her feet from the dash.

'Holy crap!' she said, pointing at the building that loomed in the foreground. 'Is that the casino?'

'That's it,' said Rolly. 'That's where we played the other night.'

'Sure is ugly.'

A small green sign on the right side of the road informed them they were entering the Jincona reservation. They passed the sign, then the casino.

'Hard to believe they could make this place even worse,' said Macy. 'I guess they're all gonna get rich.'

'Some of those casinos don't do that well,' said Rolly. 'We played this place near Julian. There were only three people in the room.'

'Maybe that was because of your band.'

'Nice. Thanks.'

'You want to see Daddy Joe's place?'

'I'm not sure that's a good idea.'

'I grew up there, you know. I got a right to visit my old house.'

'I haven't been able to get in touch with Kinnie yet.'

'So what? You called her, right?'

Rolly nodded. He'd left two messages for Kinnie. She'd left one for him.

'She might not like us snooping around.'

'If Kinnie shows up we'll just say we were

coming to see her. We've both got alibis for the other night.'

'Yeah.'

'Daddy Joe might've shown up by now, anyway.'

Rolly bit his lip. He hadn't told Macy what the man with the taser had said to him, that Daddy Joe was a dead man. He didn't want to tell her. He didn't want to tell anyone, not without some kind of proof.

'C'mon, Waters,' said Macy. 'A trip down memory lane might help me remember something important. Take a left at the intersection.'

Rolly turned at the stop sign. The road got rougher. He did what he could to avoid the larger potholes, but the bumps and ruts weren't friendly to the Tioga's suspension. They crested a small hill. Below them the road ran straight down to the edge of a triangular mesa. A small ranch-style house stood on the edge of the mesa, overlooking the intersection of two canyons.

'That's Daddy Joe's place,' said Macy.

Rolly lifted his foot off the gas. The Tioga inched down the road like a tiptoeing elephant. The house was surrounded by a yard, if your definition of yard included an open space filled with gravel and cactus and tumbleweeds. A low chain-link fence helped keep the tumbleweeds from entering or leaving the yard. He pulled to a stop in front of the gate.

'This is where you grew up?' he said.

'Yep. I lived here with Daddy Joe and Kinnie. Aunt Betty too, I guess, although I don't really remember her, just from photos.'

'How old were you then?'

'Two or three,' said Macy.

Macy opened her door and stepped down from the cab. She was all the way to the front door of the house before Rolly could protest. Macy seemed oblivious to caution, unconcerned with self-control, that imprint of age and experience. Rolly knew he'd acted that way himself once. His compulsions weren't as strong anymore, but he often found himself in conflict with his natural tendencies. Macy's impulsiveness felt exciting, almost sexy. She opened the door to the house and walked in.

He jumped out of the Tioga and looked around to make sure no one was watching. Across the canyon he could see a large house, the Beatrice House for Girls, if he'd understood Macy correctly. It looked much nicer and newer than Daddy Joe's rundown hovel. He walked to the front door. Macy had left it ajar.

'Macy?' he whispered. No one answered. He pushed the door open then raised his voice. 'Macy!'

'I'm in back,' she said. 'There's nobody home.'

'We shouldn't be in here,' said Rolly. 'What if somebody shows up?'

'Chill out, Waters. It's cool. It's my house as much as anybody's.'

'Macy . . .'

'There's something in here you need to see.'

Rolly took a deep breath and entered the house. The kitchen was piled with dishes and the living room was dusty. It had dank green carpeting and

98

a dirty brown sofa. Heavy curtains prevented any sunlight disinfectant.

'Where are you?' he said.

'In here,' said Macy, from a doorway off to his right. He walked to the doorway and peeked in. Macy sat at a small desk in the corner. The desk was piled high with papers. All sorts of papers, drawings, photos and maps covered the walls.

'What is it?' he asked. Macy turned from the desk.

'My flyer,' she said. 'Daddy Joe's got my flyer.'

She handed Rolly a flyer, just like the one she'd handed him the night they met.

'It was here on the desk?' Rolly said.

'There's a letter, too. It's not finished . . .'

'What?'

'It's addressed to me,' she said, handing him the letter.

Rolly inspected the paper in his hand. It felt coarse, like an autumnal leaf. The handwriting was rough too. You could almost see the quiver of the hand that had written it. But the words were legible.

'"My Little Alien,"' he said, reading the salutation.

'Daddy Joe called me that sometimes,' said Macy.

Rolly continued reading the note. '"I have seen a photograph of this woman. The one called DJ Crazy Macy. I know it is you. You are old enough now. I must tell you some things. About the gold charm which I see you still wear. The one stolen from me. It is yours now. I have something else for you. It is an instrument of great power."'

Rolly looked over at Macy. She nodded. Rolly turned back to the letter.

"'I had intended to make it a gift to you on your eighteenth birthday, when you would have your freedom, but you left us before that time came. There is more I still hope to give you. So that you may be free. But you must speak with me first, before I can—"

'He didn't finish,' said Rolly.

'Flip it over,' said Macy. Rolly flipped the paper over. Three words were scrawled on the back.

TEOTWAYKI? TEOTWAYKI? TEOTWAYKI?

Rolly looked over at Macy. 'What's this stuff on the walls?'

'Kinda creepy, huh?' she said. 'He's still obsessed with the UVTs. It's up there still.'

Macy pointed at the dry erase board on the wall, at the capital letters in red lettering. TEOTWAYKI.

'We shouldn't be here,' Rolly said.

'Yeah,' said Macy. 'This is totally spooky.'

'I don't want anyone finding us here,' Rolly said. 'Especially if Daddy Joe's still missing. It would look suspicious.'

He handed the letter back to Macy, who placed it back on the desk. Their fingerprints were all over it now. They trooped back out to the Tioga and climbed in.

'That was stupid,' said Rolly, as he buckled himself in. 'Let's get the hell out of here.'

'Yeah, I'm sufficiently creeped,' said Macy. 'But at least we know how Daddy Joe found me.'

Rolly turned the Tioga around and headed out the same way they'd come in. It was the only way to go.

100

'Why didn't he send me the letter?' said Macy as they jounced along the road that was more like a ditch.

'He couldn't wait, I guess. Maybe he thought you wouldn't talk to him if he only sent you a letter.'

'Shit,' said Macy. 'Everything's different now. I thought I didn't care. Coming back here, suddenly I'm worried about Daddy Joe. Maybe he's in trouble or something. Maybe he's dead.'

'Don't worry,' said Rolly, trying to manage his own sense of uneasiness. 'They'll find him soon.'

They crested the hill and started back down into the middle of the reservation. Rolly resisted the urge to drive faster. The Tioga didn't belong here. It was too large, too obvious. He felt like an alien in a crippled spacecraft. As they approached the intersection to the main road he spotted a truck, parked on the other side of the road, shaded under a tree.

'You see it?' said Macy.

'I see,' Rolly replied.

'That's tribal police.'

'I know. Be cool.'

'Too late,' said Macy. 'I'm hyperventilating. I gotta lie down, in the back.'

Macy took off her seat belt, lowered her head, snuck back to the dining room and laid down in the booth. Rolly pulled up to the stop sign facing the patrol truck across the intersection. He made a full stop, checked for traffic and turned left onto the main road.

'Was it her?' Macy whispered. 'Was it Kinnie?'

'I don't know. I couldn't see anyone.'

Macy crawled along the floor and into the bedroom. She climbed on the bed and looked out the rear window.

'Shit,' she said. 'It's her. I know it. She's pulling out.'

Rolly checked his rearview mirror. The tribal police truck came into sight, following them at a well-measured distance. He checked his speedometer, looked in the mirror again and took a deep breath. No one knew him here. He hadn't broken any rules. No one could prove he'd been in Daddy Joe's house.

'I can't see if it's her,' said Macy. 'She's staying too far back.'

'Sit down and stop staring. Don't act so suspicious.'

The police truck continued to follow them. Macy crawled back up to the front. She got up on her knees and pointed out the front window.

'That's the reservation border up ahead – that sign,' she said. 'If she's going to stop us, she'll have to do it soon.'

Rolly checked his mirror again. He relaxed his hands on the wheel. They passed the boundary sign.

'She stopped, didn't she?' said Macy.

Rolly checked his mirror. The police truck had pulled off to the side of the road. 'Yeah. How'd you know?'

'She had to. That's the rules.'

Rolly watched in the rearview mirror as the police truck turned around and headed back in the opposite direction.

102

'Sovereign nations,' said Macy. 'Tribal police can't arrest you once you're outside the rez. The county sheriff can't arrest you once you're inside.'

'Sound pretty complicated,' said Rolly.

'Oh, yeah,' said Macy. 'I took advantage of it a couple of times.'

Thirteen
The Mountain

'Oh, God, I remember that smell,' Macy said as they drove through the town of Calipatria, just south of the Salton Sea. It wasn't much of a town, more like a gathering of buildings not quite as far apart as others they'd recently passed. There was farmland for miles around, long rows of tilled earth on either side of the road – desert farms irrigated by water diverted from the Colorado River. There was a notable scent of fertilizer in the air.

'You see that weird castle thing over there?' said Macy, pointing at a long purple wall adorned with yellow turrets. 'We took some pictures there when I came out with No Pants. You ever been to Coachella?'

'Big festivals aren't my kind of thing. Not usually my kind of music, either.'

'Yeah. I hear what you're saying. It was hot as fuck during the day. I'd love to play for a big crowd like that, though, get some serious entrainment going.'

'Entrainment?'

'Yeah. You know what that means?'

'I just learned it yesterday.'

'That's what being a DJ's all about. Everybody moving to the music. Mass-altered states. In a good way.'

'Have you ever heard of something called the Solfeggio frequencies?'

'No,' said Macy. 'What's that?'

Rolly explained what he'd read on the website the day before.

'Sounds like it might be good for my downtempo stuff,' said Macy. 'Chillout or Lounge. Those are kinda like the New Age of dance beats.'

Rolly considered all the things he didn't know in the world. There were a lot of them.

'How long were you out here with Randy No Pants?' he asked.

'Less than a week. I dumped him. It was not a healthy relationship.'

'You want to tell me about it?'

Macy stared at Rolly for a moment. 'Sure, Doctor Phil,' she said. 'Let me tell you all about my dysfunctional relationships. How guys ask me to dress up in little girls' clothes, call them daddy and suck on a lollipop.'

'Really?' said Rolly.

Macy rolled her eyes. 'I'm being sarcastic, Waters. Don't be my shrink. Just be you. You're cool the way you are, almost like an adult.'

'To tell you the truth,' Rolly said, 'I thought you liked girls.'

'Because I got all hot and bothered about that butch girlfriend of yours? Bonnie the Copper?'

'Well, I did consider it a possibility.'

'She's gay, right?'

Rolly nodded. Bonnie didn't advertise, but she didn't hide either.

'Yeah, Waters, you've been trying to figure me out since we met. I saw the way you checked me out at the cantina. You been calculating the odds, trying to figure out if I'm doable, wondering if an old guy like you could get lucky.'

'I don't sleep with my clients.'

'Doesn't stop you from thinking about it though, does it?'

'Well,' said Rolly, 'some things are hard not to think about.'

'Your friend Bonnie is kinda hot. I'd let her strip-search me anytime.'

'So . . .'

'DNA, Waters. Don't try to label me. If I get a vibe, I go with it. You got a problem with that?'

'No. No problem,' said Rolly. He smiled.

'There you go,' Macy said. 'With that look. Just like Vera warned me. It makes you seem so . . . decent.'

'Sorry.'

'You ever seen the place that crazy Christian guy built? Salvation Mountain?'

'I don't think so.'

'We should stop there. You should see it.'

'I'm not exactly religious.'

'Neither am I. Not really. Not any organized shit, anyway. I just think it's cool when someone goes crazy like that, dedicates their whole life to something non-remunerative.'

'Uh huh.'

'There it is,' said Macy. 'Pull off at the sign.'

Rolly pulled off the road in front of a large sky-blue sign: *God Never Fails – Salvation Mountain*. He parked the Tioga. Salvation Mountain was an exuberant monument made of paint and plaster. A modest hill rising above the desert floor, it was covered in bright washes of green, blue, purple and yellow, adorned with the words 'Love' and 'Repent' spelled out in large letters. Biblical quotations had been lettered into the mountain's nooks and crannies. Primitive illustrations of flowers, trees and rivers flowed down the sides. A camper truck had been parked out in front with similar embellishments.

Macy opened the door and jumped out. Rolly followed her. The hot desert air hit his face like the belch of an underworld demon. He regretted letting Macy talk him into this adventure. He hoped the Tioga's air conditioning would hold up.

'Let's walk to the top,' said Macy, pointing at the cross on top of the mountain.

'It's OK to do that?'

'Oh, yeah,' Macy said. 'I've been up there before.' She pointed to a large yellow step at the base of the mountain. 'Follow the yellow brick road,' she said.

Rolly cleared his throat, wondering how long it would take heat stroke to set in. Macy could afford to be enthusiastic in this heat. She was young and skinny.

'C'mon, you infidel,' Macy said. 'Let's go find God, see if he wants to talk to us.'

Rolly followed Macy up the bright yellow stairway that curved around the mountain. They reached the peak, stood at the base of the cross and looked out at the desert panorama. You could see for miles in every direction.

'You OK?' said Macy.

'I'm fine.'

'You look a little flushed.'

'It's hot out here.'

'Hotter than fuck,' said Macy. She put her hand over her mouth. 'I really need to watch my language.'

'Don't be sacrilegious.'

'At least I wasn't taking the Lord's name in vain. I should watch my mouth, though. Out of respect for Leonard.'

'Who's Leonard?'

'The guy who built this place. The crazy guy.'

They walked around the cross, taking in the scenery and bright decorations on the sides of the mountain below them. Streams of blue and white flowed down the mountain, painted to look like waterfalls. Pink and orange paint blossoms bloomed against fields of green. A benevolent deity ruled over Salvation Mountain.

'So, Waters,' said Macy, 'you ready to repent? You have anything you need to confess?'

'Do you?'

'I asked first.'

Rolly thought for a moment. 'Yeah. Sure. OK,' he said. 'The guy in your photo – the one with Aunt Betty, the baseball player. I talked to him.'

'You found the guy?'

'Yeah. Well, this is the confession part. I knew who it was when you showed it to me. I thought I did, anyway. I was right.'

'So who is he?'

'Eric Ozzie. The Sneaker.'

'Wait. Is that the guy on TV? With those ads?'

Rolly nodded.

'What'd he say?'

'He said the photo's from his minor league days. In Hawaii. He doesn't remember your Aunt Betty.'

'That's all you found out?'

'Afraid so.'

'You think he was telling the truth?'

'He said he'd be willing to talk to you, that he'd take responsibility.'

'In case he's my daddy?'

'Yeah. I think that's what he was saying.'

'Yeah, well, like I said earlier, if he and Aunt Betty hooked up and I'm the result, there were a lot of recessive genes getting together. It'd be a million to one, ten million to one that I'd look like I do.'

'You really understand all that heredity stuff?'

'I've done some reading on it. DNA.'

'Why can't I ask?'

'No, sorry. I meant the genetic thing. That DNA.'

'I have another confession,' said Rolly. 'Something the man said to me, the guy at Desert View Tower, the one with the taser.'

'What'd he say?'

'He said Daddy Joe was a dead man.'

Macy wrinkled her nose. She sniffled. 'This dry air makes me crazy,' she said.

'Why did you take me to Daddy Joe's house?' said Rolly.

'You ever feel like you're going crazy?' said Macy.

'I used to. Not so much now.'

'The Gold Drinkers. That's what Daddy Joe called the UVTs. He said they drank gold, like the medicine man made him do once, when Daddy Joe was sick. He told me the UVTs drank gold every day.'

'That doesn't sound very healthy.'

'Actually, gold's inert. It won't hurt you. You ever seen that five-thousand-dollar chocolate sundae the guy makes in Vegas? They put gold flakes all over the thing. People eat it right down. It wasn't drinking the gold that killed them. They'd just be trace amounts anyway. The UVTs would boil this big nugget in water, then everyone drank the water. Gold soup. That's how they died.'

'You just told me it was safe,' Rolly said.

'They got something else in their soup one day. This other chemical. Some kind of cyanide. Daddy Joe told me that miners use it to separate the gold from the rocks. He arrested the guy.'

'I thought they committed suicide,' said Rolly.

'Sodium cyanide. That's what it's called. That's how they died. Fucks up your system so you can't breathe. I snuck into Daddy Joe's desk once, looked through some papers he had. There were some photographs, too. Of the dead people. And some other stuff. I wanted to check.'

'Check what?'

'One of those diddley bow things. I remember seeing it in one of the photographs.' Macy walked away from him. She pointed into the distance. 'That's Slab City, over there,' she said.

Rolly turned to look in the direction she pointed. He didn't see much: a collection of trailers and broken-down buildings.

'Something's going to happen,' said Macy. 'Something that changes things.'

'What makes you say that?'

'You'd tell me, wouldn't you, if you thought I was crazy?'

'You're not crazy.'

'I got my own confession to make, Waters, about that word. I know what it means.'

'Teotwayki?'

'It's not an Indian word. It's an acronym.'

'What does it mean?'

'The end of the world as you know it.'

A chill ran up Rolly's spine. His sweat evaporated in the dry desert heat. He rubbed the stubble on his chin, stared at the ground. *TEOTWAYKI.* Daddy Joe was obsessed with the word. The man in the rocks at Desert View Tower had chirped the word like a bird call. The end of the world.

Two years ago a preacher had purchased billboard space along the San Diego freeways, advertising his predicted apocalypse date to disgruntled commuters, providing them with a number to call for more information. You could make a good living on Doomsday predictions. Apocalypse preparers even had their own TV

110

shows now. Geeks freaked out over the Y2K bug and that collider thing the scientists had built in Switzerland. The end was coming. It always had been. It always would be.

He wondered if the UVTs knew they were going to die when they drank the poisoned soup. Had they believed that the aliens would really take them away? There was nothing anyone could do for them now. There were only the living, people with problems, with troubles and crazy thoughts, people who hadn't left Earth yet. His father and Daddy Joe. Macy Starr. He hoped he could help Macy find what she wanted without any apocalypse.

'Onward,' he said.

They walked back down the mountain and climbed up into the Tioga. Rolly started the engine and cranked up the air conditioner. He'd never done well in hot weather. Getting older and fatter hadn't made it any easier. He hoped the desert air would cool down tonight.

They left Salvation Mountain in the rearview mirror and continued down the road. Macy pointed to an abandoned concrete guardhouse on their right. Someone had painted the guardhouse like the sky, a blue background with dusty white stencils of bird and tree shapes. Words had been stenciled along the upper molding as well. *Welcome to Slab City*.

Fourteen
The Garden

Rolly and Macy stood under a rusty rebar archway. Old propane tanks were encased inside the rebar, and a spinning bicycle wheel was stuck to the top of the arch. Car doors reinforced the base, one on each side. It was the entryway to a well-tended garden of sculptural junk. A perimeter line of old tires encircled the garden, embedded halfway into the ground.

'East Jesus,' said Macy. 'The discarded afterbirth of the Industrial Age, repurposed for aesthetic enhancement.'

'What's that?'

'That's how Bob described it to me. He gets kinda philosophical. All the art in here is built out of trash and junk people collected. It's their ethos. Making art from our modern refuse.'

'Is it OK for us to go in?' asked Rolly.

'Sure. In the daytime. You need to make a reservation if you want to come by at night.'

'How do you get a reservation?'

'I don't really know. Cool Bob just told me to get here before dark. He said people start shooting at night.'

Rolly swallowed. They walked through the arch, into East Jesus.

112

'Hey, this is new,' said Macy, inspecting a spiral installation of jagged metal triangles.

'Uh huh,' said Rolly, keeping an eye out for any gunmen who might be setting up for the evening. He pulled out his cell phone and checked the time.

'It's ten after six now. You sure Bob said to meet him here?'

'Relax, Waters,' said Macy, walking towards a tall pile of black rubber. 'Cool Bob will show up. Time is fluid around here. Check this out.'

Rolly put his phone back in his pocket and walked over to Macy.

'Looks like some kind of elephant,' he said.

'A mammoth,' said Macy. 'It's called Definition of a Grievance.'

'What's that mean?'

'I don't know, but it's pretty cool, huh?'

'Yeah. Pretty cool.'

The Mammoth, or Grievance, loomed over them, raised up on its hind legs. It had been built out of reclaimed strips of automobile tires fastened together with wire and string. The Grievance had two headlights for eyes, car fenders for tusks and a corrugated rubber tube for a trunk.

'Looks like he's wearing a gas mask,' said Rolly, but Macy had already moved on. He followed her. They stopped at a low wall of reclaimed television sets, various models and sizes stacked on top of each other. Each of the TV screens had been painted white, and words were painted in red letters on the white screens. *Bad News. Some Things Never Change. Dear*

God No. Some of the screens had only one word on them.

'Blah,' Macy said, reading the screens. 'Blah, blah, blah.'

'Everyone's a critic,' said Rolly.

'I don't see the dolls,' Macy said. 'There used to be these gold dolls.'

Moving on, they saw the top half of a house, set askew, sunk halfway into the ground as if caught in a flood. They passed a group of beer keg animals that had bottles for legs and a short piece of watering hose for tails. The heads on the beer kegs were bleached animal skulls.

Macy stopped beside a circle of rusted tin cans, different sizes of cans set in the ground at varying heights.

'They're supposed to be drums,' she said.

Rolly squatted down by the cans and tapped on a couple of them.

'Bob says they sound really cool when it rains,' said Macy.

'I bet they do,' said Rolly. 'Doesn't seem like you'd get to hear them much in the desert, though.'

Macy squatted down beside him and spoke in a whisper. 'Don't freak out, but somebody's spying on us.'

'Where?'

'Over my right shoulder, behind that stand of creosote bushes.'

Rolly swiveled his head, surveying the scene. 'Yeah, I see him,' he said. There was someone standing outside the garden perimeter, hiding behind a bush. The bush covered the man's face but you could see his body. 'You think it's Cool Bob?' said Rolly.

'Bob's a lot taller.'

Rolly stood up and turned to face the man. 'Hello,' he called. The man yelped and ran away. They watched him run out of sight.

'There was this guy, when I came here with No Pants,' said Macy. 'He started following me around.'

'What'd he want?'

'I don't know. He'd stand about ten feet in front of me and just stare. That chicken-ass Randy wouldn't confront the guy. I started screaming, finally scared him off.'

'You think that was the same guy just now?'

'Maybe. The other guy made this weird sound, like a bird.'

'Teotwayki?' said Rolly. He chirped the word a couple of times, imitating the sound of the birdman at Desert View Tower.

'Holy shit, Waters!' said Macy. 'That was it. Teotwayki! Holy shit!'

'My goodness,' said a voice from behind them. 'Such fervent ejaculating.'

Rolly and Macy turned towards the voice. A tall man with a scraggly beard and long hair stood behind them. He wore shorts and sandals, and nothing else.

'Bob!' said Macy. She ran to the man and gave him an ardent hug. Rolly glanced down at the dirt.

'Hey, Bob,' said Macy, breaking the clinch, 'this is Rolly Waters.'

'Hi,' said Rolly, offering his hand. Bob shook it.

'He's older,' said Bob. 'Older than the last guy.'

'Yeah. Waters here is an adult.'

Rolly let Bob and Macy exchange niceties a bit longer, then got down to business. 'I'm trying to find a VW van,' he said. 'Macy told me you had one. A customized one that looks like a spaceship?'

Bob's face clouded over. 'Whoa,' he said. 'That's supernormal.'

'It was unusual,' said Rolly. 'I've never seen one like it.'

'No, man,' said Bob. 'I mean, this is paranormal. Fatalistic. I traded with a guy three days ago.'

'You got rid of the jam van?' said Macy.

'Temporarius only, Mace, not a mooch. The guy left some collateral. He'll bring it back.'

'When's he supposed to return it?' said Rolly.

'Could be tomorrow. Could be next week. Could be a year from now.'

'Does he live around here? Could we talk to him?'

'Not for me to say,' said Bob. 'The guy's prodigious. Totally singular.'

Bobspeak – that's what Macy had called it earlier, describing Bob's unusual speaking style. Bob's vocal inflections imparted the intended meaning but the words themselves made less sense the more you thought about them.

'What's his name?' Rolly asked.

'Can't say.'

'You don't know his name?'

'Not allowed. No designating.'

116

Rolly wasn't sure if Bob was refusing to give him the name or if the man in question didn't actually have one. It sounded like both. Macy tried to help.

'It's OK, Bob. This guy's cool,' said Macy. 'Not like the guy who was with me the last time.'

'No Pants was heinous,' said Bob. 'Left me in shambles.'

'Yeah, I know. He was an asshole.'

'What happened?' said Rolly.

'Randy broke into Bob's trailer,' said Macy. 'We figured he was looking for Scooby Snacks.'

'He was looking for dog food?'

Macy laughed. 'You see, Bob? This guy's one hundred percent. He doesn't even drink.'

'Way orthodox,' said Bob. 'Theological.'

Macy nodded. 'What did this guy give you for the van? For collateral?'

'A metal box.'

'That's it? A metal box?'

Bob nodded his head. 'I got it in the trailer,' he said. 'You wanta' see?'

Macy turned back to Rolly. Rolly nodded. Bob turned on his heels and walked away. Macy and Rolly scrambled to catch up with him. They tramped to the far end of East Jesus, stepped across the tire perimeter and headed further into the desert. Bob took long strides. It was hard for his shorter companions to keep up.

'Where are we going?' said Rolly as he and Macy dropped into a steady trot ten feet behind Bob.

'Bob's trailer is out on the range,' said Macy.

'Home, home on the range . . .' Rolly said, singing the cowboy tune.

'Not exactly. It's a shooting range.'

'That doesn't sound peaceful, or safe.'

'Depends on who's around. Bob likes guns, anyway.'

Rolly's stomach grumbled. He wished he'd eaten before they set out, but daylight had been waning. They'd wanted to find Bob before sundown.

'We're almost there,' Macy said.

Cool Bob turned in behind an embankment of dirt. Rolly and Macy followed him. There was an old Coachmen trailer parked on the other side of the embankment. An awning had been stretched from the top of the trailer, providing a rectangle of shade. A white plastic table sat under the shade, a mismatched assortment of chairs gathered around it.

'Wait there,' Bob said, indicating the table. He opened the door to his trailer and went in, then closed it behind him. Rolly and Macy sat at the table, across from each other. The sun was lower now but it still felt good to be in the shade.

'What are Scooby Snacks?' said Rolly.

'Ecstasy. MDMA. You know what that is, right?'

Rolly nodded. 'Is Bob a dealer or something?'

'No Pants thought so, I guess. I asked Bob to show me around the Slabs. Randy was going through his trailer when we got back.'

'Did Bob think you set him up?'

'At first. I found a way to make up with him.'

'Oh.'

118

'Bob's hung like a horse.'

'Didn't need that information.'

'Sorry. Oversharing again.'

The door of the trailer opened. Cool Bob stepped down, carrying an assault rifle. Rolly glanced at Macy, wondering if he should be nervous. She looked nonchalant. Bob handed Macy the gun.

'This is beautiful, Bob,' said Macy. 'Is it new?'

'Yeah,' replied Bob. 'You wanna go shoot some stuff?'

'Maybe later,' said Macy. 'We wanta' see that metal box thing.'

'Okey-doke,' said Bob. He trudged back to the trailer.

'Whattya think, Waters?' said Macy. 'You like crazy chicks with guns?'

Macy looked perfectly relaxed holding the rifle. She'd clearly handled one like it before, unperturbed by the firepower held at her fingertips. Rolly wondered if he'd have to go to the gun range with them later and peel off a few rounds to be sociable. Both Macy and Bob would outshoot him – he felt sure of that. He just hoped he wouldn't embarrass himself.

Bob returned with a black metal box and placed it on the table. He remained standing between them. The box was rectangular, about two feet wide, eight inches tall and perhaps a foot deep. It looked like a wall safe, solid black steel with a panel in the front, thickly bolted. There was no slot for a key; no keypad or combination to spin. There was only a single extruded hole in the front panel, held in place by a six-sided nut.

'You traded the van for this?' said Macy. Bob nodded.

'What is it?' she said.

'Don't know. He said it was valuable.'

'You must really trust this guy,' said Macy.

'Impeccable,' said Bob.

'That looks like a quarter-inch jack there in the front,' said Rolly. 'Like you could plug a guitar into it.'

Bob giggled and put his hand over his mouth. 'What is it?' said Macy.

'He calls it a vibrator.'

Macy laughed. 'What's it a vibrator for – Robbie the Robot?'

Rolly pursed his lips and leaned forward, put his hand on the box, inspecting it.

'Does this mean something to you?' said Macy.

'Maybe. I'm not sure.'

Rolly turned to Bob. 'The guy who gave you this – does he play guitar?' he asked.

'Not a player,' Bob said. 'He builds guitars, though, these one-stringed things, like for kids. He builds all kinds of stuff. Totally Edison.'

Rolly felt a glimmer in the back of his brain. He needed to talk to the man and show him the diddley bow to confirm it. The man could be Buddy Meeks.

'You play guitar, huh?' said Bob.

'Yeah,' said Rolly. 'I play.'

'You any good?'

'Are you kidding, Bob?' said Macy. 'This guy's the hottest guitar slinger in San Diego. He's a killer. Hall of fame.'

120

Bob folded his arms and squinted at Rolly. 'How many frets on a guitar?' he asked.

'What?'

'Macy says you're the shit. So answer the question.'

'I didn't know I'd be taking a test.'

'C'mon, Bob,' said Macy.

Bob didn't say anything. He stared at Rolly. 'How many?' he said.

'Well,' Rolly said, 'first I'd want to know what kind of guitar you were asking about. Classical or Electric?'

'Why?'

'Well, classical guitars usually have nineteen frets. The electrics I've played usually have twenty-two, though there can be more.'

'Outstanding,' said Bob. 'What's the tuning frequency?'

'Concert A, you mean?' said Rolly.

Bob nodded.

'Four hundred and forty hertz is the modern tuning,' said Rolly.

'Exemplary,' said Bob. 'Now, what's a Solfeggio?'

'That's not a guitar question, is it?'

Bob had a glint in his eye, like he'd just won the shootout. Rolly smiled. He still had a bullet left in the chamber. He sang the notes of the major scale.

'Do, Re, Mi, Fa, So, La, Ti, Do.'

Bob laughed. 'I like this one Macy. Smiling Jack.'

'Smiling Rolly Waters,' said Macy. 'The last decent man in the West.'

121

'How 'bout it, Bob?' said Rolly. 'Can you help us meet with this guy?'

Bob put his hands on top of his head and closed his eyes.

'There must be something you can do, Bob,' said Macy. She placed her hand on Bob's thigh.

Bob's eyes popped open. 'I got it,' he said. 'You can sit in with the band. If you're any good he'll want to talk to you afterwards. He always talks to the guitar players, if they're virtuoso. You up for it?'

Rolly nodded. 'Count me in,' he said.

'I'm looking forward to this,' said Macy. She leaned back in her chair.

'What?'

'Tonight only. At The Range. Rolly Waters and the Slab City Rockers.'

Fifteen
The Camper

The jam session went on past midnight, well into the morning. Cool Bob and the Slab City Rockers were better musicians than Rolly had expected. Their style leaned towards psychedelic jams with a looser groove than Rolly preferred, but still agreeable. It was fun to play without the usual worries about the schedule, the P.A., the audience or the club owner. He loosened up, had a good time just letting things rip. He even pulled out the diddley bow for a couple of songs. The crowd loved it. They cheered. They went wild.

After the concert, he and Macy returned to their camping spot. They sat in the Tioga's dining booth munching on Yo-Hos and tortilla chips they'd found in the larder. Macy drank a couple of beers. And they talked. A lot. Macy asked questions about his glory days, back when The Creatures were the hottest band in town. She asked him about everything: the gigs, the girls, the chemicals and the craziness. She even managed to get him to talk about the accident, about Matt's death, how everything had imploded. He told her about his recovery, how far he'd come, how far he still needed to go. He told her more than he'd ever told anyone.

And when he'd finished talking, when he'd told Macy all the things he'd never said to anyone but himself, she got quiet. She stopped asking questions. She leaned in to him and kissed him on the lips.

'How about we go in the back,' she said, 'and have a good fuck.'

He was more than willing to let Macy take charge at that point. She led him to the bedroom and took off his clothes. She pushed him onto the bed, then took off her own and climbed on top of him, shoving herself onto his mouth, then down on his hips, then back to his mouth, spending time in each position until they'd both had as much as they wanted, as much as they could take. Macy slid off him and turned on to her back. They stared up at the ceiling.

'You remember when we were at Salvation

Mountain,' Rolly said. 'You said I should let you know if I thought you were crazy.'

'Yeah?' said Macy. 'What?'

'Well,' Rolly said, 'that was crazy.'

'Shut up, Waters,' said Macy. 'I'm still digging on the afterglow.'

'You did sound a little crazy, you gotta admit.'

'Shut up,' she whispered, putting a finger on Rolly's lips, 'Or I'll climb on your face and make you do me again.'

Rolly massaged his jaw. 'I may have to drink through a straw for a day or two.'

'You got yours. Ungrateful bastard.'

Rolly chuckled. He stroked Macy's hair. 'Oh, I'm grateful,' he said.

'Been a while?'

'Yeah.'

'Well, you passed inspection,' said Macy.

'Glad I could . . . measure up.'

'Waters, you are pathetic.'

'What?'

'I didn't fuck Cool Bob.'

'I thought you said . . .'

'I know what you thought. You thought Macy Starr was a size queen. I've seen Bob's equipment at the hot springs. That's how I know. People get naked a lot around here.'

'Where are the hot springs?'

'Near the water tower, other side of the shooting range. You wanna go later?'

'Maybe. We'll see.'

'Everyone gets naked there. There's no hiding your junk.'

'I doubt Bob would want to.'

'Yeah. He probably picks up a few dates at the springs.'

'So how did you make up with him?'

'I posed for some pictures.'

'What kind of pictures?'

'Bob's got a thing for naked chicks shooting guns.'

'Oh.'

Rolly dropped his head back on the pillow. Macy tucked her head into his shoulder. It had been quite an evening.

'Who was that guy you were talking to?' Rolly said.

'When?'

'At The Range. Looked like you were having an argument.'

'You saw him, huh?' Macy sighed. 'That was No Pants.'

'Your old boyfriend?'

'An old mistake, coming back to haunt me.'

'What'd he want?'

'He wanted to know what I was doing, like I got no right to be here. He's a douchebag.'

'I guess you got rid of him.'

'I told him I was with you. He got really quiet, then, when he saw you on stage.'

'Rock gods have that effect on people.'

'Yeah. Just like the old days, right, Waters?'

'What's that?'

'The crowd goes wild. You nail another groupie, add a notch to your guitar.'

'Shut up, Macy.'

Rolly drifted to sleep, the half sleep that comes with a new bed and a new place. His body was past tired but his mind stood on alert. There was a lot to process. Something clattered against the window. He jolted out of his post-coital haze.

'Ow,' said Macy, rubbing her nose.

'Sorry,' said Rolly. 'What was that?'

'I don't know,' she said. 'Sounds like the wind's kicking up.'

The window clattered again.

'Someone's out there,' said Rolly. 'It's him.'

Macy turned over, crawled to the window and peered through the shades.

'Do you see anyone?' Rolly asked.

'No. Not yet.'

Pebbles scattered against the window again. Macy jerked her head away.

'Teotwayki!' The bird cry came from outside. 'Teotwayki!'

Rolly climbed out of the bed and put his pants on.

Macy sat up. 'It's that guy, isn't it? The one who followed me? It's him.'

Rolly flipped on the light, found his shirt, slipped it over his head and turned back to Macy.

'I guess Bob's plan worked,' he said.

The window clattered again. Macy climbed out of bed and started putting on her clothes.

'I'm going with you,' she said.

'No,' said Rolly. 'You need to stay here.'

'Don't pull that macho protection thing on me, Waters.'

'Just let me talk to him first,' Rolly said. 'Find out what he wants.'

'I'm your client. I got as much stake in this as you do.'

Rolly knew he couldn't stop her. 'OK,' he said. 'Just let me go out first and look around.'

'Yeah, yeah, whatever,' said Macy. 'Let's go.'

They walked to the front of the trailer. Rolly stepped down, unlatched the bolt and cracked open the door. He looked outside. There wasn't much to see except the night sky.

'Hello,' he called. 'Who's out there?'

No one responded. He pushed the door open wider and stepped down onto the dirt. The light from inside the Tioga spilled out onto the desert floor. He walked out past the circle of light and saw the gray shapes of other trailers and mobile homes. In this part of Slab City, at least, everyone was asleep.

'Who's out there?' he called again. Someone spoke, out of sight.

'You're the guitar player. The Waters.'

'Yes.'

'I remember you.'

'I remember you, too.'

'The Waters doesn't play it right. The Waters must practice.'

Macy stepped down from the trailer and took Rolly's arm. 'I think he plays great,' she said.

They heard scuttling noises, like a large beetle hurrying through the brush.

'You think I scared him away?' said Macy.

As if in answer, a stuttered sequence of vocalizations began to emanate from the other side of the Tioga. They sounded like moans of sexual pleasure. They sounded like Macy.

'Freakin' pervert,' she said.

'Ooo, aaa . . . yes, yes, yes,' the voice continued.

127

'OK,' said Rolly. 'We get it. You heard us. What do you want?'

The moaning stopped. There was silence. They waited.

'Who is the golden eyes?' the voice asked.

'My name's Macy. Who the hell are you?'

'The Macy makes funny noises.'

'Uh huh.'

The man spoke again but his voice had changed, as if he were conversing with someone behind the trailer.

'The Macy has golden eyes. The Macy has the key. The Macy is the Sachem.'

Macy looked at Rolly. She shrugged her shoulders. Rolly thought about the woman at the Alien Artifacts store – Dotty. He remembered the gold doll at the store. Dotty had called it by the same name – *the Sachem*.

'The Waters must practice now,' said the man. 'The Sachem has the key.'

'The key to what?'

'The Astral Vibrator,' said the voice, returning to its previous tone.

'What does the Astral Vibrator do?'

'The Sachem is here. The Conjoinment is near. The Waters must practice.'

'Who are you?' said Macy.

'I'm the cool Dionysian. That's my religion.'

'I've heard that line before,' Macy whispered to Rolly. 'It's from one of Bob's songs.'

'You think it's Bob back there?'

'No. Do you?'

'No. Not really. He's probably heard Bob singing it.'

128

The voice chirped. 'Teotwayki!'

Rolly chirped back, imitating the call. 'Teotwayki!'

They traded calls again. A light went on in one of the trailers nearby. Their bird calls had woken the neighbors.

'Open the Astral Vibrator,' said the voice. 'The Sachem has the key.'

'Who's out there?' It was a new voice, from one of the trailers.

'Teotwayki! Teotwayki!' the voice behind the RV called, sounding alarmed.

'Shut up!' said the voice from the trailer.

The bird calls continued. They became muted and drifted into the distance. Rolly walked to the other side of the Tioga. No one was there. He listened as the last of the bird calls faded away. Macy walked up beside him. They stared into the darkness. Macy spoke first.

'I gotta say, Waters, this is definitely the most batshit crazy date I've ever been on.'

'Me too.'

'What's he talking about? About me having the key? What's this Sachem thing?'

'I don't know exactly. Some kind of alien the UVTs believed in. That lady at the Alien Artifacts shop showed me a doll, a baby doll painted gold. She called it the Sachem.'

'This guy thinks I'm an alien?'

'It would appear so.'

'Man, this is weird. It would explain a lot, though.'

'What?'

'Like maybe I don't have any parents. I mean,

129

earthling ones. Maybe I came from that Oort place. You saw what Daddy Joe wrote in the letter. *My little alien.* He used to call me that. I used to think about it sometimes, being so different from the rest of the kids on the rez.'

Rolly faced Macy, put his hands on her shoulders. 'You are not an alien.'

'How do you know?'

'I don't sleep with aliens.'

'Too late, Waters. You told me the stories. You'll sleep with anyone.'

Rolly pulled Macy close. She buried her face in his chest.

'Do you think Daddy Joe's dead?' she said. It was the first chink he'd felt in Macy's armor, the first hint she was vulnerable.

'I don't know,' Rolly said, holding her tighter. He kept one arm around her shoulders as they walked to the end of the trailer. 'I still think he'll show up.'

'Little Alien DJ, that'll be my new name,' she said. 'I'll make some Space Disco mixes, or maybe Bleep Techno.'

'I have no idea what that means,' said Rolly.

They turned the corner of the trailer. Rolly stopped and pulled Macy back. 'Someone's coming,' he said.

They watched a dark figure approach the Tioga. The light from the window of a nearby trailer caught the man's face as he passed.

'It's Cool Bob,' Macy said.

They waited in the shadows, watching. Bob entered the dark space between the two vehicles, then into the light again as he got close to the

130

Tioga. He was carrying a box. He set the box down and knocked on their door.

Rolly stepped out from the end of the trailer, keeping Macy behind him.

'Hey, Bob,' he said.

Bob peered over at him. 'Hey man,' he said. 'That was some righteous riffage you laid on the Slabbers last night.'

'Thanks. I had fun. What can I do for you?'

Bob indicated the box. 'He liked how you played. He asked me to give this to you. The vibrator thing. He said I should give it to you.'

'What about your van?'

'It's been returned to my domicile. Accountability justified.'

Macy stepped out from behind Rolly.

'Hey Macy,' said Bob. 'Your new boyfriend's a killer.'

'Much cooler than No Pants, huh?' Macy said.

'Way cooler.'

Rolly and Macy walked over to Bob.

'You wanta' come in?' Rolly asked.

'No worries,' said Bob. 'Just wanted to make the delivery.'

Rolly looked down at the black box. 'Is this the Astral Vibrator?'

'He wants you to practice. He said you were worthy.'

'What's his name, Bob? Can I talk to him?'

Cool Bob smiled. 'See you later,' he said. They watched him walk away until he disappeared from view.

'Oww!' said Rolly. A stinging pain shot through his ankle, like a sharp needle.

131

'What's wrong?' said Macy.

'I don't know,' Rolly said, stumbling towards the door of the Tioga. 'I think something just bit me.'

Sixteen
The ER

A spider loomed in the darkness. It was huge. It had long fangs that gleamed like glittering gold sabers. Rolly turned to run, but his legs wouldn't work. It was like running in deep sand. The spider captured him in its web. It bit into his leg with its giant gold fangs.

He jolted awake and looked around. The light in the emergency ward of Brawley General Hospital seeped under the edges of curtains surrounding his bed. It was a strange shade of green, like something you'd see on the bridge of a movie spaceship. He felt better now, stronger and clearer. There were no giant spiders.

The monitoring equipment had been unhooked from his arm. He checked his left leg, lightly wrapped in white gauze. His leg felt better, too. His stomach felt settled, with only an occasional flutter to remind him of the dry heaves and retching he'd endured a few hours ago. He was going to live.

A nurse entered the room, pushing a wheelchair.

132

She looked young enough to be a high-school cheerleader.

'Looks like we're awake,' she said.

'We are,' Rolly said.

'How're you feeling?'

'OK, I guess. What time is it?'

'Almost eight. We're ready to check you out. Your mom's here.'

Rolly raised up off the pillow, rested on his elbows.

'My mother?'

'Yeah. She's a real sweetheart.'

'How'd she get here?'

'Well, most people drive their cars.'

'No, I mean, how'd she know I was here?'

'Your friends called her, I guess. They had to leave. Let's have you try standing up now.'

Rolly lifted himself to a sitting position, then swiveled his legs so they hung off the bed.

'Be careful,' said the nurse, taking his arm. 'Your left ankle and lower leg might hurt a bit when you put weight on them.'

Rolly slid down from the bed. A hot pain shot through his left ankle as his feet touched the floor. He leaned against the nurse for support. Her hair smelled like freshly cut grass.

'Just take your time,' she said.

Rolly waited for his head to clear. He nodded at the nurse and took his arm from her shoulders.

'Have you ever used crutches before?' she said.

Rolly nodded. After the car accident, he'd been on crutches for two months.

'OK, hang on to the gurney here if you need to,' the nurse said. 'We're going to put you in

133

the wheelchair first to get you out of the hospital. We'll give you the crutches to take home.'

She grabbed a pair of crutches and handed them to Rolly. He took them, placed them under his arms.

'OK on the height?' the nurse asked, stepping back and assessing the adjustment.

Rolly nodded. 'They're fine.'

'Let's go see your mom and get you checked out.'

The nurse took the crutches while Rolly lowered himself into the wheelchair. She handed them back to him and pushed him out to the waiting room. He spotted his mother in the corner, engaged in conversation with a young Latino woman and her two children.

'Mrs Waters?' said the nurse. 'He's ready to go.'

Rolly's mother said goodbye to her new friends and walked over to Rolly. 'How do you feel, dear?' she said.

'I've felt better,' said Rolly.

'You've got all the instructions?' said the nurse.

'Right here,' said Rolly's mother. 'I took care of the insurance.'

'He's all yours then, I guess,' said the nurse.

'Thank you,' said Rolly's mother.

'Yes,' Rolly said. 'Thanks.'

The nurse returned to the emergency ward.

Rolly looked up at his mother. 'Does Dad know about this?' he said.

'Alicia can worry about your father,' she said. 'It's you I think we should worry about.'

'Sorry you had to drive all the way out here.'

'That's all right, dear.'

'The Waters men sure cause you a lot of trouble, don't we?'

'That's my cross to bear.'

'How did you get here?'

'I drove my Mini, of course.'

'No, I mean how did you find out I was here?'

'A woman called. She told me what happened.'

'Macy?'

'I don't remember her name. I don't think she told me. She said they'd brought you here but she had to leave. There was something important she needed to do.'

'Did she say what it was?'

'No. I don't think so. She gave me the address and the phone number for the hospital here, and asked if I'd be able to come over and get you. She said you'd been bitten by a black widow spider and that you wouldn't be able to drive.'

'What about the Tioga?'

Rolly's mother looked perplexed. 'I don't understand, dear.'

'We drove out here in Dad's RV,' Rolly said. 'Alicia let me borrow it.'

'Was it some sort of romantic liaison you had with this Macy woman?'

Rolly shook his head. 'It's business,' he said. 'She's looking for someone.'

Rolly's mother stared down at him, parsing his statements, assessing their truthfulness.

'We have to stop somewhere,' said Rolly. 'To check on the Tioga. I'll explain on the way.'

'All right, dear,' said his mother. It was what she always said when her vigilance meter had peaked, the needle pegged to red. She had stored up a lot of questions.

His mother wheeled him out of the hospital. He waited while she went to pick up her car. His leg still hurt, but the nervous weight in his stomach worried him more. It might be the last vestiges of spider poison, but an uncertain certainty roiled his belly; the feeling that Macy had a secret she hadn't shared with him. He worried that she'd gone rogue, extemporizing on the events of last night. Macy had the diddley bow and the Astral Vibrator. She knew they were valuable. She might even know why.

It took thirty minutes for them to drive to Slab City from Brawley General. He spent most of that time explaining what had happened to him over the last several days. His mother had always been embarrassed by his day job, almost to the point of denying it existed. When asked, she told people her son was a musician. Macy Starr's case seemed to intrigue her, though. Looking for a young girl's missing parents was more reputable than his usual assignments, even noble. At least he wasn't digging up dirt for divorce lawyers and ambulance chasers.

At any rate, by the time they reached Niland, his mother had finished her interrogation and returned to her usual state of enthusiasm. New adventures were afoot, after all. They pulled off the main road and passed Salvation Mountain. She reminisced about her year on an ashram in New Mexico, reflecting on the aesthetic and spiritual appeal of stark desert landscapes.

When they arrived at Slab City, Rolly directed

his mother to the Tioga's old camping spot. The Tioga wasn't there. They drove around looking for it, to no avail. Macy had taken it. He didn't know where or why she had gone.

His mother pulled the Mini to a stop across from The Range.

'What shall we do?' she said.

'Let me think,' Rolly said.

'Perhaps she's gone home.'

Rolly checked his phone again. He'd called Macy from Brawley but she hadn't called him back. She hadn't left any message. His phone indicated there wasn't much signal in this part of the world. The battery had run down. His charger was in the Tioga. He looked out the window. A man dressed in shorts and a carpenter's belt stepped out on the stage at The Range.

'It's Bob,' he said.

'Who?'

'Cool Bob. Honk your horn.'

His mother tapped on the horn. Bob turned to look at them. Rolly rolled down his window.

'Hey, Bob, it's me, Rolly Waters, the guitar player from last night.'

Bob walked over to them. 'Hey,' he said. 'You doin' OK?'

'Yeah, I'm OK.'

'You were looking kinda gruesome the last time I saw you.'

'You were there, weren't you? You helped me get to the hospital?'

'Yeah. I tied on a tourniquet and took you down there in the rocket ship.'

'I remember. Thanks for taking care of me.'

'Macy was freaking.'

'Yeah, I expect so. Speaking of which . . .'

'I've seen folks bit by spiders before, but I never seen it that bad. You were seriously messed up. Explosive. I just got the rocket ship clean.'

'Sorry about that. Have you seen her?'

'It was really trippin' me out. Scandalous.'

'Have you seen Macy? Do you know where she went?'

'I think she went home.'

'To San Diego?'

'There was some odious spirits blowing through here last night.'

'I'm feeling better now. I'll be OK.'

'It was Macy that found him, you know. That's why the police are on location. At the hot springs.'

'Wait. What are you talking about?'

'Macy's old boyfriend. No Pants. He's dead. Extinguished.'

A cold shiver ran down Rolly's bad leg. It was at least eighty degrees outside.

'What happened?' he said.

'They sink before they float. That's what the cops told me. Never knew that before. Didn't see the guy down there 'cause the water's so cloudy.'

'You found him?'

'Macy did. We went to the hot springs after we got back from the hospital. We were both stressing, you know. She suggested we take a soak, get some relief on the musculature. I'd already gone back to my place when she comes running and shouting, all naked. I went back to the springs

138

and saw the guy floating around. That's when I called the cops.'

Bob stroked his beard, looked down at the ground. 'People are kind of hating on me,' he said. 'They don't like having cops around.'

'What can you tell me about Macy's boyfriend?' said Rolly.

'No Pants? He was mucho inquisitive,' said Bob. 'Really bugged people. Pestilential.'

'Macy said he broke into your trailer; that he was looking for something?'

'Yeah, assuredly. With massive intent.'

'You think he was looking for drugs?'

'That's what Macy conjectured. I didn't really peg him for a tweaker, though.'

Rolly stared out the front window, wondered if he should talk to the police. He decided against it and turned back to Bob. 'I saw Macy talking to him last night,' he said, 'when we were playing at The Range.'

'Yeah, I discerned that encounter too. They looked kinda quarrelsome.'

'He didn't like her being here, I guess. Said this was his territory, for some reason. That's what she told me, anyway.'

'He asked a lot of questions. Like you.'

'What kind of questions?'

'He was looking for someone, asking about gold. He brought another lady the last time he was here. Couple of weeks ago.' Bob lowered his head and peered into the car to see who was driving.

'This is my mother,' said Rolly.

'Hello,' said his mother.

139

'Hello,' said Bob. 'You got white hair. I thought maybe you were the same lady.'

'Oh, no,' said Mrs Waters. 'I don't think we've met before.'

'Yeah. She was different than you.'

'What was the other lady like?' said Rolly.

'She had some interesting postulations about stuff.'

'What kind of stuff?'

'Therapeutical frequencies and gold. She talked about aliens. Like they were real.'

Seventeen
The House

Rolly sat in the passenger seat of Tribal Police Chief Kinnie Harper's Ford Bronco, staring into the sideview mirror as the truck churned up a trail of dust in their wake. Kinnie was driving down the hardscrabble dirt road to Daddy Joe's house. Rolly's mother was tucked away in the reservation's general store, a slatted wooden structure that looked like a set piece from an old Western. There were plenty of trinkets there to keep his mother occupied, and a coffee stand where she could get a cup of tea. She might drive the elderly proprietor crazy with chitchat, but at least she'd be out of Rolly's hair for a while.

Just after driving into the reservation they'd

spotted a tribal police truck parked at the casino. It turned out to be Kinnie Harper's. After administering a short but intense interrogation Kinnie agreed to drive Rolly out to her father's house. Daddy Joe was still missing.

'Officer Harper?' said Rolly.

'I guess you can call me Kinnie,' she said. 'Since you're friends with Bonnie.'

'How'd you meet Bonnie?' he asked.

'I know Bonnie from WILES.'

'What's that?'

'Women in Law Enforcement and Security. It's a professional support group. Bonnie was president there for a while.'

Rolly smiled and nodded. Even Bonnie needed encouragement sometimes.

'Kinnie, do you remember anything about Aunt Betty?'

'Who?'

'Aunt Betty. Macy told me she lived with you. That's why she hired me. She wants me to find Aunt Betty.'

'I don't know any Aunt Betty.'

'Macy showed me a photo. It's a young black woman standing with a baseball player.'

'There was a black lady who worked for us a little while. I don't remember her name. She wasn't here long – just while my mother was in the hospital during her last days. The lady was helping us out.'

'Daddy Joe hired her?'

'I guess. I don't remember.'

Rolly felt mystified. The photo of Aunt Betty had become real to him, the story Macy had told him,

141

her memories of Aunt Betty. Kinnie's disavowal of Betty threw him off. It was unexpected.

'Do you know anything about Macy's parents?' he said.

'Her parents? No. Daddy Joe's the only one who would know something about that. We never talked about it in our house. We didn't talk about a lot of things.'

'Macy just appeared one day?'

'Yeah. That's about it. I was ten, I think. You don't really ask questions about stuff like that when you're ten. Daddy says you got a baby sister now and you just accept it.'

'How about later?'

'Macy and I used to talk sometimes. I told her she was an alien. Daddy Joe never said anything. Who's the baseball player?'

'Hmm?'

'The guy in the photo. The baseball player. Is he somebody famous?'

'He's a minor leaguer. The Hawaii Coconuts. They're not even around anymore.'

'Is it that guy on TV? Eric Ozzie?'

Rolly rubbed his chin. He felt like an imbecile. 'Why'd you say that?'

'This guy called Daddy Joe a couple days ago. Left a message. Said he was The Sneaker. He had your name too, said you were snooping around, asking questions. That's why I called Bonnie, asking about you.'

'Well, that explains a lot. I showed him the photo a couple of days ago. He said he didn't recognize the woman in the photo. Said he didn't know anything about her.'

'He must've called Daddy Joe straight afterwards,' said Kinnie.

'They don't call him The Sneaker for nothing, I guess.'

'You think maybe he's Macy's father?'

'I'm not checking him off my list yet, that's for sure.'

Rolly fell silent, ruminating on Macy's motivations. Had she known the man in the photo was Ozzie? Had she hired Rolly to help shake him loose? Did she know Ozzie would call Daddy Joe?

'Kinnie, have you ever heard of a guy named Randy Parker?'

'Yeah. I know him. He used to visit Daddy Joe sometimes.'

'Any time recently?'

'Not that I know,' Kinnie shrugged.

'You ever been to his shop?'

'Nah. I hate that stuff. Aliens. Stupid.'

'What did Randy talk to Daddy Joe about? Was it about the UVTs?'

Kinnie gave Rolly a prickly look. He was trying to pick fruit from a cactus.

'Did Macy tell you about the UVTs?' she said.

'She told me a few things,' he said. 'That they killed themselves. That Daddy Joe was obsessed with the case. I guess he arrested someone.'

'Did she tell you about the gold mine?'

'She told me the UVTs liked to drink gold,' said Rolly.

'The story goes they were hoarding it,' said Kinnie. 'Gold. For this big event when the aliens were going to arrive.'

'The Conjoinment,' said Rolly.

'Some of the people, they sold their houses and stuff. They handed the money over to the people in charge. Their leaders, that's who converted the money to gold – this one guy, anyway. The one Daddy Joe arrested. Caught him on his way to Mexico with a bag full of gold chips.'

'You remember his name?' Rolly said. 'The guy they arrested?'

'Parnell Gibbons. They couldn't prove it was murder, not first degree anyway, so they got him on manslaughter and put him away for a while. There's stuff on the Internet about what happened. Randy Parker's got a website, one of those blog things.'

'I'll look it up,' Rolly said.

'Anyway, it became kind of a legend,' Kinnie continued. 'The gold that went missing, I mean. Daddy Joe had to shoo people away. He got bat gates installed to keep people out of the mine. They'd come around looking, thinking the gold had been buried somewhere around here. The story kind of built up over the years. That Randy Parker guy had kin there that died. His parents, I think. Their names are on the marker.'

'Where's that?'

'Out on the mesa, near that home for girls.'

'That's where the UVTs lived, isn't it?'

Kinnie sighed. A dark sigh. Deep. 'It's old history, you know,' she said. 'Bad history.' She turned her head and looked out the side window. They crested the hill that led down to Daddy Joe's house.

Kinnie said, 'Is that your RV in front of the house?'

'Looks like it,' said Rolly.

'You sleep with her yet?' said Kinnie. The truck bounced through a deep pothole. Rolly winced and rubbed his hand along his lower back to make sure his spine hadn't cracked. He didn't reply. Kinnie laughed.

'Bonnie warned me, you know. She said you got some hound dog in you. All droopy-eyed and rumpled, look like you always need a nuzzling. I bet Macy had you on a leash in five minutes.'

Rolly smiled. Kinnie might be right but he wasn't going to admit it.

'Is it true she doesn't get any proceeds from the casino?' he said.

Kinnie looked over at Rolly with what he hoped was grudging respect for the way he'd slipped in the question. The grudge part was definitely there. He wasn't sure about the respect.

'She had her chance,' said Kinnie. 'Daddy Joe was going to make her official.'

'What's that?'

'He never officially adopted her. He was thinking about it, doing it before she came of age, so she'd be part of the tribe. This was before the whole casino thing. But she ran away. She can't be part of the tribe now. Not retroactively. She had her chance.'

Kinnie parked her truck in front of the Tioga, blocking its escape.

'I'm starting to regret this,' she said. 'I talk too much.'

145

'I appreciate it. You haven't done anything wrong.'

'That's not what I'm talking about. Me and Macy, we got some history. I don't like to feel like this. Not on the job. Not around some smart-ass private investigator from the big city who I know is going to turn out to be some big-shot lawyer's ass wipe.'

'Look, Kinnie,' said Rolly, making his plea, 'I'm not anybody's asswipe – not any lawyers, anyway. I like Macy. I don't really know why, except that she's younger than me and keeps pushing my buttons, some buttons I didn't even know I had anymore. I doubt she'll be able to pay me for all the time I put into this case, but I don't like to lose people like her, even if they tell me to get lost. I want to give her a chance.'

Kinnie laughed. 'Man, you're a mess.'

'Yeah, I know. I do this a lot.'

'Well,' Kinnie said, 'I like her too. I want to apologize.'

'For what?'

'For something that happened a long time ago. Between her and me.'

'What was it?'

Kinnie looked at the house. 'Let's take a look, find out what she's up to.' Kinnie opened the door of her truck and climbed out. 'You coming?' she said.

Rolly nodded, climbed down from the truck and grabbed his crutches. They walked to the front of the house. Kinnie turned the handle and opened the door. They walked in. The dim light that filtered through the drawn curtains revealed a layer of dust on the thrift store furniture. A thump, like a shutting drawer, came from the back room. Kinnie and Rolly exchanged glances. Kinnie unholstered her pistol. Macy walked into the room.

'Waters?' said Macy when she saw them. 'How's your leg?'

'Macy?' said Kinnie.

'Kinnie?' said Macy. 'What's with the gun?'

Kinnie Harper slipped her gun back into the holster. 'What the hell did you do to your arms?' she said.

'They're called tattoos,' said Macy. 'When'd you get so fat?'

'I'm sorry, Macy,' said Kinnie. 'I'm sorry what I did to you.'

'It's OK, Kinnie. Water under the bridge. I'm sorry, too.'

'Not as sorry as me. You're under arrest.'

'What?' Rolly said.

Kinnie waved her hand at Rolly and put her other hand on the butt of her gun. 'Sit down, Mr Waters. I'm taking you in as well.'

'What for?'

'Trespassing. Breaking and Entering.'

Rolly protested. 'But you brought me here.'

'You were both here the other day. I saw an RV, just like that one outside. You were driving back from here.'

'We didn't take anything,' said Rolly.

'Where'd you get that?' Kinnie asked, pointing at the gold charm on Macy's neck.

'It's mine,' Macy said. 'Daddy Joe gave it to me.'

147

'That's not true.'

'He gave it to me five years ago, before I left.'

'You stole it.'

'Cut it out, Kinnie. Stop being so mad at me.'

'Why'd you come here?' said Kinnie. 'Why'd you come back?'

'I'd like to know that, too,' said Rolly. 'Why are you here?'

Macy looked from Rolly to Kinnie and back to Rolly again. 'I think someone killed Daddy Joe,' she said. 'And now they want to kill me.'

Eighteen
The Jail

On the whole, Rolly found the accommodation at the tribal jail an improvement on his recent overnight arrangements. It was quieter than the emergency room at Brawley General and less cramped than the Tioga. He would have preferred sleeping in his own bed, but the cell cot wasn't uncomfortable. The throbbing in his leg had settled down, thanks to a couple of Tylenol Kinnie Harper had been kind enough to provide him with. He'd told his mother to go home and call Max when she got there. Max would get him out of jail. Max had done it before. Rolly lay back on the cot and closed his eyes. Fatigue settled in.

'Hey, Waters,' said Macy, who occupied the cell next to him. 'What're you thinking about?'

148

'I was trying to sleep.'

'You ever been arrested before?'

'I'm not talking to you.'

'I didn't do nothing.'

'You stole my Tioga.'

'It's not yours. It's your dad's.'

'You still stole it.'

'I only borrowed it.'

'Like you borrowed that necklace?'

'That necklace belongs to me. Besides, I didn't know you were gonna get out of the hospital so soon.'

Rolly heard Macy padding around in her cell. They were small cells – one cot and a toilet. There were three cells in the jail – metal cages set side by side – with open bars between them. Macy and Rolly could hold hands if they wanted to. There was another man, asleep, in the third cell. He snored like a boozehound.

'Kinnie's upset about Daddy Joe,' said Macy. 'I guess she thinks I killed him or something. That'd be a twist, wouldn't it, Waters? Me killing Daddy Joe?'

'Did you?'

'C'mon, Waters, what do you think?'

'I don't know. Did you kill No Pants?'

'You heard about that?'

'Cool Bob told me what happened. He said you were there.'

'Did you tell Kinnie?'

'Sure, I told her.'

'I guess she'll call the sheriff then, won't she? Out in Imperial, tell 'em she's got their suspect in custody?'

149

'I imagine she will. What happened to No Pants?'

'I don't know. That's why I'm freaked out. He said he'd met somebody who knew my parents.'

'Wait, what?'

'OK. I lied to you a little bit. About that argument you saw, with me and No Pants. He said he'd met this guy. He said it was important, that this guy knew stuff about my parents. I told him about you, how you were working for me and that you had to be there too. He got kind of quiet then, said he was going to meet with the guy anyway, that I had to come by myself if I wanted to do it. He said he'd be at the hot springs in the morning, at sunrise, to meet the guy. I wasn't going to do it, but after you ended up in the hospital I couldn't stop thinking about it. I asked Bob to go with me, just to be safe. We stayed for a while but no one showed up. Bob said he had to get back. I sat there a little longer, thinking Randy might still show up. He did, just not like I expected.' Macy shivered. 'Ugh,' she said. 'Ugh, ugh.'

'You should have waited to talk to the police.'

'Yeah. I know.'

They were silent for a few minutes. Rolly closed his eyes.

'Hey, Waters,' whispered Macy. He didn't answer.

'Are you asleep?' she said.

'I'd like to be,' he replied.

'Don't be mad at me.'

'You got us thrown in jail, Macy.'

'Let's have some fun.'

150

'What kind of fun?'

'I could give you a blow job.'

'Stop it, Macy,' he said. As attractive as the offer might be, he felt resolute.

'C'mon, Waters,' said Macy. 'I know what you got. I bet we could do it.'

'Just stop it.'

'OK, OK. It's just that I got this heavy submissive tingle going on right now. It must be the bars and the handcuffs and everything. Makes me want to get down on my knees. I feel kind of bad too, about taking the Tioga. I want to make up.'

Rolly turned on his side and faced the other cell. What did he know about women? About anyone? Ten years ago he'd walked into his apartment at three in the morning to find Matt and Leslie together because they both knew he'd be out all night with a Gauloise-smoking groupie wearing tiger-striped stretch pants – a girl he'd picked up at the bar. The only thing he really knew about women was when they were available and willing. That was all he'd learned in his forty-odd years on the planet. It didn't feel like much of an achievement.

'Kinnie's probably got cameras in here anyway,' Macy continued. 'Spying on us. I'm not into sharing that kind of way, especially with Kinnie.'

'What's the story with you and her anyway?' said Rolly.

'What do you mean?'

'That apology thing. When she saw you, and even before we went in, she said she wanted to apologize to you.'

'I don't know.'

'Yes, you do.'

'Sure was a surprise seeing Kinnie again. She's put on some weight since the last time I saw her.'

'She's put on a gun, too.'

Macy laughed. 'Yeah. That was a surprise as well. She looked like she knew what she was doing with that pistol, don't you think?'

Rolly sighed. 'Are you gonna tell me the truth?' he said.

'What about?'

'I don't know. Anything. How about your Aunt Betty, for one?'

'What about her?'

'Kinnie says she doesn't remember anyone named Aunt Betty.'

'Really? Kinnie's such a bitch. Why would she say that?'

'That's what I'm asking you.'

'Kinnie had to take care of me. That's why she hates me.'

'Can we get back to Aunt Betty?'

'It wasn't my fault. I was just a little kid. I couldn't help that Daddy Joe liked me better. It wasn't my fault her mom died.'

'Why doesn't Kinnie remember Aunt Betty?'

Macy walked around her cell – a pacing shadow. The snoring man rolled over on his cot. Macy grabbed the cell bars, facing Rolly. 'Sure you don't want a hummer?' she said.

'Macy . . .'

'OK, OK. It's just that I can't really remember Aunt Betty either, when I try to picture her for

152

real. It's mostly from Daddy Joe showing me that photo over the years, telling me about her. That's what I remember. She's like a shadow or something. Maybe she's not real. Maybe Daddy Joe just made her seem real, with those stories.'

'It would explain why Kinnie doesn't remember her.'

'Kinnie hates me because I was Daddy Joe's little pet. His little alien with the curly gold locks. Kinnie had it tough after her mama died. She was only ten or eleven when it happened. Daddy Joe expected her to take care of the house, cooking and doing the chores. And she had to look after me, of course, when Daddy Joe was out working. When he got home, he'd sit with me on his knee after dinner, in his office, while Kinnie was in the kitchen washing dishes and stuff.'

'Uh huh,' said Rolly.

'Not much in the way of child care on the rez back then. Probably still isn't. We went to school sometimes, but it was kinda sporadic, our education.'

'So you think Daddy Joe only talked about Aunt Betty with you? He didn't show Kinnie the picture?'

'Not like he did me. That's what I'm saying. Maybe she saw it a couple of times, but mostly it was me. Daddy Joe treated Kinnie like she was the maid or something. That's why she hates me.'

'That's why you left?'

'Kinnie left before me. She was older, though. After she left Daddy Joe had me doing the chores.

153

I couldn't take it anymore. That's why I skedaddled. Daddy Joe's a mean bastard.'

'How old were you when you left?'

'Sixteen.'

'Kinnie told me Daddy Joe was going to adopt you, so you could be part of the tribe, but you ran away before he could do it.'

'I never heard anything about that. Wouldn't have made a difference.'

'She says you would've been able to get some of the casino money if you hadn't left.'

'I don't care about that. I had to get out.'

Rolly considered what Macy had told him. It sounded truthful, lacking the usual embellishments. Daddy Joe had told stories, planted memories of Aunt Betty. But why? Daddy Joe was the only person who could tell them, for sure. Daddy Joe was still missing. He might be dead.

'Why'd you come back here?' said Rolly. 'I mean, today? Why'd you come back to the house?'

'I told you.'

'Macy, c'mon . . .'

'It was something No Pants told me. Kinda freaked me out. Especially after I saw him there, floating up dead. When I was with him before, when we went to Coachella that time, he would get these weird phone calls. It was just these tones, played over and over.'

'Like a modem or fax machine, that kind of thing?'

'That's what I thought too, like it was one of those robo-dial things. But when Bob and I took you to the hospital and we were sitting in the waiting room, I got a call too. Beep, beep, beep, over and over again. I disconnected the guy but he called back. Again and again. I stopped answering, but then I remembered about Randy No Pants, how he kept getting those calls. I had to talk to him, find out what he wanted to tell me. That's why I left.'

'OK, but why did you come here, to the reservation?'

'I was freaking out after seeing him dead. And then I thought about Daddy Joe, how he went missing, like maybe he was dead too. Two people I know in one week. It freaked me out. I started thinking maybe there's a psycho killer out there who's calling people with this beeper thing as a warning. Like you're next on the list.'

'You're sure it's a person who's calling, not a computer?'

'You can hear stuff in the background, like those sales calls you get where they don't pick up right away and you hear the people talking in the room. Except I think it's outside somewhere.'

'Do they say anything?'

'No. Nobody says anything. You just kind of get this sense that there's somebody there and then these beeps start going off. I got some on my voicemail. I can play 'em for you if Kinnie ever gives me my phone back.'

'Did you tell Kinnie about this?'

'Sure, I told her. Except for the part about Randy. But I guess you told her about that. I told her she needed to go back and listen to what was on Daddy Joe's phone machine.'

'That's why you went to the house?'

'I couldn't stop thinking about it. Daddy Joe's phone machine. When you and I went there the first time, it was blinking like crazy. What if Daddy Joe got those calls too?'

'Did he?'

Macy nodded. 'They were on there. The same beeps.'

Rolly stood up and walked over to her. He reached through the grate, put his hand on her shoulder. She reached up and held it there.

'I'm scared, Waters,' she said. 'I'm freakin' terrified.'

Nineteen
The Memorial

Kinnie Harper strode into the holding area. She stopped in front of Rolly's cell.

'They found Daddy Joe's car,' she said.

'Where was it?' said Rolly.

'Over near In-Ko-Pah,' said Kinnie.

Kinnie pulled a key from her belt and opened the door to Rolly's cell. 'Your lawyer called,' she said. 'I told him I'd let you go if you helped me out with something.'

'What is it?' he asked.

'We need to go someplace. You tell me what you know when you see it. It'll save your lawyer having to come out here and post bail.'

'Max said it was OK for me to do this?'

'It's up to you. Your choice. That's what he said.'

'Can I call him?'

'Sure. If you want.'

Rolly stood up and walked out of his cell.

'What about me?' said Macy as they walked past her cell. Kinnie stopped and gave Macy the evil eye.

'You got a lawyer?' she said.

'Did you listen to those messages on Daddy Joe's phone machine – those beeps?'

'Yeah. I heard 'em. You think that means some-body wants to kill you?'

'Yes. It's just like I told you. Somebody's after me.'

'In that case, the safest place for you is right here.'

'You're such a bitch, Kinnie. Did you talk to Vera at the restaurant yet?'

'Yeah. I talked to her.'

'So you know Daddy Joe was there. You know I got an alibi.'

'I still got you on breaking and entering.'

'Come on, Kinnie. It's my house as much as it's anybody's.'

'You had no right to be in there, not without me or Daddy Joe letting you in.'

'Waters, can't you do something? You know I'm right.'

Rolly looked at Macy. He didn't say anything. He followed Kinnie into the office. She motioned to a chair across from her desk. Rolly sat down.

'If you're wondering, I'm just keeping her until the Imperial County Sheriff shows up.'

'They don't really think she killed that guy, do they?'

'I don't care what they think. They want me to keep her here.'

Kinnie picked up a photograph from on top of her desk and passed it to Rolly.

'What's this?' he asked.

'I found it in Daddy Joe's files,' she said. 'From the UVTs crime scene.'

Rolly looked at the photo. It was a room in a house. There were bodies on the floor of the room, so close to each other they looked like they'd been stacked.

'You notice anything?' said Kinnie.

Rolly looked at the photo again. He looked past the bodies at the walls of the room, into the corners. He found it.

'There's a whole row of them,' he said. 'Diddley bows.'

'Here's something else,' said Kinnie, pushing a yellow sheet across the desk. It was a receipt from the San Diego Sheriff's office. Rolly had one like it in his files back home, from the confiscated property auction the sheriff ran twice a year. He'd bought a black Paul Reed Smith guitar there once for two hundred bucks. Daddy Joe had also purchased something at the auction, almost fifteen years ago. The receipt listed it as a homemade one-string guitar.

Kinnie took the documents from Rolly and put them back in the folder. She stood up. 'There's something else I want you to see,' she said. 'We gotta take the truck.'

'What about Macy?'

'What about her?'

'You aren't just going to leave her here, are you?'

'She'll be OK. She's got Bert.'

'Who's Bert?'

'The guy in cell one. Bert's pretty friendly once he's slept things off. She'll remember him from high school.'

'You're not concerned about what she said?'

'You really buy that stuff? That somebody wants to kill her?'

'Daddy Joe's missing. And this No Pants guy is dead. You don't think those phone calls are connected?'

Kinnie looked at Rolly a moment, as if to make sure he was serious. She turned her head, put two fingers to her mouth and whistled. A door in back corner of the office opened. A man stuck his head out.

'Yeah, boss?' he said.

'Manny, I'm gonna be out a little while. You see anybody suspicious hanging around, you go on lockdown and radio me right away.'

'Suspicious, like how?'

'Oh, you know, trained assassins, death squads, anything like that.'

'Really?'

'Mr Waters here thinks we got a high-security risk in back.'

'Wow. OK.'

'You remember Macy, right?'

'Your little sister, with the eyes?'

'Yeah. That's her in the tank. Opposite Bert.'

'You got your sister in the tank?'

'Just keeping her safe from herself. Keep an eye on things, will you?'

'Sure, boss.'

Kinnie turned back to Rolly and raised her eyebrows to confirm his approval. He nodded, raised himself up on his crutches and followed her out of the office. They climbed into Kinnie's truck.

'Where are we going?' said Rolly.

'Over to Beatrice House,' said Kinnie. She pulled out onto the main road.

'Macy said you don't have jurisdiction off the reservation,' said Rolly.

'I don't,' said Kinnie. 'Doesn't mean I can't take you there and show you something.' She adjusted the air conditioning and picked up speed. Rolly tugged on his ear and stared out the window. Dry blades of grass passed in battered clumps by the side of the road, quivering in the wind like frayed nerve ends of the cracked earth.

'That place where they found Daddy Joe's car,' said Rolly, 'that's the same exit you take for the Desert View Tower, right?'

'Yep.'

'I was out there the other night,' he said. 'After our gig at the casino.'

'I had a feeling that might've been you,' Kinnie said. 'I talked to the owners.'

'What did they tell you?'

'Said a couple of crazy musicians showed up yesterday morning, with this story about some guy in a rocket ship who gave them the runaround, took some fuses out of their truck. They would have thought you were high, except somebody dropped the fuses through their mail slot that same morning.'

Rolly nodded. 'What kind of car does Daddy Joe drive?' he asked.

'It's just an old Toyota.'

'Blue?'

'Yeah.'

'We saw a blue car that morning. I think it was a Toyota. It pulled out on to the road, when we were standing around, trying to figure out what to do. We tried to flag the guy down, but he drove away.'

'You get a look at the driver?'

'Not enough to tell anything. He was too far away.'

'That's the back road,' said Kinnie. 'To get down to the gold mine.'

They rounded a curve in the road. The casino came into view. Rolly opened the window and rested his arm on the frame. The truck interior felt oppressive. He needed to feel the outside air on his skin, in his eyes. They passed the casino and left the reservation. Kinnie turned in at the sign for Beatrice House. She stopped at the gate and entered some numbers in a keypad attached to a post by the side of the road. The gate opened. Kinnie drove through it and over the hill.

A white wood fence ran along the road as they descended to the mesa. A pretty white house sat behind the fence. Another gate blocked the driveway to the house.

'That's Beatrice House,' said Kinnie. 'The people that bought the place, they tore down the old one, the one where the UVTs died. They built this place, brand new for the girls. It's for unwed teens, ones that got pregnant and don't have family, on their own.'

They passed the house and continued down the mesa.

'You see across the canyon there? That's Daddy Joe's house.'

Rolly looked across the canyon and spotted the house. The Tioga was still parked there. Kinnie continued down the road to the narrow end of the mesa. She pulled up next to a circle of concrete. Two black iron benches had been set inside the circle, facing a granite tablet about four feet high. They climbed out of the truck.

'I remember the UVTs being out here on the mesa,' said Kinnie. 'I could see 'em from our house. Every morning and every night. I'm not sure what kind of music you'd call it, but you could hear it over to our place. They'd line up in pairs and start banging away on those diddley bopper things.'

'Diddley bows,' said Rolly. 'Why am I here?'

'I thought you might want to read the names,' said Kinnie, indicating the marble slab.

'Why?'

'Just read the names.'

Rolly crouched down by the monument, read through the names. He found one of interest.

'Wanda Ozzie,' he said. 'Is she related?'

'Eric Ozzie's mother,' said Kinnie. 'I looked it up in Daddy Joe's files, after Ozzie called him.'

Rolly looked up at Kinnie. She nodded and put her hands on her hips.

162

'I got this weird flashback,' she said. 'When I heard Ozzie's voice on the answering machine, I remembered this time at the house, when I was a kid. It was night. Some guy came over, sat with Daddy Joe in the living room. He was a black guy. I was pretty young, you know. You don't see many black people out here, living on the rez. Only on TV.'

'You think it was Ozzie?'

'I don't know. I hadn't thought about it until a coupla days ago, after I heard the message. Daddy Joe had people showing up all the time, all hours of night. Part of being a cop.'

'Is that what you wanted to show me?'

'There's some other names, too,' Kinnie said. 'The ones after Ozzie.'

Rolly read the names. *Tom Parker. Gladys Parker.* He looked up at Kinnie.

'Randy Parker's parents,' she said. 'They died here too. He was only a little kid. I think that's why he visits with Daddy Joe sometimes. Because of his parents. They're both kinda obsessed.'

'What do they talk about?'

'Where the gold went, I think. People were always asking Daddy Joe about that, thinking he had something to do with it – the gold that was missing. Some people straight out thought he stole it.'

'Why would they think that?'

'The amount they found didn't add up, you know. That was pulled from the bank accounts. It came out in the trial. That Gibbons guy was taking money out, converting the cash into gold. He said it was for the aliens or something. They

took that lady to court. Some of the relatives
sued her. She ended up having to sell the place
to settle with them.'

'What was her name?'

'Dorothy Coasters. She owned the place – all
this land. She got some kind of immunity for
testifying against Gibbons. Didn't protect her
in the civil court, though. She took people's
money. They gave it to her when they joined
the UVTs. That's why they sued her. She said
she didn't know where the money was, that
Gibbons or somebody took it.'

Rolly closed his eyes. He felt exhausted, over-
whelmed with the information. There was too
much to take in, about Ozzie and Randy Parker,
the whole UVT disaster. It was like a huge tangle
of tumbleweeds had piled up in one corner of
his brain. And Macy was caught in the tumbleweeds. Daddy Joe, too. Maybe Kinnie. And the
bird-call man. They all needed to find a way out.

'One more thing,' said Kinnie.

'What's that?' Rolly asked.

'Check out the other side of the slab. The
sheriff called me about it this morning.'

Rolly lifted himself up on his crutches. He
walked around to the back. A word had been
spray-painted on the reverse side of the granite
slab, sprayed across the date etched in the stone.
TEOTWAYKI.

The damn word was everywhere.

Twenty
The Return

An Imperial County Sheriff's car was parked outside the tribal police station when Kinnie and Rolly returned. They found the detective sitting inside, nursing a cup of coffee and shooting the breeze with Officer Manny. Kinnie let Macy out of her cell and listened in while the detective interviewed both Macy and Rolly. There'd been no further identification of the man who died in the hot springs other than the colorful moniker he'd gone by in Slab City. Everyone knew No Pants was dead. No one knew who he was.

The interview took twenty minutes. Afterwards, Kinnie followed the detective out to his car and re-entered the office five minutes later. Rolly and Macy signed some release papers, then she drove them out to Daddy Joe's house. She made sure they both got in the Tioga and followed them down the road until they'd left the reservation. Rolly's gimpy leg made it difficult for him to drive, so Macy took the wheel. Her mood seemed to lift as they headed back to the city, back where she could be DJ Macy again, no longer the insubordinate, outcast little sister. Back in the city, she wasn't the only alien. There were plenty of them, with weird haircuts and tattoos.

'So Waters, whatta' ya think now?' she said.

'About what?'

'About Macy Starr. You planning to dump me?
Get rid of this crazy, scheming bitch?'

'I'm not going to dump you.'

'Professionally or personally?'

'Neither.'

'You think we'll have sex again?'

'I have no idea.'

'Do you want to?'

'I'm not sure.'

'Yeah. Me neither. We might never be able to
live up to last night. Situational sex. That's my
thing, I think. You think you'll ever settle down
with somebody?'

'I thought you hated talking about "Doctor
Phil" stuff?'

'Yeah, whatever,' said Macy. 'It depends.' She
looked in the rearview mirror and switched lanes
to pass a slow-moving truck. They dropped down
through the rocky hills of Alpine and headed
into the flatlands of El Cajon.

Macy laughed. 'One thing I can't figure out,'
she said. 'It's really stupid.'

'What's that?' said Rolly.

'Why I want you to like me. I don't usually
care.'

Rolly smiled. He looked out the window. An
aqueous sliver of blue appeared in the distance
– one of the local reservoirs cradled between
mountains of rock.

'I haven't had this much fun since Vera almost
shot me,' he said.

'What was that all about, anyway?'

166

'That's between me and Vera.'

'Rolly Waters doesn't kiss and tell, huh?'

'There was no kissing involved.'

'I'm gonna get Vera drunk sometime and find out what happened.'

Macy's phone rang. She looked over at Rolly. 'You want to see who it is?' she said, indicating the phone in the cup holder between them. Rolly lifted the phone and checked the screen.

'Justin Beeper?' he said, reading the caller's name.

'That's the guy,' said Macy. 'The one who punches in tones all the time. I entered a name so I'd know it was him. Go ahead and answer if you want.'

Rolly tapped the answer button and put the phone to his ear.

'Hello,' he said. There was no answering voice, but he could hear something in the background. It sounded like a car passing. A tone beeped. Then another. A whole set of tones, nine or ten, then a pause.

'Who is this?' said Rolly.

The sequence of tones repeated, paused and repeated. He hung up and checked the number on the display. The area code was 760, which covered a lot of territory. Most of that area lay behind them in the great desert empire. It didn't mean the caller was in the desert, though, if it was a cell phone.

'Was it that tone thing?' Macy said.

Rolly nodded.

'Freaky, huh?' Macy said.

'When did this start?'

167

'In the hospital, in Brawley, while I was waiting for you.'

'It's the same pattern of beeps on Daddy Joe's answering machine?'

'Yeah. I saved one of the calls on my voicemail so I could compare 'em. Same little tune. You think it's a code or something?'

'Maybe. Did you hear anything else on Daddy Joe's machine?'

'Like what?'

'Kinnie said Eric Ozzie left him a message.'

'The Sneakers guy?'

'Yeah. Kinnie said Ozzie called Daddy Joe about me. He wanted to know how I got the photograph. Look out for that camper up there.'

Macy tapped the brakes as a truck and camper combo swerved in front of them. Its left blinker popped on halfway through the lane change.

'Asshole,' said Macy, tapping the brakes again.

'Did you hear the message from Ozzie?' asked Rolly.

'C'mon, Waters,' said Macy. 'I woulda told you about that. All I heard were those beeps. Kinnie must've erased it.'

'Someone did, I guess.'

'The Sneakers guy lied to you, didn't he, about never seeing the photo?'

'Appears so.'

'We need to confront that guy.'

'We?'

'You're going to talk to him, aren't you?'

'Yeah. Sure.'

'I want to meet him. He told you he'd be willing to meet me, right?'

Rolly put the phone back in the cup holder and considered his choices.

'Yeah,' he said. 'You should go too. I'll call when I get home, try to set something up.'

'You think I'm all wrong? That he's my father?'

'Maybe he is.'

'Aunt Betty can't be my mother then.'

'Ozzie's mother died. She was one of them. The UVTs.'

'No shit? That's crazy.'

They descended into a bank of dust and smog that hung like cement over the city of El Cajon. Macy's phone rang again. Rolly checked the name on the screen. He looked at Macy, then checked it again.

'What is it?' she asked.

'It says No Pants.'

'What? I don't . . . Randy's dead.'

'They probably found his phone. The cops. They're going through his recent calls list and contacts.'

'You gonna answer?'

'I don't know.'

'It'll go to voicemail after six rings.'

The phone had rung four times already. It rang again. Rolly tapped the screen and put the phone to his ear. 'Hello,' he said.

'Who's this?' It was a woman's voice.

'It's me,' Rolly said. 'Who are you?'

'I was looking for . . .' said the woman. 'Oh dear.' She hung up. Rolly tapped Randy's name on the screen to call back and got sent straight to voicemail, the default message. He tapped off the call.

'Who was it?' said Macy.

'Some woman,' said Rolly. 'Not the cops. She hung up.'

'How'd she get Randy's phone?'

'I don't know.'

He realized he did know as soon as he said it. Randy No Pants was Randy Parker. They were one and the same. The man he'd met in the Alien Artifacts shop was an impostor. Kinnie had said something, back at the monument, but he hadn't realized what it meant until now. *Randy was a little kid.* The man with the bad wig and the prison tats couldn't be Randy Parker. He was too old.

'Tell me about Randy,' said Rolly.

'It was just those four days I was with him, you know.'

'How did you meet him?'

'He came to the club one night, chatted me up on the break, said he dug what I was doing. He came back the next night, said he had two tickets to Coachella, the whole weekend and asked if I wanted to go. I said sure.'

'Uh huh.'

'I know. I'm a concert whore. Those tickets are like three hundred bucks.'

'What did you talk about?'

'Not much. We got high, listened to music, fucked around. I told him about rez life. He seemed pretty interested in that stuff, in my growing up. We kinda bonded because we were both orphans. I remember talking about that. His parents died when he was young. His grandparents raised him or something.'

170

'Did he say how they died?'

'No. Not that I remember. He was wearing this goofy T-shirt the night I met him. What was it? Oh, yeah. *My parents were abducted by aliens and all I got was this lousy T-shirt.*'

Rolly rubbed his forehead.

'What is it?' said Macy.

'No Pants – his name's Randy Parker. He owns that shop. Kinnie showed me some names on the memorial. His parents were UVTs too.'

'No shit? That's seriously demented.'

Rolly nodded. He thought about the woman in the Alien Artifacts store. He wondered if she could be Randy's grandmother.

'What else?' he said. 'When did you go to Slab City?'

'He told me about East Jesus and that stuff while we were at Coachella, said he wanted to check it out. I didn't need to be anywhere after the weekend. I guess he didn't either, so we spent a couple of days at the Slabs, like I told you. We walked around a lot. It was almost like he was showing off, wanting to make sure everybody saw us together. He was trying to find somebody, too.'

'Who?'

'He didn't have the guy's name. He kept asking about gold, asking people if they knew a guy with gold fingers. That's how we met Cool Bob.'

'Bob doesn't have gold fingers.'

'No, but people kept bringing up Bob's name when Randy asked about the guy, said Bob might know somebody. Maybe it had something to do with that guitar. Then there was that thing with

171

Bob's trailer, when Randy broke in. That's when I dumped him.'

'What happened with Bob's trailer?'

'We met Bob and talked to him for a while at his trailer. He wasn't giving up anything, kinda like he acted when you and me went there. He said he knew a guy that made gold, extracted it from old computers or something. He said the guy was real private, though – didn't like talking to people. Bob said he could give the guy a message, but that's all he could do.'

'Did Randy leave any message?'

'Not that I remember. He got all weird after that.'

'How so?'

'It was like he was done with me. The morning after he said he had to go see somebody. In Calipatria, I think – his brother or someone. He just took off. I thought he'd dumped me. Sad Macy, ditched in the desert. Anyway, I went to East Jesus to hang out some more and ran into Bob. I asked him if there was any other stuff I should see. He showed me the water tank. They got it all painted up. No water, though. He showed me the shooting range and the golf course. We went back to his trailer for a beer. That's when we caught Randy tearing up the place. Bob was pissed at me.'

'He thought you set him up.'

'That's what I felt like. After Bob threw him out, Randy waited for me out on the road, like I was his dog or something and I was going to follow him home. I told him to fuck off, to get out of my life. He finally gave up. That's the last time I saw him until the other night at The Range. I thought maybe he was looking for drugs.'

'Why'd you think that?'

'Nothing, really. Bob didn't make Randy for a tweaker.'

'Yeah, he told me. Did you know Randy Parker used to visit with Daddy Joe?'

'I never heard of Randy Parker until you mentioned his name at the cantina.'

Rolly looked out the window. They were entering Mission Valley, approaching the football stadium. He spotted an exit sign. 'Take Fairmount,' he said.

Macy put on the right blinker, moved over a lane. 'Where are we going?' she said.

'The Alien Artifacts store,' Rolly replied. 'You're going to call Randy.'

Twenty-One
The Relics

Macy followed Fairmount Drive south into Mid-City, then turned onto El Cajon Boulevard. Rolly pointed out the Alien Artifacts store. They pulled into a grocery store parking lot two blocks away, climbed out of the Tioga and walked to the store. Rolly leaned on his crutches and tried the doorknob. It turned. He couldn't see anyone inside but there were lights on in back, behind the partition. He looked at Macy.

'Got your phone?' he asked. Macy showed it to him. He'd outlined the plan in the parking lot before they came over. They opened the door and walked in.

'Hello?' said Rolly. 'Is anyone here?'

Something stirred in the back of the store. 'We're closed,' said a woman's voice.

'The door was open,' said Rolly. 'Is Randy here?'

'Randy's gone,' said the voice.

Rolly looked over at Macy. She inspected an elongated crystal skull displayed on the front table.

'Dotty?' said Rolly. 'Is that you?'

Dotty entered the room through the door in the back. 'Oh, hello,' she said, walking towards them.

'Hello,' said Rolly. 'Do you remember me?'

'Yes. You're that detective person, aren't you?'

'That's right. Rolly Waters. I was here a couple of days ago. I talked to you and Randy. That was Randy I met, wasn't it?'

'Yes,' said Dotty. She looked past Rolly, assessing his new companion.

'This is Macy,' said Rolly.

'Hello,' said Dotty.

'Hi,' said Macy.

'You have beautiful eyes,' said Dotty.

'Thank you.'

'Very unusual. I used to know someone with eyes like yours.'

'They're amber,' said Macy.

'They look like gold,' said Dotty. 'Have they always been that way?'

174

Macy shrugged. 'As long as I can remember,' she said.

'We'd like to talk to Randy,' said Rolly. 'It's important.'

'Randy's not here.'

'Is he still in the desert?'

Dotty pulled her fascinated gaze away from Macy and returned her attention to Rolly. 'Yes,' she said. 'In the desert. That's right.'

'When did you last hear from him?'

'Oh, goodness, that must've been when you were here the last time. When he came back to the shop to pick up his phone. Is there some way I can help you?'

'I don't think so. Unless you know why Randy called Macy.'

Dotty turned back to Macy. 'Do you know Randy?' she asked.

Macy shrugged again. 'I camped out with him once,' she said. 'At a concert.'

Dotty stroked her long white hair, fiddling with it. Her eyes stayed on Macy.

'You must be the young lady he was telling me about,' she said. 'I was so glad to hear that he'd found someone. He doesn't get out much, you know. This shop takes up all his time.'

'We were just out in the desert,' said Rolly. 'At a place called Slab City. We saw Randy there.'

Dotty tugged at the sleeves of her dress, re-arranging the diaphanous purple fabric until she found it acceptable. She went back to stroking her hair.

'There's been a disturbance,' she said. 'I feel the vibrations.'

175

'Have the police been here?' said Rolly. 'Have you talked to them?'

'Randy was supposed to come back yesterday,' Dotty said.

'Who was that man?' Rolly asked.

'What man?'

'The one with the tattoos. The man you told me was Randy. Who is he?'

'I wanted to warn you. I didn't know he'd come back.'

'Who came back? Who is he?'

Dotty turned and walked away from them.

'Randy's dead,' Rolly said.

Dotty stopped. She turned back to face them. 'I am blameless,' she said. 'I am blameless in all of this.'

Rolly and Macy exchanged glances. Dotty took a step towards the wall. She stared at the UVT paintings that hung there, of the planets and energy fields, the man playing the diddley bow.

'Randy's been preoccupied,' she said. 'Much more than usual.'

'How so?' said Rolly.

'He gets like that when he's collecting things, when he thinks he's found something exciting.'

'This lady's dotty all right,' said Macy, *sotto voce*. 'Want me to make the call?'

Rolly nodded his head. Macy tapped on her phone once then hid it behind her. A phone rang in the back of the store. Dotty looked confused.

'Would you like to answer that?' said Rolly. Dotty said nothing, so he continued, 'That's Randy's

176

phone, isn't it? The man didn't take Randy's phone with him because he wasn't Randy.'

'I don't know what you're talking about.'

'You tried to call Macy, didn't you? From Randy's phone. Twenty minutes ago. When I answered you didn't know what to do so you hung up.'

Dotty played with her hair.

'Why did you call Macy?' said Rolly.

'I warned him,' said Dotty, talking to herself. 'I am blameless in all of this.'

'You went out to Slab City with Randy a couple of weeks ago. Who were you looking for?'

Dotty stopped playing with her hair. She looked at Rolly as if she might say something. Then she bolted past them and ran out the front door. Macy dashed after her.

'Macy!' said Rolly.

Macy paused in the doorway and looked back at him. 'I'll catch the old lady,' she said. 'Find Randy's phone and I'll call you.'

And then she was gone. Rolly stumbled to the front door. He stepped out on the sidewalk and looked up and down the street. He couldn't see either woman. There was no chance he'd catch up with them. He hobbled back into the store and made his way to the back. He opened the door leading into the back office and saw a small desk, stacks of metal shelves filled to the edges with alien bric-a-brac. There was a cell phone on the desk. He laid his crutches against the side of the desk and sat down in the chair. He turned on the magnifying lamp attached to the desk. There were maps on the desk and all sorts of papers. He looked at the top map – *Geology and Mineral Deposits of the Jincona District, San Diego, California.* He looked through the other papers. They were technical articles on gold mining and chemicals. There were road maps, trail maps, elevations. They all covered the same area. They always included the Jincona Indian reservation.

He picked up Randy's cell phone and searched through the call list. Dotty's call to Macy was the most recent one listed. A call to Joe Harper was next. It had been made two days ago. The next number on the list had no name next to it, but the prefix was 760, like the beeper's number. Rolly tapped the number and put the phone to his ear. He stayed on the line, hoping to get through to the caller's voicemail, thinking he might get a name or hear a recorded voice.

As he waited for voicemail to pick up, he heard a scraping sound, like metal against metal. He swiveled in the chair to see where it came from. A thin line of sunlight leaked out from underneath the back door. There was another door, next to the exit, a bathroom or closet. He hung up the phone, grabbed his crutches and stood up. The scraping sound came from behind the interior door.

'Hello?' he said. There was a different sound, like a grunting animal, a dog perhaps, trapped behind the door. He stepped towards it and took a deep breath, hoping he wouldn't have to defend himself from any protective canines, a Pit Bull or Doberman.

'Hello?' he said. 'Is someone in there?'

He tapped out 911 on the phone's keypad but stopped short of making the call. He reached for the handle and cracked the door ajar. Nothing growled or barked at him. He opened the door further.

A pair of cowboy boots was the first thing he saw. They were standing upright in the far corner, next to the toilet. Two stockinged feet were splayed out next to them. There were two legs attached to the feet and a massive body attached to those legs. Rolly flipped on the light switch.

'Uhnnn!' said the man with the large body. He was handcuffed to base of the sink. There was a hood over the man's head and long black hair spilling out from beneath it.

'Daddy Joe?' said Rolly.

The man raised his head. He nodded. Rolly placed his crutches in the corner, hopped over to the toilet and took a seat. He placed Randy's phone on the edge of the sink.

'I'm a friend,' he said. 'I'm here with Macy.'

'Uhnnn,' the man said.

Rolly reached down and pulled the hood from the man's head. The man stared at Rolly, blinking his eyes as they burned with the light. His eyes were bloodshot and bleary, but in all other ways he was the man Macy had described, with long black hair and broad features. Rolly leaned down to peel off the duct tape that covered Daddy Joe's mouth. It was wet, covered in sweat and spittle and hard to grip. He gave up, leaned back on the toilet and picked his phone up from the sink.

'I'm calling the police,' he said, tapping the

179

button. He looked out the door to the office. 'You'll be safe now.'

A shadow moved across the line of sunshine on the floor in the office near the back door. Someone fumbled at the lock. Rolly waited, expecting Dotty or Macy to open it. The latch clicked. Rolly stood up.

'Nine-one-one. What is your emergency?' said the operator, coming on line.

'Wait a minute,' said Rolly. He bolstered himself in the doorway. The shadow moved away from the door. He glanced at the door handle. There was a double-keyed bolt on the door.

'Do you wish to report an emergency?' the voice on his phone asked.

'Yes, an emergency,' Rolly said, putting the phone back up to his ear.

'Do you need police assistance?'

'I found a man here. I think he needs help.'

A bell tinkled on the other side of the wall. It was the bell inside the front door. Someone had entered the shop.

'Macy?' said Rolly. No one answered. 'Macy?'

'Someone's here,' Rolly said to the operator.

'Do you need an ambulance?'

'Yes, an ambulance and the police. He's going to kill us.'

'Can you describe your location, sir?'

'The Alien Artifacts store. El Cajon Boulevard off Fairmount. Please hurry.'

Rolly glanced down at Joe Harper, who stared back at him with unfocused eyes.

'Who's out there?' said Rolly. 'I called nine-one-one. The police will be here soon.'

There was a sound from the other side of the partition, muted electronic pings. Rolly jammed his crutches into the floor and hurried back towards the shop. He cut the corner too close and the left crutch jabbed into his ribs, knocking him into the display shelves. A collection of plastic *Doctor Who* figurines scattered across the floor. He stepped on one of the figurines, lost his footing and joined them on the floor. A steady beep emanated from the ceiling. He looked towards the front of the shop. Dotty stood by the door, watching him.

'I am blameless in this,' she said. She opened the door, stepped outside and keyed the lock.

Rolly stood up and steadied himself on the table. He heard the bolt set. Dotty walked past the front window and out of sight. He walked towards the door. The beeping continued. He reached for the latch but it had a double-keyed bolt, just like the back exit. The electronic count-down pitched higher. The alarm bell went off, a short ring, and the shop was silent. He was trapped. The police would arrive too late. Macy was gone.

Twenty-Two
The Interview

The San Diego Police Department's Mid-City station was attractive, for a police station. It looked new, both inside and out. In matters of government largess, the Mid-City neighborhood wasn't always treated as generously as other parts of Rolly's fair metropolis. He was glad to see his tax dollars had been spent on something regular folks could appreciate.

It was still a police station, though. On general rules of principle, Rolly preferred not to be in one. He greatly preferred not arriving at one in the back of a squad car with his arms handcuffed behind him. But that was how his day had gone. He'd have to put up with these inconveniences a while longer.

After finding himself locked inside the Alien Artifacts shop, he used Randy Parker's cell phone again to call emergency services again and update them on his situation. Unfortunately, the shop's alarm system had been equipped with infrared sensors. As soon as he pulled the phone from his pocket the alarm bell went off. It left him with the difficult task of explaining his situation to the emergency operator while the alarm bell rang in the background. Within five minutes, a squad car had arrived, followed shortly by firemen and paramedics.

The arresting officers were both polite and professional. One of them took notes as the other inspected the shop. The paramedics attended to Daddy Joe. The officers gave no indication they doubted Rolly's story, or suspected Rolly had anything to do with Daddy Joe's condition. They tried calling the owner of the business, but the owner's phone was, as Rolly explained to them, the same phone he'd used to call them. Now he sat in limbo at the attractive Mid-City Police station, waiting to find out if he would be spending another night in jail, hoping he would get to go home.

He shifted his weight in the hard plastic chair and closed his eyes to ward off the nervous jitter of the fluorescent lights. The police had taken his wallet and keys, as well as Randy's phone. No one seemed concerned he might be a flight risk. No one expected a paunchy forty-something on crutches to make a break for it. They were correct in their assumptions.

He heard a familiar voice, turned his head and spotted Bonnie speaking with the officer at the front desk. She glanced Rolly's way but didn't acknowledge him. A man in a coat and tie walked up to greet Bonnie. They spoke for a moment. The two of them walked over to Rolly. The man in the coat crossed his arms.

Bonnie looked down at him. 'Breaking and entering, huh?' she said.

'I entered. I didn't break,' Rolly said.

'I hear they had to break in to get you out. That some white-haired lady got the drop on you?'

'I'm not particularly agile right now,' Rolly said, indicating the crutches.

Bonnie picked up his crutches. 'Where'd you get these?' she asked.

'I got bit by a black widow spider. Wanna see?'

'I asked where you got them, not why.'

'Brawley General Hospital. It's in the desert, north of El Centro.'

183

'I know where Brawley is. What were you doing out there?'

'I was working. On a case.'

'For this Macy Starr woman? She's your client?'

Rolly nodded.

'You say Macy ran after the old lady,' said Bonnie.

'Dotty,' said the man in the suit.

'Dotty,' said Bonnie. 'Macy chased after this Dotty and left you holding the bag.'

'I don't think Macy had anything to do with my getting locked inside.'

'You sure about that?'

'There had to be someone else there.'

'Who?'

'The man who tied up Daddy Joe. The one I met two days ago. The ex-con who pretended to be Randy Parker.'

'What makes you think he wasn't Randy Parker?'

'I think Randy Parker is dead.'

The man in the tie and coat exchanged glances with Bonnie. 'We better record this,' he said.

Bonnie nodded. 'C'mon,' she said, handing Rolly his crutches.

'What's going on?' Rolly asked.

'I'll explain in a minute.'

Rolly climbed out of his chair and followed the man in the coat and tie down the hallway. Bonnie followed behind them. The man walked into a room with a small table and some chairs and closed the door behind them. He asked Rolly to take a seat on the opposite side of the table

184

and seated himself. Bonnie pulled up another chair across from Rolly. The man in the suit pushed a red button on the table.

'Detective John Creach interviewing Roland Waters,' he said. 'Assisted by Sergeant Bonnie Hammond.'

'Are you arresting me?' Rolly asked.

'Please state your name, for the record,' said Detective Creach.

'Roland Waters,' said Rolly. 'What's this about?'

'Mr Waters,' said Detective Creach. 'Are you acquainted with Randy Parker, proprietor of the Alien Artifacts shop at 5424 El Cajon Boulevard?'

'I met someone who claimed to be him. At the store.'

'You don't believe this man was Mr Parker?'

'Not any more.'

'Can you describe the man?'

'He was an older guy – older than me anyway. Kind of tough looking, in good shape for his age. Muscular. Taller than me.'

'How tall would you say?'

'Six-two, six-three.'

'Hair color?'

'Black. I think it's a dye job, though. Or a wig.'

'Eyes?'

Rolly shrugged. 'He had sunglasses on.'

'Any other distinctive features?'

'He had tattoos on his arms and neck. One was a watch, without any hands.'

Someone knocked on the door. A young woman

185

entered the room. She handed a large envelope to Creach.

'Thank you, Denise,' said Creach. The woman left. Creach opened the envelope and pulled out some photographs. He passed one over to Rolly.

'Is this the man you met at the store?' he asked. Rolly looked at the photo – a young man in his early twenties.

'No,' Rolly said.

'Do you recognize the man in this photo?'

'It looks like Randy No Pants,' said Rolly. 'I saw him talking to Macy in Slab City.'

'We heard they were arguing.'

'It was an animated discussion.'

'Do you know what they were discussing?'

'He told Macy he'd met someone who knew her parents. He wanted her to go with him.'

'Where?'

'To the hot springs.'

'In Slab City?'

'Look, I know all about this. I know Randy No Pants drowned. I know Macy found him. We went through all this with the detective from Imperial County. Kinnie Harper was there.'

'Yes, we know. Sergeant Hammond has talked to Chief Harper.'

'So why are you asking me about this stuff?'

Creach picked up the photo and inspected it. 'Would it surprise you if I told you this was a photo of Randy Parker?'

'Two days ago, yes. But not now.'

'This is not the man you talked to in the store?'

'No,' said Rolly. He was tired of hearing

himself answer the same questions. 'I started to think that Randy Parker and Randy No Pants might be the same person, which meant the guy I talked to in the shop wasn't Randy Parker. That's why I went there with Macy. I wanted to talk to Dotty and find out for sure.'

'What did this Dotty woman say?'

'Not much.'

'You remember anything specific from your conversation?'

'She said she was blameless.'

'Blameless for what?'

Rolly shrugged. 'Blameless in all of this, that's what she said.'

'Do you have any idea what she meant by that?'

'No idea,' he said. 'She was into this alien stuff. The Randy guy was too. They were looking for a one-string guitar owned by the UVTs.'

Detective Creach looked over at Bonnie. She nodded.

Creach handed Rolly another photo – a mugshot. 'You recognize this man?' he said. Rolly nodded. 'That's him,' he said. 'The man in the store. Who is he?'

'His name's Parnell Gibbons.'

'Uh huh.'

'You've never heard of him?'

'I think Kinnie Harper mentioned his name to me earlier.'

Bonnie cleared her throat.

'What?' said Rolly.

'C'mon,' she said. 'You really don't know who this guy is?'

187

'No. Kinnie said something about Daddy Joe arresting him.'

'This lady at the store talked to you about the Universal Vibration Technologies, right? The UVTs?'

'Yeah. They were this UFO cult who thought they were aliens in human form – something like that. Macy told me they drank this gold soup. That it was poisoned and that's why they died. I guess this Gibbons guy had something to do with it. Randy Parker's parents were there. They died with the rest. Kinnie showed me the memorial. Near the reservation.'

'What's this guitar thing?' said Creach. 'The diddley whatsis?'

'Diddley bow.'

'You say they were looking for one?'

'A friend of mine runs a guitar shop. Rob Norwood. This guy was in there, gave him Randy Parker's business card, said he'd pay good money if Rob could find him a special kind of diddley bow. It has something to do with the UVTs, I guess. Kinnie showed me a crime-scene photo. There was a whole rack of them in the back. Kinnie said she remembered the UVTs playing these things out on the mesa when she was a kid.'

'Anything else?'

'Daddy Joe purchased a diddley bow from the sheriff's property auction. He was looking for one that was built by a guy Rob and I used to know. The guy worked up at Guitar Trader a long time ago. His initials are on the back. B-M, for Buddy Meeks.'

Detective Creach wrote the name down.

'Parnell Gibbons was released a few days ago. From Calipatria State Prison.'

Rolly remembered a road sign just north of Brawley. Calipatria State Prison. On the way to Slab City.

'Macy said Randy Parker went to see someone in Calipatria. He said it was his brother.'

'Mr Parker was a regular visitor at the prison,' said Creach. He shuffled through some papers. 'He talked to Gibbons many times over the last year.'

'What was Gibbons in for?' said Rolly.

'Manslaughter and embezzlement,' said Creach. 'Multiple counts.'

'He killed those people,' said Bonnie. 'Gibbons purchased the poison. The D.A. didn't think they could convince a jury the poisoning wasn't accidental so they charged him with manslaughter.'

Rolly rested his elbows on the table and put his hands over his face. 'You think Gibbons killed Randy?' he said.

'We'll wait to see what the coroner out in Imperial has to say,' said Creach. 'Intentional drowning is tough to prove, unless there's some kind of a struggle. There's some marks on the body that suggest he might have been shocked with a stungun. Joe Harper has similar marks on his body.'

'So do I,' said Rolly.

'Excuse me?' said Creach. Rolly turned around in his chair and lifted his shirt, exposing the two brown dots on his lower back. He turned back to the table.

'When did this happen?' said Bonnie.

'The other night, after we played the casino, at this place called Desert View Tower.'

Bonnie clenched her jaw and gave him her blue-eyed beam-of-death look. That was all she could do with Creach there and the recording machine going. He would get an earful later.

'Did you report this incident to anyone?' she said.

'I told Kinnie about it. Except for the stungun part.'

Creach looked through his papers for something. He found it.

'Joe Harper's car was found near there,' he said. 'Off the In-Ko-Pah exit.'

'Yes. I talked to Kinnie about that too. I saw his car that morning driving away from us.'

'You saw Joe Harper in it?'

'No. I couldn't see who was driving. It was an old blue Toyota. I saw it about a hundred feet from us, pulling out from this secondary road. We were parked near the gate.'

Creach made a note.

'Has anyone seen this Gibbons guy since he got out?' asked Rolly. 'Did anyone see him in Slab City?'

'No witnesses, so far,' said Creach. 'Did Macy Starr ever mention his name?'

'No.'

'But you believe Macy Starr was taken by force?'

'I don't know. She ran out after the woman, Dotty. That was the last time I saw her.'

'You think it's possible she ran out on you?' said Bonnie.

Rolly slumped back in his chair. Anything was possible at this point. 'What about Dotty?' he said. 'What's she got to do with this guy? Why did she keep saying she was blameless?'

'We're working on something,' said Bonnie.

'What?'

'Too soon,' said Bonnie. 'First we need you to tell us more about your case.'

'Like what?'

'How about everything?'

Rolly closed his eyes and rubbed his temples. It came out in a rush. He told them everything he could remember about Macy, the photo of Aunt Betty and Eric Ozzie on the back of the diddley bow, Cool Bob and the bird-calling gravel thrower, and the schematic he'd found in the maps display at Desert View Tower.

Bonnie and Creach let him run. He told them about TEOTWAYKI and the Astral Vibrator, about Daddy Joe and his files and the mysterious beeping phone calls. He purged his memory, vomited up everything in his brain. It kept him from vomiting up whatever was left in his stomach. He felt better when it was done. He leaned back and opened his eyes. Bonnie and Creach both stared at him. It was a lot of information to take in. He hoped they could make more sense out of it than he could.

Twenty-Three
The Patents

Rolly parked the Tioga at the Rite Aid in Hillcrest and walked to his house. Negotiating his own driveway in the motorhome seemed like too fine a task to attempt in his present condition. Backing it out would be even more problematic. No spaces of sufficient size were available on his street, but there was plenty of room in the drug-store's parking lot. Security services wouldn't call for a tow unless the Tioga had been there for more than twelve hours.

He opened the door to his house. Everything looked clean and neat, more so than when he left. His mother had been there, doing her bit in his time of duress. He sat down on the sofa. His phone rang. 'Hey,' he said, answering.

'Where you been, Brother Waters?' said Marley.

'Talking to cops,' said Rolly.

'Having an enlightened conversation with our local constabulary?'

'Something like that.'

'Everything copacetic?'

'We worked some things out. I'm at home now. What's up?'

'I found a patent abstract for the Astral Vibrator thing. There's a couple of names listed; thought you might want to hear them.'

'This would be the guys who invented it?'

'There're two names on the filing. I think the first one's the real inventor. I searched on his name after I found it. He's got three other patents.'

'What's his name?'

'Buddy Meeks. Ever heard of him?'

'Yeah. He was a guitar tech at a shop here in town. He made the diddley bow I told you about.'

'Well, other than the Astral Vibrator, the guy has patents on something called an Astrotuner and something called a Melodylocker.'

'Sounds like they might be guitar effects.'

'Irie, my friend. It's in the patent abstract, that's like the general description you have to fill out when you're filing a patent. You have to provide an abstract. All of this guy's patents are for processing audio signals. Let me read you the one for the Astral Vibrator.'

'Wait a sec,' said Rolly. He moved to the table and grabbed his notepad and pen. 'OK.'

'Here goes,' said Marley. 'The Astral Vibrator is a physical locking device for security systems. It utilizes a pitch-based system for encoding and decoding physical locking mechanisms via vibration-tuned tumblers.'

'What the hell does that mean?'

'My best guess is it uses special frequencies to unlock things. Could be a padlock or a deadbolt. So maybe you'd use this system instead of a physical key. Like instead of a keypad, you maybe have a beeper or something, and it opens the lock for you.'

Rolly made some notes. *Locks. Frequencies.*

'What's the other name on the patent?'

'I think the other guy's his business partner or something. Not a techie.'

'What makes you say that?'

'Well, on the Astrotuner, which is the patent previous to the Astral Vibrator, this guy only shows up on the revised patent. He shows up on all the revised patents, actually.'

'Revised patents . . . that's like a new version?'

'Could be. Or it could be you're just re-assigning the patent, if you sold it or something. Like if you sold half your company to somebody, you might give them fifty percent on all previous patents.'

'Is that what the other guy gets, fifty percent?'

'Ninety percent.'

'Ninety?'

'Guess he drove a hard bargain.'

'Did you find this guy's name anywhere else?'

'No. That's it. This guy never shows up on anything else. That's what I mean about this Buddy Meeks being the real inventor. This other guy's money, or management.'

'What's the guy's name?'

'Parnell Gibbons.'

'Say that again?' Rolly said, making sure he'd heard Marley correctly.

'Par-nell Gib-bons,' said Marley, accenting each syllable. 'You heard of him?'

'Yeah. I've heard of him,' Rolly said. 'He just got out of jail. The police showed me a photograph.'

'What was he in for?' said Marley. 'Embezzlement? Larceny?'

'He was part of an alien cult,' Rolly said.

'Loopy-Doopy and Crooky, huh?'

'Worse than that,' Rolly said. He rubbed his temples. 'They got him on manslaughter. Seventeen people died.'

'This wasn't that Rancho Bernardo thing, was it?'

'No, this was out in East County. In the mountains. Twenty years ago.'

'Before I arrived in this fair land.'

'I don't remember anything about it.'

'You could probably Google it.'

'Yeah. That's what everybody keeps telling me. I haven't had time.'

'I downloaded a .pdf of the Astral Vibrator patent. The schematic looks just like the one you gave me. You want me to email it to you?'

'Yeah, I guess.'

'You sound kinda beat.'

'I've felt better.'

'Stay strong, bredren.'

'Thanks.'

Rolly hung up his phone. He looked out the kitchen window to his mother's house and decided he should check in with her – let her know he was home. The last time they'd spoken he was about to be locked up in jail on the Jincona reservation. He needed to check in with Alicia, too – perhaps visit his father in the hospital. It was hard to keep up with family obligations when you were getting arrested all the time.

His phone rang again. There was no name displayed but the number looked familiar. His stomach tightened. He tapped the answer button and held the phone to his ear. The beeping tones played, followed by silence. The tones played again.

'Who is this?' he said. The tones continued to play, over and over, in the same order. He counted them: nine notes in the pattern. He hung up and checked the phone number again. He called Bonnie and left a message, telling her what had happened. He gave her the phone number for the beeper. If she hadn't looked it up already, it might prompt her to move it up on her priority list. Randy and Macy and Daddy Joe had all received calls from that number before they went missing. He didn't like being next one on the list.

Someone knocked on the door. Rolly jumped. He looked for something he could use as a weapon. He picked up his phone, ready to dial 911. There was another knock. The door opened.

'It's me,' said his mother, peeking around the door. 'Are you here?'

'Come in, Mom,' said Rolly, dropping his shoulders. 'I made it back.'

His mother closed the door and stood looking at him. She gave a weak smile. 'I talked to Max earlier,' she said. 'He said you got out this morning.'

'They let us both go.'

'I thought you'd be home sooner.'

'Sorry I didn't call. Still had some work to do.'

'How's your leg?'

'Better. I don't think I'll need the crutches tomorrow.'

His mother looked at the room for a moment, then back at him. 'How old is that Macy woman?' she said. 'She seems rather young for you.'

Rolly rubbed his forehead. 'She's in trouble, Mom. And it's my fault.'

'Is she pregnant?'

'No, no. I think she's been abducted. And I led her right into it.'

'Oh my goodness? Did you call the police?'

'I've just had a long talk with them. Bonnie was there.'

'I'm sure Bonnie will take care of it,' said his mother, as if finding a kidnapper was like paying off an overdue bill. 'It's been a quite a week.'

'Yes, it has.'

'Do you plan on getting arrested again?'

'I don't really plan on it. That's just the way it works out sometimes, depending on the case. I wasn't really arrested.'

'What do you call it, then?'

'Just having a conversation with our local constabulary,' he said, repeating Marley's line. 'Being held for questioning, maybe. Not arrested.'

'Do you remember how you used to say you were "just having a drink"?'

'This is different.'

'I hope so,' she said. She sat down at the table. His mother was at least four inches shorter than Rolly but she always seemed taller when she put on her concerned face.

'I'd hate to think you were developing a weakness for jailhouses,' she said. 'Or anything else.'

'I haven't been drinking. Or "just having a drink".'

'This job of yours seems rather stressful, and, well . . . dangerous.'

'It's not usually like this.'

'You had that man in your house a few years ago, remember? The police had to come. And there was that little Mexican girl who showed up last year. I had to stay with the neighbors that night. I worry about you.'

'How's dad doing?' said Rolly, trying to change the subject.

His mother furrowed her eyebrows and smoothed her dress. 'Your father is about as I expected,' she said. 'Back to his old unpleasantness.'

'He's feeling better then?'

'Alicia's beside herself. You really should talk to him.'

'I will,' said Rolly, hoping to end the conversation. 'After I get through this.'

'I like her, you know,' said his mother.

'Alicia's OK.'

'I meant your girlfriend. What's her name?'

'Macy. She's not . . .'

'Those tattoos, I don't know about that. All the young people seem to have them these days. But that Macy's got spirit. There's a sparkle about her. I read her flyer there, for the nightclub. I hope it's OK. I came in and cleaned up for you.'

'You didn't have to do that.'

'Things have changed so much from when I was a girl. I married your father so young. I never blamed him. We were both young. I thought it would be romantic, being a Navy wife.'

Rolly slumped into his chair. He'd heard the litany before. It was the Navy. It was the times. His mother stopped herself. Macy's flyer was still on the table. She picked it up and read it over.

'Is that her real name?' she asked. 'Macy Starr?'

'As far as I know,' he said. 'She was adopted. That's why she hired me to find her parents. She grew up on that reservation.'

'Yes, you told me.'

'The woman who arrested us, Kinnie Harper, was like her older sister. They grew up together. Kinnie's parents adopted Macy, but the mother died. Kinnie took over the household.'

'That must have been rather difficult, for both of them.'

'Macy hated it out there. She says she never fit in.'

'You really think she was kidnapped? Who was it?'

'There's this ex-con involved. His name's Parnell Gibbons. The police showed me a photo. He just got out of jail.'

'Why was he in jail?'

'It's got something to do with this cult that lived up there near the reservation. Some people were poisoned. This was about twenty years ago. They think he did it.'

'Oh, dear,' said his mother. 'I was afraid of that. I had an intuition, driving through the reservation, when I had to leave you in jail. It felt like I'd been there before.'

'What's that?'

'It was the Universal Vibration people, wasn't it?'

Rolly sat up in his chair. 'You know about the

199

UVTs?' he said. His mother inspected the finger-nails on her left hand.

'Of course, dear,' said his mother. 'I went and visited them. I thought you and I might live there for a while.'

'When was this?'

'After your father and I separated, of course – after we moved out of the house. I needed something. I had no one to turn to.'

'But Mom, I mean . . . aliens?'

'It's not that far-fetched, you know, dear. I was just reading today about these new planets the scientists have discovered with that Hubble tele-scope. There are thousands of them out there that could support life. And it's science people, real scientists, you know, saying this now.'

'Instead of crackpots.'

'They were nice people, the ones that I met. I thought you might enjoy the musical aspects of their teachings.'

'They were a cult. Everyone died.'

'Yes, I'm aware of that, dear. I'm alive. I didn't join them. I just stopped by to find out what it was all about. I didn't stay.'

'Did you ever want to?'

'I only went up to their camp that one time. Something wasn't right. I could feel it.'

'What do you mean?'

'I don't know exactly – something unhappy I felt there. I had you to take care of. I wanted to make sure you got to live your own life. It didn't feel right.'

They fell silent. Rolly's phone rang. He checked the screen. It wasn't Bonnie. It wasn't the beeper.

The phone number had a local area code but there was no name. His mother gave him a wan smile, indicating it was OK for him to take the call. She looked tired. He answered the phone. 'Hello,' he said.

'Mr Waters?' said a man's voice.

'Yes, who is this?'

'This is Eric Ozzie, Mr Waters.'

'I talked to Kinnie Harper,' said Rolly.

'Who?'

'Daddy Joe's daughter.'

'I want to explain.'

'OK. I'm listening.'

'In person. Can we meet?'

'Now?'

Ozzie didn't respond. Rolly waited.

'Max Gemeinhardt is here,' said Ozzie. 'He tells me you live close by.'

'Why is Max at your house?'

'Max is my lawyer too.'

'Oh.'

'She's my sister, Mr Waters. The girl in the photograph is my sister.'

Twenty-Four
The Sneaker

Eric Ozzie lived at the end of a cul-de-sac over-looking the wide end of Mission Valley, where the San Diego River widened into saltwater marshes and surrendered its meager waters to the Pacific Ocean. The house was an early twentieth-century mansion set in the hills behind the Spanish Presidio, as large as you might expect for a retired professional baseball player, but no larger. Max Gemeinhardt sat at the head of the table when Ozzie escorted Rolly into the dining room.

'Hey,' said Max.

'Hey,' said Rolly. 'What's going on?'

'All in good time,' said Max.

'Have a seat, Mr Waters,' said Ozzie. 'Can I get you a drink? I've got a Macallan 18.'

'Club soda if you have it,' said Rolly, not exactly sure what a Macallan 18 was. It sounded expensive. People with money never served bourbon, Scotch or vodka. It was always a brand or a label, sometimes a year.

'Pellegrino OK?' said Ozzie. Rolly nodded. Rich people used proper names for their carbonated water, as well.

Ozzie retreated to the kitchen to retrieve Rolly's drink. A large photo album sat on the dining-room table in front of Max. Rolly took a seat to the right of Max and resisted the urge to open the cover of the album and leaf through it. The album was there for a reason. It would be part of the show.

Ozzie returned with Rolly's Pellegrino and some sort of brown liquor on ice for himself. Max already had a beer. Ozzie sat down on Max's left, across the table from Rolly. He took a sip of his drink and placed the glass back on the table. He looked at Rolly, then stared down at

202

the table as he spoke. 'Thank you for coming,' he said. 'Max is here as my lawyer, but also as a witness to what I'm about to tell you.'

Rolly turned to Max. 'You knew about this when I called you?'

'Yes and no,' said Max. 'I was afraid it might come to this.'

'You could have saved me a lot of trouble.'

'I couldn't say anything,' said Max. 'Not without Eric's permission.'

Rolly knew Max had done the right thing. He turned back to Ozzie. 'Why didn't you tell me she was your sister?'

'It was a shock, Mr Waters, to see that photograph. I couldn't understand how you were able to get it. Why it was on the back of that instrument. Joe Harper and I had an arrangement, you see.'

'Daddy Joe's in the hospital. The police are involved. Another man died.'

'What was his name, the man who died?'

'His name's Randy Parker. He runs a shop called Alien Artifacts.'

'That is disturbing,' said Ozzie. He took another sip of whisky and set his other hand on top of the photo album.

'Mr Parker was here,' he said. 'About a month ago. He claimed he was writing a book. It's been so long now, I wasn't sure I could tell him much. I never knew all that much, really. He insisted.'

'He wanted to talk to you about the UVTs?'

Ozzie nodded. 'My mother and sister were there,' he said. 'My mother died with the rest of them.'

203

'I saw her name on the memorial. I'm sorry.'

'It was my first year in the majors. My first real money. I was so focused on making the team. It was overwhelming. I couldn't save either of them – my mother or sister.'

'What was your sister's name?'

'Can I show you something?' said Ozzie as he opened the photo album. Rolly glanced over at Max. Max closed his eyes, scratched his beard. He didn't object.

'OK,' said Rolly.

Ozzie found the page he wanted. He slid the album back across the table to Rolly. The page he'd selected had a photograph of a group of teenage girls. They were standing on the porch of a house. It was the house Kinnie had driven him by only yesterday.

'This is Beatrice House, isn't it?' said Rolly.

'That's right,' said Ozzie. 'Beatrice. Betty, we called her.'

'It's named for your sister?'

Ozzie nodded. Rolly studied the faces of the girls, searching for Betty's face. Or Macy's.

'Is Betty in this picture?' he said.

'No, but she's the reason it could be taken.'

Rolly rubbed his forehead, just above his right eyebrow, massaging his head to keep his brains from falling out. Betty had appeared again, and vanished as quickly.

'What happened?' he said.

'I grew up around here, you know,' said Ozzie. 'In San Diego, but not in this part of town. I grew up in a hard part of the city. My parents were pretty messed up. We never had a home for long. My father couldn't keep a job because of his drinking. Both of my parents were alcoholics. We lived on the streets for a while.'

Rolly nodded.

'My father was killed one night, by some junky. He'd taken our spot under the overpass. I was twelve when it happened.'

'I'm sorry.'

'In a weird way, it saved me. My mom cleaned herself up after that. For a while. She took us into social services, got us lodging at St Vincent's. They found her a job, got me enrolled in school again. That's when I started to play baseball. I was always good at sports, you know, but I only played pick-up games before that. Someone at the shelter gave me a new glove, that Christmas, when they gave all the kids toys.'

Ozzie took another sip from his whisky glass and wiped his mouth. 'I guess you could say the rest is history. I got on the JV team at high school the next year and moved up to varsity halfway through my first year. Baseball became my whole life. Coach Sullivan kept me going. I got drafted out of high school, which was good, 'cause I woulda had a hard time in college. Double-A first, then to Hawaii for a year and a half before I got called up to the majors.'

'That's where the picture was taken?' said Rolly. 'Betty came to Hawaii?'

'They both did,' said Ozzie. 'I paid for their tickets. My mom and Betty. That's when I first heard about the UVTs. I thought it was weird stuff, but at least my mother was sober. She said she owed it to these UVT people, how'd they helped her see the power inside her, this golden alien thing. Betty seemed happy too. I figured it was better for them to believe in aliens and have a place to stay than it was being out on the street. I gave them some money. I wasn't seeing much yet, but I did what I could. It was later that I found out all the money I sent home went straight into the UVTs bank account. And then into gold.'

Ozzie paused and took another drink. The ice clinked in his glass. He tapped his fingers on the table. Rolly rubbed his sternum.

'So Betty was there too?' he said. 'With your mother and the UVTs?'

'Yes.'

'Why isn't her name on the memorial?'

'My sister was as much a victim as the others, just not at the same time.'

'Who else knows?'

Ozzie stood up. 'I think I'll freshen my drink,' he said. 'You want anything?'

Rolly shook his head. Ozzie went into the kitchen, got a new cube of ice and poured another shot of the Macallan 18. He returned to the table.

'I didn't even know what had happened until two days after they died,' he said. 'We were on a road trip, in Houston, my first year in the majors. I was batting one-ninety-seven, stinking it up. I heard a couple of the coaches talking about something they saw in the paper. Gave me this sick feeling inside. They showed me the article. I took some days off and flew back to San Diego. Identified my mother's body. That made the papers, too. The sportswriters knew me because

206

of my prep days. I stayed at Coach Sullivan's house. That's where he called me.'

'Who?'

'Chief Harper. He'd figured it out. That she was my sister.'

'Betty was alive, then?'

Ozzie nodded. 'He asked if I'd like to see her, that we could avoid the press and the police. I wanted to make sure it was really her. He gave me directions to his place, this little house on a canyon, out there near that tower thing that looks over the desert.'

'Desert View Tower,' said Rolly.

'You know the place?'

'I had a meeting with someone there just the other night.'

Ozzie gave Rolly a funny look, as if Rolly were joking.

'So you know there's pretty much nothing out there,' he said. 'Chief Harper had my sister with him in the house. He said we could keep her out of the limelight, away from the police and the papers. He was married. He seemed like a good man. We came to an agreement.'

'Daddy Joe adopted your sister?'

'Betty, you see, she had challenges. She was kind of simple-minded. She couldn't really take care of herself. I thought I might have to put her in an institution or something. It seemed worth it just to give Chief Harper some money to keep her out of the way until the season was over and I had more time to figure out what I wanted to do.'

'How long did this last?'

'He called me a month later. He told me she was gone, that she had run away from their house one day. He promised to find her. I took him at his word. Chief Harper behaved like an honorable, decent man. He called me, once a week, then once a month. Later, we only spoke once a year.'

'Did you ever find out what happened to your sister?'

'Chief Harper had lots of theories, I guess, but none of them seemed to lead anywhere. I'd pretty much given up finding her, dead or alive. Then you showed me that photograph. All sorts of thoughts ran through my mind. I thought it might be some kind of extortion scheme you were running.'

'I understand.'

'My sister's disappearance haunts me, Mr Waters, even more so than my mother's death. I was young. I was under a great deal of pressure. I made an expedient choice instead of a wise one.'

Rolly rubbed his chin and looked over at Max. 'Did you know about this?'

'I didn't know the whole story until yesterday,' said Max. 'I helped Eric set up the trust for Beatrice House, so his name wasn't attached. I knew he named it after his sister, but I didn't know what had happened to her. Wasn't my business, really. We were able to get some money to the UVTs' relatives by buying the place.'

'When was this?'

'Maybe two years after the UVTs event. After the criminal trial there was a civil case against the lady who started the whole thing. One guy had gone to jail, but she was the one who owned the house. She had to sell the house to pay for the judgement. Eric came to me, asked if there was some way he could buy the house without the newspapers finding out. I set up a charitable trust. He put in the money and we bought the property. We set up a non-profit and folded the home into it.'

Ozzie took the photo album back and leafed through it. 'These are my girls, you know. I'm taking care of them, helping them get through a tough time. I didn't do right by my sister, but I can help these girls, give them a chance.'

Rolly nodded. It was nice to know all this, but he wasn't sure it was going to help him find Macy. He pulled Macy's flyer out of his pocket and placed it in front of Ozzie. 'Have you ever seen this woman?' he asked.

'Not in person,' said Ozzie. 'I've seen her picture before, though.'

'Where?'

Max cleared his throat. Ozzie looked over at him. Max twisted his lips to one side and nodded. Ozzie left the table. He returned in a moment. 'Randy Parker gave this to me,' he said, placing another copy of Macy's flyer on the table. 'He asked if I knew this woman, just like you did.'

'What else did he say?'

'He seemed very interested in that charm around her neck.'

Rolly took the flyer from Ozzie.

'There's something on the back,' said Ozzie.

Rolly flipped the flyer over. TEOTWAYKI. 'Do you know what this means?' he said.

'I didn't before Mr Parker told me. How did he die?'

'He drowned, at these hot springs out in the desert. The police are investigating. They haven't ruled anything out. Macy was there.'

'They think she killed him?'

'I have to tell you this, Mr Ozzie: Macy thinks she may be Betty's daughter. Do you have any reason to believe that's possible?'

'I never heard anything about Betty having a baby. But . . . well, I noticed those eyes. I got a little of that gold in my eyes. My sister Betty had even more.'

'What else did Randy ask you?' said Rolly. 'Why did he come to talk to you?'

'He told me about his business, how he collected and sold UVT stuff. He said it was urgent he find some things of theirs soon.'

'Did he say why it was urgent?'

'He just said our time was getting short. There was some event happening.'

'The Conjoinment? Is that what he meant?'

Ozzie's phone rang. He reached in his pocket, pulled it out and answered it. A puzzled look came over his face. He hung up. 'I hate that,' he said.

'What?' said Rolly.

'You know, when there's just a bunch of beeping sounds, like a computer.'

Twenty-Five
The Blog

There was a dim light on in his mother's house when Rolly got home. He changed his clothes, grabbed his composition book, slipped into a pair of hard-soled slippers he kept by the door and scrunched across the gravel driveway to his mother's back door. He needed to return her car keys and borrow her computer. He tapped on the door – two short taps, repeated three times. It was the same way he always knocked – a coded knock so she'd know it was him. He tried the door. It was locked. He found her house key on the ring with the car key, opened the door and stepped into the kitchen.

'Mom?' he said. 'It's me. I'm returning your keys.'

He continued on through the kitchen and into the dining room, where he found his mother sitting at the table, the ghostly glow of her laptop computer illuminating her face.

'Mom?' Rolly said, keeping his voice low.

'Hello, dear,' she said, without turning to look at him. 'Are you all right?'

'Sure,' he said. 'I'm fine. I wanted to use the computer.'

'I was looking up some things,' said his mother.

'It won't take long.'

211

'I should take a break, anyway,' she said, rising from the table. 'Can I get you some tea? I think I'll make chamomile.'

'Sure,' Rolly said.

'Chamomile's very soothing. For the nerves. I know I could use some.'

'That would be nice.'

His mother stood looking at him, as if she had something on her mind. 'I was reading about them,' she said. 'That's why it's on the screen.'

'Who?'

'The Universal Vibration Technologists. The UVTs.'

'Oh.'

'I couldn't sleep. I felt very agitated after we talked. It was a terrible thing that happened to them. That man you told me about, I remembered him. The one they arrested.'

'Parnell Gibbons?'

'He was quite imposing.'

'You met him?'

'Oh, yes. I think that's what gave me such unease when I visited. There was a kind of animal magnetism to him. Something dark under the surface. Very controlling. Of course, I'd just left your father, so I was hyper-aware of alpha male controlling behaviors.'

'Dad didn't start any cults,' said Rolly. If there was one thing his mother was hyper-aware of, it was pop psychology catchphrases.

'His cult was the U.S. Navy, dear,' said his mother. 'Giving orders. You've seen how he behaves when he gets around his buddies. Always making sure he's captain of the ship.'

'Dad likes to be in charge, I'll give you that.'

'Well, anyway, I left the article up there on the screen. Since you're involved with these people, you might want to read it.'

His mother went into the kitchen. It was a surprise to Rolly that there had been an event in his mother's life that she hadn't told him about. She'd dragged him to so many things when he was a teenager, from yoga sessions to music appreciation classes to lectures by mumbling dolts who thought that sending postcards would lead to world peace. It was his mother's revenge, of a sort, on his father, after the divorce. Rolly's father never wanted to go anywhere. He only cared about three things: his country, his Navy and his bourbon. The order of those allegiances changed daily, but his father remained consistent on general principles. He expected others to honor them. Dean Waters didn't want his wife attending yoga classes or his son playing the electric guitar.

Rolly sat down in front of the laptop and looked at the article his mother had been reading. He scrolled to the top of the page. It was Randy Parker's blog, also called Alien Artifacts. He read the article on screen about the trial and subsequent incarceration of Parnell Gibbons. It didn't answer all his questions but it filled in a few gaps.

The UVTs had all died from drinking their morning soup – the gold soup, as Macy had described it. Except on that particular morning, the soup had somehow been laced with sodium cyanide. There were two known survivors:

Parnell Gibbons and a woman named Dorothy Coasters. Gibbons went to jail. He'd worked as a professional exterminator, killing rats and vermin. A purchase receipt he'd signed for sodium cyanide was the key evidence against him, as well as Dorothy's testimony that Gibbons had embezzled money from the organization.

The circumstances of Gibbons' arrest went against him, as well, though anyone who had just found seventeen people dead might be expected to panic. Gibbons had been pulled over in his car, heading for the Mexican border at Tecate. Found in the car with him was a tote bag filled with one-ounce gold bars worth about thirty thousand dollars at the time. Gibbons offered the gold to the arresting officer, under the impression that tribal policemen were underpaid dupes. The arresting officer was Sergeant Joe Harper. The bribe didn't work. Rolly made a note in his composition book.

In his initial deposition, Gibbons claimed that two other members of the UVT group had been responsible for the poisonings. Neither of those people had ever been found, dead or alive. The first was a young black woman Gibbons claimed had been with him when he was arrested. Officer Joe Harper denied Gibbons' claim on the witness stand. The jury found Daddy Joe to be a more creditable witness than Gibbons. Daddy Joe had turned down the bribe, after all.

Gibbons also claimed that he'd purchased the cyanide at the request of another member, a man named Buddy Meeks. According to Gibbons, Meeks had asked him to purchase the sodium cyanide solution in order to process gold ore from other rocks and minerals they found in an old gold mine near the property. The use of sodium cyanide for this purpose was well known and accepted among gold miners. Gibbons testified that he and Meeks had explored the old mine together, looking for ways the UVTs might use it. Rolly made another note in his composition book.

At the end of the page there was a link to the next article – *Alien Gold?* Rolly clicked on the link and read through the page. Parnell's testimony, as well as the gold he had on him when he was arrested, became the subject of much speculation in the years following the trial. UVT members had sold off their personal possessions and transferred the proceeds to the bank account Gibbons had set up, but the numbers didn't add up. Gibbons had drawn on the account and converted the cash into gold, but estimates put it well above the amount of gold he had been carrying with him. His tales of the old mine inspired more speculation. There were rumors of a secret hiding place in the mountains, a designated safe spot where the UVTs would wait for the looming arrival of their alien brethren. There were documents found at the scene indicating the members were planning on leaving, and a list of items with each member's name above it had been found at the communal table. They'd been used as evidence by Parnell's defense team, who suggested the UVTs knew exactly what they were doing when they drank the fatal doses of cyanide.

Rolly's mother called to him from the kitchen. 'Your tea is ready,' she said.

Rolly got up from the table and walked into the kitchen. His mother had laid out a plate of cookies to go with the tea. They looked like cookies anyway – a chocolate color pressed into round cookie shapes. Rolly could never be sure what his mother had brought home from the natural food stores. He tried one of the cookies. It tasted like raw honey mixed with an indeterminate root vegetable, perhaps beets. It wasn't bad, but it wasn't anything like chocolate.

He sat down at the table and stared at the steam from his tea mug, waiting for it to cool.

'You look tired, dear,' said his mother.

'I guess I am.'

His mother picked up the plate and offered it to him. 'Have another one,' she said. He took one of the not-chocolate round things and chewed on it. It gave him something to do while he stared at his tea.

'That man, Parnell Gibbons,' he said. 'The leader of the UVTs?'

'He wasn't really their leader,' said his mother. 'Not spiritually. There was that woman. I found her quite fascinating. It was really her theories, you know, about the tones and the frequencies. She came up with the original vibration technologies. I found the precepts quite compelling. If it hadn't been for that horrible man I might have stayed.'

'What did she look like?'

'Beautiful corn silk hair and a radiant smile. She was wearing a long purple dress the day I went up there.'

The so-called cookie felt like sawdust in Rolly's mouth. He swallowed it and looked over at his mother. 'Do you remember her name?'

'D something, I think it was.'

'Dorothy Coasters?'

'No, that wasn't it. It was similar.'

'Dotty? Did anyone call her Dotty?'

'Now that you mention it, I think they did.'

Rolly nodded and blew on his tea. It was still too hot to drink. His phone rang. It was Bonnie.

'It's a pay phone,' she said.

'What?'

'That number you were asking about, the one that keeps calling you. It's a pay phone.'

'Where do you find a pay phone these days?'

'Out in the desert. That's where. 17817 California Route 111. It's in Coachella. I checked the satellite maps online. It's outside a 7-Eleven, right on the highway.'

Rolly walked into the living room and jotted the address down. Coachella was where Macy gone to attend the music festival with Randy Parker.

'Any sign of Macy or Parnell or Dotty yet?' he asked.

'Nothing yet. We're working on it.'

'Can't you put out one of those amber alerts?'

'Those are for kids. She's an adult. We don't know for sure she didn't dump you.'

'I told you what happened.'

'You didn't actually see anyone force her, though. I'm working on it.'

'Listen, Bonnie – that UVT thing, twenty years ago. How much do you know about it?'

'More than I did two days ago. I'm going through the case files.'

'I was looking at Randy Parker's blog. He said there was a woman named Dorothy Coasters who testified against Gibbons.'

'Sounds familiar. Give me a second.'

Rolly heard Bonnie rustling through things on her desk and other voices in the background. She was at the office, not in her car.

'Dorothy Coasters,' she said, coming back on the line. 'Yeah, she's listed here. They gave her immunity for testifying against Gibbons.'

'Is there a description?'

'Let's see. White. Long blonde hair. Five foot two. Founder of Universal Vibration Technologies and alleged companion of Parnell Gibbons.'

'I think it's her. Dotty. The woman at the shop.'

'You mean the old lady who locked you in?'

'Yes. They're in this together. She and Parnell.'

'Why would he hook up with her after she testified against him?'

'They're looking for something. Randy Parker was looking for it too. And Daddy Joe. They were trying to find it before Parnell got out of jail.'

'What are they looking for?'

'I don't know. But it's got something to do with Macy.'

'You think she knows something?'

Rolly saw Macy's face in his mind. He saw her dirty-blonde dreadlocks and her gold eyes. He saw the necklace, the gold tube hanging above her lovely jugular notch. He remembered what the birdman in Slab City had said.

The Macy has the key.

Twenty-Six
The Number

Rolly pulled up to the corner of the street next to the Villa Cantina. Marley Scratch stood outside the cantina's front door with a takeout container in one hand and the Astral Vibrator schematic in the other. Rolly opened the door of the Tioga and let Marley in.

'Where'd you get this beast?' said Marley, climbing into the cabin.

'Borrowed it from my dad.'

'Where you headed?' said Marley.

'Not sure yet. Someplace I can stay out of sight for a while.'

'Going underground, huh? Where you want this?'

'On the table,' said Rolly, nodding towards the back.

Marley placed the items on the dining-room table and glanced around the interior.

'Sir Roland's rolling crime lab,' he said. 'Stylin'!'

One of the drivers behind them started leaning on the horn. The Tioga was blocking the lane.

'Just remember,' said Marley as he headed back to the door. 'It's a sequence of specific frequencies – nine, I think. That's how it unlocks whatever it unlocks. I left you my notes.'

'Got it. Thanks.'

The car behind them honked again. Another one joined in. Marley descended back down to the street.

'I owe you one, buddy,' said Rolly.

'Good luck, bredren,' said Marley. He flashed Rolly a peace symbol and shut the door.

Rolly put the vehicle into gear and turned down Tenth Avenue. He hadn't completely worked out his plan yet, but until he knew why Gibbons was looking for the diddley bow and the Astral Vibrator, he would stay on the move. He drove to the end of Tenth Avenue and turned onto Harbor Drive. There was a public parking lot behind the Convention Center that might be empty at this time of night, assuming you were allowed to park there this late. He circled around the Convention Center and found the lot. It was open, mostly vacant. He steered the Tioga to the emptiest section of the lot, parked and ate his dinner. Then it was time to go to work.

He placed the black box, the box Cool Bob had given him, on the dining-room table, opened up the schematics plan for the Astral Vibrator and reviewed Marley's notes. The word was there in the bottom corner, just like it was on the whiteboard at Daddy Joe's house. The birdman's call. TEOTWAYKI. Maybe it did mean the end of the world, but it meant something else too. It was a code. It was a clue.

He unwrapped the diddley bow, slipped a clip-on tuner to the bridge and adjusted the peg until the tuner indicated he'd found the right note – 440Hz, concert A, the answer to one of the questions Cool Bob had asked him when they met in Slab City. He pulled the tuner off, connected one end of his guitar cable into the diddley bow and the other end into the black box. He pulled out a guitar pick and his slide and played a few notes. The slide was a metal tube, not unlike the gold tube on Macy's necklace. He was ready.

The Astral Vibrator is a locking security device utilizing a pitch interval based system for encoding and decoding physical locking mechanisms via vibration-tuned tumblers.

An hour later he was still there, contemplating defeat. He'd run out of ideas. His phone rang. He picked it up and checked the caller's ID. There was no name but he knew who was calling. It was the beeper's number. He answered. The same pattern of tones played on the other end of the line.

'Why do you keep calling me?' Rolly said. The tone pattern stopped. Rolly could hear the other man breathing.

'Teotwayki,' said the man. He played the tone pattern again. Rolly hung up and placed his phone on the table. The digital keypad stared up at him. There were three letters listed under each number on the keypad. It gave him an idea. He grabbed his composition book and a pencil and jotted the numbers down. 'T' was an 8. 'E' was 3. 'O' was 6. He wrote the whole word down as numbers. It was the numerical equivalent of *Teotwayki*, if you spelled it out on a phone's keypad. The numbers were the same as the ones on Macy's gold charm. He had the

221

combination. He knew how the lock opened. He felt sure of it.

Notes in a musical scale could be represented by numbers. Each number indicates the distance from the root, or key note. The root was the one. Other notes could be thirds, or fourths, or fifths – any whole number. Using his pencil, Rolly marked the positions of each of the notes in the sequence on the diddley bow, assessing the accuracy of the position by ear. The first note was easy. Eight was an octave above the root, exactly halfway up the neck. He could recognize the sound of an octave in his sleep. The other notes were more difficult to nail down, especially the nine, but he felt sure he had them all now. He practiced playing the whole sequence of notes. Nothing happened. He played it again. He tried it a dozen times, but still nothing happened.

Frustrated and fatigued, he decided to take a break and set the diddley bow down on the table. Assuming the numbers represented standard intervals in a major scale, he knew he'd played the correct sequence of notes. The concert pitch he'd tuned to was the standard frequency that everyone tuned to, be it guitar duos or ninety-piece orchestras.

He climbed out of the booth, went to the bathroom, turned on the faucet in the tiny sink and looked at himself in the grimy mirror. The man he saw looked like he hadn't washed his hair in a week. The man needed a shave. He suspected the man in the mirror had started to smell funny, too.

Returning to the cabin, he grabbed a Coke

from the refrigerator, seated himself at the table again and reconsidered his plan, wondering where he'd gone wrong. It came down to two things: the sequence of notes was incorrect or his execution of them wasn't accurate enough. He picked up the diddley bow and thumped out a funky rhythmic figure, singing along with it, trying to clear his mind.

> *She sells black honey,*
> *She sells black honey,*
> *She sells black honey in Tupelo*

Few people realized it, but almost all of the music they listened to, be it live or recorded was built on an arbitrary system, a series of compromises musicians had worked out over hundreds of years. A protocol had been agreed upon, one that made it easier for instruments and their owners to play together in harmonious ways. As frequencies went, an octave note was twice the frequency of the original. The octave for A440Hz was A880Hz. The octave to that note was 1760Hz.

The songs you played on your guitar, or your piano, on almost any instrument of European origin used twelve equal divisions for the notes between the octaves. But you could break the space between them into any number of frequencies. There were other types of scales, other divisions of the frequencies musicians could use. They could be found in some non-Western countries, in avant-garde experiments, in the Indonesian Gamelan scales, Wendy Carlos's electronic temperaments or Harry Partch's homemade instruments. When you considered the whole range of frequencies, a single stringed instrument, one without frets like the diddley bow could play any number of notes in-between the standard divisions of the twelve-tone scale. If the UVTs really thought they were aliens, they might have used some sort of alternate tuning and scales.

He picked up the diddley bow and looked at the marks he'd made on the neck. None of them matched up with the dots of gold filigreed into the neck. Norwood had remarked on the filigrees when Rolly first showed him the diddley bow – how they looked out of place. He and Norwood had both assumed they were decorative, but that was because he and Norwood had been playing the same guitar their whole lives. Their guitars came in different colors and shapes, with variations in the pickup configurations, and they were constructed from different types of wood, but they were all the same guitar in one important way. The position of the frets on each of them was based on the twelve-tone scale. The relative position of the frets and fingering guides was always the same.

He laughed. He understood now. The diddley bows were so simple he'd completely missed the meaning behind their design. They'd been built for beginners, people who'd never played a guitar in their life, not experts like Norwood and he. There were exactly nine gold dots on the diddley bow's neck, a filigreed inset for each note in the sequence. It was the Solfeggio frequencies, the New Age tones he'd read about in Marley's loft. There were nine of them, and nine dots on the diddley bow's neck. It was like painting by numbers. He rubbed his forehead and closed his eyes. It just might be that simple.

He pulled out his slide again and plucked the string nine times, matching the position of his slide to the proper dot on the neck of the diddley bow. He played the notes slowly, making sure to match his position with each dot before he plucked the note. When he played the last note the bolts locking the front panel of the vibrator box clicked open. He stared at the box, almost afraid to look at what was inside. He tugged on the guitar cable where it connected to the box. The front panel fell off. There was something inside. It was a postcard of the Desert View Tower. It was blank on the back. He felt cheated.

He grabbed his phone, found the beeper's number and tapped it. If the man answered, he was going to give him a piece of his mind. The pay phone at the other end of the line rang four times, then five, six, seven. He let it keep ringing. He was going to stay on the line until someone answered. He didn't care who it was.

'Hola?' said a voice at the other end of the line.

'Hello,' said Rolly. 'Who's this?'

'Manuelito.'

'Manuelito, can you speak English?'

'Sure. I speak English.'

'Did you call me just now, Manuelito?'

'I no call you. I hear the phone ring. It rings a long time, so I answer.'

225

'Where are you?'

'By the 7-Eleven. I ride my bike here. Get some Takis and a Monster drink.'

'Was there anyone else using the phone just a minute ago? Did you see anyone?'

'There was this old guy in the parking lot. The one with the crazy car. I seen it sometimes. That car.'

'Why do you call it crazy? The car?'

'He's got all this stuff on it. Flying planets and wings. I seen him before. He's kind of loco, that guy.'

'What kind of car is it?'

'It's like one of those hippie things. You know?'

'A van? A Volkswagen Van?'

'*Si*. That's it.'

'Is the man still there?'

'No. He is gone. He drive away.'

'You've seen him before? Using the pay phone?'

'I seen the van before, in the parking lot. On the street.'

'All right. Thank you, Manuelito.'

'You want me to tell the man something? You know, if I see him?'

'Tell him to call me,' said Rolly. 'Tell him Golden Eyes is in trouble. Tell him the Waters needs his help.'

'OK,' said Manuelito. 'I tell him, if I see him. I hope he helps you.'

'I hope so, too, Manuelito.'

'You buy me some Takis if I get him to help you?'

'You bet. I'll buy you a whole case of them.'

226

'OK,' said Manuelito. '*Adios.*'

'*Adios,*' said Rolly. He hung up the phone. He had to drive to Slab City. Tonight.

Twenty-Seven
The Constant

By the time Rolly pulled into Slab City and parked the Tioga he couldn't remember what parts of the drive had been real and what parts he'd only imagined. Driving through the early morning darkness – the looming shadows of the East County mountains, the heavy canopy of stars over the desert, the ghostly green streetlights of Brawley and the silhouetted cross above Salvation Mountain – had been like one long, disjointed dream.

An icy blue line hung over the eastern horizon, the cold gleaming before sunrise. He knew it would be safer to wait for the sun to break above the desolate landscape but he'd abandoned all sense of caution. He would find his way to Cool Bob's trailer in the half-light.

He grabbed the diddley bow from the dining booth, stepped down from the vehicle, locked the door and set out for Bob's trailer. His leg still hurt. He could walk without crutches now, but he still limped. He'd figured it out, almost to the finish line, but there'd been no prize at the end. There was only an empty metal box with a fancy lock he could open by playing the diddley bow. There had to be more.

He trudged down the dirt road. Clumps of creosote bush and mesquite rose up in gnarled bunches around him, interrupted by single tall spires of desert agave and spiky explosions of ocotillo plants. Finches and flycatchers twittered from inside the bristly shrubs. A family of quail marched across the road in front of him, returning home from a night's foraging. He stopped so as not to disturb them then turned his head at the sound of footsteps behind him.

'Hello,' he called. 'Is someone there?'

There was no answer. He started off again, listening to the night air. The sound of other footsteps returned. Cool Bob's trailer was close, no more than fifty yards or so by his figuring. He'd be safe once he got there, after he'd knocked on Bob's door. Unless it was Bob following him.

'Stop right there,' said a voice from behind him. Rolly kept walking.

'If you don't stop, I'll sting you,' said the voice.

Rolly stopped. The man walked up behind him and stood so close that Rolly could feel the man's breath on the back of his neck. The guy was a serious mouth-breather.

'Where are you going, jerkoff?' said the man.

'I'm going to see Bob. Cool Bob.'

'What for?'

'I just want to talk to him.'

'What's that in your hand?'

'I don't know. What do you think it is?'

'I think it's a funny-looking guitar with only one string.'

'Sorry, it's a machine gun.'

The man chuckled. 'Little Roland Waters. Always a smartass; always acting like he's the coolest shit in town.'

'Do I know you?'

'No. But I remember you. Snotty-nosed little bastard.'

'Are you Buddy Meeks?'

The man laughed. 'You would remember Buddy, wouldn't you? Yeah, of course. Buddy would've done anything for you.'

'I don't know what you're talking about.'

'Buddy fell for your bullshit. He thought you were his pal, the way you talked to him.'

'I liked Buddy. I learned a lot talking to him.'

'I spent twenty years in prison because of that little shit.'

'Buddy's here in Slab City, isn't he? Randy Parker was looking for him, wasn't he?'

'Randy Parker was a little shit, too.'

'Did you kill him?'

'Shut up,' the man said, kicking Rolly's legs out from under him. Rolly ate dirt. The man stepped on Rolly's bad leg. Rolly screamed and let go of the diddley bow. He reached for his ankle as a nauseous bolt of pain shot up the side of his leg. The man applied more pressure. Rolly squirmed. He broke loose and crawled away. The man followed and crouched down next to him. He grabbed Rolly's collar and shoved his face behind Rolly's ear.

'It's been fun, Roland Waters,' he said. 'I could do this all day. But it's time for me to go. My prize is waiting.'

'I know who you are. You're Parnell Gibbons.'

'What's in a name?'

'I met you at the Alien Artifacts shop. You pretended to be Randy Parker.'

'We met a long time ago, Roland Waters. I recognized you right away when I came in to the store, even with you being old and fat. You know what I said to myself when I saw you?'

'I have no idea.'

'Look who's a big fat loser now. That's what I said to myself. Roland Waters, the skinny little kid with the fast fingers and the big mouth.'

'I don't remember you,' said Rolly.

'You insulted me.'

'Sorry.'

Gibbons shoved Rolly back into the ground and stood up. 'Fuck you, Roland Waters,' he said.

Rolly rolled onto his side. He watched Parnell pick up the diddley bow and walk away.

'I know how to open it, the Astral Vibrator,' said Rolly. 'I have the key.'

Gibbons stopped. 'I have the key, too,' he said, turning back to Rolly. 'And I have the Sachem.'

'Let her go,' said Rolly.

'Who?' said the man.

'You know who I mean. Macy Starr. What have you done with her?'

'What have I done with her? What kind of question is that?'

'I know it was you. When we came back to the shop. It was you that locked me in the shop, wasn't it? After I found Daddy Joe.'

'That was unfortunate, having to leave the false witness behind. He's a tough old bird.'

'Daddy Joe told me everything,' said Rolly. It was a lie. The paramedics had taken Joe Harper away while Rolly was still talking to the police.

'Did he tell you what I was looking for?'

'Yes.'

'Did he say where it was?'

'Desert View Tower.'

Gibbons laughed. 'A decent guess, Roland Waters, but not the correct one.'

'I talked to the police. They know about Dotty.'

'I'll take care of that bitch when I'm done. I've waited a long time for this.'

'I want to see Macy.'

'Don't tell me you're in love with that little mongrel?'

'I don't like to lose clients.'

'You're too old for her. That would be my concern.'

'I feel like I owe her something.'

'She's done with you. You're fired. She knows her true destiny now.'

'I'd like to have her tell me that.'

Parnell took a step towards Rolly. 'Macy told me all about you,' he said. 'You're an even bigger fuckup than I thought.'

'The police are looking for you.'

'Rolly Waters is one sad sack of shit. Not the kind of man I would approve of.'

Rolly climbed to his feet and shifted his weight to his good leg. Parnell retreated two steps.

'This is mine,' he said, indicating the diddley bow. 'No one will press charges. They owe me. I can put them in jail.'

A light blinked on from a trailer nearby.

'Who's out there?' someone called. Gibbons glanced towards the trailer.

'The aliens are waking,' he said. 'Gleep, gleep. Time to go.'

'I want to see Macy.'

'She needs to spend some time with her people. Not losers like you.'

'Wait,' Rolly said, taking a step towards Gibbons. 'Are you her father?'

'Who's to say? It was so many years ago. I get confused sometimes, all those stupid, eager women. I'm sure you know how that is. You were the rock star. Oh, wait, I forgot. That never happened, did it?'

Rolly wanted to throw something at Gibbons. 'Is Macy your daughter?' he said.

'She never came to visit me. All these years. We have a lot to catch up on.'

Rolly took a wobbly step towards Gibbons. The voice from the trailer called out again.

'You'd better scram. I've got a shotgun.'

Gibbons put one finger up to his lips, turned on his heel and walked away. Rolly watched him go. Did Macy think Gibbons was her father? Had she suspected it? Growing up on the reservation, surrounded by Daddy Joe's UVT obsession, she might have read about Gibbons, seen his photograph. It was something she might have clung to, a fantasy about her bad boy father, a killer. It explained her strangeness, her separateness from the tribe. It explained the outlaw blood in her veins.

Everyone was an outlaw in Slab City. On the

232

run. They'd come to escape from themselves, to relieve the pressure and pain in their lives, away from the traffic and TV, the lost jobs and unpaid mortgages, the soul-killing demands of just staying upright in the modern world. There hadn't been enough money, or love, or purpose in that world to sustain them. They came to Slab City because it was cheap, because it was free, because no one would bother you if you didn't want to be bothered, because your time was your own instead of your company's. You could see where you stood in the universe, living under the stars. You came to Slab City to be born again, just like the man who'd built Salvation Mountain.

The UVTs had tried to escape even farther. They'd tried to escape to the stars. Their true nature was with the aliens, above and beyond the debasements of earthbound humanity. But it was a false promise, a swindle. Gibbons took their money. He cheated them. Twenty years after they'd died and he'd gone to jail he would still get to pick up his check. Rolly couldn't believe Macy would go along with it, even if Gibbons was her father. He wouldn't believe it until he'd heard Macy say it – until he looked her straight in those bright gold eyes and heard the words from her mouth.

'Help!' he shouted, breaking into a clumsy trot. Electric jolts of pain shot up his left leg. Gibbons looked back and hastened his pace, revealing a similar limp in his gait. Neither of them gained any ground on the other.

'Help!' shouted Rolly again, trying to rouse the Slab City denizens. 'He's getting away.' He didn't care who came after them or what kind of guns they might brandish. He needed to stop Gibbons. A loud blast filled the air, a warning shot from one of the trailers. Other lights went on. Gibbons ducked off the road, into the bushes. Rolly followed him. Prickly branches tore at his clothes. He crossed an open space near a trailer camp. A light went on outside the trailer, illuminating the area. Gibbons scuttled into the shadows like a big cockroach. Rolly ran to the end of the trailer and looked behind it. He couldn't see anyone. He heard a grunt from inside the trailer.

'Who's there?' someone called.

'Call the police,' Rolly yelled back.

'Who's there?'

'He's trying to kill me. Call the police.'

Rolly spotted a break in the brush on the other side of the trailer. He stepped through the break onto a new road. A dark figure moved away from him. He set out after it. Gibbons had put more space between them. Rolly had to keep Gibbons in sight and rouse the Slab City regulars. If enough people started looking, they'd find him. Gibbons couldn't taser them all.

The dark figure climbed a small hill at the end of the road. Rolly kept after him, stumbling up the slope. He paused at the crest and searched for movement below. There was an open expanse of manicured desert below him, filled with large, irregular shapes. It was East Jesus, the sculpture garden. Deep orange broke on the eastern horizon, the first curve of the sun. Rolly looked back to the Slabs. A dozen encampments now had their lights on. He shouted down to them from the summit, like an Old Testament prophet exhorting the wandering tribes.

'East Jesus,' he called to them. 'He's over here, in East Jesus.'

A shadow rose up towards him. It made a tapping sound and jolted his body with a painful shock. He wrenched away from the pain, dropped to one side and rolled down the hill into East Jesus, coming to rest against the half-buried tire perimeter. He lay on his back and stared up at the sky. He saw stars in the firmament but they might have been stars in his head. It was confusing. A shadow moved over him, an evil alien who shot people with ray guns and filled them with poisonous gold liquid.

'Help,' Rolly said.

'Shut up,' said the alien. He lifted his arm and swung something at Rolly, as if striking a kettle drum. A dissonant orchestra exploded in Rolly's brain. It faded away and he heard only ghost notes, the notes no one plays.

Twenty-Eight
The Trailer

Rolly opened his eyes to a dim yellow light and saw the particle board underside of a Formica table. He lifted himself up and took in the rest of his surroundings. It was the interior of an old trailer, small and cramped. Steam drifted up from

235

a small pot on the stove. His head pulsed in a languid jackhammer of pain. He put his hand to his face. His left nostril had been plugged with a large wad of cotton. He sat up to the table, squeezed his eyes shut and rubbed his temples.

Something rattled in the back of the trailer. He opened his eyes and looked for the exit, wondering if he should try to escape. The trailer didn't seem to be moving. They weren't on the road. He didn't have the energy to make a run for it. He hoped some Good Samaritan had delivered him here.

'Hello?' he said.

Cool Bob stepped into view. 'Hey,' he said. 'How you feeling?'

'I'm OK, I guess.'

'You want to go to the hospital?'

'You think I need to?'

'Dunno.' Bob shrugged. 'You sure got a gift for getting messed up.'

'Yeah. I'm pretty good at that. How'd I end up here?'

'Me and some of the guys found you. That was you, right, screaming for help?'

'Did you catch the guy?'

'People heard you ragin'. They thought you were baked on meth or something. I remembered what Macy said, though, about you being so orthodox.'

'Did anyone call the police?'

'As a general rule, we don't invite the authorities into our domain unless it's absolutely necessary. Only if there's some misdeed we can't handle ourselves.'

'Like Randy No Pants in the hot springs?'

'Yeah, that'd be the kind of singularity where we engage officers of the law.'

Rolly nodded. 'The guy stole my diddley bow,' he said.

'Oh, man. Odious.'

'I was coming to see you.'

'Double odiferous. You know who did the deed?'

'His name's Parnell Gibbons.'

'Not a moniker with which I'm familiarized. Definitely not native. Is he Canadian?'

'Not that I'm aware of.'

'The first blast of Mounties rolled in today. That's why I was asking. They like to set up their own section before the winter season.'

'He said he was Macy's father,' Rolly said. 'He just got out of jail.'

'Macy's dad did this to you? Dude, you need to work on your relationships.'

Rolly put his hand to his nose again, felt the cotton stuffing.

'You can probably take that out now,' said Bob. 'You were dripping pretty good when we found you. Going to have a nice shiner, too. That eye's starting to turn.'

Rolly tugged the cotton from his nose and took a look at it. It was soaked with blood but most of it had dried. He touched his nose. It felt swollen. He hoped it wasn't broken.

'Hey,' said Bob. 'Why were you looking for me?'

'I need to talk to that guy. The gold guy, the guitar maker.'

'He's not usually agreeable to conversational ambitions.'

'He's the only one who can help me.'

'He's seriously inauspicious.'

'What's his name?'

'We just call him Goldhands.'

'Listen, Bob, you care about Macy, don't you?'

'Macy's profound. Sexy with a semi-automatic, too.'

'You'd want to help her, then, if she was in trouble?'

'Irrefutably.'

'This guy that hit me, Gibbons, the one that says he's her father. I think he killed No Pants.'

'Now that's consequential,' said Bob.

Rolly nodded. 'Tell me about the other time No Pants was here,' he said. 'When he brought the other lady, the one with the white hair who talked about aliens.'

'That chick tripped me out seriously.'

'What did she say?'

'She was expounding, you know what I mean? On how we're part alien, like it's part of our heredities. She was saying everybody's got this alien blood in them – it's in their DNA or something. Some people have more than others, you know, they're closer to being full aliens. She said you could recognize people sometimes, the more alien ones. You can recognize them by certain signs.'

'What were the signs?'

'Gold was one of them. She liked to talk about gold.'

'What'd she say?'

'Well, you see these aliens, you know like the full aliens, she said they have gold in their blood, I mean it's not really blood, 'cause they're not us, but it acts like blood does in humans. She said that's why there's always gold being used in religions, because religions are always about higher powers. It's just that most people don't understand that the higher powers are aliens. She got really turned on about it. They were looking for aliens.'

'Were they looking for Goldhands?'

'I think so. They were kinda general in their questions. They wanted to know if I knew anyone who showed the signs.'

'The gold signs?'

'Yeah. Like in their eyes. They said if you saw somebody with gold eyes or gold hair that was a real connection. I asked No Pants if he thought Macy was alien.'

'What'd he say?'

'He got kinda obtuse.'

'What do you mean?'

'He pretended like he didn't know her, said I must be confusing him with someone else. I think it was 'cos of the other lady being with him, like maybe he didn't want her to know. I backed off.'

'Anything else?'

'They asked if I knew any alchemists. They said people who worked with gold, that they had some kind of connection to the aliens too. I guess they were looking for Goldhands, now that I think about it.'

'I need his help, Bob. It's important.'

Cool Bob twisted his lips to one side of his mouth. He looked out through the front of the trailer and scratched his beard.

'We got a code around here in the Slabs,' he said. 'We protect our own. If a guy doesn't want to be found, we're not gonna give him away as long as he contributes positively to the citizenry. Not a disgruntler, or something.'

'Why do you call him Goldhands?' Rolly asked.

Bob stared out the front window. His eyes moved, as if watching something outside.

'He knows how to make gold from old electrical stuff, like computers. He collects parts, stuff he finds, or people trade with him, for his help with electrical stuff. It's mostly old computer boards and electrical things. He's got chemicals and burner stuff too.'

Something rattled against the back window of the trailer. It sounded like gravel.

'It's him, isn't it?' Rolly said. 'It's Goldhands?'

Cool Bob walked to the front of the trailer, opened the door and stepped outside. He shut the door behind him. Rolly heard muffled voices, but he couldn't make out any specifics. The door to the trailer opened. Cool Bob stuck his head inside. 'Goldhands wants to talk to you. Outside.'

Rolly slid from the booth, walked to the door, stepped down onto the sand and planted himself next to Bob. The other man, Goldhands, stood about twenty feet from the trailer, just inside the shade of the overhanging canopy. He wore heavy black-rimmed glasses. The hair he had left clung to his head like a shriveled badger.

240

'Do you remember me?' Rolly asked.

The man nodded. 'I remember the Waters.'

'I remember Buddy Meeks, the best guitar tech in town. He and I used to talk a lot.'

'That man is in here,' said Goldhands, tapping his right hand with its gold fingers to his temple. 'I remember him. Before the Conjoinment.'

'Can I still talk to him? To Buddy Meeks?'

'The Waters can talk to him. Only the Waters.'

Rolly smiled. There was enough of Buddy Meeks in the man to bring back his own memories. Buddy, the nerd, behind the shop counter at the Guitar Trader, his glasses slipping down his nose, going off on a tangent, giving long, detailed explanations of what made your guitar imperfect and how he could improve it. Sometimes the boss would interrupt them, remind Buddy that he didn't pay him to stand around talking with customers all day. Rolly had enjoyed talking to Buddy. He'd learned a lot from him.

'I figured it out,' Rolly said. 'The combination. I opened the box. It was empty.'

'The box is empty. Yes. The vibrator box is only for practice.'

'What do you mean?'

'The Waters must practice. Practice makes perfect.'

'Why do I need to practice so much?'

'The Waters must be perfect. He must play the Astral Vibrator.'

'Isn't the box the Astral Vibrator?'

'The box is for practice. The Astral Vibrator is for The Conjoinment.'

Rolly thought for a moment. The real Astral

Vibrator was somewhere else. It was wherever Gibbons was going. 'Parnell Gibbons has the diddley bow,' he said. 'He stole it from me. He's got Macy, too. And the key.'

Buddy Meeks looked up at the sky and screamed. 'Teotwayki!' He paused then howled again, three times.

Rolly looked at Cool Bob, gauging his reaction. 'Why does he do that?'

'Three times like that,' said Bob. 'He's calling the Rockers.'

A response to Buddy's call echoed through the air, then another. They sounded close by, within the area inhabited by the year-round Slabbers.

'That's the Rockers,' said Bob. 'They're echolocating, so he knows where they are. It shows that they're ready and listening.'

Buddy Meeks howled again, this time with a stop and start rhythm, short, long, short.

'Whoa,' said Bob. 'SOS call.'

Cool Bob joined the chorus, repeating the start and stop rhythm, the SOS call. Calls came in response. They sounded closer than before. It was like being part of a wolf pack. Someone ran in from the road. Rolly recognized the drummer from the band. Soon others had arrived. They were all members of the band – the drummer, the bass player and the man who played saxophone and piano.

'What's up?' said the drummer, catching his breath.

'You all remember this guy?' said Bob, indicating Rolly. 'Guitar player who sat in with us at The Range a couple nights ago?'

242

The band members nodded and greeted him.

'Somebody slugged him and stole his diddley bow. Somebody in camp.'

'What's the plan?' said the keyboard player.

'Goldhands made the SOS call,' said Bob. 'It's up to him.'

All eyes turned to Buddy Meeks – Goldhands. He signaled to Bob with his hands.

'Road trip,' said Bob.

The band members cheered.

'Where we going?' said Bob.

'The Conjoinment,' Buddy said.

Bob looked over at Rolly. 'You know where that is?' he said.

'Yes, I think so,' said Rolly. It all made sense now. And it made no sense at all. 'We can take my RV.'

'OK, boys,' said Bob. 'Let's saddle up. Me and Goldhands will go with this guy. You guys get the rocket ship and meet us at the guardhouse, follow us from there.'

'Electric or acoustic?' said the bass player.

'Fully loaded,' said Bob.

'Holy shit, Bob,' said the drummer. 'You mean it?'

Bob turned to Rolly. 'This guy's dangerous, right? Him taking Macy and all.'

'He's got a stungun,' said Rolly. 'He just got out of prison.'

The men stared at Cool Bob for guidance. Bob raised his arm and clenched his fist.

'Locked and loaded,' he said. The men cheered.

'Does that mean what I think it does?' said Rolly.

243

'That's right,' replied Bob. 'We're packing heat.'

Twenty-Nine
The Ascent

As soon as they hit the main road and the signal was strong enough, Rolly put in a call to Kinnie Harper. She didn't answer, so he left her a message. He told her about Parnell Gibbons and said he was headed her way. He warned her that a group of long-haired freaks bearing firearms were coming her way, driving his Tioga and a Volkswagen van that looked like a spaceship. He hoped Kinnie got the message. With any luck she and her deputies would have Parnell Gibbons locked up by the time Rolly arrived. And the Rockers could put away their guns.

Buddy Meeks sat next to Rolly in the shotgun seat. Cool Bob sat in the dining booth, looking over Rolly's shoulder. The freeway split as they started up into the mountains. The grade became steeper and the Tioga slowed as they hit the first switchback. Rolly moved to the truck lane. He checked his rearview mirror. The rocket ship, filled with the rest of the Rockers and their guns, moved into the truck lane as well. Neither vehicle had been built for climbing mountains, let alone high-speed pursuit. The Rockers and their ordnance were a mixed blessing. There was some protection in numbers, but a lot less control. He wasn't sure how desperate Parnell Gibbons might be.

The sky grew more overcast as they climbed up the mountains. Rain would bring out the wild-flowers in the desert but it wouldn't make his job any easier. The backcountry roads would become slick with thin layers of oil, squishing mud. Flash floods might block off their access entirely.

Buddy Meeks mumbled something.

'What's that?' said Rolly.

Buddy stared out the window and mumbled again. Rolly glanced down at Buddy's hands, the gold stains on Buddy's fingers. He wondered if the stains were permanent or if Buddy just needed a cleaning regimen. Of the three men traveling in the Tioga, Buddy was the ripest, but all of them could use a little freshening.

'What's he looking for?' Rolly said. 'What's Parnell Gibbons looking for?'

Buddy mumbled something unintelligible. He traced his index finger on the window – quick little motions, as if he were playing invisible tic-tac-toe or solving equations on a chalkboard. Rolly glanced in the rearview mirror at Bob.

'Do you know what he's doing?' he asked.

'Cogitating,' said Bob. 'He gets like that some-times. Serious internals.'

Buddy continued with his calculations. He paid no attention to them.

'Do you know why his fingers are gold like that?' Rolly asked.

'He makes gold. From old computer parts. The

circuit boards have gold in them, the connectors and stuff. That stuff's too chemicalized for me, working with that stuff.'

'Can you make money doing that?'

'I don't know if he makes any money.'

'Can you make enough to get by in Slab City?'

'You don't need to make much to survive in the Slabs,' said Bob. 'He showed me how to do it once, had this big pile of old circuit boards somebody gave him. He cut off the gold parts, the connectors, then melted them down and mixed in some chemicals. Ended up with a nice little chunk of gold. Too toxic for me to mess with. They use cyanide, you know.'

'How long's he been doing this?' Rolly asked.

'As long as I've been at the Slabs.'

'How long is that?'

'It was maybe five years ago I set up my trailer. I didn't meet Goldhands for a while, though, him being so singular. People don't tell you about stuff at the Slabs unless you've been around a while, when you're one of the regulars. Don't bother people when they don't want to be bothered. That's the standard. You got to be trusted first. Don't look for people who don't want to be found.'

As a general life rule it was a good one to follow, but Rolly got paid to find people who didn't want to be found. That's why people hired him. People like Macy. There were ghosts in his clients' lives, people missing. He wondered how many of the regulars living in Slab City had become ghosts, haunting the minds of the people who used to know them, people who loved them,

246

people who hated them. Buddy Meeks had been a ghost, a haunted spirit from Rolly's past. Now he was a real person again, a weird and distracted one, but real, not a ghost.

'You say he used cyanide for the gold,' Rolly said.

'Yeah,' said Bob. 'That's nasty shit. They use that stuff to kill rats.'

'And people too.'

'Yeah, I guess. I worked for an exterminator one summer, back in Tennessee. We used it for rats.'

Rolly remembered something Gibbons had said to him. *I spent twenty years in prison because of that little shit.* He wondered if Buddy Meeks, the crazy man with gold fingers, had somehow been responsible for the UVT deaths twenty years ago. They'd been poisoned with cyanide. Was Gibbons innocent? Was he looking for revenge?

He checked the speedometer as the Tioga lumbered up the grade. Their speed had dropped to forty miles an hour. He checked the side mirror. The guys in the van had fallen even further behind. Four men and their weapons were too much for an old Volkswagen to haul up a mountain. He thought about Macy, if she would become a ghost, lost in his memory as the years went on, just like Buddy.

'He makes gold paint too,' said Bob. 'I've seen him do that.'

'Hmm?'

'That might be how he gets the gold fingers. He pulverizes this foil stuff, adds some kind of chemicals and water.'

247

'What does he do with the paint?'

'He made this sculpture in East Jesus – gold dolls, a pile of them.'

'I didn't see any gold dolls.'

'They disappeared about a week ago.'

'He painted the dolls?'

'Don't know for sure, but that's what I heard.'

Buddy turned from the window and looked at Rolly. 'Gold is an electrical conductor,' he said in a flat tone. 'Very high conductivity. Seventy percent.'

'People are always trying to sell me guitar cables with gold connectors,' said Rolly.

'Silver and copper are better conductors,' said Buddy. 'Gold is better for corrosion, more durable.'

'I didn't know that,' said Bob. 'This dude is awesome.'

'Awesome,' said Rolly.

'Gold is a noble metal,' said Buddy. 'The Ancients have gold in their veins.'

'Totally engrossing,' said Bob.

Rolly held the steering wheel tight as they curved through the second switchback and headed up another long slope of asphalt.

Buddy did some more calculations on his fingers and pointed up the hill. 'Sluggish,' he said.

'Yeah, sorry,' said Rolly. 'Tell me about the Ancients. They're supposed to be aliens, right?'

'From the Oort,' said Buddy.

'What's that?'

'It's the cloud where comets come from. The Ancients.'

'Oort, oort, oort,' said Bob.

Rolly fought back an impulse to tell Bob to shut up. He might never have found Buddy if it hadn't been for Bob.

'It is time for the Conjoinment,' said Buddy.

'What's that?'

'When the planets align. When the Ancients are closest. We will call them.'

'How do you call them?' said Rolly. He had a pretty good idea of the general concept, but was still unclear on the specifics.

'The Astral Vibrator.'

'What is the Astral Vibrator? What does it do?'

'It calls the Ancients.'

'Is that why I have to practice? So the Ancients will show up?'

'Yes. The Waters must play it. So the Ancients will see.'

Great, thought Rolly. This would be the weirdest gig he'd ever played.

'The Waters must play the Astral Vibrator so the Gentlings may join with the Ancients,' said Buddy. 'They will speak through the Sachem.'

'Whoa,' said Bob. 'He's starting to sound like that lady, the one with No Pants.'

'That lady with No Pants, I think she knows Goldhands from a long time ago. That's right, isn't it, Buddy? You know Dotty, Dorothy Coasters? You were there with her, and Gibbons, with all the UVTs.'

'UVTs?' said Buddy.

'What's a UVT?' said Bob.

Rolly realized that UVT was a term Buddy might never have heard before. It was a shortcut the police and press had started using after the event.

'The Universal Vibration Technologies. You lived with them, didn't you, in that house?'

'Meeks implemented the frequencies,' said Buddy.

'Sounds formidable,' said Bob. 'You know what he's talking about?'

'Not exactly.'

'I'm totally Kenneth, what is the frequency right now,' said Bob.

'It's an alternate scale he worked out,' said Rolly. 'Somebody worked it out, anyway. Nine tones. The Solfeggio frequencies.'

'You mean the Do, Re, Mi?'

'It's different. They claim it's the original scale of the Ancients.'

'Primordial,' said Bob.

'Exactly,' said Rolly.

He guided the Tioga through the next hairpin. They'd made it halfway up the mountain, holding steady at forty. He remembered what Kinnie had told him about the UVTs, how they paired up together, playing the diddley bows at sunrise and sunset. They'd been practicing for the Conjoinment. He took a deep breath and looked over at Buddy, who was doing his calculations again. Rolly didn't know what would happen once they got to the gold mine. With all the heat the Rockers were packing, it would be a wonder if anyone survived. He had to ask now.

'Buddy,' he said, 'can you think back for me . . . those people you were with, when you implemented the frequencies. Did you know a girl named Betty? Or Beatrice? Her mother was there too. Wanda Ozzie. Do you remember either of them?'

'Betty,' said Buddy. It didn't sound like a question. Rolly held his breath.

'Betty's gone,' said Buddy. 'Betty fell down in the hole. Couldn't get out.'

'Was there a baby?' said Rolly. 'Did Betty have a baby with her? A little girl with gold eyes?'

'The Sachem,' said Buddy.

It was the closest Rolly had come to a confirmation. Macy had been there, with the UVTs, as a baby. Bob was silent. He seemed to sense the weightiness of the situation. Rolly took the last hairpin. They were almost at the summit and the In-Ko-Pah exit. Rolly had no idea what they would find when they got to the Astral Vibrator. He took a deep breath. One more question.

'Buddy, what happened to those people?' he said. 'The UVTs?'

'The Waters must play it,' said Buddy. 'The Waters will free them.'

Thirty
The Mine

The sky had darkened considerably by the time they reached the In-Ko-Pah exit and turned off the freeway. Rain was a rare occurrence on this side of the mountains, but the slate-colored clouds above them looked menacing and heavy, as if they would open up any minute. Trees and bushes by the side of the road trembled in the rising wind. Rolly drove towards Desert View Tower while Buddy ran calculations with his fingers.

'Left turn,' said Buddy.

Rolly stopped the Tioga and spotted an access road that Buddy apparently wanted him to take. It didn't look like much. When the rain came, it would get muddy. The Tioga would slide around in the ruts, or, even worse, sink its tires into a wet spot. It was the same road he'd seen the blue Toyota exit from two days ago when he and Moogus were stranded. Daddy Joe's Toyota had been found in the area. He wondered if Daddy Joe had been driving it that morning.

A splatter of raindrops hit the window, as if warning him.

'I don't know if I can drive in there,' said Rolly. 'We might get stuck.'

'The rocket ship can handle it,' said Bob. 'Let's wait for the Rockers.'

Rolly pulled over to the side of the road. Soon the others arrived and pulled up behind them. More splatters of rain hit the ground as the three men left the Tioga behind and climbed into the van. The VW wasn't much of an off-road vehicle, either, but it was a lot lighter than the RV. Three men could lift the van out of a rut if they needed to.

They headed down the side road, packed in like sardines. Rolly looked at the faces of the

Rockers. They looked calm, almost bored, as if carrying guns along with them was an everyday experience. Nobody seemed to be in a hurry; no one was amped up for a shooting. That was good. He looked out the side window, surveying the scenery. They passed behind the boulder field where the stone animals lived. The van lurched to the right then came to a stop.

'Looks like the cops are here,' said the driver.

Rolly looked out the front window. A tribal police truck was parked at end of the road in front of the guardrail. There was another car next to it, a cheap-looking Suzuki.

'Let me find out if she's around,' Rolly said, not wanting to disgorge a gang of gunslingers on Kinnie without some discussion of their proper employment. He opened the sliding door and walked to the police truck. There was no one inside. He checked the Suzuki. It wasn't locked. He looked in the glove compartment and found the registration slip listing Randy Parker as the owner. Parnell Gibbons was here already. Kinnie had found him. Or followed him into the canyon.

Two mesas jutted out from the other side of the canyon, a solitary house located on each of them. The first one was Daddy Joe's house. The other was Beatrice House, with the UVT memorial park out on the point. They looked closer together from this angle, more like neighbors than they'd seemed before. Below them, the canyon widened out into a flat plain. There were signs of an old settlement in the canyon, ruins of wood structures.

Buddy walked up beside him. 'The Waters

253

must play it,' he said. He walked around the end of the guardrail, stepped off the ledge and disappeared into the canyon.

'Hey!' Rolly called. He hastened to the end of the guardrail and looked down. Buddy stood on a ledge ten feet below. He pointed up at a skinny path leading to his location. Rolly looked back towards the van. Bob stood outside, watching him.

'Stay here,' said Rolly. 'Don't let anyone get by you until I get back.'

Bob nodded and waved.

By the time Rolly turned back, Buddy had disappeared again. He walked down the path to the ledge where Buddy had been and looked around. Buddy appeared again, twenty feet further down the canyon.

'Wait!' Rolly called. Buddy stopped and looked back at him. He pointed at a break in the rocks below the ledge to Rolly's left. Rolly climbed down through the break, slid around the side of a large boulder, found the trail again and followed it until he'd caught up with Buddy. The rest of the trail was an easier trek, gentle switchbacks leading into the flat part of the canyon. Shrubs clumped thickly as they got to the bottom, but a narrow break let them through.

As they hiked along the canyon floor, broken-down structures of wood appeared by the side of the trail, the remains of old cabins and fences, skeletal wood grids that looked like they might have been planters or sorting bins. Three rusted train cars stood on railroad tracks next to a smashed water tower. Someone had spray-painted the word *TEOTWAYKI* on one of the cars. A steady drizzle began to fall.

The trail became wider. Buddy turned off and headed back up the slope they'd come down, but farther along, in the direction of the Desert View Tower. Rolly looked back to find the spot where they'd parked. He could see the front grill of Kinnie's truck and Randy's Suzuki, but they soon passed out of sight.

They climbed the hill a short way before Buddy stopped and cogitated for a moment. Using two of his golden fingers, he pointed at something farther up the hill, a large black hole in the side of the earth covered by a steel gate. It was the bat gate Kinnie had told Rolly about, designed to keep people out, allowing the bats to come and go as they pleased. Buddy climbed up to the gate. Rolly joined him. The edges of the hole had eroded over time, leaving gaps on either sides of the gate. They squeezed through the right side of the gate and entered the hole in the mountain, just as the rain began falling in sheets.

The inside of the mine looked like Rolly had expected – an earthen tunnel braced by criss-crosses of splintery pillars and beams. It got darker as they hiked further in. Soon he wouldn't be able to see his hand in front of his face. Buddy pulled a flashlight out of his pocket and turned it on. They continued on into the mine, snaking through the tunnels, following Buddy's light. Buddy stopped.

Rolly bumped into him. 'What is it?' he whispered.

Light blazed through the room, a string of

safety lights running along the edge of the cavern. It was too much light, too soon.

Rolly covered his eyes with one hand. 'Yah!' he said.

'Grmmph,' someone grunted.

Rolly looked towards the grunt, still shading his eyes. Someone lay on the floor.

'Kinnie?' he said.

'Grmmph,' said Kinnie. It was all she could say. She'd been gagged, with a red bandana tied over her mouth and her hands pulled behind her. Rolly stepped towards her.

'Hold on, Roland Waters,' someone said. Rolly turned towards the voice. It was Parnell Gibbons. He had the diddley bow with him. Dotty stood next to him. She had an automatic pistol in her hand, pointed in Buddy and Rolly's general direction.

'Hello, Buddy,' said Dotty. 'It's good to see you again.'

Buddy Meeks made a strangling sound in his throat. His body went rigid, almost as if he were having a seizure.

'Grmmph,' said Kinnie.

Rolly looked back at her. 'Are you OK?' he asked.

Kinnie nodded. 'Grmmph.'

'Well, everyone's here now,' said Gibbons. 'All the liars and freaks and criminals, back together again. The Conjoinment, round two.'

'Where's Macy?' said Rolly.

'A stand-in for the old chief, of course,' said Gibbons, nodding at Kinnie. 'But his daughter will have to do.'

'Where's Macy?' said Rolly again.

'Down there,' said Gibbons, pointing to a hole in the ground.

'What did you do to her?'

'She's retrieving something valuable.'

'He figured it out, Buddy,' said Dotty. 'What you did with the gold.'

'Twenty years, Buddy,' said Parnell. 'I thought about you a lot. Weird little Buddy, with his puzzles and numbers, his anal-compulsive oddities.'

'I want to see Macy,' said Rolly. 'Where is she?'

A beam of light shot up from the hole in the ground between Dotty and Gibbons.

'I'm coming up,' said a voice from inside the hole.

The flashlight beam bounced around the walls of the cave. Macy climbed out of the hole. She turned off the light that was strapped to her head, reached back down and hauled up a rope. A plastic crate appeared at the end of it. There was a metal box inside the crate.

'Is that it?' said Rolly. 'Is that the Astral Vibrator?'

'Hey, Waters,' said Macy, 'what're you doing here?'

'Trying to find you,' Rolly said. 'Among other things.'

'Well, you found me. Sorry.'

'I'm sorry too.'

'Guess this'll teach me to go chasing after old ladies.'

'Shut up,' said Gibbons. 'Let me see it.'

'Yes, boss,' said Macy. She reached into the

crate, lifted out the metal box and placed it on the floor. Gibbons leaned down and inspected the box.

'The Waters must play it,' said Buddy. He seemed to have come out of his spell.

'The what?' said Gibbons.

'The Waters must play it,' said Buddy. He sounded like a five-year-old kid, as if he'd start screaming or crying. 'The Waters must play it.'

'Screw that,' Gibbons said. He grabbed the other end of the guitar cable and plugged it into the box.

'No, no, the Waters,' pleaded Buddy.

'You heard him,' said Macy. 'Let Waters do it. Waters is the shit.'

'Fuck Roland Waters,' said Gibbons. 'I spent twenty years waiting for this.'

Gibbons sat down on a rock and placed the diddley bow on his knees. He pulled out a slide and played a sequence of notes similar to the ones Rolly had played. Nothing happened. Gibbons turned the volume knob all the way up and played the notes again with the same results. He jiggled the cable, made sure it was seated properly. He played the notes again. Again there was nothing.

Buddy giggled. 'The villain sucks,' he said. 'Teotwayki!'

'Shut up,' said Gibbons. He played the notes again, with still no result. 'I know I'm playing it right.'

'The Waters must play it,' said Buddy.

'Fuck you.'

The diddley bow clattered to the ground as

258

Gibbons jumped up from his seat. He pulled something out of his back pocket as he rushed towards Buddy. Rolly saw an arc of electricity and heard the woodpecker sound as Gibbons jabbed the prongs of his stungun into Buddy's waist. Buddy yelled and jerked backwards. He fell to the ground.

'Stop it,' said Rolly.

Gibbons turned on him. 'You want some?' he said.

Rolly held his hands up in front of him. 'No, thanks. I've had my share.'

'What does he mean?' Gibbons said. 'Why does he want you to play it?'

'I can open the box,' Rolly said. 'I've got one just like it in the RV. I opened it.'

'Was there anything in it?'

'A postcard.'

'You're a liar.'

'I'm not lying.'

'Where did you hide it?'

'I didn't hide it. You can come take a look if you want. I've got it with me, in the Tioga. There wasn't any gold, just a postcard of Desert View Tower, no writing or anything.'

Dotty walked over to Buddy, leaned down and stroked his hair with her free hand, the one without the gun. 'Buddy,' she said, 'it's almost time. What should we do?'

'The Waters must play it,' said Buddy. 'Teotwayki!'

'It's a trick,' Gibbons said.

'For God's sake,' Dotty said, turning on Gibbons. 'Just let him play the damn thing.'

The look on Parnell's face turned to pure

loathing, as if he remembered every day he'd spent in prison, every hour he'd spent planning his triumphal moment. He hadn't expected to argue with half-a-dozen people about it. He waved the stungun at Rolly.

'No tricks,' he said. 'I'll fry your ass like bacon if this is a trick.'

'Understood,' said Rolly. He picked up the diddley bow, reached into his pocket and pulled out his slide, then sat down on the rock. He laid the diddley bow on his lap and rehearsed the sequence of notes in his head. He stopped and looked at the slide on his finger. It wasn't right. He put it back in his pocket. 'Macy?' he said, looking over at her.

'Yeah?'

'Give me the key.'

Macy looked blank for a moment before recognition came into her eyes. She undid her necklace, slipped the gold tube off the end and handed it to Rolly.

'Rock my world, Waters,' she said. 'I don't want your ass getting fried.'

'Yeah. Thanks,' said Rolly. He closed his eyes and visualized the positions on the diddley bow's neck. He opened his eyes, took a deep breath, locked in and played the notes. The bolts popped on the front panel of the box.

'You did it,' said Macy. 'Right?'

'I think so,' said Rolly.

'Let me see,' said Gibbons, shoving Rolly out of the way. He picked up the box, reached inside and pulled something out. It looked like a Barbie doll, a blonde Barbie doll covered in gold paint.

260

'What the hell is this?' he said.

'Teotwayki!' cried Buddy.

No one else said anything because the lights had gone out.

Thirty-One
The Conjoinment

The stungun spit out an electrical arc. Rolly saw Gibbons' face in a halo of light, cramped and contorted in a rictus of pain. The arc light went out. Pure blackness covered their eyes again. Rolly smelled ozone. Someone moved in the darkness. There had been someone behind Gibbons, a cave monster hidden in shadow. Rolly held his breath, listened to the soft rustling sounds. Someone groaned.

'Who's there?' he said.

A flashlight beam danced on the walls. Macy had turned on her headlight. The beam settled on Gibbons. He lay prostrate on the ground, his hands tied behind him. They could see a man's boots next to him. Macy swiveled the light up the other man's body. He turned away from the light.

Gibbons screamed, 'Shoot him!'

Macy's light went out. A deafening explosion burst from the darkness. Rolly ducked into a fetal position, hugging the rocky floor. The gun went off again, three more shots. Bullets pinged through the cavern. The room went silent. He lifted his head. There was a loud smack, like a slap. Something metallic clattered onto the rocks. Someone began crying. The cave was still dark.

'Macy?' said Rolly.

'Yeah?'

'Are you OK?'

'Yeah. What happened?'

'I don't know.'

'Where's your flashlight?'

'It fell off when I ducked.'

Someone groaned in the darkness.

'Here it is,' said Macy. She turned on the light and blasted it in Rolly's face.

'Not on me,' he said, squinting his eyes. 'Over there.'

Macy turned the light towards the center of the room. Gibbons lay face down on the floor, trussed up like a hog.

Dotty lay near him, flat on her back. She was sobbing. 'I am blameless,' she said. Someone grunted, off to the right. Macy swung the light over and found Kinnie.

Rolly stood up and walked over to Kinnie. He leaned down and pulled the gag from her mouth.

'Find my gun,' she said. 'That was my gun.'

Macy turned the light and walked to the middle of the room. Rolly followed her. They looked down at Gibbons and Dotty.

'Where'd he go?' said Macy.

'I don't know. We need to find Kinnie's gun.'

'Shit,' Macy said. 'Is that blood?'

Rolly saw it as soon as Macy did: a wet red puddle.

262

Kinnie called over to them. 'Turn on the lights.'

'Where are they?' said Rolly.

'By the ladder. Watch for the hole.'

Macy swiveled her headlight around the room and found the hole in the floor. She tilted the light up to the wall.

'There,' Rolly said.

Macy walked to the wall and flipped the switch. The lights came back on. 'Shit,' she said.

'What?'

'There's more blood here. On the ladder. Hey, lady!'

Rolly turned back to the room. Parnell lay trussed up on the floor, but Dotty had risen. She stood at the edge of the tunnel with Kinnie's gun in her hand.

'Put the gun down, Dotty,' said Rolly. 'You can't get away.'

'I did before,' she said. 'I can do it again. I am blameless.'

Gibbons laughed. 'Stupid bitch,' he said. 'You're not blameless. All of this is your fault.'

'Shut up, Parnell,' she said. 'I had to testify against you. I had to protect myself and my work. You ruined me.'

'Those people got what they wanted. They did it for you.'

'That's a lie. You were unfaithful to me.'

'I'm more faithful than anyone.'

'Stop it. Stop your lies.'

'What do you think would have happened if the Conjoinment had passed and nothing changed, everyone sitting around waiting for something to happen? You made it so easy, you and your stupid rituals. Everyone synchronized, like the music, taking a drink at the same time. That's how it worked. Once the poison was in the pot, they were all done for.'

'You put the poison in there.'

'That stupid girl did it. She made the soup.'

'You gave the poison to her. You told her to do it.'

'You don't have any proof of that. No one does.'

'They were believers,' said Dotty. 'They were my disciples.'

'They knew exactly where you were leading them. They wanted to die.'

'You treated them like vermin. I made them gods.'

'They were cattle. Stupid, dumb sheep. They wouldn't have died without you taking them in, leading them on.'

Dotty moved towards Gibbons. Her voice shook. 'You left me with nothing, Parnell. I had to sell my house. I had to leave town. I had to change my name and scrape along, reading auras in Sedona. Then Randy found me. He knew my work. He believed in the universal vibrations. He seduced me. But it was you, all along, leading him on. You fed him stories. You gave him ideas. And then you killed him.'

'That was an accident,' said Gibbons. 'The little shit tried to cheat me. I knew what he was up to. Looking for Buddy, so he could get here first.'

'Can't you see, Parnell? It's not here. Buddy used it all up. It's gone.'

Rolly looked around the room. Buddy was missing.

'It's here,' Parnell replied. 'I know it is.'

'You lie to yourself, like you lied to Randy, like you lied to me.' Dotty's hand quivered. She pointed the gun at Parnell.

'Don't do it, Dotty,' said Rolly. 'He's not worth it.'

She looked over at Rolly and dropped the gun to her side. 'I have to go,' she said.

'There's a posse out there,' said Rolly. 'Friends of mine from Slab City. They've got guns. They won't let you leave.'

Dotty stared at Rolly a moment. 'All men are liars,' she said, and ran out the tunnel.

'Holy shit, Waters,' said Macy. 'That was screwed up.'

'Now that you both screwed things up,' said Kinnie, 'you think you could find the key to my handcuffs and set me loose?'

'Where are they?' said Rolly.

'Check his pockets.'

Rolly walked over to Gibbons, knelt down and began searching him.

'Think you won again, don't you, Waters,' said Gibbons.

'I don't care about winning,' said Rolly.

'You used to.'

'What are you talking about?'

'The jam contests. At McP's on Sundays. You remember when you won?'

'I won a lot of those things,' said Rolly.

Gibbons snickered. 'Asshole. I mean the first time. When you were in high school.'

265

Rolly found the key in Gibbons front pocket. He grabbed it and stood up. 'Sure, I remember,' he said. 'Some guy made me give back the prize money. He said I was too young because I used a fake ID to get in.'

'I was that guy,' said Gibbons.

'That was you, huh?'

Rolly walked over to Kinnie and unlocked her handcuffs. Kinnie sat up and rubbed her wrists.

'Where's Buddy?' said Rolly.

Gibbons laughed. 'The bitch shot him,' she said.

Kinnie stood up, walked over to Gibbons and slapped her handcuffs on him to make sure he didn't slip out of his knots.

'Somebody tied you up pretty good, didn't they?' she said. 'Who was it?'

'You know who it was,' said Gibbons. 'He's part of this too.'

'Hey, Waters,' said Macy, 'the blood. I think the bird guy went down the ladder.'

'Show me,' said Kinnie. She pulled a flashlight from her belt and walked back towards Macy. She pointed the light at the top of the ladder.

'That's fresh blood, all right,' she said. 'What's the guy's name?'

'Buddy Meeks,' said Rolly.

Kinnie leaned down into the hole. 'Mr Meeks! Buddy Meeks! Are you down there?'

No one answered.

'Let me go down,' said Macy.

'You don't know what he's got down there,' said Kinnie. 'It could be dangerous.'

'You gotta go down, then.'

Kinnie squatted down by the hole. She sighed. 'Shit,' she said. 'I'm off the rez. That lady's got my gun. I shouldn't even be here.'

'I can do it,' said Macy. 'I went down there before.'

'How'd you find this place, Kinnie?' said Rolly. 'The message I left just said we were going to the tower. How'd you end up here?'

'We can talk about that later, Mr Waters,' said Kinnie. 'I better call in support, get the sheriff on this. They can helicopter the guy out of here.'

'It's too bad about your gun, Chief Harper,' said Gibbons.

'Shut up, asshole. You're getting kicked back to the big house for a long time.' Kinnie stood up. 'My radio won't work in here,' she said. 'I'm going outside to call in support.'

'What about him?' Rolly said.

Kinnie kicked Parnell's boot. 'This asshole ain't going anywhere,' she said. 'Macy, you do whatever you want. I warned you. If you find that Meeks guy down there, if he's bleeding serious, apply pressure,' she said. 'Stuff your shirt in his wound or something, whatever you got. Try not to let him bleed out. I'll get the paramedics in here as soon as I can.'

Kinnie stomped away down the tunnel.

'Waters, I'm going in,' said Macy. She adjusted her headlight, climbed onto the ladder and stepped halfway down into the hole.

'Macy?' said Rolly.

'What?'

'Be careful.'

267

'Don't believe in careful. Hey, Waters?'

'Yeah.'

'In case something happens, just so you know.'

'What?'

'Best date ever! Awesome!' Macy disappeared into the hole.

Rolly turned back to Parnell. 'Got anything you want to tell me?' he said. 'You know, just between us.'

'Suck my dick,' said Gibbons.

'Oh, come on now. You know I like girls,' Rolly said. He looked back at the ladder. 'Crazy girls.'

'I was framed,' said Gibbons. 'I didn't kill them.'

'Who did then?'

'That girl. The stupid one. Stupid bitch put that stuff in the soup. Thought it was salt or something. All Buddy's fault, leaving it out on the counter.'

'You're telling me it was an accident?'

'It looks just like salt, you know. Buddy Meeks, smarter than shit but no brains at all, left that shit on the counter.'

'You bought the stuff. Your name was on the receipt.'

'Buddy asked for it. We were looking for gold. We found some here, in the mine.'

'What happened to the girl?'

'Big chief. He took her. Lied on the witness stand. Who's the jury gonna believe, me or some noble Indian chief bullshit?'

'It was Betty, the girl, wasn't it? Her name was Beatrice Ozzie?'

'Black girl. Nice piece of ass. Stupid girl had a baby.'

'Maybe somebody else was stupid, too.'

Gibbons chuckled. 'Yeah. Maybe.'

'Is she your daughter? Is Macy your daughter? You and Betty?'

'Ungrateful bitches, all of 'em.'

'Yeah, it's weird how women get like that. All you did was poison everyone and take their money.'

'Fuck you, Waters. All that tired blues stuff you play. It sucks.'

'What?'

'That's how you won. All those cliched licks. That's how you won all those contests.'

'Yeah, well, play what you know.'

'You don't know shit.'

Rolly decided to lay off for awhile. Gibbons might get chatty later and tell him more.

'Hey, Waters!'

It was Macy, popping up out of the hole like a gopher. She was naked to the waist.

'Where's your shirt?' he said.

'Shit, Waters. It's not like you haven't seen 'em before. I stuffed my shirt in the guy's wound just like Kinnie said I should. There's a lot of blood. He asked for you.'

'Buddy asked for me?'

'He wants you to play that thing again.'

'He wants me to bring the diddley bow down there?'

'Yeah. There's something down here. It's just like that box thing I brought up before.'

Rolly looked down at Parnell.

'I knew it,' said Parnell. 'I knew it was here.'

'Jesus shit, Waters. C'mon. This could be the guy's dying wish or something.'

Kinnie was right. Parnell wasn't going anywhere – not before she got back, anyway. Rolly grabbed the diddley bow, wrapped the cable around it and handed it to Macy. She disappeared back into the hole. He grabbed the first rung of the ladder. The blood was still wet. Buddy's blood. He lowered himself down into the hole.

They walked through the lower tunnel. Macy's light bounced off the walls.

'You're not going to believe this shit,' Macy said. 'There's something crazy down here.'

'What is it?'

'I'm not sure exactly. There's a grotto or something, this big room. There's one of those boxes stuck in the rocks, farther back than that first one I found.'

Macy stopped and aimed her headlight down at the floor. Buddy lay there, covered in blood, with Macy's T-shirt stuck in his gut. His head lolled to one side. Macy squatted down and cradled the back of Buddy's head against her small breasts. He opened his eyes and spotted Rolly.

'The Waters,' Buddy said, raising one gold finger.

'Plug the guitar thing in there,' said Macy. She pointed her light at a black box embedded in the rocks. The top of the box was covered in concrete. There was a quarter-inch input on the front of the box, just like on the others. Unlike the first two boxes, there was a thick black cable running out of the back. Rolly plugged in the diddley bow.

270

'The Waters must play it,' said Buddy, his eyes glazing over.

Rolly took Macy's gold charm out of his pocket. 'I need more light,' he said, indicating the diddley bow. Macy gave it to him. He took a deep breath then played the notes again. A switch clicked. Lights went on in the cavern.

'Holy shit,' said Macy. 'What is it?'

The cavern was burnished in gold, its walls covered in gold paint. There were diddley bows arranged in a half circle, a dozen or more, with gold filigrees. A doll had been placed in front of each diddley bow – all kinds of dolls, Barbies and GI Joes and baby dolls. The dolls were all covered in gold, with gold-painted skin and gold eyes. A flat rock slab rose in the center of the room. A human skeleton lay on the slab.

'It's a tomb,' said Rolly.

'The bones,' said Macy. 'He painted them gold.'

Buddy Meeks gurgled. 'The Conjoinment is done,' he said. 'The Gentlings are free.'

His eyes went still. Buddy Meeks was released.

Thirty-Two
The Rockers

Rolly and Macy stood just inside the entrance to the mine, watching the rain. Two deputy sheriffs had picked up Gibbons and escorted him back down the trail. A helicopter had arrived and taken

271

Buddy away. The paramedics pronounced Buddy dead where they found the body, propped up against the base of the ladder where Macy and Rolly had placed him. Neither the paramedics nor the deputies questioned their story. Kinnie had explained the situation to the deputies outside. They took her at her word. She was a cop, one of them. The details could be sorted out later. The bad guys had been identified – a man and a woman. The man was in custody. The woman had escaped with the officer's gun. No one but Rolly and Macy had seen the gold room. The lights inside it had gone out before the others arrived.

Macy shivered. The paramedics had given her a blanket to cover up when they arrived. The blanket had been replaced by Kinnie's jacket, which was at least twice the size Macy would normally wear. She'd rolled up the sleeves. The jacket came to her knees.

Kinnie came in out of the rain, along with a county sheriff who seemed to be in charge of things. 'We got a situation,' said Kinnie.

'What's that?' said Rolly.

The sheriff spoke. 'I need you to call off your guys,' he said. 'They're interfering with my operation.'

'My guys?'

'Some long hair types in a VW van up at the lookout are refusing to cooperate. My deputy says they're armed and unfriendly. I hear you're the boss. They need to stand down and let us remove the fugitive to the patrol vehicles.'

'You mean Gibbons?'

Kinnie nodded.

Rolly turned back to the deputy. 'I asked them to stop anybody that came through,' he said, 'until I came back.'

'Are you willing to go up there and talk to them?'

'Yes,' said Rolly. 'Anytime.'

The sheriff spoke into the radio clipped to his vest. 'David, listen, have everybody stand down up there. Back off. Tell them we'll have the guy up there in ten minutes so he can talk to them.'

'Roger,' came a voice over the radio.

'All right, Chief Harper,' said the deputy. 'You have charge of your prisoners. I'll meet you back at the top.'

The deputy walked down the hill and climbed into a waiting helicopter. It lifted off, leaving the three of them alone.

'Who's up there, Waters?' said Macy.

'Cool Bob and the Rockers,' said Rolly.

'Sounds like a band,' said Kinnie.

'Yeah,' said Rolly. 'It is.'

'These guys'll do what you say?' Kinnie asked.

'They have so far,' said Rolly.

'Count on it, Kinnie,' said Macy. 'The Rockers totally dig on Waters.'

'All right, let's go.'

They headed down the trail, turned up the valley and headed back to the overlook. Rolly walked in front with Macy behind him. Kinnie brought up the rear.

'Why did that guy call us your prisoners, Kinnie?' said Macy.

'I'm taking you back to the rez for your own protection.'

273

'Are you going to put us in jail again?'

'Not if you tell me what happened down there.'

'We already told you once. I found the guy. He was bleeding. I tried to bandage him up with my shirt, just like you told me.'

'He was the one made those bird calls?'

'Yes,' said Rolly. 'It's just like I explained before, to you and the deputies. His name's Buddy Meeks. He lives . . . lived in Slab City. He was one of the UVTs. Twenty years ago. All three of them, there's some kind of bad blood between them. About the money, the gold. You heard them talking.'

'Why was he doing that, making that sound?'

'It's hard to explain. It's some kind of code.'

'You really think he's the one took down Gibbons?'

Rolly and Macy were silent. They'd reached the spot where the trail started up to the outlook. They stopped and looked at each other.

'Yeah, I didn't think so either,' said Kinnie. She stopped too and waved to the deputy standing guard above, at the overlook.

'I started thinking about it,' said Kinnie. 'While I was out there waiting for the chopper. Those chirps he was making. It's that word, isn't it? On Daddy Joe's whiteboard?'

'Teotwayki,' Rolly said. 'Yes.'

'What else did you see? How did that Gibbons guy end up hogtied like that? I don't figure it was you.'

'No,' said Rolly. 'It wasn't me.'

'And it wasn't the birdman.'

'No. There was a big man, bigger than Gibbons,' said Rolly. 'I couldn't see his face. He had cowboy boots.'

'There's only one way this makes sense,' said Kinnie.

'I thought he was in the hospital.'

'I brought him home yesterday.'

'You think it was Daddy Joe who kicked that guy's ass?' said Macy.

'And saved ours,' said Kinnie. 'It's the only thing that makes sense.'

'Where did he go?' said Rolly. 'Why didn't he want us to know it was him?'

Kinnie gave them both a severe look. 'Listen,' she said. 'We gotta be careful about this. We don't know for sure yet, and I don't want him getting involved if we can help it. It was dark and you didn't see what happened. Right now, they think it was the birdman that took Gibbons down and got himself shot in the process.'

'Gibbons knows it was Daddy Joe, doesn't he?'

'That's why I'm taking you back to the rez,' said Kinnie. 'So I can get you both out of here before he starts squawking.'

'I have to talk to the Rockers first,' said Rolly.

'Let's go,' said Kinnie.

They hiked through the switchbacks, up to the guardrail at the edge of the outlook. A deputy stood behind the guardrail, waiting for them.

'Come with me,' he said. Rolly followed. Macy started after him but Kinnie grabbed her arm and held her back. The deputy led Rolly between the two cars and stopped. Two

275

deputies stood at the rear of Kinnie's truck with Parnell Gibbons between them, in handcuffs. Cool Bob had placed himself in their path, twenty feet down the road, in front of the VW van. He had his rifle strapped to his back. One of the Rockers, the bass player, stood next to the van. The side door was open. He rested his gun in his arms.

'Hey, Bob,' said Rolly. 'What's happening?'

'We did just like you said. Nobody passes.'

'I can see that.'

'It got kinda tortuous, with the cops showing up and boxing us in,' said Bob. He pointed to the rocks off to his right. 'I got two guys up there. That slowed 'em down. I told 'em no prisoner release unless I got the word from you.'

Rolly looked up into the rocks. He saw the two other band members holding their guns. He looked down the road, past the van. Three sheriff's vehicles blocked the road. The helicopter had landed behind them. The rotors spun down in slow motion.

'I'm here now,' said Rolly. 'This guy they arrested, he's the one who took my diddley bow. We'll let the police take care of him.'

'Everything's cool?' said Bob.

'Everything's cool. You can let them through.'

Bob looked up to the rocks. He shouted. 'Stand down, boys. We're letting 'em through.'

The men moved into the clear and leaned the butts of their guns on the ground. Bob checked the man outside next to the van to make sure his message was clear. The man nodded and leaned his gun against the van.

276

Cool Bob moved out of the way. 'All clear,' he said. 'Desecuritized.'

Rolly turned to the deputy. 'That enough?' he said.

'It'll do,' said the deputy. He motioned to the men with Parnell. They marched him down the road, keeping a wary eye on the Rockers.

'Where's Goldhands?' said Bob, walking over to Rolly.

'Goldhands is dead. Someone killed him.'

'Oh, man. Catastrophic.'

'I'm sorry.'

'This is gonna go down hard with the Slabbers. Debilitating. What're we going to do without Goldhands?'

As Parnell passed the Volkswagen, he turned to look at something inside. He sneered. It looked like he was talking to someone. The bass player with the gun stood outside the van. There were two other band members in the rocks, and Bob here. All four Rockers were accounted for.

'Bob?' said Rolly. 'Who's in the van?'

'Oh, yeah,' said Bob. 'Remember that alien lady I told you about?'

'She's in there?' said Rolly. 'Did she give you her gun?'

'I didn't see no gun on her. She was cool. Tranquility base.'

'You didn't search her?'

'She's an old lady.'

Someone shouted. A gun went off. Rolly turned to see the bass player diving towards the rear of the van. The deputies ducked down, fumbling at their gun holsters. Gibbons stood alone. He

277

stepped towards the van, defiant and screaming. The gun went off again from inside the van. Gibbons tottered backwards. He turned and pitched face first into the road. The deputies rolled to their feet, guns at the ready. A pistol flew out of the van and landed next to Gibbons. The deputies drew a bead on the shooter inside. Dotty stepped out of the van, with her hands up.

'I'm done,' she said. 'We're all done now. It's over.'

Thirty-Three
The Chief

The tribal police truck bounced down the back road to Daddy Joe's house. Kinnie Harper looked in the rearview mirror at the two people in the backseat. She pulled up to the house and switched off the engine. She turned back to talk to them.

'What'd you see down there?' she said. 'When you went down the hole?'

'Not much,' said Macy. 'I found that box thing I brought up.'

'When you went down the second time, to look for the bird guy. While I was gone.'

'You know what I saw, Kinnie.'

Kinnie sighed. 'I'm sorry, Macy. I don't know how many times I gotta say it. I'm sorry.'

'You tried to kill me, Kinnie.'

'Excuse me,' said Rolly. 'Could one of you explain what's going on here?'

Kinnie rubbed her forehead. 'You know how I told you about the mine, how Daddy Joe had that gate installed so people wouldn't go looking down there?'

'Sure, because of the UVTs. Because there were people looking for gold all the time.'

'That was part of it. The real reason he did it was because I left Macy down there one day. I was pissed at her. I left her in the dark to teach her a lesson. I kinda forgot about her. Daddy Joe found out when he came home for dinner. He made me tell him what happened.'

'I spent the whole night down there,' said Macy. 'Until Daddy Joe found me the next morning.'

'How old were you?' said Rolly.

'Seven,' said Macy.

'You stayed down there all night when you were seven?'

Macy looked directly at Rolly. 'Kinnie and I both went in that hole. We were exploring. We both saw that old skeleton. Just like we saw it today. That's what we saw. Kinnie and me. An old skeleton in a mine.'

Macy's gold eyes stared into Rolly's as she spoke. Her eyes told him something different than the words that came out of her mouth. They told him to keep his mouth shut, to stop asking questions. Macy turned back to the front of the truck.

'Kinnie took the ladder away,' she said. 'Left me there. She told me that skeleton was how I was gonna look after the bats ate out my eyes.'

'I was disciplining you,' said Kinnie. 'Until you'd learned your lesson.'

'You know, Kinnie, fifteen minutes woulda been disciplining. All night's more like cruel and unusual punishment.'

'I said I was sorry.'

'Shit, it was easy going down there today,' said Macy. 'I've already seen what was down there. Couldn't have been any worse than when I was seven, in the dark with the bones and the bats.'

'Yeah, well, it didn't do me any good either,' said Kinnie. 'Daddy Joe never forgave me. He stopped talking to me after that, he got so mad. It seems like he started bringing home all that stuff on the UVTs after that, too.'

'After he went in the mine?' said Rolly.

Kinnie nodded.

'You think he found something down there?'

Kinnie opened her door. 'I think it's time we found out,' she said. 'It's time for some sleeping dogs to get kicked in the pants.'

Kinnie climbed out of the truck and opened the back door to let Macy and Rolly out. They walked to the front door. Kinnie knocked once then opened the door.

'Daddy Joe?' she said. 'It's me. I got somebody here who needs to see you.'

They walked into the living room.

'Daddy Joe?'

'Shit, Kinnie, what's that on the table?' said Macy.

Kinnie walked to the side table next to the sofa. 'There's blood on it,' she said, inspecting the stungun.

'Daddy Joe!' said Macy. 'It's Macy. Where are you?'

They heard a sound in the back. Kinnie led the way. Rolly saw drops of blood on the carpet. They found Daddy Joe in the study, slumped over the desk. There was blood on the back of his shirt. Kinnie rushed to his side and jammed two fingers into his neck.

'He's still alive,' she said. She pulled her radio from her belt and made an emergency call.

'I'll get under one arm, you take the other,' she said to Rolly after she finished the call. 'Let's see if we can move him. Macy, get the chair.'

Rolly watched Kinnie slide her neck under Daddy Joe's armpit. He did the same on the opposite side. They lifted Daddy Joe, straining under his weight. Macy pulled the chair away. Daddy Joe's head lolled to one side. He groaned.

'Where to?' said Rolly.

'Just lay him on the floor here,' said Kinnie. They took a few steps back, Daddy Joe's arms hanging over their shoulders. His dead weight made it hard to maneuver, but they managed to pull him away from the desk and lay him down on the floor. A flower of blood stained Daddy Joe's shirt just above his left hip.

Kinnie inspected the wound. 'Doesn't look like they hit anything vital,' she said. 'Stupid old man. Walking all the way back here after getting yourself shot.'

Daddy Joe groaned again.

'That's right, Daddy Joe,' said Kinnie. She leaned in closer to his face and lifted his eyelids. 'You're a stupid old man, chasing after ghosts and aliens when you can't even make peace with the living.'

Daddy Joe's lips moved as if he were trying to say something.

'Macy's here,' said Kinnie. 'She found something, down in the mine. This other guy here, her friend, he figured out how to open it with that guitar thing. There was just some old doll inside, painted gold. Maybe you knew that already, maybe you didn't, but that's what it came down to. Nothing. All those years trying to figure it out. All that sneaking around. There's no gold. Nothing.'

'Cut it out, Kinnie,' said Macy.

'Macy,' said Daddy Joe.

Macy sank down to her knees and took Daddy Joe's hand. 'I'm here, Daddy Joe.'

'Tell her what happened,' said Kinnie. 'You don't have much time left. No more sleeping dogs. She needs to know. I need to know.'

Daddy Joe's lips parted again, as if he might say something, but he didn't speak.

'He's too weak to talk,' said Rolly.

'He'll just have to listen, then,' said Kinnie. 'Daddy Joe, you listen to me. I'm going to tell you a story. You just nod if I get it right. Shake your head if I'm wrong. This might be your last chance to do right by Macy. You understand me? Shake your head if you understand me.'

Daddy Joe gave an almost imperceptible nod of his head.

'That time when I left Macy in the mine, when you got so mad at me, when you found the body down there, the skeleton. You knew who it was, didn't you? That's why you closed down the mine, wasn't it?'

Daddy Joe nodded.

'You knew who it was because you found the necklace there, on the body. You found it with the bones. That's how you knew it was her. You knew it was Betty.'

Daddy Joe nodded again. His bottom lip quivered.

'Then you got them to put that gate in to keep people out. Because you knew someone else might find the body. And if they found it, the sheriff would have to investigate, try to identify who the body was. They'd find out it wasn't that old. And they might find out what you did. How you lied on the witness stand. Then they might have to let that Parnell guy go free. You perjured yourself. You told the jury he was by himself when you arrested him. But he wasn't, was he? There was a girl with him, a black girl with a little baby. You brought that girl home with you, and her baby.'

Kinnie paused, waiting for Daddy Joe's acknowledgement. Rolly could see him still breathing. He nodded.

'That's what happened, isn't it, Daddy Joe?' said Kinnie. 'Nobody else ever knew. Not even me, not until after Macy ran away and I started thinking about things, trying to figure it out. What happened to her, Daddy Joe? What happened to Betty?'

Daddy Joe nodded. His lips moved.

'What'd he say?' said Macy.

Daddy Joe spoke again, barely audible. 'Birdie,' he said.

283

'What's that mean?' said Macy.

A thumping sound floated through the air. A shadow passed across the sunlight pouring from the window.

'The paramedics are here,' said Kinnie. She stood up. 'I'm going outside. Keep talking to him. Keep him responding.'

Kinnie left the room. Macy held Daddy Joe's hand up to her chest.

'Daddy Joe? It's Macy,' she said. 'What's the birdie?'

Daddy Joe's lips parted. It was almost a smile.

'The little birdie,' said Macy. 'What's the little birdie, Daddy Joe?'

'In the dark. Led me to you.'

'Yes, Daddy Joe. I remember that now. I told you about the little birdie that was my friend. The little birdie that stayed with me all night.'

'Wait a minute,' said Rolly. 'What did this bird sound like? Do you remember?'

Daddy Joe pulled his hand away from Macy. It wavered as he pointed two fingers up at the whiteboard, the word on the board. He gave his hand back to Macy. She looked at Rolly.

'It was him, wasn't it?' she said. 'He was with me, in the cave, when Kinnie left me there. That Buddy guy was there.'

The paramedics arrived, Kinnie leading them in. Macy and Rolly retreated into the living room. They walked outside with Kinnie and watched the emergency crew load Daddy Joe onto the helicopter. The helicopter flew away over the ridge.

'Kinnie,' said Macy, 'why did you lie about Aunt Betty?'

'Daddy Joe made me promise. He was going to give you that diddley bow thing and tell you the whole story when you turned eighteen. He was going to explain it all to you.'

'I remember him, Kinnie. The birdman. We would hear him sometimes. When you and I went exploring. He helped Daddy Joe find me, that time you left me in the cave.'

'I'm sorry, Macy.'

'Was it him? Did he kill my mother?'

'He didn't mean to. It was an accident. Your mom, Betty, heard the birdman calling one night. She tried to find him. She ran away. Daddy Joe didn't tell anybody because of the trial. Those bones that we found in the cave – that was your momma.'

'I know,' said Macy.

'He didn't mean for her to die, Macy. That birdman was your daddy. He loved your mama.'

'I know, Kinnie,' said Macy. 'I know he did.'

Thirty-Four
The Homecoming

Rolly Waters stood offstage at The Range in Slab City. His Fender Telecaster hung from his shoulder as he waited to go on. It had been less than a week since he'd first played with the Slab City Rockers, a few days longer than that since he'd first met Macy Starr while eating Mexican food at two-thirty in the morning. Macy was here, sitting in the front row, the guest of honor in a beat-up reclining chair placed front and center in the audience. The Rockers would close out tonight's ceremony, a memorial service for the man the Slabbers called Goldhands: Buddy Meeks. The Rockers would play all night if they needed to. They would play until everyone in the audience felt that they'd done Buddy justice, until everyone had gone home, until they'd given the proper *adieu*. Until the sun came up, when the morning light told them it was time to move on.

The first part of the evening was for others to take the stage, a chance to express their personal feelings and appreciation. Cool Bob acted as master of ceremonies, introducing each person who offered a testimonial, poem or prayer. Many of the Slabbers told personal stories of how Goldhands had helped them, how they came to respect his eccentric ways. They talked about the weird birdman who had flitted through camp, the one who fixed their generators, hooked up their solar panels, restored old guitars so they played better than new. They talked about how they kept strangers away, protecting his privacy. One man displayed drawings of a sculpture he planned to build in East Jesus as a more permanent memorial, a large golden hand you could play like a harp, with guitar strings stretched between the various fingers.

Rolly and Macy had arrived early that afternoon in the Tioga, which they'd borrowed again from Alicia. Rolly's father had returned home from the hospital two days earlier. Macy had insisted on coming along to meet him. Her salty style seemed to amuse the old sailor. Rolly was glad to have her along to take up the slack. Their conversation remained civil, not strained. It helped Rolly avoid the big questions his mother had hoped he'd address with his father. Those questions were for another visit, one he'd make by himself when he screwed up his courage. He had enough on his plate now, keeping up with Macy and surviving a second trip to Slab City.

Sometime next week the DNA tests would come back, and Macy would find out for sure if Buddy Meeks had been her father. Then the coroner's office would honor her claim. Macy had a plan. She'd proposed it to Rolly earlier in the day. It was a crazy and reckless plan, but he'd have to give her an answer on the return trip.

After parking and setting up the Tioga, they went to meet Bob at his trailer. From there, Bob took them to Buddy's place, an old trailer parked further down the road from the East Jesus. Buddy had staked out a modest kingdom over the years, delineating his territory with a hodgepodge of barbed wire, old tires and corrugated tin sheets. A box had been set on a post at the entrance. There was a tuning fork set in the top of the box. According to Bob, anybody wanting to communicate with Buddy had to write out a message, set it inside the box and tap the tuning fork. An hour later, sometimes as long as a day, Buddy would show up at your campsite and take a look at the problem that needed to be addressed, tossing gravel and dirt at your window to announce his arrival. You could pay him in food or any discarded junk he found to his liking.

Buddy's property was covered in neatly arranged piles of junk, sorted by types. Computer parts, plastic dolls, metal wire and pieces of wood were all separated into individual piles. Two workbenches sat in the shade, close to the trailer. Bob showed them the table where he'd watched Buddy make gold, where Buddy melted down old motherboards with Bunsen burners and mixed in chemicals to separate the gold from the slurry. A half-finished diddley bow lay on the second bench, its roughed-out shape awaiting more passes with increasingly fine gradations of sandpaper.

The inside of the trailer looked surprisingly neat, even orderly, filled with papers and technical books. There were drawings and sketches taped to the walls, stacks of composition books filled with paragraphs of text and mathematical equations. There were cans of beans in the cupboards – white beans and black beans, pinto and red beans, baked, refried and barbequed. There was no identification to be found, no photos of Buddy, of any family and friends. He'd stripped away all vestiges of a personal life except for one item, a promotional flyer taped to the wall across from the dining table, a flyer for DJ Macy Starr.

Bob told Macy the trailer was hers if she wanted it. The police had already been through everything. Bob and the Rockers had set up a volunteer watch to discourage scavengers until

Macy decided what she wanted to keep. He left Rolly and Macy alone in the trailer. They sat next to each other in the dining-room booth, going through papers and notebooks.

'How much you think I can get for this trailer?' said Macy.

'I don't know.'

'How much do I owe you?' said Macy.

'I haven't figured that out yet,' said Rolly.

'You think the trailer will pay for it?'

'It would more than pay for it, I'm pretty sure.'

'I might want to keep it a while.'

'We'll work something out.'

'This piece of ass don't come cheap, if that's what you mean by working it out.'

'That's not what I meant.'

'You're done with me, right, Waters? No more boning with Macy?'

'Would you stop it?'

Macy surveyed the trailer. She seemed nervous, even more twitchy than usual. 'It's weird,' she said. 'Having a dad.'

'Tell me about it,' said Rolly.

'Your dad's OK, not as bad as you made him seem,' said Macy.

'He wasn't drunk,' said Rolly.

'What's he like when he's drunk?'

'Louder. Likes to tell you what's wrong with you. All the ways you've failed to meet his expectations.'

'That did kinda piss me off, the way he orders your stepmom around.'

'I don't think she even hears it anymore.'

'Is that how you were? When you were a drunk?'

'I was very happy when I was a drunk. I liked everybody.'

'That doesn't sound so bad.'

'I didn't always make good decisions. About people.'

Macy laughed. 'Hell, Waters, you don't make good decisions when you're sober. How else do you explain me?'

Rolly smiled. He couldn't explain Macy Starr. He didn't need to. 'Have you called Eric Ozzie yet?' he said.

'No.' Macy sighed. 'I guess I should meet him.'

'He could tell you more about Betty. He's your uncle, after all.'

Macy scrunched her nose. Her dirty-blonde dreadlocks bounced off her shoulders.

'Does this mean I'm gonna have to start going over to his place for Christmas and stuff now? I don't know if I'm ready for that shit. I like being unattached.'

'Just meet him and see how it goes. That's all I'm saying.'

'Shut up and deal with it. That's what you're saying.'

'No, I'm not.'

'Aargh,' said Macy. She waved her hands in the air. 'I don't feel connected to any of this. The weird music and the alien shit. All those people that died. It seems like I should be freaking out or something. It's all kind of horrible. I mean, I've seen four dead people in the last week. My mom's a pile of bones and my daddy died in my arms. Shouldn't I be freaking out more?'

'We all process stuff differently.'

'You've seen people die before. How did you react?'

'Well, one time I threw up.'

'Yeah, that's what I'm talking about. Something more visceral.'

'It was pretty visceral.'

'You think anyone knows about it, besides us?' said Macy.

'What's that?'

'The room, with the gold.'

'Kinnie might know. She knows about Betty.'

'You think she was testing us?'

'What do you mean?'

'She didn't say anything about the gold. All she talked about was the bones.'

'I thought that was weird too. She just told us it was Betty's body.'

'It's a freaking weird thing not to mention, right? A gold room and gold bones?'

Rolly nodded.

'We wouldn't have known about it without you playing that vibrator thing so the lights would go on.'

'No. I guess not.'

'How much do you think all that stuff is worth?'

'No idea. I'm not sure how you get it all out of there.'

'Remember that guy, Leonard, I told you about?' said Macy.

'Who?'

'The guy that built Salvation Mountain.'

'Oh, yeah.'

'You remember how I thought it was cool, when someone goes crazy and spends their whole life on something that's not all about money.'

Rolly nodded.

'My dad was like that, wasn't he?' said Macy. 'He could've kept all that gold for himself, retired down to Puerto Vallarta or something. That's what the others would've done – Gibbons or Randy or that Dotty lady. My dad must've spent a lot of time working on that room, the gold rocket ship or whatever it is. How many years you think he spent doing that? Just to help those people out, make sure they connected with the aliens, hitching a ride to the planets or whatever it was. That's what it was about, wasn't it?'

'Sounds about right.'

Macy slid out of the booth. She walked to the rear of the trailer then walked back.

'I want to go back there,' she said, 'when I get the body. I'll cremate him and take his ashes there. Put him back with my mom. That's where he belongs. I want to seal the place up.'

'How are you going to do that?'

'I'll get some cement or something, maybe some boards and rebar, get rid of that ladder and seal up the hole. I don't want any spelunkers or gold bugs or aliens finding the place. I want it to stay like that, forever. At least until that Conjoinment thing comes along again. I'm the only one left now who was there with the UVTs. I'm the Sachem. I'm in charge. It's my responsibility now.'

'I guess you could look at it that way.'

'It's a real word, you know. I looked it up.'

'Sachem? What's it mean?'

'It's an Indian word. The chief. That little gold baby is now the chief.'

'Hail to the chief.'

'So, are you in, Waters?'

'What?'

'I need your help.'

'With what?'

'I want you to go with me,' said Macy. 'I want you to play that diddley bow again, like you did before. So I can see it one last time. Then we'll leave him inside, with my mom, and seal the place up. They'll be together. I'll be free. That's what I want, Waters.'

Rolly blinked and looked out at the audience. Someone was calling his name. Cool Bob stood at the microphone, beckoning Rolly on to the center stage. The audience cheered as he stepped out from the wings. He waved and connected his guitar cord into the amplifier. He wondered if he could ever plug a guitar into an amplifier again without thinking of the Astral Vibrator and the golden room, a room in a cave in the mountains, a room that lit up when you played the right notes, golden notes for the gold-blooded aliens. He wouldn't play any golden notes tonight. He would only play notes that were dirty and rough, bent notes and blue notes and slide notes. He would play imperfect frequencies for all the flawed earthlings he knew. He would play for the heretic citizens of Slab City, his own dishonored father and the eccentric orphan girl Macy Starr, for everyone who was going to die. As they all would. Someday.

The drummer counted to four. The band launched into the song. He joined them. The sound they made was like a beautiful rocket ship, breaking through gravity and arcing into an uncertain universe, full of bright stars.

C

Steve [signature]

Science Studies Unit

Univ of Edinburgh

March 1996

The Reorganised
National Health Service

RUTH LEVITT

CROOM HELM LONDON

First published 1976
©1976 by Ruth Levitt
Revised and reprinted July 1976
Second edition published 1977
Croom Helm Ltd, 2-10 St. John's Road, London SW11

ISBN 0-85664-657-1 hardback
ISBN 0-85664-683-0 paperback

Printed and bound in Great Britain by
REDWOOD BURN LIMITED
Trowbridge & Esher

CONTENTS

LIST OF TABLES

LIST OF FIGURES

TO P.B.

PREFACE

In 1974 the National Health Service underwent a major reorganisation – the first since its creation over 25 years earlier in 1948. The intention of the reorganisation was to improve the planning and provision of effective health care through an integrated approach to the problems of ill-health and the prevention of illness. This book describes the new arrangements in detail, explaining the purpose of the various elements and the manner in which they have evolved. It discusses the work of several professional and occupational groups, analyses the complex system of finance and describes the part played by consumers.

The National Health Service that is discussed in the main part of the text refers to the arrangements existing in England and Wales. The Scottish NHS was reorganised in a similar manner in 1974, and its particular features are described in Appendix 1. The NHS in Northern Ireland was reorganised on a rather different basis in 1973, and is beyond the scope of this book.

An inevitable feature of the reorganisation is that its effects take some time to become evident, and available statistical information does not always keep pace with the changes. It would therefore be unrealistic to make a comprehensive assessment of the success of the reorganisation at this stage, although improvements over the pre-1974 system and problems of the new system are examined wherever possible.

I hope that this study of the way the NHS works will be of interest not only to those who work with it and study it in Britain, but also to those elsewhere who are concerned with comparisons between the health care systems of different countries.

This book was first published in March 1976, and a revised edition appeared in August of that year. In the Second Edition, more substantial alterations have been made to bring the facts as up to date as possible and to take account of developments since the text was originally prepared. In particular, a Royal Commission has been set up to examine the NHS since I first started work on the book, and I hope that this edition may help to clarify why this major investigation was called for and what changes it could suggest.

Several people have given very generous help at different stages in the preparation of this book and I would like to thank all of them, mentioning particularly: Brian Abel-Smith, Ronald Allen, Allan Brooking, Stephen Cang, W. Keith Davidson, Malcolm Dean, Maureen Dixon, Roger Dyson, Esme Few, Desmond Higgins, Ian Islip, Robert Jardine, M.Q. Jardine, staff of the King's Fund Centre Library, David Knowles, John Marks, Robert Maxwell, Stephen Neal, David Pace and Stuart Slatter. In addition, I would like to express my gratitude to Nigel Weaver who gave me the opportunity to write the book and provided most helpful advice and encouragement. Of course, any errors are entirely my own responsibility.

Those Figures using Crown Copyright material are reproduced with the permission of the Controller of Her Majesty's Stationery Office.

London, June 1977   RUTH LEVITT

LIST OF ABBREVIATIONS

AHA	Area Health Authority
AHA(T)	Area Health Authority (Teaching)
ATO Are	Area Team of Officers
BMA	British Medical Association
BoG	Board of Governors
CHC	Community Health Council
CPSM	Council for Professions Supplementary to Medicine
DHSS	Department of Health and Social Security
DCP	District Community Physician
DMC	District Medical Committee
DMT	District Management Team
DPT	District Planning Team
FPC	Family Practitioner Committee
GMC	General Medical Council
GNC	General Nursing Council
GNP	Gross National Product
GP	General Practitioner
HAS	Health Advisory Service
HCPT	Health Care Planning Team
HMC	Hospital Management Committee
JCC	Joint Consultative Committee
JCPT	Joint Care Planning Team
LHC	Local Health Council
LMC	Local Medical Committee
MPC	Medical Practices Committee
NHS	National Health Service
PESC	Public Expenditure Survey Committee
RAWP	Resource Allocation Working Party
RHA	Regional Health Authority
RHB	Regional Hospital Board
RTO	Regional Team of Officers
SHHD	Scottish Home and Health Department
VPRS	Voluntary Price Regulation Scheme
WHTSO	Welsh Health Technical Services Organisation

1 BACKGROUND TO THE 1974 REORGANISATION

This first chapter explores the first period of the NHS, looking at certain key events of the previous hundred years which provide important clues about why the NHS was originally created in its particular form, why a reorganisation took place after the first twenty-five years, and why the reorganisation happened in the way it did. The three essential elements of the NHS are the hospital services, the community-based services and the family practitioner services. Their separate origins will be traced to 1948 when the NHS began and will be followed through subsequent developments which culminated in their integration in 1974.

Health Services Before 1948

Developments up to 1870

The concept of public responsibility for the health of individuals can be traced back at least as far as 1834 when the Poor Laws were passed. These established that the parish workhouses should have sick wards where the able-bodied inmates could be treated when they became ill. However, the health of the community had long been neglected, and it became necessary for the workhouses to admit sick paupers living in the parish to their wards, since so many were dying in their homes being unable to obtain any medical care for themselves. By 1848 the demand for institutional care was so great that the sick wards had become entirely devoted to sick paupers. The Public Health Act of that year acknowledged for the first time the State's responsibility in this matter through its creation of a central organising body called the General Board of Health. It was only able to achieve very few reforms because it did not possess the powers necessary to counter the vested interests of the Boards of Guardians, who were the local managers of the institutions concerned.

By 1851 the first links between workhouses and the voluntary hospitals were beginning to be forged. The origins of this second group of hospitals represented a complete contrast to the workhouses. They emerged from the philanthropy and altruism of the well-to-do, and the moral obligations of religious and charitable bodies, whereas the workhouses had developed in the eighteenth century to cope with the problems of poverty and destitution. The voluntary hospitals were built and financed through donations and subscriptions and attracted the services of skilled doctors who, acting on their social conscience,

11

treated the patients often without payment. These hospitals became selective in their admissions, leaving all but acute cases to be dealt with by the workhouses. The workhouses themselves sometimes subscribed to nearby voluntary hospitals so that they could transfer their more complicated and acute cases to them. In this way, ill-health became divided to mirror the social status of the two types of hospitals, but the load was not evenly shared — in 1861 there were estimated to be 50,000 sick paupers in the workhouses and 11,000 patients in the voluntary hospitals. The Metropolitan Poor Act of 1867 represents a further landmark in health care provision as it obliged local authorities within London to provide separate institutional care for tuberculosis, smallpox, fevers and insanity. One year later, the Poor Law Amendment Act established the same provision in the provinces.

Developments from 1870 to 1919

By the 1870s, the workhouses, isolation hospitals and asylums together with the voluntary hospitals could be described as a public service through which people had access to hospital care when they became ill. Conditions were often appalling by modern standards, and medicine had few effective tools for alleviating disease; most of the activity involved care rather than treatment, and care that was sometimes harshly and unwillingly distributed. It is possible that the stimulus to alter this inadequate state of affairs only came after the experience of war — particularly the Crimean and Boer wars — in which thousands of British soldiers died from disease. For every death from combat in Southern Africa there were at least four from typhoid and other fevers. The Army's Committee on Physical Deterioration reported that 48 per cent of recruits had to be rejected on physical grounds alone. Its recommendations were the basis for the establishment of the School Medical Service in 1907. In addition, the beginning of the twentieth century saw a new era in effective medical care with discoveries that put diagnostic, therapeutic and pathological efforts on a much more scientific footing. It was clear that the nineteenth-century hospitals could not ensure a healthy fighting force were there to be another war, so interest moved for the first time towards preventive methods of health care. But this did not happen rapidly for it depended on having general practitioners with the ability to deal with the huge unmet demand for health education and care in the community.

In comparison with famous specialists in the voluntary hospitals who could build up large private practices, the general practitioners in the parishes derived much of their income from the capitation fees paid to them on contract by the friendly societies, trade unions and similar associations, in return for the provision of treatment and medicines to the members. Most of the wage earning population, including a large proportion of the middle class, received their medical care in this way, through the payment of a flat rate contribution to their association. The benefits were only available to the wage earner himself — wives, children, the old and the disabled had to rely on outpatient departments and dispensaries of the voluntary hospitals or go without. In 1911, through the British Medical Association, the doctors put pressure on Lloyd George to protect their interests, and through the passing of the National Health Insurance Act they were successful in changing the administrative control of their work to new insurance committees, on which they were represented. The Act made lower paid workers compulsorily insured for the services of a general practitioner and fixed the fee that the doctor could receive for every person on his list. However, this still left the majority of the population without any improvements in their general practitioner services.

Some local authorities had achieved many advances in public and environmental health, but since they could not be compelled to provide many health services at all, substantial differences in the amount and quality of their provision emerged across the country. In 1905, the Minority Report of the Poor Law Commission came out strongly in favour of intervention by central government in tackling poverty and ill-health. The Government chose to act indirectly, through the provision of old age pensions and unemployment benefits rather than improving the health care system itself. The Ministry of Reconstruction, which was set up towards the end of the First World War continued to approach this problem indirectly by proposing that a Ministry of Health should be established, to take on all the functions of the Local Government Board and the work of the National Health Insurance Commission.

Developments from 1919 to 1942

The new Ministry of Health was established in 1919 but it only devoted a small part of its time and efforts to health service administration since the duties transferred to it from the Local Government Board were so numerous. Nevertheless, a radical stimulus to the provision of a nationally organised, comprehensive health service was provided in the Dawson report.[1] It recommended a number of objectives including domiciliary services from doctors, pharmacists and local health authority staff; primary health centres with beds for general practitioners, diagnostic facilities, outpatient clinics, dental, ancillary and community services; secondary health centres for specialist diagnosis and treatment;

supplementary services for infectious and mental illnesses; teaching hospitals with medical schools; the promotion of research; standardised clinical records; the establishment of a single authority to administer all medical and allied services with medical representation and local medical committees. Although this report was published in 1920, it identified the issues which have been central to most of the subsequent debate on the organisation of the health services to the present day.

Then in 1926, the Royal Commission on National Health Insurance stated that the ultimate solution would lie in the direction of divorcing the medical service entirely from the insurance system, and reorganising it together with other public health activities as a service to be supplied from the general public funds. The need for greater coordination between the various parts of the system was only slowly and partially met, as for instance through the Local Government Act, 1929, which transferred to the local authorities all the responsibilities of the Poor Law Boards of Guardians, and additionally permitted them to provide the full range of hospital treatment. However, there was no compulsion, so great variations in standards existed. Some local authorities actively worked towards providing modern buildings with good equipment and the beginnings of specialist care, while others continued to have crowded, dark and understaffed wards in their old workhouse buildings.

The next important stimulus to reform in the scheme of health care did not come until 1939 when, as part of their wartime measures, the Government set up the Emergency Medical Service. This made the Minister of Health responsible for the treatment of casualties, and thus enabled the central department to direct the day-to-day work of the voluntary and local authority hospitals for the first time. In return the Government took over the financial burden of this provision, which until that time had been met by patients' contributions, local authority rates, and the funds of the voluntary hospitals. Many prefabricated buildings were erected to create more beds and to compensate for those destroyed by enemy bombings. Outpatient departments, operating theatres and X-ray departments were set up, and through the local cooperation of medical and administrative staff, a much more effective scheme of care began to develop. Special centres grew up to deal with specific types of injury, and the blood transfusion service became a nationally organised effort that could cope far better with the demands of the war emergency. This 'national hospital service' was very quickly formed without any statutory change in ownership or management and showed, for the first time, albeit under the pressure of war, what sort of developments could arise from central leadership and coordination.

In 1941, Ernest Brown, the Minister of Health announced that the Government had commissioned an independent inquiry into the state of all the country's hospitals and their ability to provide adequate facilities. These hospital surveys confirmed clearly that there were great inequalities of provision, that many of the public's needs were not being properly met and, above all, that without thorough coordination of effort there would be insufficient improvement.[2] Although the findings were hardly disputed there was a considerable divergence of views on the best way to finance the necessary reforms, and on the question of whether central government should assume ownership and control of the existing hospitals.

The Creation of the National Health Service

In 1942 the Beveridge Report was published, and it made far-reaching recommendations that formed the basis for the postwar system of social welfare services.[3] But in addition it took as its central assumption the idea that a comprehensive system of health care was essential to any scheme for improving living standards. To Sir William Beveridge, the term 'comprehensive' meant medical treatment available for every citizen, both in their homes and in hospitals, provided by general practitioners, specialists, dentists and opticians, nurses and midwives, and the provision of surgical appliances and rehabilitation services. He thought these should be available to all citizens as and when they should need them.

The Coalition Government announced in 1943 that it accepted the need for a comprehensive scheme of health care, and it started negotiations with a number of bodies. The first plan envisaged a unified health service with one administrative unit taking full responsibility for local provision. The units would be administered by regional local government or by joint local and health authorities. The hospitals would be partially taken into national ownership and general practitioners would be full-time salaried servants. The British Medical Association was outraged at these proposals which it saw as originating from the influence of the National Association of Local Government Officers, and the Society of Medical Officers of Health, so it withdrew from the discussions and progress was temporarily halted. Later in 1943 Henry Willink replaced Ernest Brown as Minister of Health and set about devising a scheme that would be acceptable to the various interest groups. In 1944 he published a White Paper, *A National Health Service*,[4] which described a system of administration with the central responsibility vested in the Ministry of Health, to be advised by an appointed Central Health Services Council. Local organisations would be based on joint local authority areas which would in turn be advised by local versions of the Central Health Services Council. They would take over the local authority hospitals and would determine the financial compensation to be paid for the voluntary hospitals boards' participation in the public scheme. General practitioners would be under contract to a central medical board with local committees and would be paid, as in the National Health Insurance system, on a per capita basis, unless they worked from a health centre provided by the local authority — in which case they would receive a salary. The central board would be able to regulate the distribution of practices all over the country. Although this plan failed to satisfy the varying interests, several of its proposals were retained in the final legislation.

The Government was indecisive, and discussions dragged on for fifteen months until a revised version was drawn up. This differed from the White Paper in proposing a two-tiered administrative structure in the form of regional and local planning authorities, and in which ownership and administration of the hospitals was to remain with the local authorities and voluntary hospital boards. Instead of the central medical board of the White Paper, local committees similar to the existing local insurance committees of the National Health Insurance system were proposed. This plan therefore dropped the idea of joint administration of the hospital and local authority services (which was not raised again until 1968), but it did establish the idea of regional and local levels of management. It did not tackle the problem of doctors' remuneration and the principle of health centre practice was relegated to 'experimental' status. These last points have been of continuing controversy in the health service, but in this case meant that Willink had to drop the idea of a fully integrated service in order to meet the negotiating demands of as many groups as possible.

Although the Labour Party conference of 1944 came out in favour of a full-time salaried service based on regional local government, Aneurin Bevan did not, as Minister of Health in the 1945-51 Government, include these points in his White Paper. In fact he adopted much of the detail worked out for earlier plans, and held few discussions before the White Paper was published. The BMA was suspicious of his intentions and organised a campaign of its members to boycott cooperation with the Government. In March 1946 the *National Health Service Bill*[5] was published, and its main new point was the proposed nationalisation of all hospitals under appointed Regional Hospital Boards, with local responsibility delegated to Hospital Management Committees. Teaching hospitals were to be separately administered under Boards of Governors with a direct link to the

Ministry of Health. There were however still a great many details to be worked out in the time between the passing of the Act in November 1946 and the 'appointed day', 5 July 1948, when the National Health Service would come into effect. The BMA resumed discussions early in 1947 since it realised that its action could no longer prevent the arrangements from going ahead, but in fact, the legislation ensured that the medical profession would have a voice on all statutory committees. Accounts of these negotiations disagree on the part Aneurin Bevan played in reaching the final compromises. Although some observers hold that he did not contribute many original points to the substance of the Act, it seems clear that he was particularly skilful in exploiting the splits within the BMA, and in getting the National Health Service under way with widespread enthusiasm amongst the staff and institutions concerned.

How the New National Health Service Worked

Although patients received broadly unchanged services at the point of delivery just before and just after 5 July 1948, the creation of the National Health Service did represent a radical change in the relationship between the individual citizen and the State, and it established a firm government commitment to developing and improving the country's system of health care. In the words of the 1946 Act, the aim was to promote ' . . . the establishment in England and Wales of a comprehensive health service designed to secure improvement in the physical and mental health of the people of England and Wales and the prevention, diagnosis and treatment of illness.'[6] The principles of freedom and choice were upheld in that all people were entitled to use the service yet they still had the opportunity to go to doctors outside the service. Equally, doctors would have no interference in their clinical judgement and were free to take private patients while participating in the service. The achievement of the Act was to make benefits available to everyone free of charge, on the basis of need, thus ending the former restrictions of provision to those who were insured or those who could afford private treatment.

The Minister of Health was made personally responsible to Parliament for the provision of all hospital and specialist services on a national basis, and for the Public Health Laboratory Service, the Blood Transfusion Service and research concerned with the prevention, diagnosis and treatment of illness. He had indirect responsibility for the family practitioner and local authority health services. The Central Health Services Council and its professional Standing Advisory Committees were established to advise the Minister on the discharge of

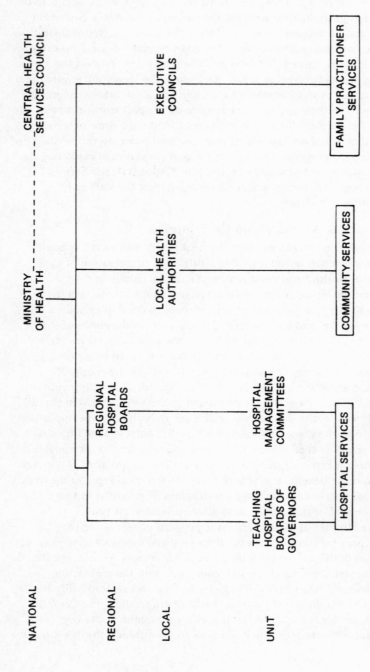

Figure 1 *The National Health Service 1948–1974*

his duties, and to keep developments in the service under review. The fourteen Regional Hospital Boards (subsequently fifteen) were each focused on a university with a medical school, and teaching hospitals were separately administered by Boards of Governors. Hospital Management Committees were appointed to run the non-teaching hospitals on a day-to-day basis. The local health authorities were the county councils and the borough councils. Through their health committees they provided community and environmental health services including maternal and child welfare, health visiting, home nurses, vaccination and immunisation, care and after-care for mental illness and mental subnormality patients and the maintainance of health centres. Some of these had already been their responsibility before 1948 whilst others had been provided by a variety of other agencies. Executive Councils were established (usually to match the local health authorities) to administer the family practitioner services and received their finance directly from the Ministry of Health (see Figure 1). The Act also recognised the contribution that voluntary organisations could make in the field of health care by absorbing some of their activities into the NHS and giving financial aid to others operating outside the NHS. The School Medical Service continued to be run by the local education authorities and provided medical and dental inspections for children in State schools, and a child guidance service. The Industrial Health Service was organised by the Ministry of Labour mainly through the factory inspectorate. The armed forces retained their own health service quite separate from the NHS.

The Problems of the NHS

Just as the final form of the NHS in 1948 represented a compromise between the demands of several interest groups, so the problems that the service encountered between 1948 and 1974 were a reflection of the failure to meet the original hopes for a fully unified and comprehensive health service that had been expressed as far back as the beginning of the century. For example, when compulsory payments by patients were introduced for some parts of the service and when the weekly NHS contribution was established, the idea of a free service for all was breached. A more important problem was, however, that the demand for NHS care rose very rapidly and resources were often insufficient to be able to meet it. The uneven distribution of services that had existed before 1948 was not eradicated by the creation of the NHS so many inequalities between regions were maintained. Because the administrative structure, with its bias towards hospital matters, had the strongest influence on policy-making in the central department, there was inadequate local liaison between hospital and community staff, with the result that services for the acutely ill tended to improve more rapidly while the needs of the chronically ill and disabled were comparatively neglected.

In 1953 the Minister of Health set up a committee to inquire into the costs of the NHS and its report, published three years later (the Guillebaud Report),[7] although acknowledging some deficiencies in the service, did not see structural alterations as a necessary measure at that time. One member of the committee, Sir John Maude, stated his reservations about this conservative position. He had identified for himself the weakness of the NHS as being its division into three parts operated by three sets of bodies having no organic connection with each other; their separate funding from central and local government sources underlined the weakness. The divisions caused preventive medicine, general practice and hospital practice to overlap, while the predominance of the hospital service had the effect of pushing general practice and social medicine into the background. Maude's view was that if local government administration and finance could be adequately reorganised then it might be possible to transfer the local responsibility of the NHS on to them, thus arranging for a truly unified service.

The Beginnings of Reform

The first notable mention of a plan to unify the health service was made in the Porritt Report[8] which was compiled independently of the Ministry of Health by representatives of the medical profession. Its suggestion for local NHS administration under Area Health Boards, although not worked out in detail, at least indicated that the medical profession accepted in principle the need for unification. However, the Gillie Report (1963)[9] rejected unification of administration in favour of much greater efforts to developing the role of general practitioners. It suggested that family doctors alone could effectively coordinate the resources of hospital and community care on behalf of their patients, in relation to individual family and working conditions.

During this period, several other reports appeared and further Acts of Parliament were passed in relation to the NHS. They can be seen, in retrospect, to have reflected the problems being encountered in trying to overcome the deficiencies of the tripartite structure and represent tentative moves towards greater integration. The Cranbrook Report (1959)[10] for example was critical of the division between local authority and hospital maternity services. The Mental Health Act, 1959, radically altered the legislation on mental illness, reducing the grounds for compulsory admission and detention in mental hospitals. This coincided with the use of several new drugs leading to quicker and more effective psychiatric treatment which could more often be given on an outpatient basis. Mental hospitals began to discharge more patients back into the community and in 1961, Enoch Powell, the Minister of Health, predicted that half of these hospitals would be closed in ten years time. Although he was wrong in detail, progressively more mental hospital patients did become transferred to community care.

In 1962, Powell published *A Hospital Plan for England and Wales*[11] which formulated the need for new hospitals in the light of projected population growth and the demand for hospital facilities in the coming ten years. It approved the development of district general hospitals for population units of about 125,000 people. The Bonham-Carter Report[12] on the functions of the district general hospital developed this concept in more detail, emphasising the need to plan hospital and community health services jointly. In 1967, the Salmon Report[13] published detailed recommendations for developing the senior nursing staff structure and the status of the profession in hospital management. The first report on the organisation of doctors in hospitals was published in 1967 (known as the Cogwheel Report)[14] and it proposed speciality groupings that would arrange clinical and administrative medical work more sensibly. These reports will be discussed in detail in later chapters, but are mentioned here to indicate the variety of efforts involved in trying to improve on the tripartite structure.

The Formal Process of Reorganisation

The necessity for a fundamental reorganisation of the service had not, however, become the subject of general discussion even though the administrative structure had remained unchanged for twenty years, and the various reports mentioned above had pointed out some of the serious faults that had arisen. The NHS was then composed of 15 Regional Hospital Boards, 36 Boards of Governors, 336 Hospital Management Committees, and 134 Executive Councils administering the services of 20,000 general practitioners while 175 local health authorities ran the community services.

The First Green Paper

The issue of reorganising these elements was first officially tackled on 6 November 1967 when Kenneth Robinson, the Minister of Health, stated in the House of Commons that he had begun a full and careful examination of the administrative structure of the NHS, not only in relation to the present, but looking twenty years ahead. He followed this in July 1968 with the publication of *The Administrative Structure*

of Medical and Related Services in England and Wales,[15] now known as
the First Green Paper. He took as his central theme the unification of
health services in an area under one new body called the Area Board.
This would replace the Regional Hospital Boards, Boards of Governors,
Hospital Management Committees and Executive Councils, and take
over certain functions previously held by the local health authorities.
There would be forty to fifty Area Boards in direct contact with the
Ministry of Health, and their boundaries would be related to those of
local government, serving populations of between 750,000 and two
to three millions.

These proposals were launched in anticipation of the reforms which
might result from two inquiries which were being held at that time. The
first was that of the Committee on Local Authority and Allied
Personal Social Services (chaired by Frederick Seebohm)[16] which
recommended, later in 1968, that all personal social services should be
unified, including those administered by local authority health
departments, in single new local authority departments with their own
committee of elected representatives, and the appointment of directors
of social services trained in social work or social administration. The
second was the Royal Commission on Local Government in England,[17]
whose report, published in 1969, recommended the creation of new
local authority areas under unitary authorities, grouped into eight
provinces each with their own provincial council. The Commission's
scheme aimed to loosen the grip of central government over the
control of planning and management in local affairs through the
communities' fuller participation in their public services. It saw the
new unitary authorities as being eminently suitable to take charge of
the health services along the lines suggested in the First Green Paper
for ending the tripartite divisions, but with the added advantage of
being able to coordinate the health services with the social services
reorganised by the Seebohm proposals. The significant stumbling
block of finance was acknowledged by the Commission — the cost of
each authority's health services would be far too great for the current
rating system to bear — but it was hoped that new sources of finance
for local government would in any case be worked out. The Layfield
Committee's report on local government finance (1976, Cmnd. 6453)
was not able to resolve this question. Of the three proposed reforms, the
First Green Paper, the Seebohm Report and the Royal Commission's
Report, only the Seebohm recommendations were accepted, and the
Government implemented them in the Social Services Act, 1970.

In 1968, Richard Crossman succeeded Kenneth Robinson to become
the first Secretary of State for Social Services in the new Department of

Health and Social Security. He published *The Future Structure of the National Health Service,*[18] known as the Second Green Paper, in February 1970, which reflected some of the criticisms received about the First Green Paper, as well as Crossman's own ideas. In it he stated that the Government had already decided on three important factors: that the new health authorities would be independent of local government and directly responsible to the central department; that the public health and personal social services would continue to be the responsibility of local government; that the boundaries of the new health authorities would match those of local government. This second scheme for the reorganisation suggested more health authorities than the first attempt — ninety instead of forty or fifty, but it inserted Regional Health Councils between them and the Department of Health and Social Security (DHSS). These bodies were to take charge of hospital and specialist planning. Crossman intended to publish a White Paper that summer so that the Bills for health and local government reform could be put before Parliament early in 1972, permitting elections for the new local authorities[19] and appointments for the new health authorities to be completed in 1973 so that they could take over in 1974.

The Consultative Document

The General Election of June 1970 did not, however, return the Labour Party to power, so future plans for the health service awaited the decision of the new Secretary of State, Sir Keith Joseph. Almost one year later, in May 1971, he issued a Consultative Document[20] to interested parties only, without officially publishing it. Two months were allowed for comment so that the legislation could be prepared to come into force on 1 April 1974, the date already set by the local government reforms embodied in the Conservative White Paper, *Local Government in England.*[21] The Consultative Document rejected much of the Second Green Paper's plan but retained the proposal to incorporate local authority health services into the duties of the new area authorities, and to match health and local authorities' boundaries. Joseph's scheme brought hospitals, health centres and community nursing services under the new authorities; occupational health service provision was left with the Department of Employment and Productivity, but there was no decision on whether to take over the School Health Service from the Department of Education and Science. The major new feature was the proposal for a strong regional tier of authority to be responsible for planning, finance and building, with power to direct the area authorities. Efficient management was the skill thought to be desirable amongst the membership of the authorities so professional representatives as such would not be necessary. The consumer's view would be voiced on Community Health Councils established outside the chain of authority. Social services would remain with the local authorities, and general practitioner services would be administered separately from the new authorities, retaining their distinct source of finance. Clinical teaching services would also be separate and organised on a regional basis. The Consultative Document also announced that two 'expert studies' had been commissioned by the DHSS; one was on the detailed management arrangements for the new authorities and their staff, and the other was on the subject of collaboration between the health and local authorities on matters of common concern. Management consultants were also brought into the DHSS itself to effect an internal reorganisation that would prepare the Department for the impending national changes.

Final Legislative Steps

The sequence of the final procedure to establish the reorganisation of the NHS involved publication of the Government's White Paper, *National Health Service Reorganisation: England*[22] in August 1972 followed by the *National Health Service Reorganisation Bill* in November 1972. After parliamentary debate, the National Health Service Reorganisation Act, 1973 was given Royal Assent on 5 July 1973 (i.e. exactly 25 years after the original 'appointed day').[23] The first phase of the Study Group on the management arrangements investigations was completed in February 1972, but the final report, *Management Arrangements for the Reorganised National Health Service,*[24] known as the Grey Book, did not appear until the end of 1972, after the White Paper had been published. The Working Party on Collaboration produced its first report in 1973. The DHSS started issuing a new series of circulars in 1972 to the existing health authorities and to members of the newly created 'shadow' authorities, detailing preparations for the reorganisation, and a news sheet called *NHS Reorganisation News,* but apart from these there was little information available and almost no public debate of the complicated issues involved. People working in the NHS began to realise that there would be a period of considerable uncertainty in relation to the jobs they might expect to obtain and the speed at which all the new appointments would be made. The National Health Service Staff Commission was appointed in 1972 to handle all the arrangements relating to recruitment and transfer of staff, and it was also made responsible for protecting the interests of staff

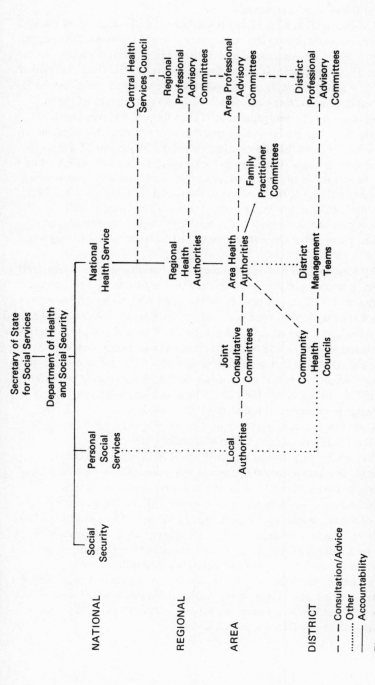

Figure 2 *The Reorganised National Health Service*

Source: Management Arrangements for the Reorganised National Health Service, HMSO, 1972

under the new arrangements.

The publication of the Grey Book provided the skeleton of the new organisation, describing the Regional and Area Health Authorities, the District Management Teams, and outlining job descriptions for some of the new posts at all levels (see Figure 2). For those unfamiliar with the particular style of language that it employed, the Grey Book represented a puzzling basis on which to develop a grasp of the implications of the reorganisation. The main problem was also that preparations had to be made at speed in order to meet the deadline of 1 April 1974, and this discouraged thorough discussions of the impending changes. The Grey Book contained proposals which could be altered as a result of consultation, but the enforced haste transformed the proposals into official edicts in the minds of many people. DHSS circular HRC(73) 3 in fact amended some of the Grey Book's statements, and the representations of certain professional groups against parts of the Grey Book continued to be discussed throughout 1974.

By June 1973 it had become clear that the programme of new staff appointments could not be completed by the following April, so the reorganised NHS would have to be launched with all but the most senior staff without formal contracts of employment. Although the need for a reorganisation of the NHS was hardly disputed and although this particular version of the reorganisation was widely supported, it is probably true that many staff working in the NHS and in outside, but related, bodies were not in a position to fully understand the thinking behind the preparations for 1974. The administrative arrangements were not as complete as the staff would have desired, but it is clear that their patients, as the focus of their efforts, were probably quite unaware that any reorganisation was taking place.

Yet on the very date at which the new NHS came into being, changes in its structure were already being planned. In February 1974 a Labour Government replaced the Conservatives and the new administration was compelled to proceed with the reorganisation timed for the coming April even though the design was not of its making. The new Secretary of State, Barbara Castle, acknowledged the problems being encountered by the staff in implementing the reorganisation, but she was also determined to influence its development immediately. She set out her proposals in a consultative paper entitled *Democracy in the National Health Service*[25] and changes based on them were announced in July 1975 — they will be dealt with in detail in Chapters 3 and 10.

2 THE DEPARTMENT OF HEALTH AND SOCIAL SECURITY AND THE REGIONAL HEALTH AUTHORITIES

This chapter and the two that follow will describe the new structure of the NHS and the way it works, looking at the various bodies and their functions in some detail. To begin, a brief summary of the whole reorganised structure will help to provide a context for each distinct part.

Summary of the New Structure

At the head is the Secretary of State for Social Services, the person ultimately responsible to Parliament for the provision of health services in England (see Figure 2). He or she is helped in this by junior ministers and civil servants at the Department of Health and Social Security (DHSS). They in turn delegate many of the detailed responsibilities to the next level of administration — the Regional Health Authorities (RHAs). These bodies, in 1974, replaced and extended the role of the former Regional Hospital Boards (in England there are fourteen RHAs, and their work will be discussed in the second part of this chapter). The RHAs also delegate activities, retaining mainly planning and supervisory work, placing responsibility for day-to-day matters in the hands of Area Health Authorities (AHAs). The AHAs (ninety in England) have no exact counterpart in the pre-1974 structure. Their boundaries are in most cases the same as those of the counties and metropolitan districts. This is of great importance in securing the collaboration between local authorities and health authorities so that their joint planning and provision of service may be enhanced. Their work will be discussed in Chapter 3. The other major administrative units exist within the health districts, each able to secure the provision of the complete range of health services for their local population (of 100,000 to 500,000 people). There are 205 districts in England administered on behalf of the AHAs by their District Management Teams (DMTs). They do the work of the former Hospital Management Committees, local authority health departments and the Boards of Governors of undergraduate teaching hospitals. Their work will be discussed in Chapter 4.

Although the arrangements in Scotland are similar, their particular features will be explained in Appendix 1. Wales has seventeen districts and eight AHAs which are directly responsible to the Secretary of State for Wales, and the Welsh Office acts for the Principality. The Secretaries of State for Social Services and for Wales work closely together on matters connected with health services, and much of the guidance both before and since 1 April 1974 has been worked out jointly before being issued to their respective health authorities.

The Department of Health and Social Security

The Functions of Government Departments

Although it is commonly understood that the DHSS takes central control
of the National Health Service, how this control is achieved and exercised
in practice is not widely known. Governments need departments which
will transform their laws and policies into action, and thus enable the
balance of political power to have its influence on the life of the country.
In Great Britain each government department is headed by a politician
who is either called a Minister or a Secretary of State. He is appointed by
the Prime Minister who determines how long he holds that office. If the
Prime Minister changes or the government is voted out of office, the
political heads of departments also change. However, the permanent staff
of the department, the civil servants, continue their work irrespective of
alterations in political leadership, and usually spend most of their careers
within the department. Although the Secretary of State is the statutory
head of the department, he will almost invariably be assisted by a number
of junior ministers who are Members of Parliament and also appointed
by the Prime Minister.

There are substantial differences between civil servants and politicians
over what they want the department to achieve, and in particular, over
the time-scale for achievement. Ministers will usually want to establish a
number of specific changes in the work of the department during their
time in office, to follow the policies of their own party and the views of
their fellow MPs. The civil servants on the other hand are expressly non-
political, and because of their longer association with the department, are
more likely to prefer a gradual process of change that will protect the
stability of their work, and inflict less sudden changes of direction on
the institutions they administer. The relations between civil servants and
their ministers will also be a function of those important but rather nebulous factors — personality and style. The result can be anywhere on the
spectrum from close and trusting cooperation to icy formality and dead-
lock. Whatever the result is, it will influence the department's achievements enormously. A key figure in this is the most senior civil servant,
the permanent secretary, who is in direct contact with the minister. (Certain government departments may have more than one permanent secretary.) He is, on behalf of the minister, responsible for the overall management and control of all aspects of the department's administration; therefore the minister needs to consult him closely in order to remain well-
informed about his department's activities. There is relatively little a
minister can do to impose his wishes on an unwilling department unless
he introduces new legislation in Parliament; if successful, this can be

done quite quickly, and ensures the formal obedience of the civil servants.

The Emergence of the DHSS

The DHSS was created in 1968 from the merging of the Ministries of Social Security and Health. (The origins of the Ministry of Social Security go back to 1916 when the Ministry of Pensions was established. A Ministry of National Insurance was created in 1944 and these two were amalgamated in 1954. Then in 1966 they were joined by the National Assistance Board to form the Ministry of Social Security.) When the Ministry of Health was first formed in 1919, it had responsibility for roads, national insurance, planning, environmental health and local government as well as the health services, but over the years these other duties were transferred to other departments. The final change came in 1951, when it lost responsibility for local government housing to the Ministry of Town and Country Planning, which was itself absorbed into the new Ministry of Housing and Local Government in the same year. This change lost the health ministry its cabinet seat; a loss of status which also meant it had to give up its Whitehall offices and half its staff.

In 1968 Richard Crossman, Lord President of the Council and Leader of the House of Commons, was involved with the Prime Minister in planning the restructuring of certain Government ministries that would further consolidate the total number of spending departments. The new Department of Health and Social Security was created in this way, with the Cabinet seat restored (although Enoch Powell was, as Minister of Health, a member of the Cabinet in 1962). The first Secretary of State for Social Services, as the head of the new department was called, was Richard Crossman himself. But the merger did little to alter the organisation of the two ministries since their functions and methods of working were and remained so strikingly different. The former Ministry of Health was a headquarters administration for each arm of the tripartite structure, with the detailed fieldwork in the hands of the hospital boards, executive councils and local authorities. After 1974 the health side of the DHSS employed over 4,500 civil servants, although the actual running of the NHS from day to day was delegated to the health authorities and their staff. On the other hand, the social security side had a much smaller headquarters staff (about 2,000 after 1974) but it employed over 75,000 civil servants in the local offices to administer the range of benefits and welfare provisions on its behalf. The status of junior ministers at the DHSS has been advanced in recent years so that now, of the two Parliamentary Under-Secretaries, one is designated Minister for the Disabled. There is one Minister of State for Health, and the Minister of Social Security has a Cabinet seat of his own. The civil servants at the DHSS remain on the whole in two distinct organisations. The Secretary of State is also responsible to Parliament for the Supplementary Benefits Commission which is a separate entity staffed by appointed commissioners who are neither civil servants nor MPs.

The Role of the Health Ministers

The Secretary of State's obligation towards the officers of his department and towards his colleagues in the Government can often be conflicting. The department will want him to put its case in the Cabinet, where he has to argue for the government's attention and for funds, in order to support departmental needs and priorities. His civil servants will also want him to represent them loyally in Parliament and effectively in public. He must also be available to take non-political departmental decisions. The Prime Minister and the Cabinet, on the other hand, will require the Secretary of State to be a political force, contributing and supporting the Government on matters away from his immediate responsibilities, experienced in Parliament and active in the party organisation. So the person who holds the position of Secretary of State has to achieve a balance between these factors which will, ideally, enable him to be successful, both in his department as an innovator and administrator, and in the Government as a politician. As government departments have greatly expanded their activities, increasing amounts of policy-making have to be done by civil servants, and the minister may at best only be able to choose between alternative policies presented to him by the senior officials, without knowing the details of departmental views on the subject. Indeed, relatively junior civil servants are often required to make important decisions by attempting to 'interpret the minister's mind', in the absence of any direct contact with the minister himself. Although this might be undesirable from the politicians' point of view, it is an inevitable consequence of the sheer quantity of work being handled in the department. For his own part the minister may introduce a group of policy advisers from outside the civil service who will, with his junior ministers, form a team as a countervailing influence to the civil servants. In the DHSS the position is as in Figure 3. In Wales the organisation is different since the Secretary of State for Wales is responsible for several other functions in addition to health, and only a section of the civil servants in the Welsh Office deal solely with health matters.

The Reorganisation of the DHSS

In 1970 the Government ordered a study of the DHSS to be made which would, in the light of the earlier reorganisation of the Personal Social Ser-

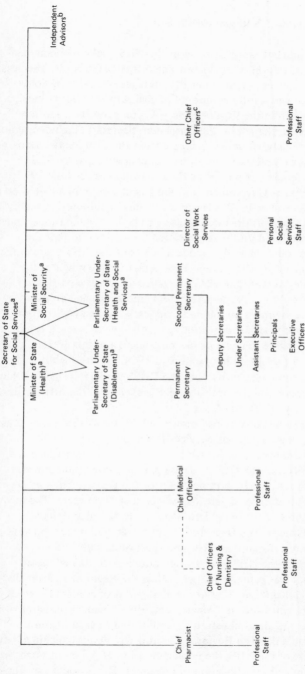

Figure 3 *The Organisation of the DHSS*

NOTES:

a   Indicates must be either a Member of Parliament (Commons) or a member of the House of Lords.

b   Ministers have increasingly, since 1964, tended to introduce their own personal advisers who are independent of both the DHSS and Parliament. Some of them are on the civil service payroll, others are seconded from their usual employment, and some are paid by the political party in power.

c   Chief Scientist, Chief Statisticians, Chief Architect, Chief Engineer, Chief Quantity Surveyor.

vices and the imminent reorganisation of the NHS, make recommendations for a reorganisation of the health side of the DHSS itself. This was
carried out by a Review Team under the guidance of a steering committee. The team was jointly composed of civil servants and of management consultants from the firm McKinsey & Company Inc., and the
steering committee, chaired by the Permanent Secretary, included senior
departmental officials, an under-secretary from the Civil Service Department, a director of McKinsey and three independent advisers. The
Review Team's report was published (in eight volumes) in June 1972,[1]
fully accepted by the Government and the DHSS, and implemented on a
single date in December 1972. Clearly the changes could not, in reality,
be as sudden as that, but the intention was to lay the foundations, and
simultaneously to build up the organisation upon them, so that the
DHSS would be well prepared to guide all parts of the NHS through their
reorganisation in 1974. The Review Team's report, like much of the
other official literature on the NHS reorganisation, uses a particular
vocabulary and style which can easily seem ambiguous and confusing.
Although the Department undoubtedly appreciates the need to communicate effectively with those working for the health service, it has
often appeared unable to make its meaning plain, and this created a lot
of uncertainty, especially in the months of 1974. So although it is important to have some idea of the way the DHSS works in order to understand how its control of the health service is exercised, the official literature does not make this easy.

The health and personal social services side of the DHSS is now organised into five groups: Regional, Services Development, Personnel,
Finance, and Administration (which is shared with the social security
side), plus the 'Top of the Office'. These groups consist of administrative staff who work closely with members of the Department's professional staff: doctors, nurses, dentists, works, social work, etc. The most
significant features of the 'new' DHSS are the Regional and Services
Development Groups. The Department previously had no regional organisation of any substance and because most of its staff had no practical experience of the NHS, it was often criticised for being out of
touch with what was actually going on. Now the Regional Liaison Division of the Regional Group acts as the main point of contact between
the health authorities and the Department. Mobile teams consisting of a
doctor, a nurse and an administrator are allocated to each region to
strengthen these links. The Regional Planning Division is concerned with
the organisation of the NHS, the implementation of policy through the
planning system and the allocation of resources. The Services Development Group has eight divisions which are organised to cut across the old

TOP OF THE OFFICE

To help the Secretary of State provide central leadership in the health and social services

To advise him on ultimate choices about the nature and scale of the NHS and national objectives and priorities

To advise him on matters of major public concern

To manage the Department's resources

SERVICE DEVELOPMENT

To help the Secretary of State decide national objectives, priorities and standards for the health and social services, and specifically to
- Advise on nature and scale of the NHS
- Develop policy needed to improve health services
- Promote local authority social services
- Identify and develop plans to meet needs of selected clients

To support the field authorities and the Regional Divisions in implementing these decisions

To support the Secretary of State in relation to allocated subjects.

REGIONAL

To guide the health and local authorities on national objectives and priorities

To support and (to the extent feasible and desirable) control them in the planning and running of services

To provide specialist support to them in building and supply

To provide specialist support to them in building and supply

To support the Secretary of State in relation to allocated subjects

---

NHS PERSONNEL

To help the Secretary of State decide fair and economic pay and conditions of service for all NHS personnel, and to see agreement is reached with staff concerned.

To help the NHS recruit, train, retain and employ wisely sufficient staff of the required calibre and experience

To support the Secretary of State in relation to allocated subjects

---

DEPARTMENT SUPPORT (to Social Security side also)

To support the Top of the Office on manpower and organisation and efficiency matters and negotiate with CSD and Treasury

To support line managers in organisation, staffing, the efficient use of resources and staff development

To provide specialist support as needed (e.g. Statistics, ADP, OR, O & M)

To support the Secretary of State in relation to allocated subjects

---

FINANCE

To represent the Department with the Treasury and the rest of government on financial matters

To provide financial advice to the Top of the Office

To provide financial advice to the Department as a whole and to review the financial implications of proposed and current policies

To exercise financial control of the income and expenditure of the Department, the NHS and other agencies under DHSS supervision of other agencies under DHSS supervision

To support the Secretary of State in relation to allocated matters

Figure 4 *The Six Main Groups in the DHSS and Their Primary Objectives*
Source: Management Arrangements for the Reorganised National Health Service, HMSO, 1972

boundaries (hospital services, GP services) and look at provision in terms of patients' needs (e.g. children, the mentally ill and handicapped). The Group is concerned both with the formulation of policy and with its execution and therefore has a very broad responsibility.

The Personnel Group has four divisions, three of which are concerned with all aspects of the pay and conditions of NHS staff that are negotiated through the Whitley Council system. The fourth division deals with doctors' pay and conditions, and the administration of the family practitioner services. The Finance Group has one division dealing with negotiations with central government for the Department's share of money through the PESC system, and one division dealing with allocations to the health authorities, accounting systems and the NHS audit. The Administration Group is concerned with internal DHSS affairs such as staffing, computers and research, statistics and management services. The Top of the Office consists of the most senior civil servants who advise ministers directly on important matters of policy. In addition, each minister and permanent secretary has his own private office which acts as the channel of communication with the rest of the Department and also handles correspondence and arranges meetings and visits.

In 1976, three regional health authority chairmen conducted an investigation into the work of the DHSS in relation to the RHAs, at the invitation of the Minister of State for Health, Dr David Owen. They assessed the performance of the five Groups and made a number of radical suggestions for 'encouraging delegation, eliminating duplication and effecting economies'. In response, a joint working group was established to recommend to the Secretary of State what action should be taken on the proposals. In January 1977, before the working group had reported, a further investigation into the work of the DHSS was announced. It was not so much concerned with the relationship between the Department and the health authorities as with improvements in the top management of the DHSS. The inquiry was conducted by senior officials from the DHSS and the Civil Service Department with help from outside consultants.

The Personal Social Services

The reorganisation of the DHSS also emphasised the relationship between the Personal Social Services and the NHS. Although the metropolitan districts and non-metropolitan counties are locally responsible for the provision of personal social services which are not part of the NHS, they act under the general guidance of the Secretary of State. Within the DHSS there is a small section of staff working with the Director of Social Work Services in this area, and their influence on health service policy is potentially far-reaching. The welfare of children and people suffering from

Table 1 *Personal Social Services*

CHILD CARE	regional planning of community homes
	approved schools and remand homes
	youth treatment centres
	adoption
	intermediate treatment
	control of employment
	day care for pre-school children
	registration of nurseries and child minders
	supervision of private foster homes
	non-accidental injury to children

RESIDENTIAL SERVICES FOR THE ELDERLY AND DISABLED
DOMICILIARY SERVICES (home helps, meals)
CARE OF THE HANDICAPPED
MENTAL HEALTH SERVICES
TRAINING (social workers, nursery nurses, teachers for the mentally handicapped)
VOLUNTARY SERVICES SUPPORT AND LIAISON
BUILDING AND DESIGN PROGRAMMES
URBAN PROGRAMME
CARE OF THE HOMELESS

Source: DHSS Annual Report 1974

long-term illness and handicap depends on the liaison between health and social service agencies, and departmental responsibility for supporting and encouraging it is vital in the years ahead. Table 1 shows the main personal social services that the DHSS supervises.

Monitoring DHSS Activity

There are three ways in which external checks on the policy and administration of the DHSS are exercised. Early on, when new schemes are being thought out, or alterations in existing services are being planned, civil servants in the DHSS are joined by civil servants from the expenditure divisions of the Treasury, so that jointly acceptable proposals can be constructed. Then the Department has to submit estimates of its spending in the next financial year (and overall for the next five years) to the Treasury. At the end of the financial year the Department also has to construct a complete account of its income and expenditure for that year. Preparation of the estimates and accounts are the responsibility of the Finance Group.

However, apart from the Treasury, Parliament has further means of keeping a check on departments. The annual account is passed to the Comptroller and Auditor-General who is an independent officer of Parliament. He audits the account and reports on it to the House of

Commons, drawing attention to any waste or inefficiency that he has detected. These points will be taken up by the fifteen MPs who are members of the Public Accounts Committee. They hear evidence from the Accounting Officer of the Department (who is the Permanent Secretary) and members of his staff, and recommend ways in which they decide the Department could work more economically or administer its affairs more efficiently. The other instrument of control is the House of Commons Select Committee on Expenditure. Its members are divided into a number of specialist sub-committees; the appropriate one takes the Department's estimates as a basis for examining the way the Department makes plans and intends to execute them. It hears evidence from departmental officials and also from those in the field, and provides its critical assessments to the House of Commons. This combination of the Secretary of State's personal responsibility to Parliament, the Treasury's involvement in departmental planning, the investigations of the Comptroller and Auditor-General, the Public Accounts Committee and the Select Committee on Expenditure provides a basis for thorough and ongoing scrutiny of the Department's work. It is interesting to note that this system has been operating effectively in many aspects of government administration without interfering with ministerial responsibility and authority, or making judgements on party lines.

The convention that each minister is personally responsible for the work of his department is strongly maintained as a safeguard against the abuse of the Government's extensive powers over individual citizens. Through the mechanism of parliamentary questions, individuals' grievances can be raised in the full light of publicity, so the preparation of the answers is given serious attention by the department in order to maintain its credibility and authority. The procedures through which individual complaints can be made will be discussed more fully in Chapter 10, but the work of the Health Service Commissioner should be mentioned here. The NHS Reorganisation Act 1973 provided for the creation of the Health Service Commissioner for England and Wales as an independent officer of Parliament, empowered to investigate individual complaints arising from administrative failures by health authorities. This could include bad communications, delays in hospital admission from the waiting list, inadequate facilities or unsuitable accommodation, or failure on the part of the authority to deal soon enough or properly with an aggrieved person's complaints. The Health Service Commissioner was specifically excluded from investigating complaints concerning the diagnosis, care and treatment of a patient's illness involving a doctor's exercise of 'clinical judgement', or in

pursuing complaints against family practitioners or their Family
Practitioner Committee. He can investigate matters referred to him by
health authorities where they have been unable to settle satisfactorily
with the complainant. There was initially some concern that the
restrictions on the Health Service Commissioner's scope would limit
his effectiveness on behalf of the public, but through an imaginative
interpretation of his role a wide range of health services can be
covered. The first occupant of this post was Sir Alan Marre, who had
since 1967 been the Parliamentary Commissioner for Administration,
(the Ombudsman) and who, from 1973, combined those two posts
as well as being the Health Service Commissioner for Scotland.

The Role of Professional Staff

Returning now to the policy-making duties of the DHSS, a particular
characteristic to be considered is the involvement of doctors, nurses and
members of other health professions, both as civil servants and in the
advisory machinery. They provide expert opinion on the many technical
issues involved in the Department's work, and there are Chief Officers
of Dentistry, Nursing and Pharmacy as well as the more well-known
positions of Chief Medical Officer and Chief Scientist. They enable the
DHSS to approach its work in a multi-disciplinary way, and staff from
the Permanent Secretary downwards are acutely aware of the need to
take the professionals with them on most policy matters of any
substance. The Chief Medical Officer (CMO) is in a particularly
influential position since he can consult and advise the Secretary of
State personally as of right, without the prior intervention of any
other officer and he is likely to be in post for far longer than the
ministers or the Permanent Secretary. He works in close liaison with
the Permanent Secretary (whose equal in status he is), and he and the
other chief officers are consulted on issues that have a bearing on their
professional practices and attitudes. The CMO independently publishes
an annual report (entitled *On the State of the Public Health*) giving an
account of the health care activities of the past year, and in which he
can also make his personal comments on the policy and administration
of the NHS. These comments are likely to be widely reported and
respected. The CMO also has duties as Medical Officer of the Home
Office and the Department of Education and Science, and he advises
on medical matters to the Ministry of Agriculture, Fisheries and Food,
and the Department of the Environment. Such pre-eminence being
given to one member of a particular profession is unique within the
Civil Service, and is a significant acknowledgement of the medical
profession's power and influence. Sir George Godber was Chief Medical

Officer from 1960 to 1973, and this exceptionally long service, coupled with his personal reputation and dedication made the post unusually influential on NHS policy.

The tradition of involving professional opinion and advice in the work of the DHSS is also maintained through the advisory machinery mentioned in the last paragraph. The National Health Service Act, 1946 established a Central Health Services Council to advise the Minister on any matters relating to the service that were either referred to them or that they themselves thought fit to consider. After reorganisation, this Council was retained, but with a modified constitution. It is made up of between forty and forty-four people: the Presidents of the thirteen Royal Medical Colleges (e.g. physicians, surgeons, obstetricians and gynaecologists); twenty-three professional representatives (e.g. family practitioners, nurses, social workers and health administrators); four representatives of the public; up to four more may be appointed by the Secretary of State. They have to publish an annual report to the Secretary of State, describing the issues they have considered, and they can publish additional reports on particular matters, which may often receive publicity in the general and specialist press, and are sometimes discussed in Parliament. Five Standing Advisory Committees of the Central Health Services Council (for medical, dental, pharmaceutical, ophthalmic and nursing and midwifery services) also look into issues that have particular reference to their professional sphere, and publish reports. These bodies together supplement the knowledge available to the DHSS and can be used as a vehicle to obtain wider support for a new departure policy, or to strengthen the Secretary of State's position in taking decisions on specific controversial matters. For the first twenty-five years of their existence, these bodies rarely deliberated on matters of their own choosing but many of their published reports are recognised as important contributions to developments in the National Health Service (e.g. the Bradbeer Report,[2] the Platt Report,[3] the Bonham-Carter Report[4]).

A more recent addition to the advisory machinery is the Hospital Advisory Service. It was created by Richard Crossman in 1969 following the recommendation in a report of the Committee of Inquiry into conditions at Ely Hospital, Cardiff, for the mentally ill and subnormal.[5] It operated through four multidisciplinary teams: two for mental handicap, one for mental illness and one for hospitals for the elderly and chronic sick. The teams visited hospitals and units all over England and Wales, and inquired into the details of their day-to-day activities. After each visit they would write a report which was sent in confidence to the hospital authorities and senior staff concerned, as well as to the Secretary of State. The authorit would then discuss the report with the DHSS and agree on responsibility for implementing the recommendations. In 1972 one mental handicap team was disbanded and a second team set up for the elderly, but when the NHS reorganisation was imminent, HAS activity was reduced to just two teams — one for the elderly and one for mental illness. In 1976 the HAS was changed into the new Health Advisory Service to work through joint multi-disciplinary teams with the Social Work Service of the DHSS. These five or six member teams look at hospital services, community services and the links between the two. There are three new teams: one for the mentally ill, one for the elderly and one for children receiving long-term hospital care. Their job is to encourage and disseminate good practice, new ideas and constructive attitudes and relationships, and to act as catalysts to stimulate local solutions to local problems. Like the old HAS they are not able to investigate individual complaints or matters of clinical judgement. Before each visit the DHSS and authorities are asked to supply information about the services to be visited. They are invited to submit their comments, as are the CHCs and Family Practitioner Committees. Senior staff of the health and local authorities concerned, joint consultative committees, staff organisations and any other local bodies may also be invited to make comments. The teams try to reach agreement during the visit about each issue they raise with the staff. Their full report goes to the Secretary of State and the authorities involved. Six months later the HAS asks the health and local authorities about matters raised in the report which have not yet been resolved, and they may make follow-up visits.

The Regional Health Authorities

The Concept of Regional Administration

The next statutory tier of administrative authority in the NHS has been placed at regional level. In the original pre-1974 arrangements there were Regional Hospital Boards in each of the ten provincial areas whose boundaries had been defined in relation to the universities which had medical schools. London and South-East England were covered by the four metropolitan Regional Hospital Boards which together included the twenty-six teaching hospitals situated in London. These Boards represented a definite tier of authority between the Ministry/Department and local managers, but only in relation to the hospital services. Community health and family practitioner services had no regional administration. During the debate on the reorganisation, successive schemes for achieving an integration of the tripartite structure took differing views on the necessity for regional administration.

In the First Green Paper the idea was absent and in the Second Green Paper, the role was limited to planning and advisory functions only. In the Consultative Document however, a strong regional element in the chain of command from the centre to the periphery was proposed. The reason for this trend in thinking was probably caused by the growing conviction of the Ministers and their expert advisers that there was a need for a coordinating body between the DHSS and the area administration. The reason was that it seemed necessary to reduce the Department's span of control, and to make the NHS less subject to political pressure.

In that sense, the Regional Health Authorities can be said to have succeeded the Regional Hospital Boards by taking over a number of their functions in relation to the hospital sector, including the appointment of specialist medical staff and the distribution of clinical work across the hospitals within the region, and the planning and management of capital works and expenditure. Although the intention behind the linking of each RHB to a university medical school and teaching hospital was to improve the distribution of medical manpower throughout the country, inequalities between regions in the standards of provision were strongly in evidence all the time. The responsibility for failing to iron out these differences seems to be shared by the Ministry/Department and the RHBs. Not until 1971 did the DHSS begin to allocate revenue funds to the regions according to a formula that took account of critical local factors such as the projections of population growth. Before then, the statistical information on which comparisons between regions could be based was not really sufficiently sophisticated to permit meaningful analyses. However, the RHBs did not influence the development and planning of teaching hospital facilities so that there could be greater integration of the hospital service, and the Department did not encourage them to do this.

The relationship between the RHBs and their Hospital Management Committees was also responsible for some difficulties. In Scotland the arrangement was a strict hierarchy of three tiers: Department of Health for Scotland; Regional Hospital Boards; Boards of Management (the equivalents to the HMCs in England and Wales, although they did also have responsibility for the teaching hospitals). Each level explicitly gave orders to the subordinate one below it. In England and Wales, although the RHBs received their orders from the Ministry/Department, they were charged with 'general oversight and supervision' of the HMCs in their regions. This led to the paradoxical situation where some HMCs resented the degree of control exerted over them by their RHB, while other RHBs were criticised for leaving their HMCs alone too much, and allowing administration of an inadequate quality to result. The First Green Paper focused on the first of these points when it said, ' . . . the interest which Regional Hospital Boards have taken in the performance of management functions by Hospital Management Committees, although not outside their statutory powers, may go beyond what was envisaged when the structure was established. Their primary task as originally conceived was planning and coordinating development; their intervention in matters of management has grown out of their responsibility for allocating financial resources, but it is sometimes unwelcome. Confused responsibilities tend to create unsatisfactory relationships.'[6]

On the other hand, following inquiries at Ely and other hospitals which exposed poor standards of care for long-stay patients, RHBs were criticised for being insufficiently involved, and Richard Crossman held them directly responsible for the activities of their HMCs in this respect.

In the White Paper, however, the reasons explicitly given for needing a strong regional tier did not take up these arguments,[7] and discussions on the most desirable extent of control that should be exerted by regional authorities over local administration have continued vigorously. Nevertheless, from 1 April 1974, fourteen RHAs came into being in England (see Figure 5). The Regions are called Northern, Yorkshire, Trent, East Anglia, North West Thames, North East Thames, South East Thames, South West Thames, Wessex, Oxford, South Western, West Midlands, Mersey and North Western. Their boundaries have altered slightly from the RHB boundaries, to accommodate the new local authority boundaries which their constituent Areas observe: each Region has between three and eleven Area Health Authorities. The chairman and members of each RHA are appointed by the Secretary of State after consultation with interested organisations, including the main health professions, the main local authorities, the universities, appropriate trade unions and voluntary bodies. The work of the RHAs is in some respects similar to that of the old RHBs, including the selection, design and construction of major capital building projects, manpower planning, and major computer and operational research services. But since one important aspect of the reorganisation is to bring together the elements of the tripartite structure, the RHAs have to look beyond the hospital service to include the community health services in their planning. Although most 'operational' functions are delegated from the Secretary of State through the RHAs to the Area Health Authorities (and this delegation will be discussed further in the next chapter), RHAs are responsible for employing the consultants and senior registrars of non-teaching hospitals, the blood transfusion service, the ambulance service in metropolitan counties, management services, the training of administrators, and for some services better

Figure 5 *Regional Health Authority Boundaries*

Source: National Health Service Reorganisation, HMSO, 1971

provided on a regional basis (such as the computer processing of payrolls).

The Regional Team of Officers

Clearly these duties cannot be carried out by the RHA members themselves, who serve on a voluntary basis and meet about ten times each year, although the RHA Chairman receives an emolument in recognition of the extra work which he undertakes. The day-to-day work of the RHA is performed by the five designated officers: the Regional Administrator, the Regional Treasurer, the Regional Works Officer, the Regional Medical Officer and the Regional Nursing Officer. The main work involved is to arrange the distribution of the region's health service resources in line with nationally and regionally determined policies; in other words, seeing that people, buildings and equipment are in the right place and of the right quality to ensure that the National Health Service can achieve its objectives. For example, this could involve an active policy to reduce the numbers of chronic psychiatric inpatients, or deciding where to site a renal dialysis centre and what its workload should be, or arranging for the right balance between hospital and community care of geriatric patients, and so on. This kind of strategic planning is absolutely necessary in order to spread the limited resources of a region reasonably across all fronts. The scale of the regional organisation is large: several of the RHAs serve populations in excess of three million, and have annual budgets in 1977/ 78 of approaching £250 million,[8] and staff numbering over 50,000. The Grey Book proposed a specific management structure which focuses on the five designated officers named above. As members of the Regional Team of Officers (RTO) they are collectively responsible for framing regional plans, proposing the allocation of resources, monitoring AHA plans, and providing certain services on a regional basis. The individual officers have particular specified responsibilities as well, and departmental organisations to support them (see Figure 6).

The Regional Administrator is responsible for preparing plans for the region's administrative services and seeing that these are carried out. Capital and services planning, personnel, supplies, management services, information services and public relations departments, each with their own senior officer, are managed by him. He also has to provide secretarial services to the RHA, its committees and the professional advisory committees. He manages the services planning and capital building arrangements and acts as the formal channel of communication between the RHA and the DHSS. The Regional Treasurer is responsible for providing information to the RHA and its senior officers on the capital and revenue implications of the region's work through

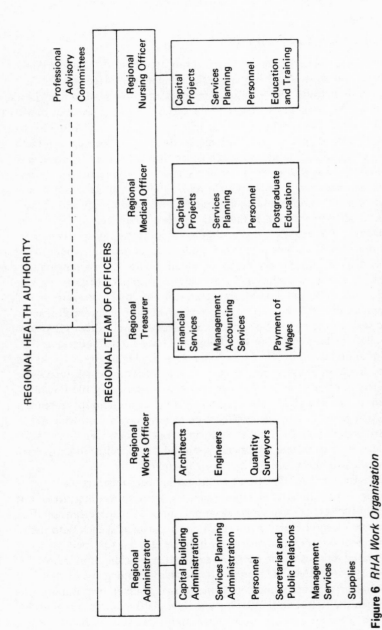

Figure 6 *RHA Work Organisation*

Source: Management Arrangements for the Reorganised National Health Service, HMSO, 1972

management accounting and internal auditing systems, and for arranging the computation and payment of wages to staff. He also advises the area treasurers on the management of their income and expenditure. The Regional Works Officer has a large staff of architects, engineers and quantity surveyors who carry out the building work of the region. Administrators in charge of capital projects and forward planning work in liaison with the Regional Administrator and the Regional Works Officer. The Regional Medical Officer is in charge of planning the distribution of medical manpower throughout the region, and coordinates the work of multi-disciplinary groups which study the development of operational health care services. He has to ensure that medical education and research facilities are suitably developed, through cooperation with the university and teaching hospital authorities, and that personnel services are available for regionally employed medical staff. The Regional Nursing Officer is responsible for the provision of personnel services for regionally employed nurses, and for the provision of adequate education and training facilities throughout the region. She also contributes with the other members of the RTO to the development of plans for health care services and for capital building.

In Wales there is no tier of authority placed between the AHAs and the government departments (the DHSS and the Welsh Office) to compare with the Regional Health Authorities in England. However, it was thought that some functions could be more effectively provided at an 'all-Wales' level, and for this purpose the Welsh Health Technical Services Organisation (WHTSO) was established. It does not have managerial authority over the AHAs but carries out executive tasks and provides professional advice to the AHAs and to the Welsh Office. Its five main areas of activity are: building services, management services, supplies, prescription pricing and administrative services. A small Board of the WHTSO is appointed by, and responsible to, the Secretary of State for Wales, and there are designated senior officers for each area of activity, who are employed by the Board.

Since the planning role of the region is so important, the staff need to have a rational system to ensure the synthesis of their individual efforts. This happens in two ways: through service planning teams and project teams. The teams can include medical, nursing, finance, works, and administrative staff, and any other professional and technical members with appropriate skills. The service planning teams have to study and coordinate the region-wide health care services in much the same way that the Services Development Divisions of the DHSS do so on a national basis. Project teams are set up for each major capital project that the service planning team has defined a need. Depending on the project an administrator or a medical officer takes the lead responsibility for briefing the members in order to ensure that projects progress satisfactorily through all stages from design to final completion.

Returning again to the Regional Team of Officers, their description as a 'consensus-forming' group of equals needs to be noted. The concept of consensus management will be discussed further in relation to the teams of officers working at area and district levels, but its definition of the style in which RTOs are meant to work can be seen as an interesting departure from former arrangements. The origins of 'consensus' come from academic research into the ways groups of people solve problems together, which has suggested that team methods can often be more effective than either committee or individual efforts, in given situations. Traditionally, the leadership of a committee always rested with the same person, the chairman, who was not necessarily informed about the subjects under discussion. Decisions were taken, when necessary, by majority vote, and this often failed to recognise or reconcile the different opinions of members. The new arrangements, however, require teams to arrive at unanimous decisions after thorough discussion of individual points of view and their respective implications. The consequence is that no one member is necessarily more powerful than another, and that the collective decisions reached are a statement of the members' commitment to the action that will result from their decision.

Just as the DHSS has arrangements for obtaining expert professional advice, so the RHAs have advisory committees of health service staff which may cover medical, dental, nursing and midwifery, pharmaceutical, optical and other categories of services. These committees enable RHAs to make development plans in consultation with the professions, and ensure the participation of individuals outside the RHA staff in the all important planning process.

Management Relationships and the Planning Process

The architects of the reorganisation based many of the detailed arrangements for improved administration on the complementary concepts of 'maximum responsibility delegated downwards' matched by 'clear lines of accountability upwards', which would be exercised through the creation of sound management structures at each level.[9] In effect this means a division of labour between the levels of authority which is designed to ensure that the DHSS' policy intentions will be put into effect, more or less uniformly, across the country. An oversimplified way of saying the same thing is that the DHSS does the strategic planning on a national scale and the RHAs do the strategic planning on a local scale remaining faithful to the DHSS' guidelines; the AHAs handle details of staffing and services that make the RHAs' plans possible, and the districts deal with the 'delivery' of health care to their populations, with the resources that are made available by the AHAs. The result is that each level allocates resources to the next one down, which in turn redistributes them and passes them on. This delegated responsibility for using resources is mirrored by accountability up through the levels, which is achieved through the medium of plans and budgets. So districts submit plans to areas, area plans are submitted to the regions, and regional plans go to the DHSS. The plans are in each case scrutinised by the 'senior' authority who allocates budgets to cover the items in the plans that have been approved. It thereby sanctions the carrying out of the approved plans by its 'junior' authority. There are paradoxes in this scheme, particularly because an inevitable fact is that the NHS has to operate in the context of a continuously growing demand for its services. Therefore whatever services are being arranged are likely to fall short of the current level of demand or the state of medical knowledge. This state of affairs forces each level of authority to choose between alternative priorities, since it will never have enough money or staff to provide everything it ideally should. Although the reorganisation envisages a shift of emphasis from the hospital services to the community health services, this cannot easily be achieved with the limitations on available resources, since it would entail allowing the hospital services to deteriorate so that the community services can benefit. Such a move is unacceptable, and the only alternative is to devise ways of using the existing resources more economically thus spreading their effect more widely. 'Sound management structures' are held to be the way that appropriate handling of this delicate situation will be achieved. Nevertheless, there is concern that instead of delegated responsibility being matched by accountability, the pressure on the structure will tip the balance in favour of accountability. The effect of this will be that higher levels of authority will keep too tight a grip on the plans and expenditure of the lower levels so the greater freedom to distribute resources according to local circumstances will be minimised.

In the case of RHAs and their areas, the regions have to judge the correct balance between their areas' claims, and monitor their subsequent performance according to the approved plans. 'Monitoring' is another important aspect of the reorganisation which, although not new to the NHS, has been given greater emphasis in the new structure. There is no question of a manager-subordinate relationship between regional officers and their counterparts at area level. It is, rather, a matter of the regional officer giving advice and guidance on the interpretation of RHA policies in general, and in connection with specific problems which may arise. He cannot give the area officer orders, but he may try to persuade him to get particular things done in particular ways. The relationship between the DHSS and the RHAs is slightly different although adhering to the same general principles. Through its establishment of a Regional Planning Division the DHSS is attempting to forge much closer and developing links with the RHAs so that it can be in touch with operational problems and trends that will make its picture of the way the NHS works more accurate. There are regular meetings with the RHA chairmen and with particular regional officers, and individual RTOs meet with the Regional Planning Division of the DHSS.

Until 1974 there was no formal or explicit planning system in the NHS, and the Department found itself constantly being asked to react to changes and crises that it was not well equipped to understand or deal with. Now its intention is to think ahead and analyse alternative ways of achieving its national objectives, and thereby assign priorities between them for the use of its limited resources. The working of the NHS is in many respects regular and predictable, so a formal planning process is a suitable way to organise its administration. The problem is that there are no objective ways of measuring performance in the service that are equally acceptable, so some of the planning judgements take on the status of informed guesses. Nevertheless, the DHSS has decided to operate an annual planning cycle in which each level is simultaneously involved in an ongoing assessment of its targets. The DHSS decides on its priorities with the Secretary of State and then agrees with the RHAs on how these may broadly be achieved. They pass guidelines on to the AHAs that are tailored to fit specific local circumstances, and give an idea of the financial allocations that may be expected. Districts are anyway involved in charting the services that they need to provide for their local populations, and they work in collaboration with officers from the AHA to agree on ways of achieving the best arrangements for providing their services. The RHAs' role is to coordinate and approve area plans, and neither the DHSS or the RHAs are involved in the detail of district plans, but only in satisfying themselves that the latter fit into the overall strategy at regional and national levels. However, further details of the timing of the planning cycle, together with a diagram, will follow in Chapter 4.

3 THE AREA HEALTH AUTHORITIES

In order to understand why it was thought necessary to establish a tier of authority at area level for the integrated administration of the NHS, it is helpful to return briefly to the criticisms that were being made about the NHS during the 1960s; the key arguments can be found in the Porritt Report,[1] and the two Green Papers.[2] The theme running through them was that despite its considerable achievements, the NHS was not organised in such a way that the three arms of the service could work efficiently and cooperatively. Without better dovetailing, satisfactory standards of patient care could not be assured because the poor liaison between hospitals, community services and general practitioners too often lead to unacceptable delays and unnecessary suffering on the part of many patients.

The Medical Services Review Committee was appointed in the autumn of 1958 under the chairmanship of Sir Arthur Porritt with representatives from the Royal Colleges of Physicians, Surgeons, Obstetricians and Gynaecologists, the Society of Medical Officers of Health, the College of General Practitioners and the British Medical Association. Their report, published four years later, can reasonably be taken as the expression of the opinion of the medical profession at that time, and its unequivocal conclusion was that ' . . . one administrative unit should become the focal point for all the medical services of an appropriate area, and that doctors and other personnel in all branches of the Service should be under contract with this one authority',[3] and that, ' . . . the full advantages of the preventive and personal health services and their effective integration with the family doctor and hospital services can only be achieved by transferring both services and staff to the Area Health Boards'.[4]

But this view illustrates only part of what the NHS is intended to do. In fact it is not only concerned with the delivery of care to patients, but is also required to allocate and reallocate resources, and these two functions are not the same — they are rather interdependent on each other. If the NHS was simply about the day-to-day treatment and prevention of illness, the arguments about a reorganisation would have focused on ensuring closer cooperation between all the staff involved in this activity. The additional emphasis given to 'management' of the services[5] indicates that it is also about planning for the future. The last chapter illustrated this in terms of the DHSS's internal reorganisation which was intended to enable better planning and improved delegation of its authority to become possible.

49

In his foreword to the White Paper of 1972, the Secretary of State wrote of the reorganisation: 'It is about administration, not about treatment and care.'[6] The significance of the new authorities at area level now becomes clearer. The DHSS and the RHAs have to concentrate on strategic planning, whether nationally or regionally, while the districts are concerned with the day-to-day delivery of health care. Only the Area Health Authorities are in a position to do some of both activities, and as such it may be helpful to regard them as the embodiment of an 'integrated' service. Put another way, if each part of the new structure had a clear precedent in the pre-1974 organisation, critics could have expressed the opinion that the reorganisation had simply given new names to all the old jobs and committees without really altering very much. But with the existing reorganisation although many of its features are not wholly new, an exact ancestor of the Area Health Authorities is difficult to identify. In that sense, their existence could be said to represent a focus for the hopes that that the administrative rearrangement would prove to be a successful attempt to improve both the management and the delivery of health care.

Boundaries of the New Authorities

It must be remembered that the NHS reorganisation was planned in the context of the new arrangements for local authority personal social services and the reorganisation of local government. Both these reforms set down new geographical boundaries for their respective spheres of administration, facts which could not be ignored by the health service. Therefore another important element in the debate about the NHS was the administrative boundaries that the new area authorities would observe. The First Green Paper, which was published in advance of the report from the Royal Commission on Local Government, did not specify boundaries of the area authorities, but did entertain the possibility that health and local government could be jointly administered. However, the Second Green Paper favoured the separate administration of health services, but within the same geographical areas as were defined for local authorities.

The question is, what boundaries are most suitable for decentralised administration of the NHS — should they reflect the incidence of ill-health or should they conform to existing boundaries of complementary agencies? The answer depends on the previous point about whether the NHS administration is concerned with delivery of care to people or about strategic planning of its available resources. It would seem that if provision of services is the primary purpose, then organisation should take account of the distribution and relative prevalence of disease. However, if realistic planning is the aim, then coterminosity with local authority boundaries (i.e. identical boundaries) would be desirable. Few people would be happy to state a preference between these options, and the creation of Area Health Authorities with the same boundaries as local government, although emphasising the planning function does also underline the recognition of the need for close collaboration between all parts of the health service and the staff of other agencies.[7]

Regional Inequalities

Epidemiological studies have demonstrated that ill-health is associated with a number of social factors such that urban areas of declining employment with a high degree of overcrowding, low standards of housing and low wages are those with high mortality rates. Yet the pattern of health service provision has been a patchwork, essentially unrelated to population and mortality rates from particular diseases; this is partly what is meant by 'regional inequalities'. However, the difficulty of altering the balance of local services to handle local needs (which is the job of the Area Health Authorities) should not be underestimated. The historical pattern of distribution of resources and the comparative rigidity of financial allocation because of established revenue expenditure commitments, makes substantial changes slow and difficult to achieve.

The failure of the tripartite structure in ironing out regional inequalities arose partly because the interdependence of hospital and community facilities was not properly understood. The hospital service worked through numbers of hospital beds and supporting services per thousand population. Thus the Porritt report recommended a ratio of eight beds to one thousand population distributed on the basis of 3.4 acute beds, 0.6 maternity beds, 1.6 psychiatric beds, 2.0 geriatric beds and 0.2 beds for other categories, including infectious diseases.[8] But it gradually became evident to the Ministry of Health that it did not really matter how many beds and accompanying hospital services they allocated: if the community health services were poorly staffed or badly equipped to receive patients back from hospital, then the episodes of both acute and chronic illness in the population were not going to decline. Indeed, a pamphlet on the reorganisation issued by the Office of Health Economics stated that, ' . . . the regions themselves have little epidemiological significance',[9] implying that although the NHS is about the provision of health care, the reorganisation has very slender demonstrable links with this duty — it has more to do with administrative convenience. The DHSS obviously

Figure 7 *Area Health Authority Boundaries in England & Wales*
Source: National Health Service Reorganisation, HMSO, 1971

Key to numbered Area Health Authorities

1	Newcastle Upon Tyne (T)
2	Northern Tyneside
3	Gateshead
4	Sunderland
5	Southern Tyneside
6	Wirral
7	Sefton
8	Liverpool (T)
9	St. Helens and Knowsley
10	Wigan
11	Bolton
12	Bury
13	Salford (T)
14	Trafford
15	Manchester (T)
16	Stockport
17	Tameside
18	Rochdale
19	Oldham
20	Calderdale
21	Bradford
22	Kirklees
23	Leeds (T)
24	Wakefield
25	Barnsley
26	Sheffield (T)
27	Rotherham
28	Doncaster
29	Walsall
30	Wolverhampton
31	Dudley
32	Sandwell
33	Birmingham (T)
34	Solihull
35	Coventry
36	Hillingdon
37	Ealing, Hammersmith & Hounslow (T)
38	Brent & Harrow
39	Barnet
40	Kensington, Chelsea & Westminster (T)
41	Camden & Islington (T)
42	Enfield & Haringey
43	City & East London (T)
44	Redbridge & Waltham Forest
45	Barking & Havering
46	Greenwich & Bexley
47	Bromley
48	Lambeth, Southwark & Lewisham (T)
49	Croydon
50	Merton, Sutton & Wandsworth (T)
51	Kingston & Richmond
52	Isle of Wight
53	West Glamorgan
54	Mid Glamorgan
55	South Glamorgan (T)

does not share this view and would maintain that through the Area Health Authorities and the rest of the new management structure, improvements in both health care and the future planning of the NHS resources will be more effectively managed, because the interests of administration and health care coincide. An examination of the structure and functions of the Area Health Authorities will show the basis for these expectations.

The Administrative Structure

There are ninety Area Health Authorities (AHAs) in England, and their boundaries are in most cases identical with those of the metropolitan districts and non-metropolitan counties established by the Local Government Act 1972; in Wales there are eight counties matched by eight Area Health Authorities (see Figure 7). The populations served by AHAs range from under 250,000 in some of the metropolitan districts to over 1 million in some of the larger non-metropolitan counties. In a little more detail the arrangements are as follows: the conurbations designated metropolitan counties are Tyne and Wear, West Yorkshire, South Yorkshire, West Midlands, Merseyside and Greater Manchester, each divided into between four and nine metropolitan districts. Together they comprise thirty-six metropolitan districts each matched by an AHA; the remaining thirty-eight counties are also each matched by an AHA. In London, where local government reorganisation was carried out in 1963, the thirty-two boroughs plus the City of London are arranged into sixteen AHAs, each consisting of between one and three boroughs, and following their boundaries in most cases. There is a further detail in so far that each AHA which contains university medical school and hospital teaching facilities is designated Area Health Authority (Teaching) (or AHA(T)), and in England outside London there are thirteen AHA(T)s – Newcastle, Leeds, Leicestershire, Nottinghamshire, Sheffield, Cambridgeshire, Hampshire, Oxfordshire, Avon, Birmingham, Liverpool, Manchester and Salford. In Wales the one AHA(T) is South Glamorgan; in London there are six AHA(T)s which together administer twelve undergraduate teaching hospitals of the University of London and one postgraduate teaching hospital (the Hammersmith Hospital). The Boards of Governors of twelve other London postgraduate teaching hospitals were preserved for a period of up to five years by Section 15(1) and Schedule 2 of the 1973 Reorganisation Act.

The Grey Book identified the preferred size of community for which the full range of personal health and social services could be provided as about 250,000, and therefore 34 AHAs have a single

Table 2 *Regional and Area Health Authorities and Health Districts: Analysis of Populations (England & Wales) (thousands)*

Regional Health Authority	Population	AHAs' Population					Districts' Population				
		<250	250–499	500–749	750–999	1000+	<150	150–249	250–349	350–449	450+
West Midlands	5112	1	7	1	1	1	4	8	9	–	1
Trent	4501	2	1	2	3	–	2	8	6	2	–
North Western	4095	5	4	1	–	1	2	9	7	–	–
North East Thames	3809	–	3	2	–	1	2	10	5	–	–
South East Thames	3652	1	2	1	1	1	1	10	5	–	–
Yorkshire	3528	1	2	3	1	–	4	9	2	2	–
North West Thames	3526	1	4	1	1	–	1	15	1	–	–
Northern	3141	3	4	1	–	–	5	7	4	–	–
South West Thames	2968	–	2	2	–	1	2	8	4	–	–
South Western	2858	1	3	–	2	–	3	4	5	1	–
Wessex	2571	1	–	2	1	1	2	4	–	3	1
Mersey	2519	–	4	–	1	–	3	6	2	1	–
Oxford	2074	–	3	1	–	–	–	3	2	1	1
East Anglia	1677	–	2	1	–	–	–	4	2	1	–
	46031	14	41	19	10	6	32	105	54	11	3
WALES	2749	2	5	1	–	–	10	5	1	1	–
	48780	16	46	20	10	6	42	110	55	12	3

Source: DHSS Circular HRC(74)23 and Welsh Health and Personal Social Services Statistics 1974

Table 3 *Regional Health Authorities and Wales: Analysis of Area Health Authorities and Health Districts*

Regional Health Authority	AHAs	AHA(T)s	No. of Districts per AHA						Districts	Teaching Districts
			1	2	3	4	5	6		
West Midlands	11	1	7	–	2	1	1	–	22	1
Trent	8	3	3	1	3	1	–	1	18	7
North Western	11	2	9	–	1	–	–	1	18	3
North East Thames	6	2	–	3	2	–	1	–	17	4
South East Thames	5	1	1	1	1	1	–	1	16	3
Yorkshire	7	1	1	4	–	2	–	–	17	2
North West Thames	7	2	1	3	1	1	–	–	18	5
Northern	9	1	6	–	2	1	–	–	16	1
South West Thames	5	1	2	–	2	–	–	1	14	1
South Western	5	1	1	2	–	2	–	–	13	1
Wessex	4	1	1	2	1	1	–	–	10	1
Mersey	5	1	1	3	–	–	1	–	12	2
Oxford	4	1	–	1	2	–	–	–	7	1
East Anglia	3	1	–	1	2	–	–	–	7	1
	90	19	34	23	17	10	3	5	205	33
WALES	8	1	3	3	–	2	–	–	17	1
	98	20	37	26	17	12	3	3	222	34

Source: DHSS Circular, HRC(74)23 and Welsh Health and Personal Social Services Statistics 1974

district, 23 are divided into two districts, 16 have three districts, 11 have four districts, 3 have five districts and 3 have six districts (see Tables 2 and 3). In Wales there are 3 single district areas, 3 two-district areas, and 2 AHAs have four districts. The organisation and work of these districts will be described in the next chapter, but the arrangements for the single district areas are of relevance here, since their Area Teams of Officers have additional responsibilities.

Membership of the AHAs

The Chairman of each AHA is appointed by the Secretary of State, and paid a part-time salary. Some of the members are appointed directly by the Regional Health Authority, some by the RHA on the nomination of the university associated with the provision of health services in the region, some members directly by specified local authorities, and some additional members are appointed for each AHA(T). There were variations in the exact pattern of the initial appointments in England and Wales, but the majority of AHAs had fourteen members not including the Chairman, nine of them appointed by the RHA, four appointed by the local authority(ies) and one nominated by the university. For AHA(T)s there were two or three additional university nominations, and one or two people with experience of teaching hospital administration (e.g. members of former Boards of Governors of the teaching hospitals within the area) were also appointed by the RHA. (In Areas where more than one local authority is covered by the AHA, each local authority appointed two members, and in appropriate London AHAs there is one additional place for a nomination by the Inner London Education Authority.) Non-local authority members were appointed for four years, with half the members retiring after two years. Local authorities' members' tenure is determined by the local authority itself. Officers of the AHA or of its Districts are disqualified from being members of that particular AHA, although they could be appointed to other RHAs or AHAs.

The Labour Government which came to power after the General Election of February 1974 deemed their predecessor's scheme of health authority membership to be inadequate. In May of that year it published the consultative paper *Democracy in the National Health Service* that has been referred to in Chapter 1, and Barbara Castle (the new Secretary of State for Social Services) said of it: '[The Health Service] ... is run for the benefit of people. I believe that it will be better run and more democratically run, if those who use the service, through their local councillors, and those who work in it, through their representatives, have a greater say in the health authorities, and if the

Community Health Councils are strengthened. This Government is committed to transform the Area Health Authorities into democratic bodies.'[10] The proposals in the consultative paper were: each community health council (CHC) should have two of its members appointed to the AHA (and at least one of these should be a district councillor); one-third of the total AHA membership should be drawn from the local authorities; similarly one-third of the total RHA membership should be drawn from local authorities; two members of NHS staff other than doctors and nurses should serve on each of the RHAs and AHAs; a number of changes relating to CHCs should be made. (The latter will be discussed in Chapter 10.)

In July 1975, Mrs Castle announced that on the basis of comments received on these proposals, she had decided that one-third of the membership of AHAs and RHAs should be nominated by local authorities. However, in order to ensure that the membership did not, as a result, grow to an unwieldy size, she stated that after 1977, when the current terms of appointment would end, the number of new appointments would be restricted while preserving the proportionate balance between local authority and other members. She confirmed that provision had been made for two NHS staff (other than doctors and nurses) to become members of each RHA and AHA. In relation to CHCs, the decision was to allow one member from each CHC to attend meetings of their AHA with speaking but not with voting rights.

Originally people considered suitable for membership of authorities were defined by the DHSS not as representatives of either professional or consumer interests (which had channels of expression in the form of professional advisory committees and the community health councils) but as 'generalists' who would be free from partisan interests in relation to the health service. The Department nevertheless specified that at least two doctors and a nurse or midwife should be included in the membership. They thought that some younger people would, as members, make a useful contribution and that a range of backgrounds and perspectives amongst the membership would be likely to construct an authority capable of providing good leadership and sound judgement.

These decisions and recommendations about the AHA membership deserve closer scrutiny because they illustrate the DHSS's stand on certain controversial issues in the reorganisation debate. First, on the question of whether members should be representatives of particular interest groups, there is clearly a paradox since members of local authorities explicitly belong to political parties, and are elected by their constituents on the basis of their political intentions for the administration of the local authority. Yet on becoming members of the Area Health Authority, they are supposed to ignore this in favour of their knowledge and experience of local affairs. Similarly the interests of the users of the health services and the staff are not directly represented but referred instead to bodies which are outside the chain of authority. Formerly, some members of Hospital Management Committees and Boards of Governors were appointed precisely to give the consumers a voice in the management of the hospital. It was stated that the new authorities need to be responsive to local needs and views, both from the providers and consumers of the service, but the DHSS maintains that these are best placed outside the formal decision-taking structure, advising and commenting from the side-lines.

The belief expressed in the consultative paper that greater democracy could be achieved through these proposals represented an attempt to tackle the issue of health authority members' accountability to the users and providers of the services without having to make major revisions in the 1973 Act. It has already been shown that the RHAs have considerable power at their disposal through their own use of resources, and particularly through their control over the allocation of capital and revenue funds to the areas and districts. Similarly, although on a reduced scale, the AHAs have substantial power through their manipulation of budgets ranging from £30-£80 million.[11] The point is that because members of health authorities are appointed by (or on behalf of) the Secretary of State, they cannot be held directly responsible for their actions by the consumers and staff whose lives and work they influence. Corporate accountability means that the decisions of the authority are assessed as a whole, and are not differentiated into an assessment of the contribution of each member of the authority to those decisions. The implication is that local authority appointees take part in their AHA's deliberations without being bound by the interests of their local authority or political party. They are expected to abide by the consensus view of the AHA and support it publicly. Chairmen are also bound by the corporate accountability of their authority, and the salary they receive does not permit them to act as the 'manager' of their members, officers or any employees of the authority. The salary is merely meant to reflect the greater amount of time that the chairmen devote to the work of their authority. The consultative paper's proposals for achieving greater democracy are therefore somewhat confusing since it is acknowledged that the local authority appointees are not responsible for *representing* local authority interests on the AHA, but that they ' . . . provide a link with the people whom they have been elected to represent on the local authority'.[12] It still remains to be made explicit how they can really strengthen the democratic element in the local administration of the NHS, given their obligation to participate 'objectively' in the counsels of the health authority. Unless they can somehow bridge the gap between their conflicting local authority and health authority roles, they can play no special part in making the health authorities answerable to the staff and users of the NHS, in the matter of creating and implementing local policies for the administration of the services that necessarily take account of the views of those groups.[13]

The Work of AHAs

A distinctive feature of AHAs' duties is their dual responsibility for planning and providing services. They have not only to provide comprehensive health services including hospitals, community and domiciliary care, but also to study the health needs of the area, and find out where provision falls below required standards. Each AHA has to determine policies for provision and find the best way of putting them into effect with the resources allocated to it by the RHA. In addition, it has to give special attention to planning and providing services in conjunction with the matching local authority(ies). Again, as was the case with the RHAs, there has to be a division of labour because members serve on a voluntary basis, giving perhaps two or three days a month to the policy-making and resource allocation matters. The day-to-day executive responsibilities are delegated to the Area Team of Officers (ATO), to individual officers at area level, to the District Management Teams (DMTs) and individual district officers. The activities handled in the districts (in other than single-district areas) are the basic services associated with the district hospital, the community health services formerly run by the local authority health departments, and the school health service. These functions will be discussed in Chapter 4. The Area Team of Officers has to coordinate the work of the DMTs, but it also has to advise the AHA on developing area-wide policies, informing them of particular local needs and circumstances to be taken into consideration.

Individual Members of the ATO

The ATO is composed of the Area Medical Officer, Area Nursing Officer, Area Treasurer and Area Administrator. Each officer has a departmental organisation to support him in carrying out his particular professional responsibilities as well as his duties as a member of the ATO. The Area Medical Officer advised the ATO on health care policies and recommends planning guidelines for the districts in line with these

policies. He also advises the AHA on the interpretation and use of
advice from his professional colleagues and promotes research and
trials into improving health care methods. He has particular
responsibilities for child health services in connection with the local
authority, and for developing the work of clinicians in the public
health field. The Area Nursing Officer contributes to the ATO on
matters of planning and policy, and is particularly responsible for the
development of integrated nursing services between the hospitals and

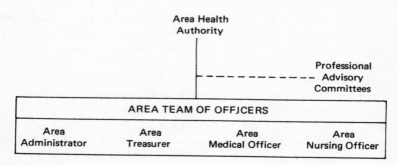

Figure 8 *The Area Team of Officers*

Source: Management Arrangement for the Reorganised National Health Service,
HMSO, 1972

the community. She has to advise on the running of the school nursing
services and on staffing provision for residential care institutions
in the area. Professional training facilities are also her concern and she
advises on nursing personnel policies. The Area Treasurer provides
financial advice to the AHA in respect of its budget and expenditure.
He prepares the area accounts and ensures proper adherence to its
policies by the districts, and is responsible for the complete paymaster
function, including salaries and wages and the payment of all accounts.
The Family Practitioner Committee receives financial services from his
department. The Area Administrator has several roles. He acts as
secretary to the Area Health Authority and coordinator of the Area
Team of Officers. He prepares advice for the AHA on the development
of area-wide policies, issues policy guidelines to the District
Management Teams and implements approved Area plans. He
contributes to the Area Team of Officers on planning and policy and
is responsible for coordinating and preparing the AHA's formal
planning proposals. He is directly responsible for a number of functions

managed by other officers, namely, personnel, supplies, ambulance and capital planning. The Family Practitioner Services Administrator is also responsible to him for some aspects of his job. In addition the Area Administrator coordinates the work of the Area Works Officer and Area Pharmaceutical Officer. He provides administrative support for all the AHA headquarters activities.

It is clear that if AHAs are to function as an effective link in the chain of delegated authority, much depends on the ATO's ability to moderate policies handed down from the region in a manner that is sensitive to district circumstances, and that is respectful of the DMTs' sphere of authority. The DMT and ATO officers are on the same managerial level, so the ATO cannot give orders to the DMT nor be held accountable for their work. It is (in all but single district areas) the DMT and not the ATO which is responsible for the actual operation of health care services. The role of the ATO in relation to the districts is a monitoring one, which means that the area officers can persuade their counterparts in the districts to conform to policies, and can interpret AHA intentions to them. But if they are not satisfied with the outcome they must refer the issue to the AHA for a decision about what action might be taken. In the case of the relationship between the ATO and the Regional Team of Officers, each set of officers is accountable to its own authority, so in no sense does a manager-subordinate relationship exist between them. Regional officers can give advice and guidance to their counterparts on the ATO and persuade them to act in particular ways, but if they are dissatisfied with the Area Officers' performance, their recourse is only to the RHA, which must decide what to do.[14]

In AHAs with relatively small populations there are no subdivisions into districts, and these areas therefore have no DMTs, district officers or district budgets. The four members of the ATO are joined by a representative consultant and a representative general practitioner to form an Area Management Team who, in addition to the activities described, also take on the work of a District Management Team (to be described in the next chapter). This arrangement applies to thirty-four of the ninety AHAs in England and three of the eight AHAs in Wales, i.e. 37 per cent of all AHAs.[15]

Collaboration with Local Authorities

Throughout the debate on the reorganisation it was accepted that improved health care could not become effective without the involvement of the personal social services at all stages from planning to delivery. The Porritt report stated, '. . .the separation of the social services . . .

from the other health services has proved in our view one of the main stumbling blocks to a properly coordinated service'.[16] But when the Second Green Paper announced that health would be administered separately from local government, ways of bringing health and social services closer together had to be found, in order that the concept of comprehensive community care might become a reality. The two relevant features of the reorganisation in this respect are (a) the creation of Joint Consultative Committees, and (b) the added emphasis given to community medicine, particularly through the work of doctors designated Area Specialists in Community Medicine. First the Joint Consultative Committees (JCCs) — the Working Party on Collaboration between the NHS and Local Government (set up by the Secretary of State in 1971) recommended that in each AHA matched to a metropolitan district, a single JCC with membership from the AHA and the metropolitan district council should cover health, social services and education. In AHAs matched to a non-metropolitan county, one JCC with membership from the AHA and the county council should cover social services and education, and a second JCC with common AHA membership and district and county council members should cover environmental health and housing. (The reasons for this lie in the different allocation of functions between metropolitan and non-metropolitan authorities.[17]) The JCCs meet four or more times each year, and are supported by working groups of senior officers who meet regularly to ensure that day-to-day operation of the services is working smoothly, that joint development plans in fields of mutual concern are worked out for the JCC, and that early action is taken on the JCC's decisions.[18] For each AHA the Area Specialist in Community Medicine (Social Services) is the link between it and the local authority Social Services Department. Dental and nursing officers are also appointed to provide the local authority with appropriate professional advice and services. Reciprocally, a senior officer of the Social Services Department gives advice and social work support to the AHA.

The Social Services Department is a single agency concerned with the whole range of problems affecting families, deploying its social work and other limited resources to cope with needs that are being identified on a rapidly advancing scale. Implementation of the Seebohm report recommendations initially followed the 'generic' approach in which each social worker dealt with the whole range of problems, rather than specialising in children, the deaf, the handicapped, or family casework, for example. But the tendency has, since then, been rather more in favour of maintaining these distinct professional abilities while still unifying the

first point of contact between a client and the whole resources of the
Social Services Department, and the Working Party on Collaboration
supported this trend. It also recognised that medical social workers
formerly employed as a unit by the hospital authorities should still
work in the same way, even though they had become employees of the
local authority Social Services Department, in order to preserve their
contribution to the teamwork approach to care of hospital patients.
The Working Party further recommended that attachment of social
workers to general practices should be developed, especially in health
centres.[19]

The local authorities in their role as education authorities have had
their responsibility for the school health service transferred to the AHAs,
although they still operate some parts of the special education services
for handicapped children in conjunction with the health authority. The
detailed aspects of the school health service are operated at district
level, and the Area Specialist in Community Medicine (Child Health)
coordinates these with support from the Area Dental and Nursing
Officers. Environmental health has remained outside the NHS with
the local authorities, and includes the removal of refuse, the sanitary
inspection of public hygiene, orders under the Clean Air Act 1958,
open spaces, public baths, disinfestation, inspections under the Food
and Drugs Act 1955, inspections under the Offices Shops and Railway
Premises Act 1963. (Water supply and sewerage are managed by the
new water authorities.) An Area Specialist in Community Medicine
is recognised in non-metropolitan counties matched to single district
areas as their 'proper officer' responsible for environmental health,
and in all other cases the District Community Physician is so
recognised. The designation, formerly given to the Medical Officer
of Health, is a legal requirement under the Local Government Act
1972, Section 112.[20]

The tone of the advice issued to authorities by the DHSS on
collaboration was general, in order to allow local arrangements to be
made that would suit local circumstances and it stated that
'. . . the aim of the collaborative proposals is to create an atmosphere
of ready and informal cooperation at member and officer level so
that the two sets of authorities can, despite their differing functions
and structures, coordinate their services for the benefit of people
in their area'.[21]   In its reports the Working Party made a number of
other recommendations in connection with housing, publicity, supplies,
building and engineering, management services and statistics, ancillary
services, and some other topics. It did not deal with the joint planning
of capital projects, which would have been an anticipated area of vital

cooperation, albeit a complicated one, given the two authorities' different sources of finance, and the absence of established national norms for such provision (but see final paragraph on p. 87).

To complete this account of AHAs' work, four other items should be mentioned: (a) health education, (b) liaison with voluntary organisations, (c) liaison with universities, and (d) the family practitioner services. Health education, transferred from the local authorities, is intended to be an important contribution to the prevention of ill-health. The Area Medical Officer is usually assisted by an Area Health Education Officer (and supporting staff transferred from the local authority) in promoting health education in the schools and colleges of the area, and in giving advice to professionals working in the health service. This subject had been seriously neglected in the past, and it was hoped that the setting up of a national Health Education Council would give a boost to local efforts, although any really notable developments remain to become effective.[22] On the other hand, the tradition of voluntary effort, particularly in the hospital service, is a long and successful one. Many hospitals have employed a voluntary services organiser to coordinate this work. Many health and welfare services that have been missing from public provision have, through single-minded voluntary effort, become well established, and later subsidised or even taken over by the State. An example current at the time of the reorganisation was the work of the Family Planning Association which, through sessional employment of doctors and nurses in its own clinics had been providing professional advice and supplies of contraceptive pills and appliances to a steadily broadening part of the population. The Secretary of State decided to take this work into the NHS over a two-year period from 1975-76, during which the Family Planning Association would be paid on a fee basis for providing their services on behalf of the NHS, and after which the Area Health Authorities would themselves run the services. In other cases, the National Health Service Reorganisation Act 1973 empowers health authorities to make grants and payments to voluntary organisations acting in the personal health and social services fields, and to make premises and facilities available to them.

Liaison with universities was given new emphasis in the reorganisation, particularly since the management of undergraduate teaching hospitals has been brought into the scope of the AHA(T)s, and their membership reflects this added responsibility. The intention is to improve facilities available for teaching and research to the universities, and equally, to enable a wider spectrum of the population to benefit from the specialist knowledge and skills of staff employed by them. Liaison committees have been set up at regional and area levels to facilitate this collaboration, and the participation of the Dean of the Medical School in teaching DMTs will also help these links.

The family practitioner services involve the work of general practitioners, dentists, pharmacists and opticians, which will be discussed in Chapters 5 and 6. Responsibility for administration of these services resides at area level, with the Family Practitioner Committee (FPC) set up by the AHA. FPCs are very similar to their predecessors, the Executive Councils, in terms of their membership and duties. The FPC consists of 30 members, 11 appointed by the AHA, 4 appointed by the local authority, 8 by the local medical committee (one of whom must be an ophthalmic medical practitioner), 3 by the local dental committee, 2 by the local pharmaceutical committee, and 2 by the local optical committee (1 of whom must be an ophthalmic optician, and the other a dispensing optician). The FPC has to make arrangements for the provision of family practitioner services, to publish lists of all practitioners undertaking NHS work in the area, to pay those practitioners under contract with it from Exchequer funds (i.e. direct finance from the DHSS channelled through the AHA but separate from the AHA's budget), and to investigate complaints. The Executive Councils were quite independent bodies, like their predecessors the Insurance Committees, but the FPC is a statutory health authority established, staffed and funded by the Area Health Authority. Its chief officer, the Administrator (Family Practitioners Services) as well as serving the Family Practitioner Committee, is also directly accountable to the Area Administrator in respect of his work on health centres and attachment schemes. He has to work closely with area and district staff in these matters, and can therefore contribute significantly to the AHA's plans for professional manpower and services development. Although the arrangement is not an integrated one *in so far as family practitioners remain independent contractors administered separately from the hospital and community services) by making the Family Practitioner Services Administrator accountable to the Area Administrator and having some common membership between the AHA and the FPC, the intention clearly is to bring this part of the service closer to the rest of the NHS, especially for planning purposes.[23]

The AHA needs to appoint 'managers' to undertake its obligations in respect of the Mental Health Act 1959[24] (including the discharge of patients detained in psychiatric hospitals), some of whom are members of the authority. *Ad hoc* committees including authority members are also necessary for the selection of certain staff (senior medical and dental staff in AHA(T)s as well as all other senior staff), and to hear disciplinary matters.

However the DHSS guidance discourages AHAs from appointing standing committees to deal with parts of its functions, preferring the membership as a whole to be involved. But the AHA has the statutory duty to recognise advisory committees of the professions, just as the regions and the DHSS do. Area Advisory Committees may be formed for medical, nursing and midwifery, dental, pharmaceutical and optical services, to advise the AHA on matters relating to their professional spheres, and to be consulted on important developments in the area's health services.

4 THE DISTRICTS

The Definition of Districts

There are two distinct but related principles associated with the reorganisation — improved management and improved health care. From the management point of view, the districts represent the level of organisation at which health services are provided to people. From the health care point of view, the districts represent the scale of units within which the NHS can respond efficiently to the specific needs of the local people. But improved management does not necessarily mean improved health care, especially if the authority to direct the use of resources (at a level of management that is remote from the central department) is limited. And this point is at the centre of the argument about what health districts can and should achieve. They are not a statutory tier of authority, which means that they are not recognised or mentioned by name in the National Health Service Reorganisation Act, 1973. The legislation is worded in such a way as to permit RHAs and AHAs, as agents of the Secretary of State, to delegate certain of their functions to other bodies, while retaining responsibility for the end result.

Nevertheless, AHAs did not have a free choice as to whether they should delegate some of their functions to districts, because the Second Green Paper, the Consultative Document and the White Paper all laid down that districts should exist to manage the operation of the NHS at a local level. The latitude was in deciding how many districts each AHA should create, and the Joint Liaison Committees (the forerunners of the Joint Consultative Committees) were given the task of recommending district boundaries within each area. Thirty-seven areas in England and Wales were found suitable for management as single-district areas, and the rest arranged for between two and six districts each. Single-district areas should not be regarded as areas without districts, but as areas where the Area Team of Officers can satisfactorily handle the detailed arrangements for the delivery of health care to their population, with the addition of a consultant and a general practitioner to form an Area Management Team.

The concept of a 'natural' health care district put forward by the Grey Book[1] is sketched out on the basis of the number of patients on an average general practitioner's list. It suggests that if each GP looks after about 2,500 people, then a group practice of five GPs might have a combined list of 12,500. Two such group practices working together from a health centre with attached home nurses and health visitors (and forming a 'primary care team') could serve a population of 25,000. A social work area team consisting of ten social workers could expect to cover a population of 50,000, and therefore complement the work of two 'primary care teams'. The Grey Book goes on to suggest that ten primary care teams, with responsibility for 250,000 people, would expect to look after 60,000 children, 35,000 people over the age of 65, 7,000 severely handicapped people of all ages, 700 mentally handicapped people, 2,500 people with mental illness. 19,000 of their patients would have acute episodes of medical or surgical illness requiring admission to hospital each year, 550 of them being inpatients at any one time. This pattern of illness has for some time been thought best catered for by a district general hospital with consultant specialist staff including 5 general surgeons, 5 general physicians, 6 psychiatrists, 3 obstetricians and gynaecologists, 2 paediatricians, 1 geriatrician and 1 dental surgeon, together with appropriate community health services. This is only a 'model' district, and district populations actually range from about 85,000 to about 500,000 as Table 2 in the last chapter shows. The actual population range indicates that district boundaries have in practice often been defined according to parameters other than GPs' work patterns. The most likely one is the catchment area of a hospital — the surrounding locality from which patients admitted to and attending the hospital most frequently come. In a minority of places, the district boundaries have been defined either in relation to well-established district or parish boundaries, or following physical features (a large river or a range of hills) that have traditionally identified neighbouring communities as being distinct. The Joint Liaison Committees were instructed to make their recommendations in the light of patient flow patterns primarily, even if these did cut across existing boundaries for local government or other agencies. In London, however, the situation is so complex that a committee specially appointed to determine the best way for districts to be defined, decided that even catchment areas would have to be ignored in some cases. However, even though the boundaries for all districts were finally decided, it is worth pointing out that the variety of hospital and community resources between districts is considerable. Many districts do not have a single general hospital, but a number of small specialist and general hospitals which together provide the necessary inpatient and outpatient facilities. But very many districts are seriously underprovided, either with hospitals or with community services.[2]

The District Management Team

The responsibility for the district health services rests, initially, with the District Management Team (DMT). This is composed of a nursing officer and a finance officer, an administrator and a community physician, together with the Chairman and Vice-Chairman of the District Medical Committee (who represent the local consultants and general practitioners). The team is assisted by a number of district officers, and, in districts which contain a teaching hospital, a university representative (usually the Dean of the Medical School) attends DMT meetings. Almost all district officers manage aspects of the day-to-day operational work of the health services, and those four officers who are also members of the DMT have additional responsibilities for planning the overall development of their local services (see Figure 9). An interesting feature of the DMT is that of the basic six members, three are doctors, one from each branch of the profession: a general practitioner, a hospital consultant and a specialist in community medicine. Their membership represents the DHSS's acknowledgement of the necessity to involve doctors more closely in the detailed management of the health service, particularly because clinicians are in a position to influence the rate and range of consumption of resources. Maintaining the principle of clinical freedom means that health authorities have to rely on the cooperation of their doctors in trying to achieve a balanced and economical distribution of resources; it must have been realised that by involving doctors more closely in the problems of resource allocation, a greater degree of control might be achieved.

Accordingly, the District Medical Committee is an innovation of the reorganisation which permits medical professional advice to be made to the DMT while at the same time bringing together GPs, hospital and community doctors in a formal body. About eighteen members are nominated — six from the local representative committee of GPs, six from the hospital doctors, probably through the 'Cogwheel' divisions (these will be explained in the next chapter) and six doctors working in community medicine, including the District Community Physician. The District Medical Committee makes recommendations to the DMT on matters of medical policy and practice, and exists particularly to influence district plans in line with its views for spending the district's resources appropriately. Its Chairman and Vice-Chairman, as full member of the DMT, can voice these views directly to the DMT, so the new arrangements secure a far greater scope for doctors' involvement in decision-making. However, in practice, there is evidence that some DMCs have not been contributing views and ideas to their DMTs with sustained enthusiasm. This may be because the discussions of planning

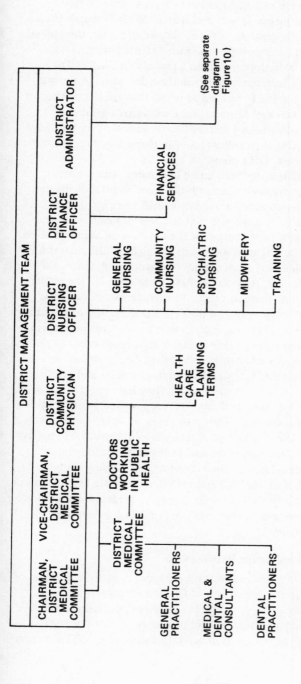

Figure 9 *District Organisation*

Source: Management Arrangements for the Reorganised National Health Service, HMSO, 1972

proposals that they are required to have lack immediate interest. General practitioner members may feel that since the hospitals automatically consume the great majority of district resources, the general level of interest and commitment they wish to foster towards their sector through the DMC does not stand a reasonable chance. The Chairman and Vice-Chairman have to use their discretion in the way they participate in the DMT, which also works through the method of consensus decision-making. Although they will learn a great deal about the business of managing district health services, they may have difficulty in interesting their colleagues or in persuading them of the advantages of particular DMT plans.

Some DMTs have initially been based in existing NHS premises, which in some cases are associated with the main hospital of the district, even though separate accommodation might be regarded as preferable, in order to demonstrate that the present health service administration is not a continuation of the old hospital administration. DMT meetings are usually held weekly or fortnightly, although the pattern varies considerably from district to district, and, unlike the RHA and AHA meetings, they do not have to be open for the public and press to attend. At these meetings the members work out their objectives for the coming year, and the detailed allocation of resources between departments. Their major concern is to allocate and monitor the use of the limited money made available to them in order to provide the quantity and quality of health services that they regard as necessary. They give detailed attention to capital building projects and priorities for minor building and maintenance work. They have constantly to review the staffing situation, and may become involved in negotiations concerning industrial disputes. They make seek to work cooperatively with neighbouring DMTs over such matters as joint consultant appointments or the payroll arrangements, and foster close working relations with the environmental health, social services and housing departments. Each member of the DMT needs to communicate team decisions to colleagues and senior staff, in order to ensure these are understood as widely as possible, and to take many minor decisions covering all aspects of local activity.

Monitoring and Coordinating Relationships

The DMT's freedom to make executive decisions is partly a function of its relationship with the Area Team of Officers (except in single-district areas); if for example the ATO exercises tight budgetary and administrative policy control, this will obviously restrict the DMT's ability to carry out autonomous policies. In theory, the ATO members each *monitor* their counterparts on the DMT, while all the officers are *accountable* to the AHA. The distinction is very important because in the monitoring relationship, there must be no suggestion of a manager-subordinate arrangement. A monitor cannot tell people what to do, he can merely try to persuade them to conform to policies. Equally he is not responsible for the work of the people he monitors, and therefore does not have or need the authority to give them orders. Taking the Area Administrator's relationship with a District Administrator as an example, both officers are accountable to the Area Health Authority and may be held responsible by the AHA for the standard of their own work and the work of their subordinates; hence they have legitimate authority to tell their subordinates what to do. But the Area Administrator may not tell the District Administrator what to do, nor may he be held responsible for the District Administrator's work by the AHA. He is only allowed to work cooperatively with the District Administrator, although he is obliged to tell him what the AHA requires of him and his fellow DMT members. The Area Administrator is the voice and spokesman of the AHA, and it is he who judges whether issues that arise must be referred to the AHA, to the chairman, or to be dealt with by officers. The District Administrator does, however, have the right to go directly to the AHA or to the chairman, and it is becoming more common for DMTS to be represented at the regular meetings of the AHA. In practice some ATO/DMT relationships have developed into the situation where members of the ATO have effectively assumed line management control over those working at district level. The serious implication of this is that in any dispute they may have with the area officers, the DMT come to feel that the outcome will always favour the ATO, jeopardising their sense of local responsibility and autonomy. (A similar imbalance has also developed between some ATOs and their counterparts at regional level.)

One member of the DMT often acts as chairman in order to ensure the orderly running of the meetings although some DMTs have preferred a more flexible arrangement, whereby each member initiates discussions on matters falling within his area of concern. Like the teams of officers in area and regional administration, DMTs also operate through consensus management. So although each DMT member has the power to veto a decision, this is very rarely used since it would tend to work against that member's interests in the longer term. If open disagreements do arise, they must be referred to the AHA. The administrator provides the secretarial support for DMT meetings. He is also responsible for *coordinating* the work of the DMT — this means that the AHA can hold him responsible for seeing that DMT gets its work done. None of the DMT members are each other's managers or subordinates, so the administrator cannot be held responsible for the quality of the members' work; but he can monitor their progress on agreed plans, make firm proposals for action, and decide what should be done in situations of uncertainty. In addition to this, the district administrator is responsible for all non-medical and non-nursing aspects of the hospital and community services. A typical arrangement is shown in Figure 10. There are two senior officers under the district administrator who are responsible (with the help of outposted sector administrators) for all the hospital services, for office and secretarial support for the DMT and other committees, and for liaison with outside bodies such as the social services department, the community health council, and other public relations duties. The sector administrators are each responsible for managing or coordinating the institutional and support services within single large institutions or within groups of institutions within sectors of the district. Individual districts vary in the way they have identified their sectors, although there appears to be a tendency to separate the administration of hospital and community services along the lines of the pre-1974 arrangements.[3]

The District Community Physician (DCP) gives advice to the DMT on the planning and improvement of health care facilities, and has a particularly important role in coordinating the health care planning teams, which will be described later in this chapter. He is closely involved with the community medical staff (those doctors who formerly worked for the department of the Medical Officer of Health) covering aspects of the child and school health services, and he gives advice to the local authority on environmental health matters and may act as their proper officer for the local control and action following outbreaks of infectious diseases. Through his membership of the District Medical Committee he has important links with the hospital doctors and GPs and can be influential in encouraging them to consider ideas for improving the health services. A problem concerning the role of the DCP is that he has virtually no exclusive responsibilities for managing staff and services, and some of his senior colleagues (the Area Medical Officer and Area Specialists in Community Medicine, in particular) may be unwilling to see this change. The consequence of being allocated a mainly advisory and coordinating role without directly subordinate staff can be to weaken the DCP's effective influence over district health services planning and management.

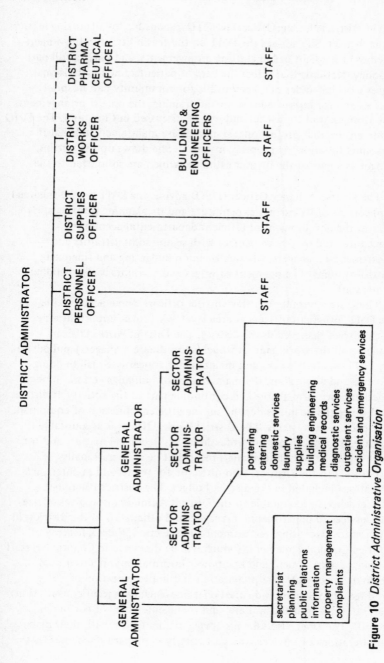

Figure 10 *District Administrative Organisation*

Source: Management Arrangements for the Reorganised National Health Service, HMSO, 1972

The District Nursing Officer (DNO) is responsible for all nursing matters in the district. She advises the DMT on the feasibility of improvement schemes in the light of her staffing arrangements, and plays a full part in policy decisions that affect the care of patients. She has divisional nurses working under her, responsible for community and hospital services and for nurses' education and training; the precise arrangements vary from district to district and will be discussed in Chapter 7. The DNO has to ensure that professional standards are maintained and that the personnel function[4] is properly managed. She draws up the nursing budget as a part of the district estimates which are submitted to the AHA.

The District Finance Officer (DFO) advises the DMT on the financial implications of its current expenditure and its planning proposals. He ensures the development of efficient departmental accounting procedures and may have contact with sector administrators and departmental managers, advising them on budgeting and financial control systems. The payment of wages and accounts is also handled by his staff.

There are a number of other district officers, some accountable to the DMT, others to officers at area level, who cover important aspects of the duties managed in the district. The District Works Officer manages all the works staff (through subordinate managers) and advises the DMT on all its works and maintenance concerns. Small building projects and alterations, the maintenance of buildings and machinery together constitute a large and continuing part of the activity at district level, since the hospitals depend on the efficient function of equipment and mechanical systems. The District Works Officer is accountable to the Area Works Officer on professional and technical matters and for some aspect of personnel management, but he is operationally responsible to the District Administrator for works and maintenance operations included in the district budget. The District Personnel Officer, who is accountable to the District Administrator, gives advice and services to departmental managers and other staff in the district, in relation to advertising; recruitment and selection; the application of Whitley Council agreements (which will be discussed in Chapter 8); staff training; establishment and manpower information; organisational deployment of staff; the preparation and implementation of productivity schemes; industrial relations (including joint consultation), staff safety, health and welfare, and the maintenance of personnel records. The DMT also take his advice in connection with their plans for alterations of services, and particularly in preparing schemes that involve multi-disciplinary work. The District Pharmaceutical Officer manages the pharmaceutical services of hospitals and clinics through principal and staff pharmacists. This involves maintaining their dispensing facilities to inpatients and outpatients and supervising security measures. He gives advice to the DMC on the economical use of medicines and on new technical developments in the pharmaceutical industry, and maintains contact with dispensing chemists in the district who are under contract to the Family Practitioner Committee. The District Pharmaceutical Officer is monitored by the District Administrator and is held accountable to the Area Pharmaceutical Officer, although the District Administrator is responsible for the coordination of the district-wide pharmaceutical services.

District Health Services

'Primary care' covers those services that people can generally obtain by making a direct approach, and therefore includes the four family practitioner services and various community-based services. 'Secondary care' refers to hospital and residential services which usually have to be obtained by referral on from the first point of contact. This division is not absolute and clearly should not be since the more integrated the services are, the more rational will be the care that they offer. But for the purposes of description it is convenient to look at the range of health services available in a district under these headings.

Primary Care

The focus for primary care has for many years been seen as the health centre. For purpose built premises a great range of preventive and curative services can be provided. Several GPs can practice individually or in groups from the health centre, and their patients also have access to chiropody, family planning, cervical cytology, vaccination, speech therapy and many other services. Dentists can also have surgeries in the health centre and chemists and opticians can have premises associated with it. This is an ideal description which fits very few existing health centres, and it is also true that the rate of building health centres has been very slow. The result is that standards of primary care are very variable, and lack the degree of coordination which health centres could provide. Before 1974 the local authorities built and owned health centres and rented them to GPs. Now the AHAs have this responsibility, although the DMT is closely involved in plans for new developments, as is the FPC Administrator.[5] The other community services falling within the DMT's management include clinics for expectant and nursing mothers, child health and school health examinations and clinics, family planning, cytology, chiropody, speech therapy, physiotherapy and vaccination and immunisation. Medical staff, nursing staff and para-medical staff working in the community sector attend clinics through-out the district on a sessional basis, and hold some school-health sessions on school premises.

There is a certain amount of domiciliary work — home nurses and health visitors particularly have very close contact with certain groups of patients and their families. Much of the reorganisation's hopes for a radical development of community care rests on the work of these people. Home nurses attend to patients who, living at home, are unable to arrange for adequate care of their health; this includes old people, disabled people, patients convalescing after discharge from hospital and patients with terminal illness. The nurses may be required to change dressings, give injections and other medication, bath people and attend to those who are incontinent. Health visitors visit every mother within ten days of the birth of a new baby, and continue to observe the baby's development until it is 5 years old. They also visit families to give advice on all sorts of health matters, and can act as a vital link between individuals and many aspects of the personal health and social services. Some general practitioners work closely with home nurses and health visitors, and depend on them to complement the services that they can give to patients on their lists. The community services are, by their nature, better known to the local population, partly because they are associated with preventive and health care work rather than with acute illness, and also because the siting of clinics in or near shopping streets makes them and their staff familiar in the locality.

Hospital and Residential Care

As a contrast, the district general hospitals may often be more remote places to most of the local population. The optimum size for a district general hospital is about 800 beds, for which the range of support services are provided, including catering, portering and domestic services, laundry, centrally sterilised and other supplies, medical records and engineering, as well as paramedical and laboratory staff and the range of outpatients facil-ities. Most of the district general hospital's work has not been affected by the reorganisation, and the supporting services are provided from depart-ments with often long established routines and relations with each other. The sector administrator's work is very similar to that of the former hos-pital secretary in coordinating all aspects of these services, although some individual departmental managers may have contact with colleagues and senior officers in their occupation at district or area level.[6] Not all districts yet have a district general hospital, their services being provided by a number of smaller and specialist hospitals.

However, in August 1974 the DHSS issued a paper on community hospitals which confirmed that as a long term aim, hospitals situated nearer where people live, for those patients who do not require or no longer need the specialist services of the district general hospitals, should be provided in the districts. Some existing local and cottage hospitals are suitable for adaptation while some new community hospitals may be built. With between fifty and 150 beds they can offer outpatient, day-patient and inpatient care for people who cannot receive adequate care in their own homes, or who do not require highly specialised investigations and care, or who would benefit from being cared for closer to their families and community. The facilities can act as a bridge between hospital care and the work of the 'primary care team', and to that extent, should have close links with local health centres in addition to holding some consultant outpatient clinics. Geriatric patients, some chronically sick and disabled people, and those with terminal illnesses could be appropriately admitted to community hospitals as a preferable alternative to the district general hospital. Other patients requiring minor medical or surgical treatment (that a general practitioner would be able to provide in his surgery) would also be preferably cared for with the treatment facilities of the community hospital; dental treatment and minor surgery could also be provided for the inpatients and for the local people. Community hospitals depend largely on staff already living in the locality, including some who prefer to work part-time. The twenty-four-hour nursing service is staffed by both full- and part-time nurses and nursing auxiliaries, with some nurse members of the primary care team joining them, while local general practitioners are responsible for the day-to-day medical care of the patients, in cooperation with appropriate consultants from the district general hospital. Community hospitals could be a significant asset in both urban and rural districts, and will probably be established gradually where buildings suitable for conversion already exist. The enormous sums of money needed to build and run district general hospitals are now much scarcer, and there is also a feeling that these very large scale developments have limitations in terms of the personal quality of care they can provide. In 1975 in response to these trends the DHSS offered an alternative concept for hospital design and construction, called the nucleus hospital. It is a standardised scheme for a 300 bed unit with the usual range of supporting departments, costing up to £6m (1975 prices). The flexible design permits further modules to be added as the need arises; the first nucleus hospital will open in Newham in about 1979. Throughout the country the entire hospital building programme has had to be modified because of financial difficulties, and in some districts small, under-used hospitals are being closed down to release resources for other services. Purpose built community hospitals and nucleus hospitals are therefore unlikely to be built in significant numbers for many years to come.

The hospitals where people with psychiatric disorders and mental handicaps are cared for represent a distinct category with special problems. Historically they have been built separately from other hospitals and away from residential areas, and for a number of reasons have attracted too little money and interest from staff. Although mental illness and mental handicap patients occupy 44 per cent of all hospital beds, they form the most disadvantaged group in terms of the quality of services provided for them. These hospitals and their associated outpatient and day care services fall within the DMT's responsibility and present a major challenge if conditions are to improve.

Residential care is provided in the community for old people, people with mental and physical handicaps, patients convalescing after hospital treatment, and people returning to the community after discharge from a mental hospital. These homes and hostels are for the most part the responsibility of the social services department, and although the numbers of fully trained medical and nursing staff working in them may be small, health authorities need to arrange for close liaison with the social services departments so that these valuable resources are used to the full. The status of residential community care is changing as long stays in hospitals are being regarded as an increasingly unsatisfactory way of helping these sections of the population. Comparatively little money has been spent nationally on sheltered housing schemes, but as the policy to confine most hospital admissions to episodes of acute illness continues, much more attention will need to be paid to these alternative forms of care.

In addition, more imaginative uses of hospital facilities can develop if the supporting services in the community are properly organised. For example, a study of the number of days people may stay in hospital for routine surgical procedures or diagnostic tests shows that these types of admissions may be wasteful of patients' time and hospital resources. There are a few centres where programmed discharge policies are being used for such conditions as surgical repair of hernia and varicose veins, termination of pregnancy and diagnostic assessment of cardiac functioning. Patients stay in the hospital for up to five days, depending on the treatment they are to receive, and their convalescence is managed in their own homes with the support of community nursing staff and GPs. If any complications arise, they can continue to stay in the hospital, but the idea is that the very costly and limited resources of the hospital are exploited fully for treating acute episodes that require specialist facilities, and recovery is managed in the home, where it is much less expensive, and preferable for the patient. Success of these schemes depends on an intelligent hospital admissions policy and on very close liaison between the professional staff in the hospital and community. The intention of the NHS reorganisation is to facilitate just this type of cooperation, but as one critic has observed, ' . . . the hopes or fears entertained of the . . . new structure are probably extravagant. The same people will be providing and managing services as now [pre-1974], and the existing deficiencies are probably less susceptible to improvement through mere administrative change than through adjustments in deep-rooted professional attitudes. Future developments in the administrative relationships between the various sectors of health care will be severely conditioned, as they have been in the past, by attitudes to the role of the hospital.'[7]

Health Care Planning Teams

Nevertheless, the foundations for a serious attempt to bring the health care sectors together through joint involvement of individual members of the professions has been made through the creation of health care planning teams. Their task is to consider the whole range of health and related services which people with common characteristics or problems need to use. These groups of people would probably be identified as the elderly; children; the mentally ill; the mentally handicapped; expectant and nursing mothers; the physically handicapped, to mention some of them. The idea is that each team should examine the present provision of services for their patient group and make recommendations to the DMT for improvements, based on their assessment of the needs of that group. The teams are therefore a formal part of the planning process, and through sensitive attention to the findings of health care planning teams, the DMTs have a real chance to alter the distribution of resources within the district, in response to local needs.

The teams are set up by the AHA, with advice from the ATO and DMT, and the DMT determines the remit and membership of each team so established. Most teams will include a general practitioner, a hospital and a community nurse, a health visitor, a hospital doctor and a member of the relevant paramedical profession, each with intimate knowledge of the patient group being studied. People outside the health service, such as members of voluntary organisations or local authorities may well also become members because of their particular experience, and some other individuals such as members of community health councils may be coopted. Each

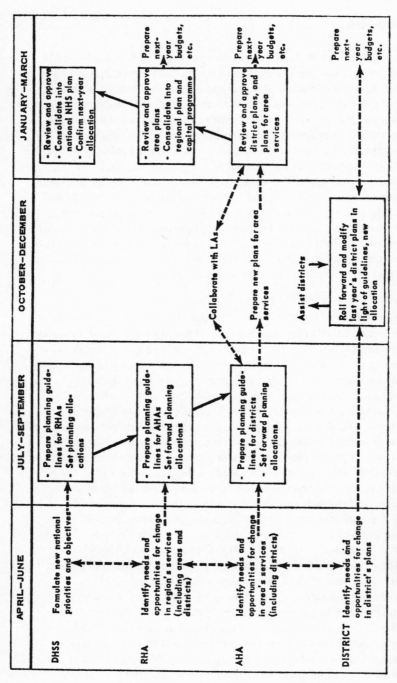

Figure 11 *Annual NHS Planning Cycle*

Source: Management Arrangements for the Reorganised National Health Service, HMSO, 1972

district may have several of these teams, some with permanent membership, which aim to review the care of their patient group over a ten-year period, while other teams may have a shorter life, in order to study a more specific problem of care, such as the introduction of day surgery or the reorganisation of an outpatient department. The success of the health care planning teams really depends on the interest and enthusiasm of their members, and on the attention that the DMT pays to their work when drawing up its planning proposals. The work can demand a lot of time and effort, and the DCP's role in organising and supporting the teams is a particularly important factor. He is a member of each team and, with administrative assistance, convenes the meeting, attends to the documentation, and may carry out special studies and projects for the teams. His contact with the DCPs in neighbouring districts and with the Area Specialists in Community Medicine, combined with his role as a member of the DMT means that he can be the key figure in stimulating beneficial change.

The Planning Cycle

The planning cycle (which was mentioned in Chapter 2) is the formal system through which plans made at district level can be reconciled with objectives conceived at national level, while taking into account the need to establish priorities for action at all levels with each year (see Figure 11). The district plan is a comprehensive assessment of all the health needs of the community, and proposals for deploying the broad range of health services required to meet those needs. It is drawn up in the light of resources expected to be available to the district, based on early guidelines from the DHSS, identifying the total revenue expenditure, capital building and personnel requirements necessary in order to achieve the planned level of service. The plan also specifies short, medium and long-term objectives, giving detailed requirements for the coming year, and looking forward as much as ten years on, outlining the broad directions of change. The area team of officers (who may be consulted by DMTs) assess the plans prepared by the districts, and recommend the balance between the claims that the AHA should submit to the RHA. Similarly the RTO suggests the balance between AHAs' claims that the RHA should submit to the Department. The establishment of broad criteria through consultation between the levels and with other bodies, including the community health councils, permits detailed proposals to be filtered up from the districts to the DHSS in the first quarter of the planning cycle, from April to June.

In the light of these proposals put forward by each level to its superior one, the broad picture of approved items is handed down from the DHSS to the RHAs in the second quarter, from July to September. In turn, the RHAs pass on guidelines to the AHAs for their planning, and the areas modify these in respect of their districts. In the third quarter, from October to December, the DMTs with assistance from the ATO draw up a final plan which takes into account the guidelines that have been established, working out detailed estimates of expenditure and other parameters. The ATO also works out plans for the services provided at area level, and in the final quarter, from January to March, the AHA reviews the district plans and submits them with its own to the RHA. The RHA reviews the plans from all its AHAs and consolidates them into a regional plan that includes their capital building programme. This is passed up to the DHSS where all the regional plans are consolidated into a national plan, on the basis of which the allocations for the coming year are confirmed. This timetable did not come into operation for the first two years following reorganisation, so the plans for 1974/75 and 1975/76 had to be worked out in a less ordered way. In March 1975 the DHSS published a large and comprehensive handbook called *Guide to Planning in the National Health Service*[8] which set out the detailed tasks of each level in the structure, and explained the concepts involved in constructing both annual and strategic plans. Later that year a circular (DS 85/75) amplified the planning tasks for the health authorities in 1975/76. These were replaced in 1976 by a new working manual called *NHS Planning System* and circular HC (76) 29 which together revised the guidance to health authorities on constructing their plans. In particular they took account of the stricter financial constraints in which spending — and therefore planning — would have to be managed over the ensuing years. There were a number of delays during 1974 and 1975 which meant that during those two years the authorities had to work to extremely compressed schedule for drawing up their plans and organising consultation with the CHCs, JCCs and statutory advisory committees.

It is worth pointing out that there was no formal planning system in operation in the DHSS before 1974; plans were made of course, but on a piecemeal basis and certainly without regard for necessary integration of services between all the sectors of health care. The new system was not expected to work smoothly until the officers at each level had become familiar with it and developed their own planning skills. So during the first few years after the reorganisation there was likely to be closer involvement of each level over their next one down than the system should finally require. There are also some provisos to be made about the system which indicate that it may not be able to work as neatly as it has been described. First, government decisions about the balance of public expenditure may change between the second and fourth quarters of the cycle. This implies that the final plans submitted through to the DHSS may have to be altered at a late stage, to conform to the new government decisions. A second point is that public expenditure levels may actually be changed in the following year, thus altering the context in which the plans are being implemented or, districts may inevitably have to overspend, and this in turn will affect the overall level of public expenditure. Thirdly, the system as a whole depends on ongoing activity at all levels, and unless each level knows what the others are doing, they may be hindered in making appropriate proposals or in assessing the relevance of plans submitted to them. Despite these possible problems, such a cycle is the only logical mechanism for achieving rational change. As administrators have begun to grasp the planning aspects of their work, many have become concerned about the availability of capital and revenue funds for development. In some regions the level of allocation is only sufficient to maintain existing provision, making real growth an impossible achievement. Therefore the planning cycle must be capable of adaptation so that it can support active change through a primary concentration on the redistribution of existing resources. However, the ability to do this depends largely on the imagination and perception of area and district officers. A bureaucratic planning system may not be flexible enough to help them in attaining their redeployment objectives.

There are two additional factors that complicate this planning task — scale and overlap. The scale of health district management (optimally set at a population of 250,000) is smaller than that of the non-metropolitan local government districts, yet greater than that of social work area teams, The need to collaborate with social services departments has already been discussed. But collaboration over housing between local government and area health authorities and DMTs is far from straightforward, since it involves both the housing and social services departments, although housing is the responsibility of the non-metropolitan district council, while social services are managed at county council level. A single AHA may cover two or more local authorities, so the number of separate departments with which it has to deal may discourage even the most enthusiastic health planners. A similar situation arises in relation to the school health services, which involve the health and education authorities, and where the matching may also be complicated.

Overlap, on the other hand, arises because health districts are defined in different terms to AHA and RHA boundaries, so some districts

extend beyond the boundary of the area to which they belong. This
has arisen where the catchment area of the district general hospital
covers populations living in a neighbouring area, or where the communit
services or smaller hospitals are actually situated both sides of an area
boundary. In these cases, the AHAs have to decide which FPC should
contract the general practitioners, and which District Medical
Committee should represent them. Additionally, some special hospitals,
such as long-stay mental hospitals, serve a catchment population that
covers several districts, which may even exclude the district where this
hospital is located. Management of the hospital has therefore to be
assigned to the most convenient DMT, and there have to be good
communications between health care planning teams covering services
for the mentally ill, in each of the districts concerned.

Whether all the districts can manage to be viable units for planning
integrated health services is not clear. The pre-1974 focus of organisational control for many community services was at area level. The
demands of various health and local authority groups had an influence
on the way districts were defined, and in many parts of the country the
result is really an enlarged hospital organisation. Another interesting
point is that the number of new administrative posts created by the
reorganisation that do not relate directly to service needs is notable.
Although the NHS as a whole does not devote a greater proportion of
its budget to administration than do many large industrial concerns, the
ability of the new NHS structure to facilitate better planning for
efficient health services is not yet proven.

It clearly takes a number of years before something as complicated
as the planning system can be properly assessed, yet the pressures
acting on it now to enable planners to adapt to very low growth targets
are considerable. Two policy modifications that the government has
had to explore as a result need to be mentioned. The first involves
redefining district boundaries. All multi-district areas have been told to
investigate the possibility of amalgamating some or all of their districts
so that a greater number of single-district areas can be established.
Financial savings could result if a number of senior posts were thus
removed, although the effect of making sector level staff yet more
distant from the planning authority must be carefully assessed.

The second change involves the question of collaboration between
health and social services through planning. Local authority planning
has – like the NHS – had to modify its goals in the face of less money
being available, and the result has been to put a brake on those
developments that can enable community-based health care to expand.
Residential accommodation for the mentally ill and handicapped, day

centres for the elderly, and assistance for disabled people living at home are some of the provisions which are essential if the use of expensive hospital facilities is to be controlled. So in 1976 the government announced a scheme for joint planning which would make specific sums of money available to health authorities for projects that could over a period be taken into local authority responsibility. This was modified in 1977 (Circular HC(77)17) which clarified the arrangements for using the special allocations and announced a target of £50 million annually for these schemes by 1980/81. Joint Consultative Committees have set up a Joint Care Planning Team to advise the local and health authorities on the services and client groups that can most benefit from a joint approach to planning. In the districts, special planning teams (which can be modified health care planning teams) are responsible for drawing up detailed schemes to be financed through the special allocations. The schemes have to specify certain criteria including the proportion of health authority and local authority support in financial terms for several years ahead, and the amounts of capital and revenue spending involved. Although the total sum of joint planning money each health authority can receive is relatively small, this initiative offers a real chance to develop services quickly for the vulnerable client groups, and it puts into practice the guiding principle of the reorganisation — integration of services.

5 MEDICAL SERVICES

This chapter is concerned with the professional organisation of doctors, their education and training, their working arrangements in the NHS and their remuneration. The development of medicine as a scientifically-based understanding of health and disease has depended on the pace of discoveries in the natural sciences. The last 100 years have seen the most rapid changes, although important landmarks date earlier than that.

Professional Organisation

Before 1700 the medical profession was firmly divided into three groups: the physicians, surgeons and apothecaries. The physicians had the highest status, and the Royal College of Physicians of London was founded in 1518. The members were graduates of Oxford and Cambridge universities, who had received religious and classical education, and subsequently often studied medical subjects in European universities. The surgeons were not scholars but craftsmen organised in a guild that was associated with the barbers, and they were licensed to perform the small range of procedures that could be carried out on unanaesthetised patients. Apothecaries were tradesmen who, from 1617 were licensed by the Society of Apothecaries to sell drugs prescribed by physicians. Until 1700 treatment was essentially carried out in the patients' homes. However, the position changed between 1700 and about 1850, partly because that period saw the rise of the great voluntary hospitals which provided the setting for developments in surgery; in comparison, the physicians hardly advanced their techniques and abilities. The prestige of surgeons rose and in 1745 the Company of Surgeons was founded, cementing their independence from the barbers and enabling educational standards to improve; by 1800 the Company had become the Royal College of Surgeons of England.

Apothecaries also advanced, and by 1703 they were entitled to see patients and prescribe medicines themselves. The result was that they became the 'general practitioners' for the middle classes and the poor. The Apothecaries Act of 1815 gave the Society of Apothecaries the right to license those who had served a five year apprenticeship and passed examinations, and some physicians took this qualification as well. As the voluntary hospitals were closed to these practitioners and only employed the services of those recognised by the Royal Colleges, the distinction between consultants and general practitioners became established. The Society of Apothecaries pioneered improvements in the standard of education and in raising the status of practitioners far more than the universities or Royal Colleges did — from 1842 to 1844 sixteen practitioners were licensed by the universities of Oxford and Cambridge, thirty-seven by the Royal College of Physicians, and 953 by the Society of Apothecaries. Despite this success, unqualified practitioners flourished (the 1841 census showed over 30,000 doctors, while the first Medical Directory published in 1845 listed only 11,000 qualified practitioners), and demand for a single licensing authority and a single professional qualification permitting practice in any branch of the profession arose. The strongest pressure for such a licence came from the Provincial Medical and Surgical Association. This body was founded in Worcester in 1832, and drew so much support that by 1855 it had changed its name to the British Medical Association. The campaign resulted in the passing of the Medical Act in 1858, which created the General Council of Medical Education and Registration.[1] It is now called the General Medical Council (GMC) and has forty-seven members representing the Royal Colleges, the universities, the Crown and the profession at large. Their duty is to maintain a register of practitioners licensed by recognised authorities, and to supervise the educational standards of training institutions. They also take disciplinary action in cases of criminal conviction or serious professional misconduct. In April 1975 the Merrison report was published, containing the results of an inquiry, instituted by the Secretary of State, into the workings of the GMC. It had been set up in response to some complaints that the GMC was not operating in the best interests of the medical profession.[2] The report recommended changes in the constitution of the Council, and proposed a new three-tiered system of registration for doctors. It covered other aspects of the regulation of the profession including standards of professional conduct and the proficiency of doctors practising in Britain, but who had been trained overseas.

Other medical corporations to have been established include the Royal College of Obstetricians and Gynaecologists (1929), the Royal College of General Practitioners (1952), the Royal College of Pathologists (1962) and the Royal College of Psychiatrists (1971).

The Royal Colleges and other medical corporations are not trade unions for doctors, but bodies mainly concerned with post-registration training and development, and until comparatively recently they only represented the elite specialties of the profession. The British Medical Association (BMA) emerged as the spokesman for the 'underdog' general practitioners. For example, it threatened Lloyd George's government with destruction of the National Health Insurance Scheme through the refusal of GPs' cooperation just as the scheme was about to be implemented. The opposition was dropped in 1912 when the government agreed to the demand for a higher rate of remuneration for GPs. Before that time, the outpatient departments and dispensaries of the voluntary hospitals provided treatment subsidised by the charitable organisations, and thus represented an alternative source of treatment for people which might be chosen instead of going to a general practitioner who contracted to work for a friendly society, if private treatment could not be afforded. But the 1911 Act had the effect of greatly increasing the numbers of people entitled to medical benefit through membership of the approved societies, and hence safeguarded the level of GPs' incomes under the National Health Insurance Scheme. The rivalry between the GPs and the hospital doctors was considerable and the BMA set out the terms of their relationships in a code of ethics which made the GP responsible for his patients while the specialists could be consulted for opinion and advice on diagnosis and treatment. This enabled GPs to maintain their list of patients without the fear that if any of them were referred to a hospital doctor, he would take them over; to the present day hospital doctors do not have a list of registered patients for whom they assume continuing responsibility.

Other bodies have emerged to protect doctors' interests, including the Junior Hospital Doctors' Association (5,500 members), the Hospital Consultants' and Specialists' Association (5,000 members) and the Medical Practitioners Union (about 4,000 members), but the BMA (with a membership of about 50,000 in the UK) is still regarded as the foremost and legitimate spokesman for all doctors, whether or not they are members. Its role in the setting up of the NHS in the 1940s has been described in Chapter 1, and since that time its internal organisation has been modified such that it mirrors the structure of the NHS — hospital doctors are represented in the BMA by its Central Committee for Hospital Medical Services, while GPs are separately represented by its General Medical Services Committee. The constituents of these two committees are the Local Medical Committees and Regional Committees for Hospital Medical Staffs on which doctors working in the NHS are represented. The BMA leadership has not always been regarded by individual doctors as being in touch with their interests and there have been a number of occasions when it has been unable publicly to present a convincing view of the profession's position. One factor which may contribute to this impression is that there are three separate bodies (or sets of bodies) acting for the profession — the medical corporations for professional representation, the GMC for discipline and self-regulation, and the BMA for pay negotiations.

Figure 12 *Medical Schools in the United Kingdom*

Medicine was being taught in several of these centres before a medical school was formally established or incorporated into an existing university.

ENGLAND

Birmingham	1828
Bristol	1833
Cambridge	14th century
Leeds	1831
Leicester	1975
Liverpool	1834
Manchester	1814
Newcastle	1834
Nottingham	1970
Oxford	14th century
Sheffield	1828
Southampton	1971

LONDON

Charing Cross	1834
Guy's	1769
King's College	1831
London	1785
Middlesex	1835
Royal Free	1874
St. Bartholemew's	1726
St. George's	1831
St. Mary's	1854
St. Thomas's	1723
University College	1828
Westminster	1834

WALES

Welsh National School of Medicine	1931

SCOTLAND

Aberdeen	1840
Dundee	1898
Edinburgh	1726
Glasgow	1714
St. Andrew's	1898

NORTHERN IRELAND

Belfast	1849

Medical Education

The training of doctors involves a large element of practical experience and in the past, students were apprenticed to physicians, surgeons and apothecaries, the university part of their training representing a relatively small element. The balance has now altered, although this tradition has had a substantial influence on the style of undergraduate curricula, and postgraduate education is still mainly in the hands of the professional organisations rather than the universities. By 1858 there were eleven medical schools in London and at least ten in the provinces apart from the universities of Oxford and Cambridge. By 1914 all except four of the present provincial university medical schools were open. Currently there are thirty-one undergraduate medical schools in the UK (see Figure 12).

Before the First World War, teaching of clinical subjects was provided by physicians and surgeons who although in private practice gave their services to the hospitals where students were apprenticed as clerks and dressers for short periods. Pre-clinical subjects were taught by doctors engaged in clinical work who often did not specialise in these subjects. The Haldane report published in 1912 strongly criticised these features and recommended there should be full-time clinical teachers of university status and that units of medicine and surgery under clinicians with professorial status should organise and provide the clinical teaching. It was not until the 1920s however that things began to change, and this was partly due to the establishment of the University Grants Committee which was given the responsibility for the financing of the universities. The medical schools were becoming steadily more dependent on the universities for funds. Research and specialisation extended as a result, but by 1944 the idea of full-time specialist units had not really been implemented and there were only seven full-time chairs in medicine, four in surgery and two in obstetrics. In that year, the Inter-departmental Committee on Medical Schools published its report (the Goodenough report).[3] It reaffirmed the main points of the Haldane report and proposed full-time professorial units in obstetrics and gynaecology as well as in medicine and surgery. It suggested premedical studies should be started by potential medical students at secondary school and continued at medical school, and that after qualification, one year of pre-registration hospital work under supervision should provide the necessary practical experience before a newly qualified doctor could work on his own.

The pattern of undergraduate education was further investigated by a Royal Commission chaired by Lord Todd, from 1965-68.[4] At that time students with high passes in biology, chemistry and physics 'A' level examinations were admitted to medical schools for five terms of pre-clinical instruction which basically covered anatomy, physiology and biochemistry. After examination the students then studied for three more years, partly in the hospital wards and partly in formal lectures. The subjects included medicine, surgery and sometimes psychiatry. They took examinations in these subjects too before obtaining their qualifying degree (M.B., B.S. or M.B., Ch.B. or M.B., B.Chir.),[5] and then had to spend one further year in approved training posts as house officers before being registered. There was subsequently no compulsory further education, although if a junior doctor wanted to advance his career in certain specialties, he would have to take further instruction and examination, leading to Membership of the Royal College of Physicians (MRCP) or Fellowship of the Royal College of Surgeons (FRCS), for example.

The Todd report is a comprehensive document that questioned the basic assumptions on which medical education had been based, and made several radical recommendations about its future organisation. It suggested that the undergraduate curriculum should be broad and flexible, to include sociological subjects and to cover the whole concept of human biology in the pre-clinical stage, possibly leading to a medical science degree after three years. Four broad modules covering (1) medicine and surgery, (2) psychiatry, (3) obstetrics, gynaecology and paediatrics, and (4) community medicine and general practice should constitute the clinical stage, but the qualifying doctor should not be expected to be fully trained. Subsequently the programme for postgraduate training should be systematically planned to give wide-ranging experience in carefully allotted posts, for both hospital specialists and general practitioners, through the development of postgraduate training centres in the district general hospitals. The report also suggested that the number of places in medical schools should be doubled by 1990, that the twelve London schools be merged into six expanded schools and the postgraduate schools consolidated with them, closer links being forged all over the country between the medical schools and multifaculty universities.

The philosophy of the Todd report has had an influence throughout medical education, and undergraduate curricula are changing quite substantially. Central Councils for Postgraduate Medical Education exist for England and Wales, Scotland and Northern Ireland, with the responsibility for monitoring standards and advising the Regional Postgraduate Committees. Joint Higher Training Committees have now been set up for a number of specialities, to define the scope of special education within the specialities, to establish criteria for posts and inspect them, to recommend patterns of appointments and to provide accreditation. There is, similarly, a Postgraduate Training Committee for General Practice. In

1976 the National Health Service (Vocational Training) Act was passed, creating a legal framework for the future regulation of training for doctors wishing to become general practitioners. Currently, newly registered doctors can voluntarily undertake a programme of vocational training which involves two further years of hospital work in three or more designated specialties (e.g. obstetrics and gynaecology, paediatrics, psychiatry, general medicine, etc.) and then one year as a trainee in an approved general practice. The new Act will require doctors who wish to become unrestricted principals (i.e. GPs providing the full range of services) to have taken the prescribed vocational training, which will probably be similar to the voluntary scheme. The DHSS is drafting regulations which will bring the Act into force by about 1980. However, general professional training as conceived in the Todd report does not yet exist for all specialties because of the lack of suitable posts, and the proposal for structural control of specialist education has not been implemented.

Doctors in the NHS

When the NHS was created in 1946 the three arms of the tripartite structure were already established. General practitioners combined private practice with work under the National Health Insurance scheme, whereby they had 'panels' of insured patients who could be treated by them. Hospital consultants were basically private practitioners who gave their services to the voluntary hospitals for a nominal fee, while local authorities employed full-time doctors to work in their hospitals and in the school and public health services. The NHS created Executive Councils to administer arrangements for general practice, and Regional Hospital Boards and Boards of Governors to manage the hospital services. Local authorities retained responsibility for the school and public health services. The reorganisation of the NHS in 1974 attempted to integrate the tripartite structure by bringing the elements under the control of the health authorities. This made the AHAs responsible for hospital and school health services, and brought administration of the general practitioners' contracts under a separate committee of the AHA — the Family Practitioner Committee. Local authorities however retained responsibility for environmental health and for social services. Details of the pay and conditions of service will be discussed in the next section, while here the clinical work of doctors and their development under the influence of the NHS is the subject.

General Practitioners

The split between general practitioners and hospital specialists that emerged in the eighteenth and nineteenth centuries still exists, and general practice, although it has in the lifetime of the NHS consistently attracted about 50 per cent of qualifying doctors, remains the less prestigious career choice. Both the Royal College of General Practitioners and the General Medical Services Committee of the BMA have worked hard to improve research and understanding and there is a growing recognition of the fact that general practice, as the key element of primary medical care, is the area where more planning of services and scrutiny of the outcome of treatment will be able to alter the balance in the whole pattern of health care. There are about 24,500 GPs who each provide the full range of services to, on average, 2,307 patients. The trend since 1948 has gradually moved away from single-handed practice towards group practice so that by 1975 about 18 per cent of GPs were single-handed, about 45 per cent were in groups of two or three doctors and about 37 per cent were in groups of four or more. They see patients in surgeries that may be in purpose-built premises or health centres, or in modified rooms of their own homes, but also visit patients at home or in hospital. Table 4 shows the pattern of minor, major and chronic illnesses that the average GP sees in a year, and indicates that about 62 per cent of the common conditions are 'minor', with no risk to life or permanent disability and are mostly not treated by hospital doctors; about 13 per cent are 'major' life-threatening situations mainly referred for hospital treatment, and about 25 per cent are chronic conditions involving permanent disabilities. Patients have direct access to their GPs and studies have shown that about 5 per cent of the population regard themselves as healthy at any one time, yet 75 per cent of symptoms are treated by the patients themselves, without going to see a doctor. The people most frequently seen by a GP are the young, the old, and people living alone, and certain occupational groups such as miners attend more often than average. There is also evidence of a social class difference, with unskilled male manual workers consulting their doctors more frequently than men in other classes. It is difficult to interpret from the available information how long and how often doctors see their patients – some consultations can be for short matters such as obtaining certificates or repeat prescriptions, while others can be lengthy discussions of emotional or social problems. Studies do however show that the trend is for a reduction in home visiting of the order of 60 per cent over the last twenty-five years and about 15 per cent in surgery consultations, but these factors are strongly influenced by the locality and the type of practice, the way it is organised and the age and experience of the GP.[6]

The great majority of practices now employ secretaries or receptionists, and increasingly, health visitors, home nurses and social workers are being attached to practices to provide a more comprehensive team of primary care workers. These developments are related to the acceptance of the concept of health centres as the most rational way of organising primary care. The Dawson report (see Chapter 1) of 1920 laid down these principles but developments have been slow until recently. From 1948 to 1968 — the first twenty years of the NHS — about 100 health centres were built. Then, as a result of renewed interest in the concept and a restructuring of the financial arrangements (which will be discussed later), 250 new health centres were opened between 1969 and 1971, and there was a total of nearly 800 by 1975. However, there are still less than 20 per cent of all GPs working from health centres, so the major change in general practice has really been the switch to group practice rather than specifically to practice from health centres. (However in Scotland, health centres have been built rather more energetically [see Appendix 1].) They usually house five or six GPs, and another important organisational factor is the use of appointment systems. At first, not more than about 6 per cent of all practices used them but by 1970 over 50 per cent were doing so. Studies have shown that appointment systems reduce patients' waiting time by up to half, and the more orderly flow of work can reduce the length of the doctors' working day. Additionally, many GPs use commercial deputising services to cover for them at night time and weekends, and some are also involved in outside activities, such as work in hospitals, industrial medicine and the school health services.

It is estimated that the GP is the first point of contact for about 90 per cent of people seeking treatment for ill-health, and about one in three of a GP's patients will receive some form of hospital treatment each year. GPs also need access to diagnostic facilities (pathology and X-ray) housed in hospitals, and although use of these facilities has been improving, the pattern is for about 25 per cent of all GPs to account for 75 per cent of requests for these diagnostic tests, younger and more recently qualified doctors being more likely to make requests than older doctors in large group practices.

The quality of the relationship between GPs and hospital doctors is clearly very important, and critics of the former tripartite structure maintained that continuity of care between the hospitals and the community was very vulnerable to the administrative problems caused by this structure. The reorganisation acknowledged this point, and attempts to encourage closer contact and discussion by involving all doctors more closely, through their representative committees, in the planning of local provision of services. GPs are represented on local medical committees, which cover the same areas as the Family Practitioner Committees. They are officially recognised bodies, and they

Table 4 *Annual Morbidity Experience in Average British General Practice of 2,500 Persons* (i.e. numbers of patients suffering from the diseases that the doctor may expect to see each year)

Minor Illness (Illness of short duration or minimal disability)

Upper respiratory infections	674
Skin disorders	256
Emotional disorders	115
Acute otitis media	84
Common digestive disorders	53
Acute urinary infections	51
Wax in ears	50
Acute backache	34
Hay fever	28
Migraine	20

Major Illness (Illness of severe degree, or marked effect on living)

Pneumonia and acute bronchitis			184
Coronary heart disease			37
Anaemia			23
Killed or injured in road accidents			16
Severe depression			14
All new cancers:	breast	1.1	
	lung	1.0	
	cervix	0.6	
	stomach	0.4	7
Acute appendicitis			5
Glaucoma			2

Chronic Illness

Chronic emotional illness	238
Chronic arthritis	111
Hypertension	57
Chronic bronchitis	36
Asthma	34
Peptic ulcer	18
Stroke	15
Rheumatoid arthritis	15
Diabetes mellitus	14
Epilepsy	9
Pernicious anaemia	4
Parkinsonism	3
Multiple sclerosis	2
Pulmonary tuberculosis	1
Mental retardation	1

Source: Morbidity Statistics from General Practice, Second National Study 1970-71. OPCS, HMSO, 1974

elect members onto the FPCs, they investigate allegations of excessive prescribing by their colleagues and they appoint members to the Service Committees of FPCs which hear allegations of breaches in Terms of Service. Although they are not bodies of the BMA, the executive of their Annual Conference is the General Medical Services Committee which is a standing committee of the BMA. The District Medical Committee is composed of GPs, hospital and community doctors, with a total membership of up to fifteen, and as has been described, the chairman and vice-chairman of that committee are members of the District Management Team, and some of the GP members of the local medical committee will be members of the District Medical Committee. GPs are also represented on the statutory Area Medical Advisory Committee, and there is one GP on the Regional Medical Advisory Committee.

Two notable studies of the work of GPs have been carried out by the Standing Medical Advisory Committee of the Central Health Service Council. In 1963, the Gillie report: *The Field Work of The Family Doctor*[7] recommended improvements in the total education of general practitioners which were broadly echoed in the Todd report. It stated that the professional isolation of GPs had been a serious handicap, and should be overcome through group working arrangements, part-time hospital appointments and continuing education. Interestingly, this report did not consider a reorganisation of the administrative structure of the NHS as critical as the ability of the family doctor himself to coordinate the resources of hospital and community care on behalf of his patient. The Harvard Davis report[8] suggested that the optimum size for group practice was about five or six doctors with appropriate nursing and secretarial staff. It suggested community services should be given financial priority so that the GPs would be well supported in their provision of conti care for a defined group of patients. Organisational factors were also taken up by the Joint Working Party on General Medical Services which (in 1974) reported on its studies of the use of deputising services, appointment systems, and support from hospital diagnostic facilities.

Hospital Doctors

The organisation of hospital doctors in the NHS was first set out by the Spens committee on the remuneration of consultants and specialists, in 1948,[9] but there have been a number of modifications since that time, notably as a result of the recommendations of the Joint Working Party on Medical Staffing Structure in the Hospital Service (the Platt report[10]) in 1961. The present position is that following registration a young hospital doctor can expect to spend at least one year as a senior house officer, followed by one to three years as a registrar and three to

ive years as a senior registrar before becoming a consultant in his late
hirties. However, the actual position varies a great deal and orderly pro-
ression is not ensured since there are many more aspiring junior doctors
han there are consultant posts which they stand a chance of obtaining.
Some of the junior (i.e. non-consultant) posts are regarded as service
ather than training posts, implying that the manpower is needed to fulfil
hospital's clinical obligations and not to provide training and experience
vhich will entitle the holder to automatic promotion.

The clinical work is organised around a basic unit called a 'firm', com-
osed of one consultant and a varying number from the junior grades.
atients referred to hospital by a GP for inpatient or outpatient treat-
ent become the responsibility of the consultant, who has to make deci-
ions about their diagnosis, treatment, referral and discharge. He is helped
y his junior doctors and by a variety of nursing and paramedical staff,
nd delegates some of the work to them while retaining full personal re-
ponsibility. In practice the senior registrars and registrars have some
utonomy although they are responsible to their consultant, and they
upervise the work of the house officers. The discretion given to each
rade of junior doctor varies considerably from 'firm' to 'firm', and de-
epends on the nature of the clinical work, the number of staff involved
nd the inevitable personality influences. Teaching of junior medical
taff, medical students and other hospital staff may also play a part in
e work of the 'firm'.

At the next level, clinical work done by the 'firms' is organised into
pecialties (see Figure 13). Figures from the DHSS show that some
pecialties are much more popular than others, and the competition in
ome is so severe that a trainee is not assured a career post in any of the
ollowing specialties: clinical physiology, nephrology, cardiology, infec-
ous diseases, general surgery, obstetrics and gynaecology, ophthalmo-
gy, urology, neurosurgery and paediatric surgery. On the other hand,
egistrars specialising in geriatrics, venereology, chemical pathology and
naesthetics can be sure of obtaining senior registrar posts; and all senior
egistrars in these same four specialties plus child psychiatry and radio-
gy can expect to obtain a consultant post on completion of their
raining. The prestige of a hospital (particularly whether it is a teaching
ospital or not) and its geographical location also influence the competi-
on for training posts, and these and other factors have contributed to
e mistakes made in planning the number and distribution of hospital
octors. Two particular elements of this situation are the intake of stu-
ents into medical schools and the emigration of doctors qualified in
ritain. In 1957, the Willink report[11] recommended a 10 per cent cut in
edical schools' intake, and this subsequently proved to be a serious un-

Figure 13 *Clinical Specialties 1975*

Accident and Emergency	Immunopathology
Anaesthetics	Infectious Diseases
Blood Transfusions	Medical Microbiology
Cardiology	Mental Handicap
Chemical Pathology	Mental Illness
Clinical Pharmacology and Therapeutics	Mental Illness — children
Clinical Neurological Physiology	Nephrology
Clinical Physiology	Neurology
Dermatology	Neuropathology
Diseases of the Chest	Neurosurgery
Ear, Nose and Throat	Nuclear Medicine
Endocrinology	Ophthalmology
Forensic Psychiatry	Other
Gastroenterology	Paediatrics
General Medicine	Plastic Surgery
General Pathology	Psychotherapy
General Surgery	Radiology
Genito-Urinary Medicine	Radiotherapy
Geriatrics	Rheumatology and Rehabilitation
Gynaecology and Obstetrics	Thoracic Surgery
Haematology	Traumatic and Orthopaedic Surgery
Histopathology	Urology

Source: Health and Personal Social Services Statistics, 1976

derestimation, partly because the extent of doctors' emigration out of Britain was not realised. The Government's 1976 statement of priorities set the target of an annual intake of 4,000 students into the medical schools by 1980 to enable a higher proportion of posts in hospitals and general practice to be filled by British graduates.

Successive committees and working parties have assessed the structure of hospital medical staffing, and in 1972 the Central Manpower Committee was set up to advise the Health Departments on implementing improvements in the position that had been agreed between the profession and the Government. It has aimed to increase consultant posts differentially between regions to achieve a nearly uniform number of consultants per head of population, while allowing for regional variations in specialty choice. It has further attempted to redress the balance of registrar and senior registrar posts by relocating them from the well-staffed to the badly staffed authorities, and by creating new posts wherever good and professionally recognised training programmes have been identified. [12]

The participation of hospital doctors in administration, and their contribution to the efficiency of the hospital service is a major theme of the reorganisation, and stems from the fact that the doctors are in a position o direct the use of costly resources with varying, but often considerable, degrees of autonomy. After discussions between the Minister of Health and the profession in 1965, a joint working party was set up to discuss the progress of the NHS and particularly to review the hospital service. t has produced three reports (1967, 1972, 1974) known as the 'Cogwheel' reports because of the design printed on their covers. The first report[13] recommended the creation of divisions of broadly linked specialies to include consultants and junior medical staff, which would contantly appraise their services and methods of provision. Representatives of each division were to come together in each hospital as a Medical Executive Committee which would coordinate the work and views of the divisions and provide a link with nursing and administration. The sort of problems they might consider included bed management and the organiation of outpatient and inpatient resources. Hospitals gradually implemented this scheme, and by 1972 the second report[14] was able to identify the essential elements of an effective 'Cogwheel' system and to report hat in large acute hospitals particularly, the system had been helpful in dealing with improved communications, reductions of inpatient waiting lists and the progressive control of medical expenditure.

The third report[15] clarified the role of 'Cogwheel' systems in the newly-reorganised NHS, because an emphasis of the reorganisation was the part to be played by multi–disciplinary teams in the integrated mangement, whereas 'Cogwheel' is a doctor-dominated and hospitals-based rrangement. The report suggested that 'Cogwheel' should continue to eal with issues where the agreement and action of hospital doctors was he main need, while problems requiring strong collaboration between all he professional groups, both within the hospitals and in community serices should be the province of the district management teams and their ealth care planning teams. It would still be appropriate for 'Cogwheel' ystems to concentrate on efficiency issues, and would be helpful for ospital doctors to see their clinical freedom in the context of teamwork and the necessity of sharing resources.

Community Physicians

The first major attempts to improve public health conditions occurred in the Victorian period and owe much to Sir Edwin Chadwick and Sir John Simon. They were at the forefront of the move to create sanitary reforms through improvements in water supply and sewerage systems and better housing conditions, particularly for the poor. Chadwick was instrumental in getting the Public Health Act of 1848 passed (see p. 11) but the General Board of Health was not a success, partly because Chadwick in his zeal for reform did not realise how necessary it was to involve doctors and administrators as well as engineers in the battle for improved public health. However, Chadwick recognised earlier than mar the relationship between poverty and disease. In 1848 Sir John Simon b came Medical Officer of Health for the City of London, where he concerned himself with housing and water supply, and dealt with the chole epidemic. Later he successfuly promoted further legislative measures wh established a sanitary code for England by recognising that a 'partnership of experts' was necessary to achieve improvements in public healtl

By 1872 all sanitary authorities were required to appoint a Medical Officer of Health. This practice continued until 1974 when the reorgan sation of the NHS transferred responsibility for personal health service: from the local authorities to the new health authorities. The Medical Officer of Health had been the chief executive of the local authority's health department, with overall responsibility for the clinical and publi health services provided for the local community. He was foremost an administrator and planner. The Todd report had articulated a view whi was developing during the 1960s that doctors working in community medicine formed a distinct group requiring a specialised training. In 1972 the Faculty of Community Medicine of the Royal College of Physicians was founded, thus recognising the discipline as a specialty in its own right. It defined community medicine as ' . . . that branch of me medicine which deals with populations or groups rather than with indivi dual patients . . . It requires special knowledge of the principles of epid emiology, of the organisation and evaluation of medical care systems, o the medical aspects of the administration of health services and of the techniques of health education and rehabilitation which are comprised within the field of social and preventive medicine.'[16] In 1972 the Hunter report[17] was published, setting out the role of those doctors working in the reorganised NHS would would form a distinct group, being neither clinicians nor purely health service administrators. It explained the contribution that these 'community medicine specialists' would be able to make at each level in the new structure, emphasising the need for special training programmes to prepare doctors for this particularly important work in the near future.

The reorganisation has laid great stress on the development of community medicine and it has created posts for doctors in this specialty a each level in the new structure. The role of the Medical Officer of Heal has been incorporated and extended in the functions of the District Co munity Physician who, in addition to supervising the provision of community-based personal health services, has to assess and plan the whole range of integrated services that are organised at district level. He make use of mortality and morbidity figures and a range of statistical inform tion to sort out the priorities that are appropriate to the district popul.

tion, and thereby decides on the emphases of coordination between hospital and community services. Effective systems of record linkage, immunisation and screening programmes, health education and staff training schemes and the research and recommendations of the health care planning teams are among the items at the District Community Physician's disposal. They help him to carry out his responsibilities which may be considered as the pivot on which the development of integrated health care rests. His links with the local authority's environmental health, education, housing and social services departments are also very important and need to be fully developed in order for health services improvements to be complemented by developments in the social standards of the community. At area level, the Area Medical Officer has a team of Specialists in Community Medicine who between them cover health services planning and information, child health (including school health) services, services for the mentally ill and handicapped, the elderly and the physically handicapped (in conjunction with the local authority Social Services Departments), environmental health and medical personnel services. Similarly at regional level, the Regional Medical Officer has a number of Specialists in Community Medicine, but they are more concerned with the planning and development of integrated services over the region as a whole.

Since the specialty of community medicine was established so recently, the number of appropriately trained doctors falls far short of the number of new posts and, as expected, many former medical officers of health transferred into the new structure, mainly to districts and areas. Although training courses have become available, much of the development of community medicine has had to take place 'on the job' because the work is so different from that of the medical officers of health. The emphasis on epidemiology, especially in relation to the non-communicable and chronic diseases and the health changes of middle and old age requires a fresh approach and a willingness to challenge the old assumptions about priorities between acute and non-acute illness.

Doctors' Pay

The reasons for the current problems over doctors' pay only become clear when the history of their pay negotiations between the inception of the NHS in 1948 and the present is examined in some detail. When the NHS began, the systems for employing the services of doctors had had to be carefully worked out and negotiated between the Government and the profession. Two committees under the chairmanship of Sir Will Spens reported in 1948 on the remuneration of general practitioners[18] and consultants and specialists respectively. They recommended scales for consultants and junior hospital doctors, arrangements for part-time contracts for consultants and a system of distinction awards which would ' . . . provide for a significant minority the opportunity to earn incomes comparable with the highest which can be earned in other professions'.[19] For GPs the Spens committee recommended a graded scale of incomes leading to an average net income for doctors of forty to fifty years of age, which would be paid out of a central pool. The GPs' income would be made up of a capitation fee for each patient on his list, which included a fixed allowance for practice expenses, plus payments for certain individual items of service. The figures for all doctors were quoted at 1939 values of money, it being left to the Government to decide what increases would establish and protect the status of these incomes relative to each other and to other professional incomes, in the context of rising inflation.

The adjustments that were accordingly fixed by the Government were not acceptable to the BMA in respect of GPs' incomes, and after negotiations had broken down, the matter was referred to adjudication in 1953 Mr Justice Danckwerts awarded the GPs a substantial increase and said that the size of the central pool should be related to the total number of GPs and not to the population covered by the NHS, in order that required increases in the numbers of GPs would not be discouraged. The result was that some of the increased incomes were paid directly into a special fund from which GPs could draw if they spent money on improving or building new surgery premises.

The BMA again made a claim for increases in 1956, but this time on behalf of hospital doctors as well as GPs. The Health Ministers could not agree to it and the matter was referred to a Royal Commission under Sir Harry Pilkington, which sat from 1957-60.[20] It recommended new levels of remuneration but also that a standing Review Body of ' . . . eminent persons of experience in various fields of national life'[21] should keep medical and dental remuneration under review, making recommendations directly to the Prime Minister, which were on the whole to be accepted without alteration. The BMA refused to give evidence to the Royal Commission, but when the Presidents of the Royal Colleges announced that they would cooperate by putting the view of hospital consultants and specialists, the BMA was left no alternative if it wished the GPs to have a voice, but to submit a brief to the Commission. The effect of setting up a review body was to end the practice initiated by Spens of calculating doctors' pay increases in relation to the rate of inflation, but at the same time it left the pay settlements in the hands of a body separate from the Ministry that could be advised but not instructed by the Government. Chapter 8 will describe how the Whitley Council system for collective bargaining and determination of the pay of all NHS staff was set up and how it has operated. In the case of doctors, the Royal Commission was persuaded to recommend the end of direct negotiations between representatives of the health departments and the profession on Whitley Councils through the creation of a permanent independent review body.

The Review Body on Doctors' and Dentists Remuneration was duly set up, consisting of six members and the Chairman, Lord Kindersly. Its terms of reference were 'to advise the Prime Minister on the remuneration of doctors and dentists taking any part in the National Health Service'. Twelve reports were issued between 1963 and 1970 and these concerned the basic rates of pay for different grades of doctors and dentists as well as particular aspects of remuneration including distinction awards. The Review Body constructed its recommendations after receiving evidence from doctors' and dentists' representatives, from the Ministry/DHSS, and factual information about changes in the cost of living, the movement of earnings in other professions and the state of recruitment in the professions. However, general practitioners were not satisfied with the awards made to them by the Review Body, and in 1965 the BMA submitted a memorandum demanding direct reimbursement of practice expenses and of income from local authority and hospital sessional work, a system of seniority payments and a number of other items. The Review Body made an award of £5½ million, on the condition that most of it would be used to reimburse those doctors employing ancillary help or spending above-average amounts in improving their services for patients. The BMA replied (through its General Medical Services Committee) that this award and previous awards which maintained the pool system could not enable GPs to secure 'just' remuneration. They demanded an immediate unconditional credit of the £5½ million award to the pool — thus raising the value of the capitation fees — as an interim measure, and asked GPs throughout the country to sign undated resignation forms which would be used or not, depending on the outcome of negotiations with the Minister.[22] In March 1965, Kenneth Robinson (the Minister of Health since October 1964) agreed to add the £5½ million unconditionally to the pool, and began discussing the GPs' suggestion for a completely new contract, as outlined in the BMA's publication *A Charter for the Family Doctor Service*.[23] This set out a radically revised scheme of payments, including a five and one half day working week, six weeks paid annual holiday, payments for out-of-hours services, an independent corporation to make long-term loans to GPs for building or improving surgery premises, the ending of the pool system, direct reimbursement for practice expenses, ancillary help, and several other items. Long negotiations on the Charter ensued and a contract jointly agreed to by the Minister and the profession which embodied some but not all of the demands was submitted to the Review Body for pricing, later in 1965. It consisted of a basic payment, available at the full rate to doctors with at least 1,000 patients providing full services for a minimum period in each week, and available to other doctors at proportionally reduced rates. Additions to this were made in respect of group practice and practice in unattractive areas. Two levels of distinction awards were available to about 30 per cent of GPs aged between forty-five and sixty-five, dependent on attendance at a required number of postgraduate training courses. Additional services provided by GPs in accordance with national policy, e.g. cervical cytology and vaccination and immunisation were to be paid on an item-of-service basis, as were maternity and emergency work. The capitation fees for ordinary weekday work were fixed at two rates, that for patients over sixty-five being about 30 per cent higher than for other patients. Night-time and weekend work earned the GP an additional standby allowance, and extra capitation fee for over 1,000 patients, and a flat rate for home visits made between midnight and 7.00 a.m.. Six weeks paid annual holiday plus a notional five and a half day week were established, provided that the GP could make arrangements for the complete care of his patients while he was not working. The BMA's Charter would have cost an extra £38 million, but the Review Body's recommendations on the jointly agreed package resulted in an extra cost of about £24 million to the NHS. Although the GPs did not get exactly what they had demanded, the gap between the incomes of GPs and hospital consultants was narrowed. A notable achievement of the whole dispute was, however to encourage group practice from purpose built or modified premises, through the setting up of the General Practice Finance Corporation, and the reimbursement of a greater proportion of practice expenses which encouraged employment of ancillary staff. It also reduced the burden of signing National Insurance certificates, which the GPs strongly objected to.

In March 1970 the Twelfth Report of the Review Body[24] recommended a general increase of 30 per cent for doctors and dentists to be introduced over two years, because their pay had been falling behind increases for other professions. The Government accepted this for the training grades of doctors and dentists but only agreed to half the awards for career grades in hospital and general practice work, referring the balance to the National Board for Prices and Incomes, in June. Lord Kindersley and the members of the Review Body resigned on the day after this announcement, and the BMA advised its members not to cooperate with the NHS administration. These sanctions were lifted after the General Election in 1970 in return for assurances from the new Conservative Government that the reference to the National

Board for Prices and Incomes would be withdrawn. In November 1970 the Government set up three new Review Bodies to handle the pay negotiations for groups in the public sector where the negotiating machinery had been unsatisfactory, namely, doctors and dentists in the NHS, the chairmen and board members of the nationalised industries and the armed forces. These review bodies have interlocking membership and their secretariat is provided from the Office of Manpower Economics. The new terms of reference for the doctors' and dentists' review body (chaired by Lord Halsbury) laid down that their recommendations would not be referred to another body (this had been the reason for Lord Kindersley's resignation) and would not be rejected or modified unless it was unavoidable.

Lord Halsbury resigned as Chairman of the Review Body after the fourth report,[25] published in July 1974, had been rejected by the profession who expressed their lack of confidence in him. The Review Body continued its work without a Chairman, and published a supplement[26] to the fourth report, at the end of the year. This was accepted by the Government and the profession. Sir Ernest Woodroofe became the new Chairman of the Review Body in February 1975, and its fifth report[27] was published in April 1975 and brought GPs' annual income to £8,485.

For hospital doctors relations with the Government were not so troublesome until about 1972 when dissatisfactions with the form of consultants' contracts arose. The consultants' view, expressed mainly through the BMA, was that they had been required to take on several new responsibilities without adequate pay adjustments. At that time their contracts specified the minimum number of hours to be worked, depending on whether the doctor had opted to work whole-time for the NHS, or part-time in order to take on private work also. The system of distinction awards also made extra annual payments of between £1,500 and £8,000 (approx.) to a proportion of consultants. Discussions between the consultants and the Department continued inconclusively, and in 1974 a general election replaced the Conservatives with a Labour Government. The new Secretary of State for Social Services, Mrs Barbara Castle, took up the consultants' problem by proposing to make full-time NHS work more financially attractive than part-time work. In addition she proposed to recast the distinction awards system entirely by creating two new pay supplements: a medical progress supplement (to reward valuable innovations in medical research or academic study, like the old awards) and a service supplement (to reward overburdened consultants in unpopular regions or unfashionable specialties, which the old awards neglected). Negotiations on these proposals were stormy, and took place in the context of the Review Body's deliberations on a claim from the consultants for a large interim backdated increase. At the beginning of 1975 the BMA called on consultants to 'work to contract' — i.e. to do no more than the minimum they were required to do — to demonstrate their opposition to the government's proposals and their rejection of the Review Body's decision not to grant them an interim award. The disruption caused by the consultants' action was quite widespread, but it ceased later in 1975.

At about the same time, however, junior hospital doctors commenced to 'work to contract' in support of their claims for a new contract to recognise the long hours and heavy responsibilities they had to shoulder. Again, the negotiations were acrimonious but a settlement was reached later in 1975 when the Review Body priced two new types of supplement that junior doctors could receive if they worked extra hours over a newly defined basic working week of 40 hours. The cost of this settlement turned out to be more expensive than the Review Body had calculated, because of the way the health authorities awarded the new supplements. In addition, hospital work levels were significantly reduced as a result of the consultants' and junior doctors' 'working to contract', and this showed up as increased waiting times for outpatient appointments and inpatient admissions.

The junior doctors' new contract took effect from February 1976, but by 1977 the consultants still had no new contract. They have agreed outline proposals with the DHSS but detailed negotiations on implementing them will have to wait until the pay policy permits the kinds of increases envisaged. No further progress on changing the system of distinction awards has been made. The task of the Review Body, in the light of these disputes and under the constraints imposed by the Government's pay policy, has been made extremely difficult. The Review Body was after all set up to avoid recurrent disputes and to arrive at settlements which would be fair to the profession and to the taxpayer who foots the bill. In the event, the effect of increasing militancy amongst members of the medical profession, and Government attempts to control the rate of pay increases has put great strains on the ability of both sides to negotiate acceptable pay and terms of work under the NHS.

6 DENTAL, OPHTHALMIC AND PHARMACEUTICAL SERVICES

In the community sector of the NHS, dental, ophthalmic and pharmaceutical services are provided by independent practitioners. They hold contracts for their work with the NHS that are administered through the Family Practitioner Committees. In the hospital service, these and all other staff are directly employed by the Health Authorities. Therefore these three professions will be described in this chapter and the work of other NHS staff follows in Chapters 7 and 8.

Dental Services

In the seventeenth and eighteenth centuries there was no distinct profession of dentistry, but some barber-surgeons became known as 'operators for the teeth'. As scientific study of the teeth advanced, some practitioners were able to become very skilled specialists while others, who remained unskilled and unqualified, obtained their work through advertising. In 1878 the Dentists Act empowered the General Medical Council to examine and register suitably qualified dentists, but it did not outlaw unqualified practitioners. The British Dental Association was founded in 1890, and dentistry became recognised as a profession. Unregistered practitioners continued to flourish, and many of them were unscrupulous and dangerous, but it was not until 1921 that a new Dentists Act dealt with these abuses by effectively closing the profession to anyone who was not trained at a school of dentistry recognised by the newly created Dental Board. The Act made the Dental Board responsible for keeping a register and for investigating cases of misconduct, but the GMC retained control over disciplinary action and the power to license practitioners.

A further Dentists Act in 1957 established the General Dental Council as the single statutory licensing and registering body which took on the functions of the Dental Board and the GMC (in relation to dentistry). It supervises the standard of dental examinations and teaching and keeps the register of dentists who have obtained the professional qualifications – either a degree (Bachelor of Dental Surgery, B.D.S.) or a diploma (Licentiate in Dental Surgery, L.D.S.) – from an approved school of dentistry. The training takes between four and six years, and dentists pay an entry and retention fee to have their name on the register. Practitioners' names can be erased if they commit a felony or if they are found guilty of professional misconduct by the Council's disciplinary committee. The Council has twenty-eight members: eleven elected by registered practitioners, six nominated on the advice of the Privy Council, two registered dentists nominated by the University of London and one from every other university with a school of dentistry. Six members of the GMC join the Council for its discussions on dental education and examination.

Dental Services Before the Reorganisation

Before the NHS was founded, the general state of dental health was very poor, and although dental benefits were available under the National Health Insurance scheme to thirteen million of the working population, only about 6 per cent claimed for it. After 1948, the NHS provided dental services in each arm of the tripartite structure. Hospital dentists specialised in dental and oral surgery or orthodontics (the straightening of children's teeth) and were graded in the same way as hospital medical staff. Some worked in dental departments of general hospitals and others worked within specialist dental hospitals. Local authorities were obliged by the 1944 Education Act to provide free dental inspection and treatment for all children in maintained schools, and they also cared for the dental health of expectant and nursing mothers. In fact the School Medical Service, established in 1907, made provision for dental care of the mothers and children of pre-school age, but less than 2 per cent of the eligible population made use of this. The explicit aim of the local authority dental services was to conserve teeth and to prevent premature loss of first teeth in children. The services were organised by a Principal School Dental Officer (responsible to the Medical Officer of Health) and his staff of School Dental Officers worked in the schools, clinics and treatment centres run by the local authority.

The largest sector of the dental services was provided by dentists in general practice. These were qualified registered dentists who worked from their own homes or other premises, obtained their own equipment and supplies, and employed ancillary staff. They held contracts with the Executive Councils which paid them for treating patients under the NHS. The majority combined this with private practice, and they were not obliged to undertake any more NHS work than they wished.

Dental Services Since 1974

In 1974, the reorganisation only changed the administration of dental services — it did not alter this pattern of clinical work. Hospital dentists became employees of the AHA(T)s or RHAs in the same way as hospital doctors; local authority dentists were transferred to the AHAs; general dental practitioners' contracts became administered by the Family Practitioner Committees. AHAs appointed an Area Dental Officer who took on the work of the former Principal School Dental Officer as well as being responsible for promoting improvements in all the dental services of the AHA, and advising them and the local authority accordingly. In large multi-district areas the Area Dental Officer is a full-time administrator, while in small areas he can combine administration with some clinical work. There is also provision for District Dental Officers to be appointed.

Professional advice is provided to the AHA through the statutory Area Dental Committee comprised of seven dentists nominated by the Local Dental Committee (the representative body of local dentists), three dentists working in the child and school health services, three registered general dental practitioners and three hospital dentists (two dental teachers in AHA(T)s) together with the Area Dental Officer (*ex officio*) and one member of the medical profession. The advisory committee at regional level consists of the chairman and two members of each Area Dental Committee (between them covering hospital, community and general practice dentistry), the Regional Dental Officer (*ex officio*), one member of the medical profession and one senior adviser in postgraduate dental education for the region. These advisory committees (mentioned in Chapters 2 and 3) are consulted by the health authorities in order to reach decisions on the planning and provision of services that include expert knowledge and opinion, but they are not concerned with the relations between the profession and its employers or with the internal organisation of the profession.

Dentists' Pay

As with doctors, dentists have one body to represent them professionally (the British Dental Association), one statutory body to regulate and control their practice (the General Dental Council) and separate bodies to negotiate their pay. For most NHS staff pay and conditions of service are determined through the Whitley Council machinery, and its origins and details are fully discussed in Chapter 8. Although a Whitley Council exists, in name, for hospital dental staff, their pay has, since 1960, been determined by the permanent Review Body which was established following the recommendations of the Royal Commission on Doctors' and Dentists' Remuneration.[1] Since 1974, community dentists have also become NHS employees, and their pay has therefore also come within the scope of the Review Body.

Before 1948, general dental practitioners received most of their income from private practice, and a committee[2] was appointed to work out a scheme for paying them under the NHS. It fixed a target net income for the average weekly chairside hours being worked, and the Health Departments and the profession jointly worked out fees for different items of service that would provide this level of income. However, the initial demand for dentures and dental treatment was enormous, so dentists worked more hours and received higher incomes than had been anticipated. The Government imposed limits on top earnings and charges for dentures were introduced in 1951. Demand gradually declined, but because full information about dentists' total earnings (i.e. including private practice) and practice expenses was not available, the Health Departments and the BDA jointly discussed how to fix future levels of remuneration. The BDA demanded removal of the limit on top earnings, but the Department was insistent, although it suggested new rates for items of service which could raise the ceiling for top incomes. The BDA were not enthusiastic about this, but a survey of their members showed that a majority were not against this system of payment, so they accepted. The Royal Commission on Doctors' and Dentists' Remuneration made some specific recommendations about the pay of dentists, and it confirmed that general dental practitioners' pay should be based on fees for items of service. In order to fix the timings and rates for each dental operation so that when a dentist with average expenses works for the standard number of hours and takes the standard time per operation, he receives the standard remuneration, the Dental Rates Study Group was set up. It fixes relative times, determines gross fees per item and ascertains the total number of hours worked, and reviews these constantly. It assesses the level of practice expenses annually from information on dentists' incomes obtained through the Inland Revenue and adds this into the target net income. The Dental Rates Study Group consists of representatives of the profession and the DHSS under an independent chairman, and is assisted by statisticians appointed by both sides.

The system of paying general dental practitioners is complicated. The Doctors' and Dentists' Review Body advises the Government on the average net income that dentists should receive for working a specified number of chairside hours per year. The Dental Rates Study Group (a committee of representatives from the profession and the DHSS under an independent Chairman) assesses from time to time the level of dentists' practice expenses from information provided by the Inland

Revenue in order to determine average gross earnings, and hence to draw up a scale of fees to produce average earnings of that level. The effect of this system is gradually to reduce the fee for a given treatment as more of those treatments are being carried out faster or more efficiently. The system has been called 'the treadmill' because it rewards dentists for doing a greater number of those treatments. It also inherently rewards restorative work (i.e. crowns and fillings) and under the NHS no fees are paid for specific preventive treatments nor for giving advice to patients about dental hygiene. The costs of general dental services to the NHS are therefore controlled to some extent by the degree of accuracy of the Dental Rates Study Group's calculations. The Dental Estimates Board has to give prior approval for concessionary fees which can be claimed for treatments where a range of possible costs exists. Its records indicate the number and range of different courses of treatment that are given under the NHS, but no comparable figures exist for the extent of private treatment and for the number of people who do not go to a dentist at all.

Dental Manpower

Regional variations in the distribution of dentists have always been marked, and are associated with the social class structure, such that there tend to be proportionally more dentists in areas with proportionally more people in the higher social classes. In order to strengthen the professional manpower, some observers favour greater use of ancillary dental staff. Dental technicians are anyway needed to make dentures, crowns and inlays, and to construct special clips and springs used to straighten children's teeth. They serve an apprenticeship with a dental surgeon or in a dental laboratory, a hospital or a commercial firm, or can undergo full-time training. Most general dental practitioners use the services of a central commercial laboratory, while in hospital departments, the technicians may also do work in connection with the treatment of facial injuries. Dental surgery assistants work with general dental practitioners, dealing with all the administrative duties as well as preparing instruments, mixing fillings materials and processing X-rays. Dental hygienists are trained in schools of dentistry to be able to clean, scale and polish teeth, and they also play an important part in giving advice to patients about dental hygiene. In the school dental service, dental auxiliaries are trained women who carry out simple fillings, extract milk teeth, and clean, scale and polish the teeth of school children, and also teach them about the importance of proper oral hygiene. Although all these auxiliary staff are small in number (their remuneration is negotiated through Professional and Technical Whitley Council 'B') they can clearly take on the routine work under supervision and allow the dentist to apply his specialist skills and knowledge more widely.

Ophthalmic Services

The Worshipful Company of Spectacle Makers was given a Royal Charter in 1629, and opticians date their professional origins back to this time. However, it was not until the mid-nineteenth century that instruments for examining the eye and investigating refractive errors were invented, thus enabling the scientific diagnosis and treatment of sight disorders to develop. Qualified doctors specialising in the study of the eye took on the work of sight testing as did the opticians who also sold spectacles. In 1895 the British Optical Association was founded, its aim being to achieve state registration for opticians, which would eliminate unqualified practitioners and establish professional status for the duly qualified. In 1923, a register of the Joint Council of Qualified Opticians was instituted, and the Council promoted a bill for state registration. But the BMA were against it since they regarded doctors as being exclusively qualified to detect disease , and stated that all sight testing should be carried out under medical supervision. Most of the approved societies under the National Health Insurance scheme required the people they covered to go only to a practitioner on this register or to a doctor for sight testing.

At the time of the introduction of the NHS there were several different groups testing sight and supplying spectacles, of varying standards of professional qualification. In order to regularise the situation it was decided to place all sight testing in the hospital sector under specialist doctors (called ophthalmologists) while the dispensing of spectacles could go on inside or outside the hospitals. However, since the hospitals in 1948 were not able to take on the full service a Supplementary Ophthalmic Service was instituted.[3] It allowed for ophthalmic medical practitioners and ophthalmic opticians to continue as independent operators, placing them under contracts with the NHS administered through the Executive Councils. But the intended shift to a hospital service never happened and in the Health Service and Public Health Acts 1968,[4] the word 'supplementary' was removed, and the name changed to General Ophthalmic Service. Ophthalmic medical practitioners only test sight and prescribe lenses, ophthalmic opticians test sight and prescribe and dispense lenses to their patients, and dispensing opticians supply spectacles and contact lenses prescribed by ophthalmic medical practitioners or ophthalmic opticians. Most of the work is done in the community, although orthoptists, who treat squints in children (see Chapter 8) work entirely in hospitals. Under the school health service sight testing is provided for children, but if treatment is required, they have to attend a hospital or consult an optician.

In 1953 the Crook report[5] recommended a General Optical Council should be established to maintain a register of ophthalmic and dispensing opticians, and to exercise governing and disciplinary powers over them. This was accepted by the Government but it was not until 1958 that the Council was established under the Opticians Act, partly because of strong opposition by sections of the medical profession. The General Optical Council gave opticians their independent professional status and restricted the legal prescribing and dispensing of spectacles to them (or registered medical practitioners). The necessary qualifications for registration of ophthalmic opticians are granted after three years full-time study by the Worshipful Company, the British Optical Association and the Institute of Ophthalmic Science. Dispensing opticians can obtain qualifications for registration through two years full-time study, three years day release or four years correspondence course, from the Association of Dispensing Opticians or with the Dispensing Certificate of the British Optical Association. Most dispensing opticians are members of the National Ophthalmic Treatment Board (NOTB) Association, and practise from medical eye centres that this body monitors.

As with dental services, the demand for ophthalmic services at the start of the NHS was very high, and it appeared that removing the barrier of cost enabled many people who needed spectacles to come forward and obtain them. Opticians' pay is negotiated through the Optical Whitley Council although most of them dispense non-NHS lenses and frames as well. An optician does not have a list of patients like a GP, but is paid a separate fee for each item of service, under the terms of his contract with the Family Practitioner Committee. Patients also pay a charge for lenses and frames, and these payments virtually cover the cost of them to the optician. Ophthalmic and dispensing opticians obtain spectacles made up to their specification from prescription houses, at prices fixed by negotiations between the DHSS and the prescription houses, set out in the 'Statement of Fees and Charges'.[6] Prescription houses purchase lenses and frames from manufacturing firms either unfinished or in semi-finished form, and fit the lenses to the frames according to prescriptions placed with them by the opticians. Some of the dispensing opticians' businesses are owned by multiple chains, some of which also own prescription houses. Non-NHS frames are very popular, and NHS lenses can be fitted to them, although they cost the patient and the optician more to obtain. Similarly, if an optician dispenses private lenses and frames, his fee will be higher than under the NHS, and it will be borne by the patient.

There are a number of factors contributing to the stability of the general ophthalmic services. First, apart from the development of plastic, multifocal and contact lenses, there have been no major technical advance in the production of spectacle lenses. Secondly, over the age of forty-five, an increasingly large section of the population needs to wear spectacles. Thirdly, the manufacturing process for NHS lenses is basically unchanged so that increased production costs have been less than increases in manufacturing costs in general. This stability has helped the NHS considerably because the constant and wide demand for spectacles can be met by opticians who can extend their incomes through non-NHS work. The NHS has therefore been able to provide an adequate comprehensive service that is not fully integrated with the medical services, yet the existence of demand for private treatment has made it worthwhile for opticians to undertake NHS work as well.

Opticians have a representative body called the Local Optical Committee at area level, which is consulted by the FPC and elects members to the FPC and its committees. It is joined by one ophthalmic and one dispensing optician from the hospital side to form the Area Optical Committee, which is the statutory advisory committee to the AHA. At regional level the advisory committee consists of two ophthalmic and one dispensing optician from each Area Optical Committee with two or three regional representatives of hospital opticians, and representatives of training establishments in the region.

Pharmaceutical Services

The pharmacists' profession can also trace its origins back three or four hundred years, but it developed from two distinct lines. The Society of Apothecaries was founded in 1617, and its members dispensed medicines on the orders of physicians as well as prescribing and dispensing medicines for patients themselves; the chemists and druggists were retail shopkeepers who did not prescribe, but prepared and sold medicines in competition with the apothecaries. The Apothecaries Act of 1815 allowed apothecaries to charge for their professional advice to patients as well as for the medicines they dispensed, and this encouraged them to become more like general medical practitioners. The chemists and druggists progressively took over as the dispensers of physicians' prescriptions. The Pharmaceutical Society of Great Britain was formed in 1841, and the Pharmacy Acts of 1852 and 1868 gave it the statutory duty to register pharmaceutical chemists who had obtained its diploma after training and examination, and to prevent those who were not pharmaceutical chemists or chemists or druggists from dispensing medicines or selling poisons. Under the National Health Insurance scheme only registered pharmacists could dispense medicines prescribed for insured people (except in remote areas where the doctors themselves could dispense their prescriptions).

Under the National Health Service, separate arrangements are made for dispensing medicines in the hospitals and the community. The Hospital Pharmaceutical Service employs registered pharmacists and technicians to prepare and dispense medicines to hospital inpatients and outpatients as prescribed by hospital doctors. The General Pharmaceutical Service involves retail pharmacists in dispensing medicines prescribed by general practitioners, under contract with the Family Practitioner Committees (Executive Councils before 1974). Area Health Authorities are responsible for the hospital pharmaceutical service and have appointed Area and District Pharmaceutical Officers to manage it. There is also a statutory Area Pharmaceutical Advisory Committee which brings together views from both the hospital and community side, and the Area Pharmaceutical Officer attends their meetings as of right. At regional level the advisory committee has one hospital and one retail pharmacist from each advisory committee and a representative from the schools of pharmacy servicing the region, and the Regional Pharmaceutical Officer attends their meetings.

The General Pharmaceutical Service

The system of providing general pharmaceutical services under the NHS exists to provide patients free of charge (subject to a nominal prescription charge for some categories of patients) with drugs and appliances that have been prescribed by their doctors for them. The system is also designed to impose a number of controls which will contain the costs of drugs within reasonable limits. Doctors are free to prescribe any drugs and appliances (but not foods or toiletries) which will, in their opinion, benefit the health of their patients. They write out the prescription on a standard form which is taken to a chemist for dispensing, or sometimes is dispensed by the doctor. The chemist supplies the prescribed drugs from stocks which he has purchased from the manufacturers or a wholesaler. He pays the supplier on normal credit terms, and is reimbursed by the Family Practitioner Committee for the prescriptions he has dispensed. At the end of each month the chemist sends the prescription forms to the Prescription Pricing Authority which calculates the costs of the ingredients according to the Drug Tariff. This is a list of the prices of drugs which is issued annually by the DHSS together with amendments during the year. For each prescription, the Prescription Pricing Authority also calculates the on-cost allowance for the chemist's overhead expenses and

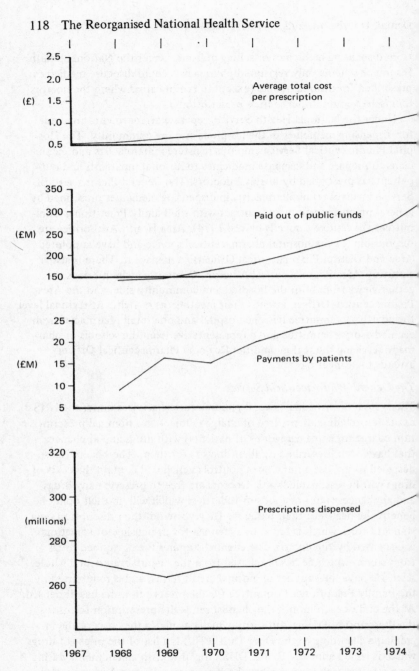

Figure 14 *Pharmaceutical Services (England and Wales)*
Source: Annual Abstract of Statistics, 1976

profits, his dispensing fee and an allowance for containers. It then notifies the Family Practitioner Committee of the amount to be paid to the chemist for the month's prescriptions.

The Prescription Pricing Authority came into existence in 1974 to continue the work that had been carried out since 1948 by the Joint Pricing Committee, and before that by Joint Pricing Bureaux under the National Health Insurance Scheme. Its main offices are in Newcastle upon Tyne and there are eight other offices in the north of England which each price the NHS prescriptions for specified parts of England. The Authority has eight members nominated from the FPCs, and the DHSS nominates one doctor and three pharmacists. It has almost 2,000 staff who process about 275 million prescriptions annually (see Figure 14). In Wales the Welsh Health Technical Services Organisation does this pricing work for the FPCs.

The Prescription Pricing Authority also uses the information from a sample of prescriptions it prices in order to prepare estimates of drug use by therapeutic group, class of preparation, etc. and to give indications of the number of prescriptions submitted and the average cost per prescription each month. In addition, once every year each general practitioner is sent a statement of the number and cost of the prescriptions he has issued during one month. From these calculations the average costs of all doctors in that FPC area can be compared with that individual doctor's costs.

In 1976 an inquiry into the work of the Prescription Pricing Authority was initiated because of concern over delays in paying the accounts of chemist contractors and dispensing doctors, and because of difficulties in obtaining information about prescribing patterns in order to tackle the problem of the cost of the pharmaceutical services. The report of the inquiry was published in January 1977,[7] making a number of short-term recommendations for speeding up the settlement of accounts. It also suggested that the Authority should give doctors information about their prescribing patterns, and give more information generally to the DHSS, the Committee on Safety of Medicines and the pharmaceutical industry.

If a chemist (who may be an individual, a firm or a corporate body) wishes to open a shop as a pharmacy, he first has to have the premises registered in accordance with the Medicines Act 1968, and this is done through the mediation of the Pharmaceutical Society of Great Britain. A pharmacist who wishes to dispense NHS medicines then has to apply to the FPC for a contract which specifies the terms and conditions of service, and includes requirements relating to opening hours and participation in the out-of-hours rota service. If a pharmacist wishes to have different opening hours from those specified he has to apply to the Hours of Service Committee of the FPC. This committee specifies the minimum opening hours and the rota service that chemists are obliged to observe, and keeps these arrangements and any special cases under review. Pay negotiations for retail pharmacists are handled by the Pharmaceutical Whitley Council, and their central representative body is the Pharmaceutical Services Negotiating Committee. The National Pharmaceutical Union was founded in 1920 as a trade association for individual retail pharmacists. In recent years it has changed its brief to include the interests of employee pharmacists, and has also admitted company chemists to membership — this group now forms the majority of its members and it has changed its name to the National Pharmaceutical Association.

Just as there are local medical, dental and optical committees, so the retail pharmacists are represented by a body called the Area Pharmaceutical Committee. Its membership is nominated by independent contractor chemists, the Company Chemists Association (a grouping of those companies who own multiple stores that dispense pharmaceuticals under the NHS, e.g. Boots and Westons), the Cooperative Society (which owns several retail pharmacies registered with the NHS) and employee pharmacists of contractor chemists, all of whom are connected with contract premises within the area. The Area Pharmaceutical Committee is consulted by the Family Practitioner Committee and it appoints members of the FPC and those of its committees where pharmaceutical representation is required.

A chemist is only likely to open a shop on a given site if the balance of NHS work and over-the-counter sales he could expect there would be economically worthwhile. As a result, pharmacies have been closing at the rate of approximately 300 each year, and comprehensive pharmaceutical coverage throughout England and Wales has been jeopardised. For a number of years a 'rural area subsidy' payment had been available to certain chemists in order to preserve services to rural communities, but this was not able to prevent closures. However in 1977 after protracted discussions between the DHSS and the Pharmaceutical Services Negotiating Committee, a new system called the 'Essential Small Pharmacies Scheme' was implemented. It provides for supplementary payments to be made to pharmacies which are 3 kilometers or more from the nearest pharmacy, dispense between 6,000 and 30,000 prescriptions annually, have a non-NHS turnover of less than £25,000 per annum (at March 1976 prices) and provide a full pharmaceutical service. It has also been agreed that pharmacies which do not meet these stringent criteria but are also in difficulties will in future be considered for extra payments under the new scheme.

Hospital Pharmaceutical Service

The hospital pharmaceutical service is now organised on the basis of the recommendations of the Noel Hall report,[7] published in 1970. The operational unit is the area, and hospitals within it are served by principal and staff pharmacists managed by the Area Pharmaceutical Officer, in sections covering inpatients, outpatients, the manufacture of sterile equipment, and quality control. There are at least eight pharmacists per 4,000-6,000 beds (with supporting staff) and they handle the acquisition and storage of drugs, dressings and medical gases, the distribution and dispensing of medicines within the hospital, bulk preparation and quality control as well as checking ward and departmental stocks. The Noel Hall report recommended that new gradings and salaries for principal and staff pharmacists and technicians should be introduced in order to make hospital pharmacy a more attractive career, especially for younger people.[8] The pay negotiations are handled by the Professional and Technical Whitley Council 'A'.

The Relationship Between the NHS and the Pharmaceutical Industry

Because doctors decide which medicines to prescribe, the manufacturers aim their sales promotion efforts at the doctors, but under the arrangements which have been described, neither the doctor nor the patient pays for the medicines (the prescription charge paid by patients represents only a portion of the prescription cost — at present averaging about 16 per cent). Ministers are responsible to Parliament for their departments' spending of Exchequer funds and from the earliest days of the NHS, successive health ministers have been under pressure from the Public Accounts Committee to ensure that prices paid to pharmaceutical companies are reasonable. The problem is that the companies sell most of their pharmaceuticals in the UK to the National Health Services since there is comparatively little non-NHS prescribing. The pharmaceutical industry has insisted that it needs a high level of profitability in order to finance research and to cover the high risks in developing new drugs. Over the years a number of attempts to control the cost of prescribed medicines have been made by successive governments. In 1949 the Joint Committee on the Classification of Proprietary Preparations was set up by the Central and Scottish Health Services Councils to advise the health ministers on the status of proprietary preparations and to indicate where less expensive standard forms of these preparations existed.

The point was that pharmaceutical manufacturers market certain

medicines under brand names to ensure continuity of sales if they are
the originator of the product, or to distinguish their formulation from
similar ones of the same basic chemicals. Often, therapeutically identical
unbranded (or non-proprietary) preparations can be obtained at lower
cost. The Joint Committee's classification (which was periodically revised) together with the British National Formulary, the British Pharma-
copaeia, the British Pharmaceutical Codex, Data Sheets and Prescribers'
Notes all provide listings which are intended to guide doctors away
from the expensive proprietary medicines wherever a standard and less
expensive alternative exists. The Hinchliffe Committee[9] was set up in
1957 to investigate the cost of prescribing and it recommended that
where a GP habitually exceeded the local average for prescription costs
(as shown in returns from the pricing offices to the Executive Councils)
the Local Medical Committee should investigate the case. Penalties
imposed on GPs for overprescribing should be severe. (In fact, a
negligible number of GPs have been investigated by LMCs, the highest
penalty being in the region of £100. Since 1971 no penalties have been
imposed, although some GPs (about 2,000 in 1974) are visited by
Regional Medical Officers of the DHSS to discuss the pattern and cost
of their prescribing.)

Another facet of the pharmaceutical industry's relationship with the
NHS was that most of the research and clinical trials on new products
were controlled by the manufacturers and not the consumers. Few
medicines that are introduced can be entirely free from risks and
preparatory testing for safety is required before general issue. The
Committee on Safety of Drugs (Chairman, Sir Derrick Dunlop) was set
up in 1963 to monitor the process of testing used by the industry
before its products could be allowed on the market. In 1964 the Joint
Committee was dissolved while the Dunlop Committee remained to
regulate the safety of drugs. A new committee was also set up
(Chairman, Sir Alastair McGregor) to classify medicines into therapeutic
categories, and thus to advise practitioners on whether, in the
Committee's expert view, particular drugs were worth using.

As well as influencing the prescribing habits of doctors governments
have also attempted to determine fair prices for their NHS drug
purchases, and in 1958 a Voluntary Price Regulation Scheme (VPRS)
was negotiated with the industry, which related the price of prescribed
medicines to their prices in overseas markets (on the assumption that
where patients or private insurance companies had to pay for the
medicines, the prices were likely to be reasonable).[10] However, continued
pressure from the Public Accounts Committee to reduce the NHS drugs
bill, and political concern over the incidence of price fixing by

manufacturers of patented medicines brought about negotiations for a second VPRS in 1961. This established that the prices of major products should be the subject of direct price negotiations on the basis of the supplying companies' overall profitability. In 1964 and 1972, further modifications to the VPRS were negotiated. However, these arrangements did not cover all the products purchased by the NHS and there were significant problems in isolating those profits resulting solely from the UK pharmaceutical trading of international companies. In 1977 after further negotiations between the Government and the pharmaceutical industry a new agreement was reached: the Pharmaceutical Price Regulation Scheme (PPRS) which superceded the VPRS. Under the new arrangements, more stringent controls have been imposed on the contents of drug advertisements, the manufacturers are obliged to submit forecasts of profitability of medicines sales to the NHS before the end of the financial year (thus improving the ability of the government to check unacceptably high profits) and the government's power to obtain compulsory licensing of pharmaceutical patents has been removed.

An event that shocked the pharmaceutical industry occurred in 1961 when it became known that some hospital pharmacists had been buying cheaper but chemically identical supplies from unlicensed manufacturers in countries which did not operate schemes for granting patents to pharmaceutical products.[11] Technically the pharmacists were breaking the law (although they were saving money for the NHS), so the Minister of Health (Enoch Powell) decided to invoke Section 46 of the Patents Act 1948, which legalised these imports for 'the services of the crown' in relation to hospital pharmaceutical supplies. In 1965, the Government discontinued these imports in return for satisfactory price settlements between regular UK suppliers and the NHS. Nevertheless, the Government's wish to rationalise the form of its negotiations with the manufacturing companies and its concern to control the continually rising cost of pharmaceuticals resulted in the setting up of the Committee of Inquiry into the Relationship of the Pharmaceutical Industry and the National Health Service in 1965 (the Sainsbury Committee).[12] Its report, published two years later, contained four major recommendations:

(1) Companies should provide annual financial returns to the Ministry of Health showing in prescribed form the returns from its pharmaceutical business.

(2) Problems associated with financial transfers and transactions with associated companies should be controlled.

(3) Companies should submit 'Standard Cost Returns' showing proposed prices and costs for new products, and eventually for

major products already on the market.

(4)   A Medicines Commission should be set up.

Points 1 and 2 were accepted and taken up in discussion between the industry and the NHS on further revisions of the VPRS. Point 3 was rejected by the Association of the British Pharmaceutical Industry (the representative body for pharmaceutical manufacturers) on the grounds that because of the high costs of innovation, operating ratios could only be reviewed as a whole rather than in relation to individual products. The Ministry of Health also made it clear that they would not have enough civil servants of suitable ability to scrutinise these returns.

The Medicines Act was passed in 1968 and embodies the Sainsbury recommendation for a Medicines Commission. This has replaced the Dunlop Committee and under it a new Committee on the Safety of Medicines has been set up. The Act completely recast the legal basis for research, manufacture and development of medicinal products.[13]

Although all these steps represent a considerable effort to regularise the supply and prescription of pharmaceuticals under the NHS, the apparently incompatible requirements of governments and the industry make it difficult for smooth negotiations on prices to be maintained. The pharmaceutical industry is more profitable than industry as a whole: in the UK, about 14 per cent return on money invested is the average for all industry while the pharmaceutical sector achieves an average return of 25 per cent. The industry maintains that this profit is earned by its efficiency and is a necessary buffer to the high risk factor, but critics reply that patented brand names and heavy sales promotions give the manufacturers quasi-monopolistic powers. The situation can be illustrated by the case of Hoffmann-La Roche.

Hoffman-La Roche is a Swiss-based pharmaceutical company which developed two particularly successful tranquillisers marketed in the UK by its operating company Roche Products Ltd under the brand names Valium and Librium. By 1970 Valium and Librium accounted for 68 per cent of all tranquillisers prescribed under the NHS and, since they were relatively highly priced, the company was able to make substantial profits on these sales. Roche Products had chosen not to participate in the VPRS but the DHSS suspected that unacceptably high profits were being made at its expense from Valium and Librium, so it took the unprecedented step of referring the case through the Secretary of State for Trade and Industry to the Monopolies Commission. In February 1973 the Monopolies Commission reported that 'monopoly' conditions did prevail and recommended price cuts of 60 per cent for Librium and 75 per cent for Valium. Roche Products appealed against this and after a protracted legal battle the dispute was settled out of court in November

1975. Roche was required to join the VPRS and to repay part of the estimated £12 million excess profits. The balance was allowed to Roche to offset losses caused by inflation and exchange rate changes. From then on, prices for Valium and Librium were allowed to rise in accordance with the terms of the VPRS.

Hoffman-La Roche is not necessarily representative of other pharmaceutical companies either in terms of its organisation or its relations with governments. The description of this case however reflects the problems that can arise when an unavoidably dependent relationship develops between the government and a sector of private industry. Although most pharmaceutical manufacturers would, in the case of the NHS, acknowledge the need for some government involvement in their affairs, they fundamentally criticise government's accuracy in defining reasonable levels of profitability.[14]

7 NURSING SERVICES

The senior posts for nurses at region, area and district levels have already been mentioned, but this chapter will go into nursing organisation more thoroughly and will consider the arrangements for nurses' education and training. The next chapter will discuss the various scientific, technical and paramedical services that are, in addition to medicine and nursing, essential elements in the total scheme of health care.

Hospital Nursing

Nursing began as a vocation — a call to a life of devotion through the alleviation of suffering of others — which was associated with the monks and nuns of some religious orders at about the time that hospitals such as St. Bartholemew's (1123) and St. Thomas's (1215) were founded. The services were given by men and women who were unskilled, but of 'respectable' parentage and generous outlook. However, from the Reformation (sixteenth century) to the nineteenth century, this tradition lapsed, and care given to the sick was haphazard and became associated with the servant classes of the community. Although several of the great voluntary hospitals were founded during this period, there was little or no provision for nursing, and the work was regarded as a sordid duty fit only for 'broken down and drunk old widows'.[1]

After the mid-nineteenth century attitudes began to change, and the idea of nursing as a vocation was revived. In 1840, Elizabeth Fry founded an Institute of Nursing at Guy's Hospital, where women were trained to nurse under Quaker influence. Florence Nightingale (1820—1910) who came from a cultured and influential upper-class family was herself at the heart of these changes. She went to Paris and to Prussia to train as a nurse, with the intention of returning to improve hospital conditions in Britain. However, when the Crimean war broke out, the reports of chaos and suffering amongst the forces urged her to go there herself with thirty trained nurses where she cared for the wounded and was able to improve the medical services substantially. After her return to England, she was regarded as an influential and publicly respected person, and was thus able to found the Nightingale Training School in 1860 at St. Thomas's Hospital. The entrants to it were all respectable ladies, and they were trained in the principles and skills of nursing, such as they were at that time. As a result, three grades of trained nurses became established.

126

Sisters were nurses in charge of a ward, who carried out the doctors' orders and trained and worked with probationer nurses. Night superintendents were in charge of the night staff, and deputised for the matron. The matron herself was a gentlewoman (like the others) and responsible to the hospital authorities not only for the employment and training of nurses, but for a variety of housekeeping and administrative arrangements.

Many of the voluntary hospitals adopted this scheme of training and organisation, but the poor law infirmaries, fever hospitals and asylums were much slower to follow. There was no recognised qualification for psychiatric nursing until 1891, when the Royal Medico-Psychological Society started to issue certificates. There was a long and complicated struggle over the issue of registration for nurses and the medical profession in particular was determined to see that measures to regulate the practice of nursing were improved. Finally in 1919 the Nurses' Act was passed, establishing the General Nursing Council (GNC) as the registering authority. The GNC was made responsible for keeping a register and a roll of nurses who had trained in approved institutions and passed examinations, usually after two or three years of study. After this time, professions other than nursing began to be open to women (e.g. physiotherapy and radiography) and training schools were set up for them in some hospitals, under the direction of the matron, although the medical superintendent or the secretary of the hospital gradually assumed responsibility for some of the other non-nursing activities. Following the Local Government Act (1929)[2] local authorities took charge of the poor law infirmaries and administered them and the maternity homes through their Medical Officers of Health.

During the Second World War several improvements in techniques of health care took place, and these were adopted after 1945, so that by the time the NHS was created, hospital administrators had taken over most if not all of the housekeeping and personnel arrangements and appointed service managers, leaving the matron in charge of nursing matters alone. The status of matrons in the former local authority hospitals definitely improved, but with the moves towards grouping hospitals together and administering them as consolidated units, group secretaries and senior medical staff assumed effective control, and the matrons were left with a reduced but more specialised sphere of responsibility, there being no collective voice for the nursing staff at the level of group administration.

The Salmon Report

Shortages of trained nurses and this apparent decline in the status of the profession prompted the Government to set up a committee in 1963. Its report, known as the Salmon report,[3] noted that the title 'matron' was applied equally to nursing heads of hospitals with ten beds and with 1,000 beds, and that a distinction between their different duties and rights was not made clear. Furthermore, as men were increasingly joining the profession the titles 'matron' and 'sister' had become anachronistic. It also found that the role of nurses as administrators was poorly defined, and that there was confusion over the relative status of general nursing, midwifery, psychiatric nursing and teaching. The report proposed that status should be determined by the kinds of decisions being made and not by the number of beds controlled or the type of patients nursed. Most senior nurses deciding policy were called 'top managers', those programming policy were called 'middle managers', and those controlling the execution of policy were called 'first-line managers'. The report further introduced the terms: section, unit, area and division, to define a nurse's span of control, and named the senior nursing posts accordingly (see Figure15).

The Minister of Health and the Secretary of State for Scotland accepted these recommendations and it was suggested that sixteen pilot schemes for introducing the new structure should be set up and evaluated over a period of years. Of course the structure outlined needed to be flexible enough to fit in with the differing local circumstances. It is not therefore possible to generalise about the precise structure adopted in each case, but the idea was that the Chief Nursing Officer was responsible for all nursing services and education in the Group and was not identified with an individual hospital within it. She was to be accepted as the head of nursing services by the Hospital Management Committee or Board of Governors, and was to voice nursing opinion at group level. The Principal Nursing Officer (PNO) became responsible to him or her for the management of a division. A division could be planned on an institutional or a functional basis, to cover, for example, general nursing or maternity work or psychiatric nursing, or teaching. The Senior Nursing Officer would be responsible to the PNO for the management of services within an area; this might be the whole of a separate medium-sized hospital or a number of small hospitals. The Nursing Officer was in charge of a unit, that is three to six medical or surgical wards, or for example, a small suite of operating theatres, a specialised unit or an accident and emergency centre. Charge

LEVEL	GRADE	TITLE	SPHERE
Top managers	10	Chief Nursing Officer	Group
Top managers	9	Principal Nursing Officer	Division
Middle managers	8	Senior Nursing Officer	Area
Middle managers	7	Nursing Officer	Unit
First-line managers	6	Charge Nurse/Ward Sister	Section
	5	Staff Nurse	

Figure 15 *Senior Nursing Staff Organisation*

Source: Report of the Committee on Senior Nursing Staff Structure, HMSO, 1966

Nurses (male) or Ward Sisters (female) would control an individual section, which could be a ward or an operating theatre.

Community Nursing

Community nurses include home or district nurses, midwives and health visitors. Their work, unlike that of hospital nurses, owes its development to the voluntary organisations of the nineteenth century. Whereas hospital nurses followed doctors' orders in the care of patients, community nurses worked more independently, under the auspices of voluntary organisations. The title 'health visitor' probably first came into use in 1862 when one such body, the Ladies' Sanitary Reform Association of Manchester and Salford, paid staff to visit people in their district, concentrating on cleanliness, helping the sick and advising mothers on the care of their children. In 1875 the Royal Sanitary Institute (now the Royal Society of Health) was founded 'to promote the health of the people' and began to set examinations for sanitary inspectors. In 1892 Florence Nightingale started a course at North Buckinghamshire Technical College where 'health missionaries' were trained to meet the needs of 'home health-bringing', and the women thus trained were employed by the local council to visit people in need. The Royal Sanitary Institute set examinations for health visitors and school nurses from 1906, and in 1908 the London County Council passed an act specifying that health visitors should hold a certificate from a society approved by the Local Government Board.

By the turn of the century, infant mortality had risen to the rate of 163 per 1,000, and the need for health visitors to advise and instruct mothers on the proper care of their babies was no longer in doubt. Acts passed in 1907 and 1915 requiring births to be registered provided the means of identifying the problem, and health visitors' work concentrated particularly on infant and maternal welfare. From 1925 to 1962 the Royal Sanitary Institute was the body responsible for examining trained health visitors, after which the Council for Training of Health Visitors became the central body for the whole of the UK. In 1962, the Council for Training Health Visitors was jointly set up with the Central Council for the Education and Training of Social Workers by an Act of Parliament, with a common chairman. After the Seebohm report was accepted in 1970, the separation took place, and the body became the Council for the Education and Training of Health Visitors (CETHV). It consists of thirty-one members representing health visitors, nursing education, medicine, educational interests and some others.

Midwives had been recognised from earliest times. In the seventeenth century they were often well-paid and well-respected women, recognised by the bishop. But the rise of the medical profession caused their status to decline, as the richer families employed doctors to deliver their babies. In the nineteenth century the majority of midwives were 'not only untrained and inexperienced, but ignorant, superstitious and of very low character'.[4] However, the Midwives Institute was founded in 1881 by a group of women who wished to improve the standards and status of midwifery. The Midwives Act was passed in 1902 and it established the Central Midwives Board to keep a roll of approved midwives and to ensure adequate training programmes and standards for good practice. The Ministry of Health was created in 1919 and it took on the supervision of the Central Midwives Board.

Midwifery was practised both in hospital and in the community, but staff came essentially from the voluntary organisations. After 1948, the local health authorities were given the statutory duty under the NHS to provide a domiciliary midwifery service and to supervise standards of practice. The hospitals were required to provide sufficient facilities so that every mother could have her baby delivered in hospital if she so wished. The trend has indeed favoured hospital deliveries, but more recently, some areas have found their hospital maternity services under-used partly because of the declining birth rate.

District nursing differs from health visiting and midwifery in that it remained a service provided by voluntary organisations for a much longer period, and in the nineteenth century it had not yet become a well-defined occupation. The history of district nursing is closely connected with the benevolence of William Rathbone in Liverpool, and others, such as the Ranyard nurses. The Queen's Institute of District Nursing was founded with money given to Queen Victoria on her Golden and Diamond Jubilees. It accepted for training nurses who had completed the basic training for registration or enrolment. Under the 1946 NHS Act, local health authorities became responsible for organising the home nursing services and they tended to use the established local Queen's Institute nurses on an agency basis until later, when they began to recruit and employ their nursing staff directly.

The creation of the National Health Service rationalised the separate community nursing services under the local authorities, and the Medical Officers of Health were in charge of virtually all their health services, including nursing. Superintendent Nursing Officers were appointed for home nursing services (some already existed under the

Queen's Institute pattern); midwives were usually managed by a head of services designated Non-Medical Supervisor of Midwives and health visitors by a Superintendent Health Visitor. However, with the growth of local authority health services provision this pattern altered, and by 1968, forty-two county councils, thirty-four county boroughs and seventeen London borough councils had appointed a chief nursing officer to organise and direct the work of their community nursing services. A notable development has been the closer association of community nurses with general practitioners, resulting in improved clinical and preventive services for patients on GPs' lists. However, the single greatest hope for transforming the NHS into an integrated system of preventive care is represented in the concepts of the primary health care team and health centre practice. GPs and community nurses working in conjunction with dentists, chiropodists, social workers and others can aim to provide a comprehensive range of services to the local population, depending on the hospitals for those acute and specialist services which cannot easily be provided from a health centre. Although the development of health centres has been relatively slow, the management and organisation of community nursing services could respond to these concepts.

The Mayston Report

In 1968 the National Board for Prices and Incomes reported on the pay of nurses and midwives,[5] and it recommended implementation of the Salmon structures and salaries in the hospitals on a national scale. It also noted that the fragmented community nursing services should be coordinated by a designated head nursing officer, and this was one of the forces that motivated the DHSS to set up a working party (under the chairmanship of E.L. Mayston) to consider the extent to which the Salmon report's proposals were applicable to the community nursing services. Its report[6] was published in 1969 and commended to the local authorities by the Secretary of State. It noted that health visitors were concerned with the health of the household as a whole, health education, the early detection of abnormalities in children, the school health service and general assistance to families in difficulties. It recognised that home nurses provided skilled care under the clinical direction of GPs in patients' homes and in health centres, and recommended that they work in attachment to general practices, concentrating on rehabilitation, elementary home physiotherapy and care of the elderly and chronic sick. It also proposed that (1) every local authority should appoint a chief nursing officer; (2) their senior nursing staff structure should be reviewed immediately; (3) three levels of managers (top, middle and first-line) should be appointed, and (4) management training should be provided for senior community nurses.

The result was that local authorities gradually reorganised their nursing arrangements. The title Director of Nursing Services was given to the head, and second-level 'top managers' were appointed to the larger authorities with the title Divisional Nursing Officer. Area Nursing Officers coordinated groups of nursing officers to comprise the 'middle-management' tier, leaving the qualified field workers as 'first-line managers', parallel to the Charge Nurse/Ward Sister grade of the Salmon scheme.

The Effect of the NHS Reorganisation

The effect that the 1974 reorganisation had on the changes being instituted as a result of the Salmon and Mayston reports was one of consolidation, mainly within the districts. Its aim was, in this respect, to integrate the hospital and community nursing services and to improve the contact and cooperation between nursing and other disciplines at all levels throughout the structure. The posts of Chief Nursing Officer (Salmon) and Director of Nursing Services (Mayston) were both superseded by the creation of the District Nursing Officer (DNO) who became head of both the hospital and community nursing services. As a result, the 'top management' tasks are now handled by the DNO and a number of Divisional Nursing Officers (and to avoid confusion, the titles Divisional Nursing Officer and Area Nursing Officer in the Mayston scheme were changed to Principal Nursing Officer and Senior Nursing Officer respectively, as their equivalent grades in the Salmon scheme were already named). The guidance from the DHSS suggested three alternative models of organisation, and left the precise arrangements for Area Health Authorities to decide as best suited their particular circumstances.

The models were (1) a community nursing division and one or more hospital divisions, there being separate heads of each side individually responsible to the DNO; (2) functional nursing divisions reflecting 'health care groups' each managed by a divisional nursing officer accountable to the DNO; (3) functional nursing divisions integrating the hospital and community elements for management purposes. (In each case the nursing education division can serve more than one district (in multi-district areas), and district nurse and health visitor training is in any case organised on an area basis.)

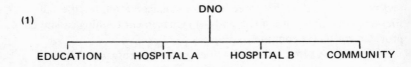

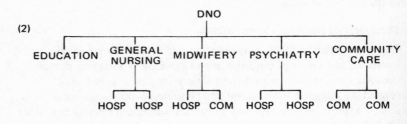

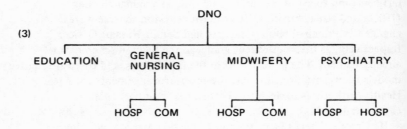

Figure 16 *District Nursing Organisation: Alternatives*

Source: Management Arrangements for the Reorganised National Health Service, HMSO, 1972

The nursing staff at first-line management level and below experienced few changes as a result of the reorganisation except, perhaps, in connection with the midwifery services. At area level, the Area Nursing Officer is a member of the Area Team of Officers, and advises the Area Health Authority on all nursing matters within the Area, but does not have line-management powers over nursing services within the districts. She is head of the nursing services provided from AHA headquarters and is closely involved in the planning process and in the establishment of close liaison with the local authority. To that extent he or she may have up to five Area Nurses (depending on the Area's size and organisation) and, of course, in single-district areas, the ANO also performs the executive functions of the District Nursing Officer. The Area Nurses cover work in relation to minor capital projects, services planning, personnel, local authority liaison and child health services. These posts are all administrative and advisory in content, and although their holders are highly trained and experienced nurses, they are well removed from direct contact with the care of patients. Similarly at the regional level, the Regional Nursing Officer may have three supporting Regional Nurses, and all are involved in detailed administrative work in relation to the planning and development of nursing services, professional education and personnel matters, as a vital part of the whole responsibility vested in the RHA and its staff.

One year after the reorganisation, most of the new posts that had been created for nurses were filled, and schemes of management had been drawn up. In September 1974 the report of a special committee of inquiry was published[7] recommending new rates of pay for nurses and midwives. Considerable unrest in the nursing profession, particularly on the hospital side, erupted earlier that year, over the conditions of NHS nursing work, and following unprecedented demonstrations by nursing staff, the Secretary of State set up this Committee of Inquiry, chaired by Lord Halsbury (who had been chairman of the Doctors' and Dentists' Review Body). The result was a substantial increase in salary for most grades of nursing staff and some increase in the holiday allowance. The Halsbury award (as it became known) was implemented by the Government in late 1974 and early 1975.

Education and Training

The General Nursing Council consists of seventeen elected members, twelve members appointed by the Secretary of State for Social Services, two by the Secretary of State for Education, and two appointed by the Privy Council (one of whom represents the universities of England and Wales). Of the elected members, fourteen must be nurses registered in the general part of the register, elected by persons on the register, two must be registered mental nurses (one male, one female) and one must be a registered sick children's nurse. The Council is required to establish a Mental Nurses' Committee, an Enrolled Nurses' Committee and a Finance Committee. Apart from its statutory duty of keeping a register of nurses of different types, e.g. general, mental illness and subnormality, sick childrens', and a Roll (general and psychiatric), the GNC has the authority to decide the content and form of training and to hold examinations for different parts of the register, and to make arrangements for assessment for admission to the roll. It also has the power to approve nurse training schools and to determine qualifications of nurse tutors. The Nurses Act 1957 (which has its origins in the Nurses Act 1919, and was itself amended by the National Health Service Reorganisation Act 1973) provides for regional nurse training committees for the regions and for Wales. Their members are appointed by the RHAs, the GNC, the Central Midwives Board and by the Minister. The GNC works in cooperation with these committees to supervise schemes of training and in developing new courses. There are minimum age and entrance requirements for student nurses, and hospitals have to meet certain minimum standards in order to be approved for practical nurse training. Nurse Education Committees may be established locally for approved student and pupil nurse training schools. The GNC has the authority to determine admission to the Register and Roll of nurses trained other than in England and Wales, and also a disciplinary function over nurses who lapse from acceptable standards of conduct. The Joint Board of Clinical Nursing Studies was established in 1970 to supervise and develop the provision of post-basic courses.

In the case of midwifery, the Central Midwives Board has control, quite separately from the GNC, for the education and training of midwives. It consists of seventeen members, seven (including two midwives) are nominated by the Secretary of State, four are medical practitioners nominated by the Royal Colleges of Physicians, Surgeons, Obstetricians and Gynaecologists and the Society of Community Medicine, four are certified midwives nominated by the Royal College of Midwives, and there are two others. The Board has disciplinary powers over trained midwives as well as the responsibility for approving training schools. Part I of the training is carried out in hospitals and Part II in the community midwifery service, and a student must pass both parts to become a state certified midwife.

Teaching is carried out by midwives who hold the teacher's diploma granted by the Board. If state registered nurses undergo the training in midwifery, Parts I and II take six months each. Student midwives without a nursing qualification train for eighteen months before taking the Part I examinations, and then do six months more before Part II. The Area Health Authorities are appointed by the Central Midwives Board to supervise local training, and refresher courses are compulsory every five years.

The situation for health visitors is different again. From 1948 the prescribed qualifications were that potential health visitors should have passed Part I of the midwifery course before a minimum of six months further training at an approved centre, and students for the Health Visiting Certificate took the examinations specially set by the Royal Society of Health. The alternative training involved a two year health visiting course for students who had six months experience of hospital nursing. The first scheme proved more acceptable to Medical Officers of Health and became the preferred method. The effect of the creation of the NHS in 1948 was to make health visiting the statutory responsibility of the counties and county boroughs to the exclusion of the districts, and therefore, voluntary effort tended to disappear. Once the Council for the Education and Training of Health Visitors became involved, the requirements changed so that student health visitors had to be registered nurses who had undergone prescribed obstetric or midwifery training before the special one year course, controlled statutorily by the CETHV. In recent years men have become increasingly interested in working in community nursing. Until 1973, however, although certain health visiting training courses were open to them, they could not become legally recognised health visitors because the requisite obstetric or midwifery training was confined to women only. Regulations which came into operation in that year amended the legislation so that they could study obstetrics, and this paved the way for their qualified entry into health visiting. (In 1975, it also became possible for men to qualify as midwives.)

The education and training of district nurses is not prescribed by statute although most employing authorities have recognised the desirability of having all their nurses properly trained. The Queen's Institute of District Nursing (now called the Queen's Nursing Institute) was practically the only body originally providing training for district nurses. It organised a post-registration (or post-enrolment) course which became the recognised qualification until 1959. In that year, following publication of an advisory committee's report, the

Minister of Health appointed a Panel of Assessors to investigate the various training schemes of the local health authorities so that recommendations for their approval by him could be made. The Panel also assessed samples of marked examination scripts, and successful candidates were thereafter awarded the National Certificate in District Nursing. (Candidates who had trained under the auspices of the Queen's Institute were simultaneously awarded the Queen's Certificate.) About 70 per cent of district nurses now have the National Certificate in District Nursing, although it is not a prerequisite for employment. The role of the Queen's Nursing Institute has changed as a result of the Panel of Assessors' activities and it is now mainly concerned with research and information services and with benevolent work for district nurses. However, the Panel of Assessors advised further integration of district nursing schemes to ensure that local health authorities' programmes were designed to meet required standards, and in 1968, a single national examination paper was introduced, reflecting an improved standard syllabus for training.[8]

In 1974 the DHSS issued guidance on the new arrangements for the organisation of nursing, midwifery and health visiting training and education to take account of the reorganisation of the NHS. It suggested that all facilities other than those for health visitor and district nurse training should be grouped together in Nurse Education Divisions based on districts or, in some cases, on whole areas. The division should arrange all basic and post-basic educational training as well as the educational aspects of in-service training for all nursing auxiliaries and assistants. Midwifery training should be handled within the new integrated midwifery divisions. The approved theoretical training centres for home nurse training should be the responsibility of the Area Nursing Officer. The AHAs should also be responsible for sponsoring health visitors' attendance at training centres such as polytechnics or colleges of further education offering courses for health visitors. The Joint Board of Clinical Nursing Studies was reconstituted in 1973 to include responsibility for community as well as hospital nursing subjects. This Board would liaise with the AHAs. Regional nurse training committees would continue to promote the secondment of nurses for training as nurse tutors. Most of the new arrangements in this guidance have been implemented and basic and post-basic courses are organised at district level in the Education Divisions under the control of the Directors of Nurse Education.

Current Developments

Since the inception of the NHS various aspects of the nursing
profession have been the subjects of inquiries and investigations;
there has been an ongoing concern to maintain developments in the
profession so that it does not lag behind the rest of the Service.
The Standing Nursing and Midwifery Advisory Committee of the
Central Health Services Council has, for example, made
recommendations on such topics as the role of the state enrolled
nurse, the organisation of midwifery services, psychiatric nurses
and relieving nurses from non-nursing duties. Many critics have felt
the profession to be in a state of crisis for some time, and that the
changes brought about by the Salmon and Mayston reports,
for example, have had serious disadvantages as well as more positive
elements. One view is that the administrative nursing grades
newly created have tended to penalise those nurses who want
to remain in clinical practice, by associating the more attractive
salary scales with administration. Another view is that the standards
of nurse training and the quality of the teachers has not been
radically improved because the teaching grades have been relatively
poorly paid and have offered less attractive career prospects, and
that the use of students as part of the 'work force' detracts from
the quality of education available. The Halsbury award mentioned
earlier acknowledged that the pay of nurses and midwives had not
kept pace with other comparable professions, and that better
recruitment to the profession depended on more attractive
conditions of service, in relation to the clinical as well as the
administrative grades.

   In 1970 the Committee on Nursing (chaired by Professor
Asa Briggs) was set up by the Secretary of State to review the
role of the nurse and the midwife and the education and training
required for that role. The Committee published its report (the
Briggs report)[9] in October 1972 which made a number of far-
reaching proposals for change, covering the statutory framework
of the profession, education and training, manpower and
recruitment, conditions of work and the professional organisation
and career structure. The detailed recommendations are too
numerous (seventy-five) to discuss exhaustively here, and reference
to the text of the report itself is strongly advised. However,
important points that relate to the discussion above include
the following proposals:

Statutory Framework

1 There should be a single central body responsible for professional standards, education and discipline in nursing and midwifery in Great Britain – the Central Nursing and Midwifery Council.

2 There should be three distinct Educational Boards for England, Scotland and Wales, responsible to the Council, and there should be a Standing Midwifery Committee.

3 Below each Board there should be Area Committees for nursing and midwifery education.

(These all require new legislation to be enacted by Parliament, and arrangements to be made for the creation of the Boards and a redefinition of the regulating functions they would have. When the report was published, it was estimated that the new legislation, etc. could not be forthcoming before the 1980s.)

Education

1 Colleges of nursing and midwifery should be established throughout the country, financed through Area Committees.

2 There should be an increase in the number and range of pre-nursing courses including nursing cadet schemes, under the title Preparation for Nursing Courses.

3 Entry to the training should not be determined by O levels alone.

4 The age of entry should be reduced in two stages from eighteen to seventeen and a half and then to seventeen.

5 There should be one basic course for eighteen months for all entrants which would lead to the award of a statutory qualification, the Certificate in Nursing Practice. (The course would be comprised of modules including general and psychiatric nursing of all age groups in the hospital and the community.) It should be common to prospective nurses and midwives.

6 A further eighteen months course open only to holders of the certificate should be provided, to lead to the second statutory qualification, Registration. The Register should not have separate parts.

7 There should be two ways of becoming a midwife: a twelve month course following registration or an eighteen months course following certification.

8 Post-registration courses, including clinical refresher courses, should be organised by the Education Boards. There should be more 'back-to-nursing' and 'back-to-midwifery' courses for

qualified returners, and 'keep-in-touch' courses for non-practising qualified nurses and midwives who might subsequently return. There should be planned in-service training for nursing aides, based on a nationally-agreed syllabus, and higher qualifications for ward sisters, family care sisters and family health sisters.

9 Nursing and midwifery education should include an introduction to the work of related professions such as the professions supplementary to medicine and social work.

10 There should be a major drive to produce more nursing and midwifery teachers.

(These points represent the steps necessary to equip student and trained nurses for their developing role in an integrated health service. They strongly depend on the quality and availability of nurse teachers, and new legislation would again be required.)

Manpower

1 Efforts should be made to increase male recruitment.

2 Steps should be taken to encourage nurses and midwives whose careers are interrupted to return to the profession.

3 As a matter of urgency, about 100 people should be trained to work at SNO level in AHAs, specially trained in the manpower/personnel function.

(Although the Committee found no evidence of a serious overall shortage of staff, there were particular areas where recruitment was difficult and wastage rates high.)

Conditions of Work

1 Wherever possible the twelve-hour day should be discontinued.

2 Serious consideration should be given to arranging permanent night shifts in suitable areas, in preference to rotation.

3 National agreement should be reached on a definition of the working week for community nurses and midwives.

4 Authorities should give consideration to the provision of day nurseries and play facilities.

(As well as making working conditions more satisfactory, these points would facilitate the recruitment of married staff or qualified staff returning to the profession, by making it easier to combine with their home commitments.)

Organisation and Career Structure

1 Ward organisation should, like the organisation of field work

in the community, be, where possible, 'patient' rather than task orientated.

2   Differences in degrees of responsibility and expertise among ward sisters and their counterparts in community nursing and midwifery should be recognised by increased status and reward.

3   A new caring profession for the mentally handicapped should emerge gradually. In the meantime, in the training of nurses in the field of mental handicap, increased emphasis should be placed on the social aspects of care.

(These points all serve to improve the quality of nursing care to patients by enabling those nurses who prefer clinical work to administration to be duly rewarded and to emphasise the importance of sensitivity in the relations between nurses and thier patients. On point 3 particularly, action commenced in 1975 when the Secretary of State established the Committee of Inquiry into Nursing and Care of the Mentally Handicapped. Under its chairman, Mrs Peggy Jay, the committee is reviewing the work and responsibilities of mental handicap nurses and residential care staff, the inter-relationship with other health and social services staffs, recruitment and training. It is expected to report before the end of 1977.)

Although this is only a selection of the report's recommendations, it is clear that they represent a thorough and radical attempt to overhaul the profession and to place it on a more up-to-date and rational footing for its role in the reorganised NHS. The report was published in October 1972 and broadly welcomed by the profession, but it was not until May 1974 that the Government responded in detail. The Secretary of State, Mrs Barbara Castle, stated in the House of Commons that the main recommendations were accepted, particularly a new pattern of education and training and a new structure of statutory bodies for the nursing and midwifery professions. She said that the age of entry would be reduced when safeguards against using students merely as 'pairs of hands' could be met. The Government was aware of the health visitors' concern about a loss of identity, and agreed that the name of health visitors should be retained in the new statutory body, i.e. Central Council for Nurses, Midwives and Health Visitors, which should have a Standing Health Visiting Committee. Mrs Castle also announced that she wished to give further consideration to the structure of nursing education below national level, and to the relationship between this and the new NHS structure. She promised a future announcement about the timetable for building up adequate teaching staff and said that, in preparation, there needed to be an increase in the number of nurse tutors and clinical teachers, and a strengthening of the career structure at the level of ward sister, nurse tutor, staff nurse and equivalents. She had invited the Nurses and Midwives Whitley Council to negotiate the details within an additional expenditure of up to £18 million (3 per cent of the 1974 nurses' bill). She added that there would be consultation with the profession on what other preparatory measures could be provided within the existing statutory framework.

Accordingly, a discussion document was issued in September 1974 and various bodies within the nursing profession were asked to make their comments to the DHSS. Then in 1976 an outline of the proposals for introducing legislation to cover the sections of the Briggs report concerning the statutory framework and education was issued. In 1977 the Briggs Coordinating Committee was set up to advise on the implementation of the report's main recommendations. Although the process of reorganising such a large and complex entity as the nursing profession is slow, and whenever legislation is necessary this adds to the time factor, the status of nurse managers (and therefore the profession) has been considerably advanced by their inclusion in all the important decision-making teams of the reorganised NHS.

8 HEALTH SERVICE STAFFS AND INDUSTRIAL RELATIONS

In this chapter the work of all the other staff in the NHS will be discussed. They can broadly be grouped under five headings: paramedical; scientific and technical; ancillary; works; administrative and clerical. In addition, the arrangements for determining pay and conditions of service will be considered, and the chapter will end with a discussion of the crucial state of industrial relations between these staff and the authorities.

Paramedical Staff

The work of the different types of paramedical staff is extremely varied, but as a whole it represents an identifiable and essential component in the whole programme of clinical care, without which medicine and nursing would be of limited effectiveness. In 1975 there were over 57,000 paramedical staff in the hospitals, compared with about 62,000 doctors and 400,000 nurses. (These figures represent whole time equivalents, in order to make the

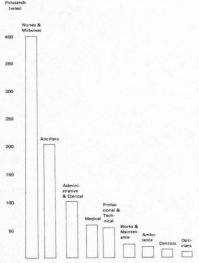

Figure 17 *NHS Manpower 1975 (Great Britain)*

Source: Health and Personal Social Services Statistics, 1976

144

contribution of part-time staff comparable; see Figure 17). When medical social workers became employed by the Local Authorities following the reorganisation in 1974, community para-medical staff simultaneously transferred to the Area Health Authorities.

Many of the staff discussed in this section share the fact that their work is supervised directly or indirectly by doctors, and that most of them undergo training that is as long and thorough as nurses' training. Most of the occupations owe their development to the clinical and technical advances in medical science of the twentieth century. As medicine has become more sophisticated, specialisation within the profession has increased, and with it has come the need for specialist supporting staff to provide the necessary back-up services. There are a number of landmarks which should be mentioned before the individual professions are discussed. The first was in 1936, when the British Medical Association set up an independent Board of Registration of Medical Auxiliaries, incorporated under the Companies Act. Its object was to maintain and publish the National Register of Medical Auxiliary Services, listing those people who had satisfied the Board of their qualifications to practise. This arose because the doctors had become concerned that some of the techniques could involve risks if administered by untrained people. The result was that the professional organisations of dispensing opticians, dieticians, orthoptists, physiotherapists, speech therapists, chiropodists and radiographers became recognised by the Board, and their members were bound not to work except under the direction of a doctor, while the doctors undertook to refer patients only to duly qualified practitioners. This arrangement could not stop unqualified practitioners from working, since registration was entirely voluntary.

In this context, a committee was set up by the Minister of Health after the inception of the NHS, to consider 'the supply and demand training and qualifications of certain medical auxiliaries employed in the NHS'. The result was the Cope report[1] which comprised separate analyses of the situation for almoners, chiropodists, dieticians, medical laboratory technicians, occupational therapists, physiotherapists and remedial gymnasts, radiographers and speech therapists. It recommended that statutory registration for medical auxiliaries working in the NHS should be necessary through separate registers. These registers and the recognition of approved training courses and examinations should be the responsibility of a single council with a number of constituent professional committees. Although these proposals were welcomed by the doctors and medical auxiliaries alike (but for different reasons), a long debate ensued between them over membership of the new bodies. In 1954, as an interim measure, regulations were introduced for the qualifications required for state registration of eight categories of staff by the NHS: chiropodists, dieticians, medical laboratory technicians, occupational therapists, physiotherapists, radiographers, remedial gymnasts and speech therapists.

Finally in 1960, the Professions Supplementary to Medicine Act was passed. This established the Council for Professions Supplementary to Medicine (CPSM), and seven Boards, one for each of the professions mentioned above, excluding speech therapists. The Boards were made legally responsible for the preparation and maintenance of registers, for prescribing qualifications required for state registration, and for approving entrance requirements, training syllabuses and training institutions. They can remove practitioners from the register for professional misconduct, and impose penalties for the improper use of the designation 'state registered'; they can also withdraw approval from training courses that fall below required standards. In 1966 the provisions of the Act were extended to include orthoptists. The Board of Registration of Medical Auxiliaries continued to provide for voluntary registration of chiropodists, orthoptists, dispensing opticians, operating theatre technicians, technicians in venereology, audiology technicians and certified ambulance personnel. The Council for Professions Supplementary to Medicine is itself composed of one member from each of the Boards, six nominees of the medical corporations and the GMC, four nominees of the Privy Council (including the Chairman) and five ministerial nominees, giving a total of twenty-three.

One further point to be made at this stage is that these paramedical and scientific occupations share problems of status and managerial authority in relation to other groups, particularly the doctors. It might be said that the move by the BMA to institute registration of medical auxiliaries was an attempt to exert control over other professions that it regarded as a threat rather than an asset. Equally, these professions probably welcomed registration since they saw it as an opportunity to expose charlatans, and to close the ranks of truly qualified practitioners.[2] The wranglings over the constitutions of the boards recommended in the Cope report arose because the medical profession wanted to secure majority representation, but this did not eventually happen. The overall problem is that each of the occupations has to reconcile its desire for independent professional status with the inevitable fact that it serves the medical profession. They have to accept some degree of direction and control by the doctors, yet they regard themselves as competent specialists in their own right. Chapter 7 of the Grey Book,[3] on the organisation of paramedical services, did not meet with the agreement of the professions concerned when it was published in 1972. The disagreements centred on this problem of their accountability to doctors, particularly in the predominantly hospital-based professions. After consultation with them, new guidance for their management arrangements had to be issued separately, taking some account of these difficulties.

Chiropody

This is the treatment of superficial ailments of the feet, and the maintenance of the feet in good condition. In the eighteenth century chiropodists also cared for hands, but now they specialise in the treatment of existing deformities with appliances and special footwear; diagnosing and treating local infections; preventive care also, including the inspection of children's feet. Most chiropodists work in the community, holding clinics and making domicilary visits. They work independently and do not require referral from a doctor, whereas those working in the hospitals work far more through referrals.

The Incorporated Society of Chiropodists was founded in 1912 to promote study and training and to improve services for poor people. In 1913 the London Foot Hospital was founded — the first specialist hospital of its kind. A number of other professional organisations grew up and in 1937 five of these were recognised by the Board of Registration of Medical Auxiliaries. They amalgamated to form the Society of Chiropodists in 1945, but there continued to be a range of bodies examining and registering chiropodists. The 1954 regulations laid down conditions for state registration and employment in the NHS, and the Chiropodists Board of the Council for Professions Supplementary to Medicine replaced these in 1963, when it became the single body responsible for state registration, following a three year full-time course at an approved training centre. In 1975 there were 1,336 chiropodists in the NHS in England and Wales of whom about two thirds were full-time employees. However, about one third of all NHS treatments including those done at patients' homes were carried out by private chiropodists who received a fee from the NHS. The DHSS admits that chiropody services are inadequate, even for the priority groups (the elderly, the handicapped, expectant mothers, school children and some hospital patients). In 1977 it issued a circular (HC(77)9) which recommended various measures to the Area Health Authorities to enable them to make better use of their existing resources. Of particular importance was the suggestion that 'foot care assistants' could be employed to carry out simple treatments such as basic foot care and hygiene, for which the skills of the fully-trained chiropodist were not necessary.

Dietetics

A dietician applies knowledge of nutrients contained in food, the effect of preparation and cooking on them and their use by the body, to advise on suitable diets as part of the treatment of illness, as well as constructing diets for people with chronic disorders (e.g. diabetes, kidney disease). Most dieticians work in hospitals, in conjunction with the catering manager, and also follow up patients through outpatient clinics, although there are some openings for them in the community services, for instance in advising mothers at ante-natal and post-natal clinics on the balanced diets required for their babies, and in the nutritional values of meals on wheels.

The first training schools for dieticians were established in the United States in the 1920s, and their students were trained nurses. In 1925 special diet kitchens were opened at one or two hospitals in London, Edinburgh and Glasgow, and they accepted students who had pure science or domestic science qualifications. In 1933 a special training course for dieticians was started at the King's College of Household and Social Science, and the therapeutic work of these 'early' dieticians mostly involved the weighing and preparing of foods. Later, the development of drugs partly overtook the effect of dietetics in treatment of certain conditions. The British Dietetic Association was founded in 1936, and joined the voluntary registration scheme before the institution of requirements for state registration in 1954. Since 1963 the Dieticians Board of the Council for Professions Supplementary to Medicine has been the responsible regulating body.

In the reorganised NHS, dietetic services are managed on a district basis through the appointment of a District Dietician, who gives advice to the DMT and the AHA on the planning and provision of a nutrition and dietetic service. The District Dietician is accountable to the District Administrator for these management tasks while she and her colleagues work in a service-giving relationship to doctors.[4] In 1975 there were 484 dieticians (whole time equivalents) in England and Wales of whom a small number were based in the community, although the community side of dietetics was expected to develop gradually into a more substantial organisation.

Occupational Therapy

This covers any work or recreation prescribed and guided by a doctor for the purpose of facilitating recovery from disease or injury. Patients are referred to the occupational therapist by a doctor, and most work is done in general and psychiatric hospitals and rehabilitation centres. There are some, though, who work in the community, in units for emotionally disturbed and autistic children, in work and day centres, and who make domiciliary visits. A number work in local authority social services departments, advising on adaptations and other requirements for the disabled. Occupational therapy has long had a place in mental hospitals, where it was provided by untrained craft workers, until 1930 when the first training courses were started. The last war influenced its development through the need to provide for soldiers who were injured or shocked from combat.

The Association of Occupational Therapists was formed in 1936 and it registered occupational therapists who had passed the professional examinations after a prescribed three year course. After 1963, qualified practitioners became registered by the Occupational Therapists Board of the Council for Professions Supplementary to Medicine. The Halsbury report[5] noted that recruitment difficulties were accounted for by the fact that the NHS offered occupational therapists lower salaries than they could receive in local authority work. In 1975 there were 2,036 occupational therapists (whole time equivalents) in England and Wales of whom about 7 per cent were working in the community health services.

Physiotherapy

Physiotherapy is the use of physical means to prevent and treat injury or disease, and to assist rehabilitation. People of all ages with a great variety of conditions can receive physiotherapy. The methods include therapeutic movement, electrotherapy, hydrotherapy, manipulation and massage. Most hospitals have departments treating outpatients and inpatients, and community work includes clinic sessions, work at rehabilitation centres and special schools for handicapped children. Treatment follows referral from a doctor, and, as with many other state registered professions, physiotherapists undertake to treat only those who have been so referred.

The origins of physiotherapy started in a body called the Society of Trained Masseuses, founded in 1895. It was open to women only but in 1920 it became known as the Chartered Society of Massage and Medical Gymnastics, and men were then admitted. The profession developed in scope and to reflect this the name was changed in 1943 to the Chartered Society of Physiotherapy. The society registered qualified practitioners, conducted examinations and approved training schools. After the Cope Report and the 1960 Act, the Physiotherapists Board of the Council for Professions

Supplementary to Medicine became the regulating body. The three year training courses at the Society are the only ones recognised for state registration. In 1975 there were 5,298 physiotherapists '(whole time equivalents in England and Wales) of whom about 11 per cent were working in the community health services.

Remedial Gymnastics

This profession is concerned with the treatment and rehabilitation of patients through active exercise. Special apparatus, games and exercises may be used, following medical diagnosis and referral, for a range of conditions including functional training in preparation for work and special work with mentally ill and handicapped patients. After the last war this more active type of physiotherapy was develoiped and training courses were set up.

The Society of Remedial Gymnasts issues a certificate after successful completion of the six months course, which is recognised by the Remedial Gymnasts Board of the Council for Professions Supplementary to Medicine. In 1975 there were 256 remedial gymnasts (whole time equivalents) working in the NHS (England and Wales).

The Remedial Professions

These three professions – occupational therapy, physiotherapy and remedial gymnastics – form a subgroup known as the remedial professions. Although they each have a distinct part to play, there are also some similarities, and their work may sometimes overlap. In 1969 a government committee was set up (chaired by Professor Sir Ronald Tunbridge) to consider their interrelationships, since the professions felt dissatisfied with their pay, career prospects and professional status. The Committee's statement in 1972[6] recommended representation on advisory committees to the health authorities, adequate departmental establishments, better provision for aides (unqualified assistants), clerical staff and porters, integrated departments, re-employment of trained married women, and a review of the training syllabuses leading to an integration of the schools.

The professions were far from pleased with these points since they felt strongly about their independence and the lack of recognition. The Oddie report (Report of the Committee on Remedial Professions of the CPSM)[7] tried to press their case further but it was not until 1975 that they felt the problems had been acknowledged. A working party was set up by the Secretary of State to make urgent recommendations, and their report (the McMillan report)[8] suggested that the professions of physiotherapy and remedial gymnastics should amalgamate, and in the long term the three should evolve into a single comprehensive profession;

increased professional and managerial responsibility should rest with
the practitioners; new career structures should be devised to reflect this;
new methods of training, increased use and recognition of aides and
recognition of the need for research should all be develo|ped. A coordin-
ating committee to deal with the implementation of these recommendations was set up in March 1975, and in particular to work out the
details on some of the more complicated points such as the managerial
relations between the professions, greater flexibility in the training, and
the use of aides. The DHSS also issued detailed guidance for the
organisation of the remedial professions in the reorganised NHS.[9]
However, by 1977 the coordinating committee could not report that
significant progress had been made in its discussions.

Radiography

X-rays were discovered in 1895 and they are used to help diagnose
illness and injury, and to provide treatment for certain malignant
and other conditions. Until 1920, non-medical assistants were employed,
but in that year the Society of Radiographers was formed to organise
training courses and examinations and to register qualified practitioners.
Both diagnostic and therapeutic radiographers work under the direction
of doctors and there are standard protective and monitoring devices to
ensure they are not excessively exposed. Apart from the mobile
mass X-ray units, radiography is a hospital-based service.

There is a two year course of which the first year is common to
students of both branches; the second year differs for diagnostic or
therapeutic qualifications. Regulations for qualifications followed the
pattern mentioned earlier, and in 1964 the Radiographers Board of the
Council for Professions Supplementary to Medicine became the regulating body. In 1975 there were 5,880 diagnostic and therapeutic radiographers working in the NHS (whole time equivalents in England and
Wales) of whom about 85 per cent were engaged in diagnostic work and
15 per cent in therapeutic work.

Orthoptics

This is the investigation of squints and other defects of binocular vision.
Orthoptists work with medically qualified eye specialists and only treat
patients referred to them by doctors. The majority of patients are
children and most orthoptists are women. The British Orthoptic
Council was founded in 1930 and runs a full-time two year course
leading to a diploma. The Board of Registration of Medical Auxiliaries
registered orthoptists until 1966, when the Orthoptists Board of the
CPSM was set up to take this over. In 1975 there were 355 state

registered orthoptists (whole time equivalents in England and Wales
of whom about 12 per cent were based in the community.

Speech Therapy

This is the treatment of defects and disorders of the voice and speech.
Originally the work concentrated on stammering, but after about 1912,
hospital departments and local authority clinics began to be set up to
offer treatment for the range of disorders. The 1944 Education Act
obliged local education authorities to provide treatment for children
with speech disorders, so the profession became split between those
working in the education and health services (the ratio is about 3 : 1,
education : health). There was a great demand for speech therapists
as a result and the College of Speech Therapists was formed in 1945 to
press for independent status of the practitioners. The profession has
faced serious problems for some time: the small numbers of fully
trained members; the fact that most of them give less than five years
service; few senior posts make the career structure unattractive;
research and preventive work has not developed; there is poor
communication between the profession and medicine.

In 1972 the Quirk report (on speech therapy service) was published[10]
and it contained proposals for reorganising and developing the profession
so that it could cope with its expanding role in the NHS and the
education service. It recommended that AHAs should be responsible for
organising the practitioners in a suitable career structure and that
training courses should be jointly arranged with universities so that
the quality of the training might be enhanced. It also proposed a new
central council to handle course assessment and registration of qualified
practitioners, and that the College of Speech Therapists should remain
as a professional body only, its present examining role being taken on
by the central council. The Government approved the recommendations
and in April 1974 issued guidance to AHAs on how they might begin
to integrate their speech therapy services along these lines through
the appointment of Area Speech Therapists.[11] It was acknowledged
that the transformation of the profession would take some time. In
1975 there were 930 speech therapists (whole time equivalents in England and Wales) of whom about 64 per cent were community-based.

The Halsbury Report

Towards the end of 1974 Lord Halsbury and the committee who were
investigating nurses' and midwives' pay at the special request of the
Secretary of State (see Chapter 7) were asked to inquire also into the

pay and conditions of service for the 8 paramedical professions that have been discussed above. Their report was published early in 1975,[12] and it gave these staff substantial pay increases. Traditionally, their pay has been linked to nurses' pay — there are some similarities, since they share the same employer and places of work, and they are (except for chiropody and remedial gymnastics) predominantly women's professions in which many work on a part-time basis. Halsbury found that no job evaluations comparing the training and skills required for each of the professions had been carried out, and he strongly recommended that this should be done. He noted that substantial staffing shortages existed for most of them in relation to NHS work, and suggested more full-time working should be encouraged, since the actual numbers of individuals with state registration indicated a potentially larger workforce. He justified the large awards (made in the context of a statutory incomes policy) by saying that they were ' . . . no more than have been due to these professions in recognition of their responsibilities and bearing in mind the critical manpower shortages'. The effect of the awards has been to improve recruitment into these professions considerably. Staff shortages are less than they were and in radiography, for example, sufficient staff can now be employed.

Medical Laboratory Technicians

This group of staff is concerned with facilities for diagnosis and treatment of illness through examination of pathological specimens from outpatients, inpatients, and sent in from GPs' patients, under the supervision of consultant pathologists in the hospitals. The Pathological and Bacteriological Assistants' Association was founded in 1912 and in 1921 an examining council of the Pathological Society was set up to develop a system of certification. The Institute of Medical Laboratory Technology was incorporated in 1942 as their single professional organisation. It registered qualified technicians who had worked in approved laboratories and attended part-time courses. The 1954 regulations for medical auxiliaries laid down the requisites for state registration and in 1963 the Medical Laboratory Technicians Board of the Council for Professions Supplementary to Medicine became the regulating body. In 1967 the Institute started an improved two year course of one day's attendance per week for trainee technicians leading to the recognised qualification, and in 1975 there were 12,956 (whole time equivalent) medical laboratory technicians in the hospital service in England and Wales.

Scientific and Technical Staff

The Zuckerman report (1968)[13] proposed a reorganisation of the scientific and technical services provided by medical laboratory technicians, some of the professions supplementary to medicine and others in the hospital service. The report included the following professions in its scheme:

Biochemists
Physicists
Other scientific officers
Audiology technicians
Cardiology technicians
Darkroom technicians
Dental technicians
Electroencephalography technicians
Medical laboratory technicians
Medical physics technicians
Radiographers
Dieticians
Animal technicians
Artificial kidney technicians
Contact lens technicians
Electronics technicians
Glaucoma technicians
Heart and lung machine technicians
Respiratory function technicians
Surgical instrument curators
Surgical and orthopaedic appliance technicians and fitters

Figure 18 *Main Classes of Non-Medical Staff to Be Included in the Hospital Scientific Service*

Source: Hospital Scientific and Technical Services, HMSO, 1968

The report recommended the creation of a National Hospital Scientific Council to advise the Ministers on the organisation of the Hospital Scientific Service, that might become one of the Standing Advisory Committees of the Central Health Services Council. Each Regional Hospital Board was to have an advisory committee, and at district general hospital level the report recommended a Division of Scientific Services to include medical and scientific staff involved in clinical biochemistry, computer science and statistics, genetics, haematology and blood transfusion, immunology, medical microbiology, morbid anatomy and histopathology, physics with biomedical engineering, nuclear medicine and physiological measurement. Four classes of staff were proposed: scientific officer, technical officer, technical assistant and technical aide, to reflect different degrees of responsibility and knowledge and to provide an improved career structure.

In 1970, DHSS circular HM(70)50[14] recommended that area laboratories managed by Board of Governors or Hospital Management Committees should combine certain departments, each under their medically qualified consultant: (1) microbiology, histopathology and cytology; (2) chemical pathology; (3) haematology and blood transfusion; (4) microbiology; and that there should be collaboration with the Public Health Laboratory Service over microbiology services. However these recommendations were modified when the new reorganised structure of the NHS was implemented in 1974. The DHSS's subsequent guidance[15] suggested alternative patterns of organisation at district level relating the Zuckerman proposals to the pattern of medical organisation in 'Cogwheel' divisions for hospital scientic and technical staff. At area level it was suggested that Area Scientific Committees be set up to advise the AHA, consisting of doctors, scientists and representatives of users' interests. Similarly at regional level it proposed a Regional Scientific Committee to advise the RHA on the planning and organisation of all the scientific services, including supervision of accommodation, larger items of equipment, staffing and training policy under the guidance of the Regional Scientific Officer.

Ancillary Staff

There are well over 400,000 patients in hospital on any one day in the year, who have the sheets on their beds provided by the laundry staff, who eat three meals cooked and served by the catering staff in wards cleaned by domestic staff. Equipment and sterile dressings are provided by the supplies staff, while porters fetch and carry specimens and equipment and conduct patients around the hospital. In addition, certain staff live in the hospital, so some of the 'hotel' services are required for them. Most of the ancillary functions are not exclusive to the NHS, and arise wherever meals and residential accommodation need to be provided. The community health services clearly require these services on a smaller scale since they are mostly concerned with non-residential care. Hostels and homes in the community are run by the social services departments unless they provide medically supervised care, in which case the ancillary staff would be employees of the Area Health Authority (see Figure 19).

The nature of ancillary work is such that the majority of the staff are unskilled or semi-skilled, and as a consequence the pattern of professional organisation that has developed is different from that of

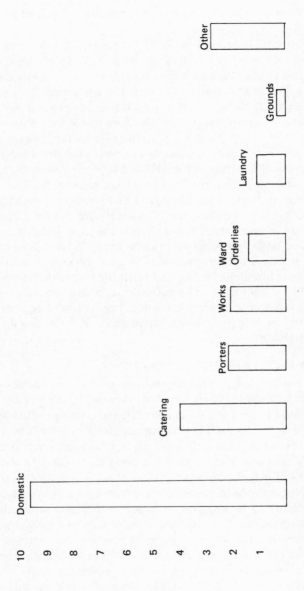

Figure 19 *Ancillary Staff in the NHS (England and Wales) 1974*

Source: Health and Personal Social Services Statistics, 1975 and Welsh Health and Personal Social Services Statistics, 1975

nursing or the paramedical and scientific occupations. State registration is not required, and formal training is only available for a few of the senior posts. The trend has been for the distinct occupations to be under the supervision of functional managers responsible to the hospital administrator, while the staff have belonged to trade unions which represent their interests both locally and nationally. In 1967, the National Board for Prices and Incomes investigated the status of ancillary workers in the NHS[16] and found that the male workers were amongst the lowest paid in the country. It recommended that urgent improvements in their pay and productivity should be achieved through the incentive bonus schemes that could be developed by overhauling the pay structure on the basis of job evaluation. The Board's recommendations were accepted by the Government, but in 1971 the Board's second report[17] revealed that only 6 per cent of the ancillary workers were or were due to be covered by such schemes. They criticised the management's failure to raise the efficiency of ancillary work, identifying the following crucial factors: (1) the methods of financial control of the hospital service; (2) the relationship between the central department and the Regional Hospital Boards; (3) the relationships between the Regional Hospital Boards and the local managers; (4) the relationship between ancillary and other hospital workers; (5) the poor definition of responsibility for ancillary workers.

Trade unions were also criticised by the Board for not being more active locally or encouraging participation by the staff. The second report proposed a fresh introduction of local interim incentive bonus schemes, in which the details were to be worked out locally between the staff and the management for setting manning standards and rewarding workers' productivity. The result was expected to yield substantial savings in this labour-intensive part of the NHS. However, in 1972, the ancillary workers went on strike in support of a £4 a week wage claim that had been negotiated, but was postponed by the restrictions in Phase II of the Government's incomes policy. Hospital services were severely disrupted by this strike which lasted intermittently for several months. The workers' request for a special inquiry into their case was rejected, and they finally returned to work without winning their claim.

Incentive Bonus Schemes

In hospitals there are only a limited number of jobs which are appropriate for incentive bonus schemes, since they need to be fairly repetitive, consisting of short-cycle operations, with the pace of work determined by the worker rather than a machine. The work

needs to be measurable and directly attributable to an individual or group
of workers, and the rate of demand and output should not fluctuate widely
A variety of schemes exist for determining how bonuses over the basic
rate should be earned, once the required performance for the basic rate
has been analysed through work study methods. Laundry, domestic and
catering jobs have been assessed in this way, but the attitude and cooperation of other staff is needed to enable these schemes to succeed. The
DHSS instructed authorities to introduce interim schemes initially, since
the preparation for a full scheme is lengthy, and there was a shortage of
suitably skilled work study staff to handle them. Interim schemes are negotiated locally between management and workers' representatives, and
aim to achieve of the order of a 10 per cent saving in total labour costs,
which is distributed to the workers involved. By mid-1975 about 40 per
cent of maintenance and ancillary workers were covered by some form
of incentive bonus scheme, and between 1970 and 1974 the number of
ancillary staff fell by 3,000, although other groups of health workers
were increasing their numbers in this period.

Works Staff

This group of staff includes architects, quantity surveyors, engineers, building supervisors, electricians, painters, carpenters, ground maintenance
staff and labourers. They deal with the planning construction and maintenance of the buildings, plant and grounds of the health service, and as
with the ancillary staff, they are concentrated on the hospital side. The
senior works staff based with the Regional Health Authorities hold professional qualifications such as those of the Royal Institute of British Architects, the Royal Institution of Quantity Surveyors and the various engineering institutions. Senior works staff of the districts have technical qualifications, but the pattern amongst them and the skilled and other works
staff is to belong to a trade union rather than a professional organisation.

   The stock of hospitals taken over by the NHS in 1948 included
over 1,200 (45 per cent) that had been erected before 1891, and
many were obsolete, poorly maintained, or in unsuitable locations.
In the late 1950s, money began to be specially earmarked for the
development of hospital bulding, and in 1962 the publication of
A Hospital Plan for England and Wales[18] specified ninety new and
134 substantially remodelled hospitals to be started by 1970/71. It
acknowledged the shortage of architects and engineers skilled in
hospital planning, and in the same year the report of a study group
investigating hospital engineering was published.[19] It recommended
a number of steps to improve the training and quality of engineers,
and suggested a minimum qualification requirement for employment
in the NHS, as well as recognition of the group engineer as a chief

officer. The Woodbine Parish report[20] published in 1970 made further recommendations for the improvement of building maintenance and the training of supervisory staff. When the Grey Book's scheme for works staff in the reorganised NHS was published, it met with opposition from the professions concerned. Revised guidance was issued in 1974[21] acknowledging some degree of autonomy for works staff such that responsibility was shared between senior works officers and administrators for the execution of building and maintenance. This specified the new posts and their management arrangements, particularly the area and district works and building officers and engineers, their departmental organisation and degree of accountability to administrators. Nevertheless, because these functions constitute such a costly element in spending by authorities, the Department has always been concerned to monitor standards and local practices carefully, and it does this through a series of publications which give detailed advice and specifications about all aspects of health authorities' building, upgrading and maintenance work.[22]

Administrative and Clerical Staff

The Grey Book gives three reasons for employing administrators in the NHS: to manage institutional and support services, to provide administrative services, and to act as general coordinators. In practice this means that ambulances, laundry and central sterile supply, medical records, catering, portering and domestic services, supplies and personnel each have a manager who is responsible for the work of his department at district level and sometimes at area level (but not usually at regional level, since institutional and support services are rarely organised there) to a senior administrator. Administrative services play a part in every aspect of the NHS and include secretarial support, management services and personnel management, public relations and legal advice for the range of staff and managers. General administrative coordination involves assisting different departments and professions to work cooperatively through multi-disciplinary teams and through informal methods, in the interests of providing integrated patient care. The senior administrative posts created by the reorganisation at each level, that were mentioned in earlier chapters, are a key element of the new structure because of their role in moderating the balance between the authority of the central Department and the delegated responsibility alloted to Regional and Area Health Authorities and District Management Teams. A new element of managerial responsibility has been introduced, with specific

	Total	NHS	
TGWU	1,950,000		
GMWU	916,000	45,000	(end 76)
NALGO	683,000	80,950	
NUPE	650,000	225,000	
ASTMS	400,000	24,000	(6%)
COHSE	208,000	208,000	

Figure 20 *Trade Union Membership of Health Service Staffs*
(approximate figures at April 1977 — larger unions only)
Source: The Individual Unions

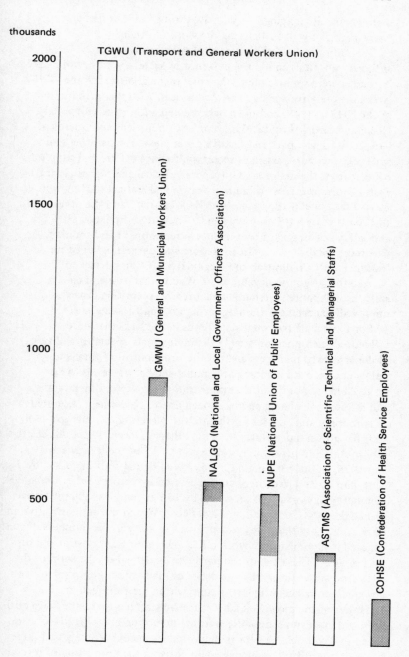

methods for discharging it — namely, through monitoring and coordinating as well as directing the work of others.

The early hospital administrators (called stewards in the local authority hospitals and house governor or secretary in the voluntary hospitals) were responsible to the chief medical officer or the governing body for the day-to-day business. With the introduction of the NHS in 1948, and the newly created authorities (Regional Hospital Boards, Hospital Management Committees and Boards of Governors) a new pattern of staffing was created, separating senior staff (e.g. secretary, assistant secretary, finance officer and supplies officer) from the junior grades (general, clerical and higher clerical). Two important reviews of administrative and clerical staffing were carried out, one in 1957 (the Noel Hall report)[23] and the other in 1963 (the Lycett Green report).[24] They promoted new gradings and salary scales, and improvements in recruitment and training. One result of the Lycett Green Report was the setting up of the National Staff Committee and Regional Staff Committees to oversee the long-term development of administrative and clerical staff through more systematic and effective recruiting drives and improved management training for senior and first-line posts.

For these staff two opposing trends in the NHS that have influenced their position are (1) the increasingly specialist ability of departmental managers and (2) the firm control of financial policy and forward planning at regional and central levels. As a result, some senior hospital administrators have found their status and influence declining and have been unable to define a clear area of autonomy and control for themselves. Nevertheless, this group of staff has grown much faster than the others in recent years. All health service staff and practitioners increased by 13 per cent between 1971 and 1975. In the same period, medical and dental staff increased by 7 per cent, nursing and midwifery staff increased by 18 per cent, professional, technical and works staff increased by 15 per cent, but administrative and clerical staff increased by 31 per cent. Within the administrative and clerical category there was a 73 per cent increase in the numbers of staff engaged in administrative work other than secretarial, clerical and support services. These trends can partly be explained by the form of the NHS reorganisation and by the desire of many other groups of staff to develop hierarchical career structures within their professions.

However, the growth of administrative staff has met with sharp criticism and moves to economise were set in motion in 1975. RHAs were asked to devise schemes for reducing management spending, and there has been a standstill in 'management costs' at the proportion of revenue which existed at 31 March 1976. In effect this has meant that health authorities have been unable to recruit new senior management staff, in order to achieve a 5 per cent annual reduction in spending. By 1980 the total proportion of NHS money spent on management costs will have fallen from 6 per cent to 5½ per cent. For its part, the DHSS has also undertaken to reduce its management costs by 10 per cent over the same period.

NHS Industrial Relations

Whitley Councils

The pay and conditions of service of most NHS staff are negotiated nationally through a system of collective bargaining, that is, a formal procedure in which representatives of organised workers (see Figure 20) meet representatives of management to discuss claims and arrive at joint decisions. The Whitley system itself originated in attempts to improve industrial relations during and after the First World War. J.H. Whitley (Deputy Speaker of the House of Commons) chaired a committee which recommended a three tiered organisation for voluntary improvement in relations within industries, consisting of a national joint industrial council, district councils and local works committees as well as a permanent arbitration body. A number of industries tried to implement such schemes, but many were not sustained, although a notable exception was the Civil Service, which operates through Whitley Councils to this day.

Before 1939 there was little application of the idea to health service staff, but during the Second World War, hospital labour was in short supply although urgently needed. The Government intervened by fixing minimum wages for student nurses prepared to work in hospitals where the shortages were particularly acute, and by guaranteeing higher wages for assistant and trained nurses working in hospitals that were part of the War Emergency scheme. In 1943 the Rushcliffe (England and Wales)[25] and Guthrie (Scotland)[26] reports were published, recommending the wage rates for all ranks of hospital nurses and the committees remained in being to deal with revisions of their scales. In 1945, the Mowbray Committee[27] was set up to deal with domestic and similar hospital workers' pay, on a voluntary basis. It fixed national minimum rates and empowered provincial councils to fix higher local rates and to deal with local disputes. During the War, the National Joint Council for Local Authority Administrative, Professional Technical and Clerical Staff handled the negotiations for administrative and clerical staff of the local authority hospitals, while the British Hospitals Association and the Association of Hospital Officers (later the Institute of Health Service Administrators) held formal negotiations with the same groups of staff in the voluntary hospitals. In 1942, the Association of Clerks and Stewards of Mental Hospitals was wound up and members were advised to join the Association of Hospital Officers which then dealt with the administrative and clerical staffs' claims in the mental hospitals. In 1945, several of the paramedical professions arranged for joint negotiations with the employers through a voluntary committee, but the medical laboratory technicians remained outside this arrangement because their professional organisation did not want to jeopardise its status by entering into formally negotiated arrangements. The hospital owners therefore had to deal with those trade unions who had medical laboratory technicians as members.

The 1946 NHS Act laid down that all employees of non-teaching hospitals would work under the instruction of the Hospital Management Committee, although their employer at law was the Regional Hospital Board. Schedule 66 of the Act empowered the Minister of Health to make regulations about the qualifications, remuneration and conditions of service of any employee of the NHS. In 1947, the Ministry and the Secretary of State for Scotland drew up a scheme for a central joint body covering the whole service and for separate negotiating bodies for the main groups of staff.

The existing joint councils and committees naturally influenced the form of the new bodies, and all organisations with a claim to represent staff were appointed to the appropriate body. The result was one General Whitley Council and nine functional Whitley Councils. The functional councils determine pay and all those conditions of service requiring a national decision, affecting directly only those staff within its scope. The General Council's activities are, in practice, limited to matters of general application, e.g. determining travelling and subsistence allowances and the procedure for certain types of leave. The nine functional councils that were constituted are: Administrative and Clerical Staffs Council; Ancillary Staffs Council; Dental Whitley Council (Local Authorities); Medical and (Hospital) Dental Whitley Council; Nurses and Midwives Council; Optical Council; Pharmaceutical Council; Professional and Technical Staffs Council 'A'; Professional and Technical Staffs Council 'B' and in addition, there is a Scottish Advisory Committee to ensure that Scottish interests are properly represented. The General Council also has a staff side and a management side, the staff representatives being members of the functional councils.

The Mowbray Committee became the Ancillary Staffs Council, the Rushcliffe and Guthrie Committees together became the Nurses and Midwives Council, and the staff members of the three bargaining bodies from the voluntary, local authority and mental hospitals amalgamated to form the Administrative and Clerical Staffs Council. For paramedical, scientific and technical staff there was unwillingness between the trade unions and professional associations to handle pay negotiations together, because these would involve the pay of professional workers who had paid for their own training as well as technicians who had served an apprenticeship. Many professional associations are registered as companies, and this restricts their freedom to act as bodies representing their members' interests in formal wage negotiations. Trade unions, on the other hand, are disbarred from registration under the Companies Act, and are able to force an unwilling employer to arbitration. The result was that two councils were set up for these staff which broadly (but not entirely) separate the trade unions and professional associations. On Professional and Technical Staffs Council 'A' staff who deal directly with patients are represented predominantly through professional organisations and on Professional and Technical Staffs Council 'B' the rest (technicians, works staff, etc.) are represented mainly through trade unions. Separate councils were set up for those professional groups who could work as full-time employees in hospitals or for the local authorities, as well as being paid fees by the Executive Councils. Thus the Medical, Dental, Optical and Pharmaceutical Councils were set up.

By 1949, seven functional councils and the General Council were working, and in 1950 the Medical Council and the (Local Authority) Dental Council were set up. Hospital dental staff were brought within the scope of the Medical Council in 1962, and its name was changed to Medical and (Hospital) Dental Council. (However the Doctors' and Dentists' Review Body took over the work of the functional Whitley Councils in relation to doctors and dentists from 1963 – see p. 104.) Following the transfer of responsibility for ambulance services to the health authorities in 1974, a new Ambulancemen's Council was created.

On most functional councils staff organisations with relatively small membership claimed places alongside the major ones, and some trade unions with members in several branches of the health service gained places on more than one council. The composition of the management side reflects the curious position that the hospital authorities were in (as the health authorities now are) as a party to collective bargaining.

Regional Hospital Boards and Boards of Governors were dependent on the Government for all the money they spent. Clearly they could not agree to grant concessions to their staff unless the Government was prepared to make money available, but at the same time, the Ministry wanted to be involved in any discussions that might commit them to increased expenditure on wages. The management sides of the functional councils therefore consisted of officials from the Ministry of Health and Scottish Office, representatives from the Regional Hospital Boards, Hospital Management Committees and Boards of Governors, the Executive Councils (on Administrative and Clerical) and the local authorities (except on Administrative and Clerical). The relative under-representation of the RHBs, HMCs and BoGs in relation to the local authorities was perhaps surprising, but the hospital authorities were in no position to object. Following the reorganisation, representatives from the Regional and Area Health Authorities and the Scottish and Welsh authorities became members of the management sides, and local authority membership ceased.

The way the Whitley Councils work is for each side to meet separately to determine their attitudes and then as a joint body to discuss the issues together. Each side has a chairman and a secretary, the chair of the council alternating between the two sides from year to year, while the secretaries are joint secretaries of the full council. The staff side secretary is elected from staff representatives, and the management side secretary is an official of the DHSS. Regional and national appeals committees exist to hear the cases of employees who are aggrieved in any matter of their employment excluding disciplinary action or dismissal. Staff and management sides appoint equal numbers to the committees who jointly agree on a decision, but the appeal can only be made by a trade union or staff association represented on a health service Whitley Council or a nationally recognised negotiating body, on behalf of the aggrieved employee. In addition, the Industrial Court, which was created in 1919 exists as the final arbitrating body in disputes that cannot be settled through the appeals committees.

Despite the Whitley Councils' existence it is widely thought that the NHS has had worse industrial relations than any other public sector industry that is served by joint negotiating machinery. This may be because the negotiations at a national level are seen to be isolated from people at the workplace, with the result that meaningful bargaining is precluded from hospital level as long as management is not in a position to meet the demands of its staff and make concessions. Additionally, the management is not directly participant to the Whitley Council negotiations and employees also only have their say through their representatives. The Government is in control of a very large sector of industry and employment — several health service occupations barely exist outside the NHS — but at the same time it is bound to manage the economy of the country. These roles appear to conflict and there is undisputed evidence that sections of NHS staff, and the ancillary workers in particular, have as a result not been rewarded with acceptable income levels. In other words, the Treasury's influence and effective control over the management side representatives on the Whitley Councils has ensured that government economic policy is firmly upheld and maintained through the wage negotiations as a priority over the demands of the staff sides.

This is illustrated in the case of the award agreed by the Administrative and Clerical Staffs Council in 1957. They worked out a 3 per cent increase on salaries up to £1,200, covering about 30,000 NHS staff on 22 October. At that time the Government was pursuing an incomes policy to contain the rising rate of inflation, and Derek Walker-Smith, the Minister of Health, announced on 1 November that the award was refused by him, in defence of his Government's policy. This was the first time that a Whitley Council agreement had been subject to Government veto, and it was regarded as a major threat to the status and viability of the collective bargaining machinery of the NHS. Administrative and clerical staff in a number of hospitals instituted a ban on overtime working, drawing attention to the fact that they represented a relatively low paid section of NHS staff whose previous awards had not enabled their salaries to keep up with general increases in wages.

Since then, no further veto has been imposed by a Health Minister, although it is thought that the management sides of the Whitley Councils have been very thoroughly briefed so that they do not agree to any awards that would embarrass the Government.

Apart from government policy, other interdependent factors that have influenced the determination of wages are shortages of labour, changes in the cost of living, relativities between the incomes of different occupations and arbitration. In recent years there has been a concerted move to improve the quality of management in the NHS and to instill greater cost consciousness at all levels of administration, but these trends cannot automatically solve industrial relations problems. Trade unions representing health service staff have been changing their image in line with their opposite numbers who they see as negotiating deals more effectively and militantly in the private sector.

The introduction of incentive bonus schemes for manual workers has been adopted as an attempt to improve efficiency as well as satisfying demands for higher pay, but this has influenced the nature of workplace bargaining and increased shop steward activity. The national militancy of the ancillary workers in 1972-3 marked a turning point in the style of NHS management-worker relations: it has been described as the 'strike threshold' which could make it relatively easier for workers to adopt militancy subsequently. It is unlikely to be a coincidence that in the first year of the reorganisation there were disputes (of newsworthy proportions) involving nurses, radiographers, physics and laboratory technicians, engineers, clerical staff, general practitioners and hospital consultants. The Whitley Council machinery is effectively unchanged since its introduction and the signs that it was not designed to cope with the pressures and problems of current industrial relations are clear. The absence of a definite policy to appoint specialist personnel officers is another feature that appears outdated. Line managers have not been well trained in the relevant skills and so are not always able to handle problems sensitively. Furthermore the disciplinary machinery was only modified in 1975, before that time, the sole guidance to authorities on the resolution of locally determined disputes being a Ministry of Health 'interim memorandum' issued in 1951.[28] The General Whitley Council negotiated a procedure in 1975 to cover all NHS staff and students, and this was the first time in over twenty-five years that discipline had been covered by a Whitley Council agreement.[29] It now brings NHS practice into that statutorily established, and gives staff a greater measure of protection, particularly through its provision for written warnings to staff who may be subject to disciplinary action, and a detailed appeals procedure.

However, in April 1975 the Secretary of State announced that a special adviser, Dr W.E.J. (later Lord) McCarthy, had been appointed to assist in efforts to review the Whitley Council methods, and to evaluate views and suggestions for improvements from interested parties.

His report, *Making Whitley Work,*[30] was published in December 1976 and circulated widely for comment. It did not propose a radically new system for NHS wage negotiations although most of the criticisms of the current arrangements were acknowledged. The report said that the Whitley Councils should be retained and strengthened, and that several important modifications should be made to ensure this. The major innovation suggested was that Regional Whitley Councils should be established as the forum for local negotiation, with the scope to fix specific details of settlements. As a consequence, the national Councils should negotiate more flexible agreements which leave room for interpretation and adaptation by the Regional Councils. In addition, the DHSS should loosen its grip over the management sides of the national Councils by only itself being concerned with the overall cost to Government of settlements, and with any effects of agreements on major aspect aspects of government policy. The health authorities should in turn take greater care to select experienced and committed representatives who will be well brief and required to report back.

Lord McCarthy's other main finding was the lack of coordination between organisations representing staff. He recommended a reduction in the total number through amalgamations, to produce more effective bodies, with agreed areas of recruitment in the NHS. He said that NHS employees should be consulted on all important management decisions and that his proposed improvements in the negotiating machinery should dovetail with improvements in the consultative procedures at national, regional and local levels.

9 FINANCING THE NATIONAL HEALTH SERVICE

This chapter is concerned with three basic questions: what does it cost to run the NHS?; from where does the money to pay for the service come?; what are the implications of the system?

Capital and Revenue Expenditure

Traditionally, NHS expenditure is divided into two categories — capital and revenue. Capital expenditure is the purchase cost of an asset which generates benefits over more than one year. Examples of such assets in the NHS include the purchase of land to site buildings, the erection of new buildings, the extension of old buildings and the adaptation of existing buildings for health purposes, and the cost of initial equipment, furniture and stores of these buildings. These costs are incurred in relation to hospitals, clinics, health centres and for offices of administrative bodies such as the health authorities themselves. Revenue expenditure, on the other hand, covers the costs of services and assets which generate in the current year. These include the remuneration of medical, nursing, paramedical and other professional staff; the remuneration of administrators, accountants, storekeepers, cooks, cleaners, porters, engineers and maintenance staff; the cost of goods and services needed to provide residential care for patients and accommodation for staff; the cost of drugs, appliances, fuel and the replacement of equipment and maintenance of buildings. These lists of items are not exhaustive but simply indicate how the whole range of health service costs have been classified.

The reason for making a distinction between NHS capital and revenue expenditure may not immediately be clear, since in private industry it is essential for the calculation of the annual profit margin. Profit is the income derived from a given level of expenditure, and this calculation is obviously difficult to transfer to the accounts of the NHS, where the 'income' is not represented in monetary terms. There are, however, four reasons why the capital/revenue distinction is made in the financing of the NHS.

First, a decision on spending priorities must involve some analysis of whether the expenditure is part of a commitment made in the past (e.g. the staffing of a hospital built many years ago) or as expenditure which will require funding over future periods (e.g. the maintenance of a new operating theatre installed during the current year). Second, in order to analyse trends of expenditure over several years it is wise to separate out those items which represent the cost of maintaining existing services from the provision for new services, for which very large sums of money are required at the very start. If this distinction is not made, there is a danger that total expenditure patterns over a period of several years will not reflect the fact that expensive projects were started in some years and not in others. Taking an example over ten years, it can be seen from Table 5 that a project was started in year 2 and another in year 6. Assuming for simplicity's sake that these two projects were new wings of an existing hospital and that the building was completed in one year, it can be seen that each of the new wings requires revenue expenditure in all subsequent years for running costs. If only the bottom line (total expenditure) was taken, this would give a distorting picture for analysis of increased costs over the period.

Third, it is necessary for purposes of comparison between NHS regions and also for comparison of expenditure on the NHS and other government spending departments to make such a distinction. Capital expenditure almost always involves large sums of money and unless the distinction was made, public expenditure would be difficult to plan. Capital projects which were necessary for the adequate maintenance of existing assets (e.g. replacing worn-out equipment) might otherwise not get sufficient priority, bearing in mind the scarce resources available to the public sector. Fourth, in judging the timing of expenditure, current items represent a continuing financial commitment which cannot normally be significantly reduced. Capital commitments on the other hand can be brought forward or postponed depending on a government's overall economic strategy. In precise terms, this means that there is normally no possibility of deciding that hospital sheets should not be laundered or that nurses should not be paid, whereas the building of a new hospital can be delayed for one or two years if the Government wishes to save money in the current year.

The rigid application of the distinction between capital and revenue expenditure has, in the past, been criticised for discouraging local managers from using their discretion to finance services in a flexible and economic way. It also used to be the rule that all unspent money should be returned at the end of the financial year, thus penalising those authorities who had, through wise financial management, been able to achieve economies. They found that their underspending could result in a reduced financial allocation for the following year. However, these anomalies have recently been recognised and health authorities are now permitted to carry over underspendings of up to 1 per cent of their bud-

Table 5 *Illustration of the Difference Between Capital and Current Expenditure*

£ million — excluding inflation

YEARS	1	2	3	4	5	6	7	8	9	10
Current expenditure: original hospital premises	5	5	5	5	5	5	5	5	5	5
Current expenditure: first new wing			1	1	1	1	1	1	1	1
Current expenditure: second new wing							1	1	1	1
TOTAL CURRENT EXPENDITURE	5	5	6	6	6	6	7	7	7	7
Capital expenditure: first new wing		5								
Capital expenditure: second new wing						5				
TOTAL CAPITAL EXPENDITURE		5				5				
TOTAL (CAPITAL & CURRENT) EXPENDITURE	5	10	6	6	6	11	7	7	7	7

gets into the following year and to transfer up to 1 per cent of revenue allocation for capital spending and up to 10 per cent of capital allocation for revenue. Capital spending is now defined as acquisition of land or premises, individual works schemes costing £10,000 or more, purchases of equipment and vehicles costing £5,000 or more, and pay and expenses of works department staff.[1]

In addition however, the discipline of cash limits has been introduced into the NHS (and other public services). This means that the health authorities are notified of their capital and revenue allocations for the year, out of which they are obliged to meet all their commitments for that year. Any overspending they make is recovered from them by making a corresponding deduction from their allocation for the following year. One further discipline which was introduced in 1976 relates to the revenue consequences of capital schemes (RCCS). As Table 5 shows, the consequence of making capital spending is to increase revenue spending in subsequent years (if the capital was spent in order to develop services). Previously this was acknowledged by adding the estimated amount of the increase to health authorities' allocations. This process has now ceased, so in order to finance the RCCS that health authorities incur, they have to use part of their ordinary revenue allocation, which does not contain any special extra amount. The effect, because of cash limits, is to require the health authorities to make savings from other elements of their revenue expenditure.

Table 6(a) shows the way that costs of the NHS and Personal Social Services are now being recorded. (Previously the heading on the left hand side reflected the three elements of the former tripartite structure.) The most notable figure is the one opposite Health Authorities: Revenue Expenditure, and indicates the point made above, that previous capital investment (i.e. the creation of new hospitals) has a substantial influence on subsequent revenue commitments.

In order to pay for these items, money is derived from three sources as shown in Table 6(b): general taxation, a portion of the social security contribution and payments by users. Until the reorganisation community health services were further paid for out of the local authority rates and Exchequer rate support grants, but they are now financed from the health authorities' allocations. However, personal social services and environmental health services continue to be financed through the local authorities. The Consolidated Fund means the same thing as 'The Exchequer' and is the Government's central cash account, held at the Bank of England. Revenue from taxation is paid into the Consolidated Fund and in return it provides money for public expenditure through government departments.

Table 6 *Costs and Sources of Finance for the NHS*

(a)   Costs of Services 1975/76 (England)

	£ million	%
Health Authorities: Revenue Expenditure	3,118	57.50
Personal Social Services	847	15.50
Pharmaceutical Services	390	7.25
Health Authorities: Capital Expenditure	317	5.75
General Medical Services	281	5.25
General Dental Services	199	3.75
General Ophthalmic Services	64	1.25
Central Administration	33	0.75
Welfare Foods	12	0.25
Other	150	2.75
	5,411	100.00

(b)   Sources of Finance 1975/76 (England)

	£ million	%
Consolidated Fund (excluding grants to local authorities)	4,059	75.00
Local Authority Rates and Consolidated Fund grants	759	14.00
NHS Contributions	397	7.50
Payments by patients	182	3.25
Other	14	0.25
	5,411	100.00

Source: DHSS Annual Report, 1975

The NHS contribution is an earmarked sum that was paid by employers and employees as part of their weekly National Insurance stamps. After April 1975 this contribution was derived mainly from the National Insurance payments which were collected through the PAYE system. Payments to the NHS by users of its services were not included in the original conception — which had aimed to secure a comprehensive system of health care, available free of charge on the basis of need alone. But from 1949, onwards, Governments found that an accelerating rate of public expenditure in an unstable economic climate forced them to re-coup some of the cost through charges to patients. These include payments for prescriptions, dentures, courses of dental treatment, spectacle lenses, surgical and medical applicances. Of course, payments for patients occupying beds in NHS hospitals for private treatment were instituted right at the beginning, as they were not part of the NHS's financial responsibility, and this income is now included as a part of the authorities' funds for revenue spending.

How the Government Pays

The major source of income, from the Consolidated Fund, is not automatically administered from year to year, but only made available after an intricate process of negotiation within the central government machinery. Reference was made, in Chapter 2, to the relationship between the DHSS and the Treasury in connection with the development of policies. This relationship is at the heart of the way money is obtained for spending on the health service, and particularly concerns the public services divisions of the Treasury. These divisions are key elements of the Treasury, where all national government expenditure is supervised, through a series of consultations throughout the year with the spending departments, Treasury Ministers and the Cabinet. Each spring, all the spending departments (e.g. the DHSS, the Department of the Environment, the Department of Trade and Industry, the Ministry of Defence) submit preliminary returns to the Treasury. These are prepared in accordance with guidelines agreed by the Cabinet. They outline the revalued figures for the four years covered by the previous plan, with proposals for any new expenditure and for possible savings, together with figures for the new fifth year. They take account of a Cabinet discussion of the medium-term economic outlook and of their priorities, as well as of detailed economic assumptions provided by the Treasury. In proposing them, the departmental officials confer with their Ministers in order to work out their proposals for the continuation of existing policies and the development of new ones. This process is not always straightforward since there may well be disagreement about what current policy actually is. Then from March to May the officials of the departments have very detailed discussions with officials from the public services divisions in order to agree on statistical assumptions and their effect on the projected future cost of existing policies. In May the Principal Finance Officers from each spending department meet together with officials from the General Expenditure Division of the Treasury, and write a report which projects the future cost of all the national policies as they stand, and defines the areas where agreement has yet to be reached.

Their report is called the Public Expenditure Survey Committee (PESC) Report, and it is a key document on which the Government's subsequent deliberations are based. The Principal Finance Officers, although officials of their own departments, need to foster the closest confidential relations with the Treasury in order that they may give their own department an accurate picture of the proposals that are likely to be successful with the Treasury, and those that will need more persuasion to be acceptable. When they meet their opposite numbers to draw up the PESC report, they are in a position to assess the likely balance of demands for new spending between competing departments and they attempt to get as much as they reasonably can for their own departments, without antagonising the Treasury officials. The process depends very much at this stage on the trusting and cooperative nature of the relationships between these officials.

The next stage of the process involves the Treasury Ministers. They receive the PESC report (as do each of the departments) and, together with Treasury officials study the effect of its expenditure proposals in the light of their assessment of the economic climate and the Government's strategy. They have to decide whether the proposals could actually be paid for with the resources that are likely to be available. The Chancellor of the Exchequer's view is presented to the Cabinet, and exceptionally he may find that increased spending will be possible in some areas, but more often he suggests that some cuts in the projections of individual departments will have to be made. The Cabinet argues over these points, and individual Ministers have to try to persuade their colleagues over the precedence of their claims for resources. Much may depend on whether the Prime Minister (who chairs Cabinet meetings) is in favour of certain policies rather than others. He will have already had confidential meetings with the Chancellor and the Secretary of the Cabinet, and his own mind may be made up before the Cabinet meets. Nevertheless, the discussions continue from June to November after which the Cabinet's decisions are embodied in the White Paper on Public Expenditure, which is published around December. It is subsequently debated for two days in the House of Commons, but this is now usually a formality in which few if any amendments are made to it. The House's Select Committee on Expenditure (which succeeded the Select Committee on Estimates in 1970) chooses topics in the White Paper for study by each of its six sub-committees, and reports on its findings to the House of Commons. Although this represents a more critical look at policy decisions than the debate on the White Paper achieves, its influence on the proposals which are, after all, largely constructed by departmental officials, is relatively small, because the MPs do not always have the grasp of the broad issues and forward implications of decisions that the full-time officials can develop. This is, however, an area where MPs could exert more influence over future government policy, if they chose to play a more active part. The PESC plans are converted to up-to-date prices and set out in a form in which Parliament actually votes the money for the year ahead. At the same time, a cash limit is calculated incorporating projections of future inflation and represents the limit on the amount of extra money which the departments can expect on grounds of price increases.

Once Parliament has agreed to the allocations for each department, through the annual 'Votes', its involvement is temporarily ended. Later in the financial year that the vote covers, departments may, through their Ministers, come back for more money (subject to the overall cash limits); the Treasury puts forward requests for supplementary allocations after discussion with the departments, and Parliament agrees to allow the additional money. Parliament is subsequently involved in the scrutiny of departmental spending through the work of the Comptroller and Auditor General, and the investigations of its Public Accounts Committee — both of these were discussed in Chapter 2.

When the DHSS finally receives its allocation for the current year, it is able to pass money on to the regions, areas and districts in accordance with their previously agreed budgets. Requests for new cash are made in the middle of the week for the five days of the next week. This amount is sufficient for the officers to write cheques in payments of goods and services. At area level, some requests for money go straight to the DHSS and some go to the RHA, depending partly on how the regional finance department is equipped — many have computers to handle the payroll, in which case all salaries and wages for regional, area and district staff (i.e. the biggest single element of spending) may be paid through it.

The Cost of the NHS

The amount of money being spent on the NHS has risen substantially. There are three ways of looking at the increase, and each of them are represented in Figure 21. The gross annual cost of the NHS produces

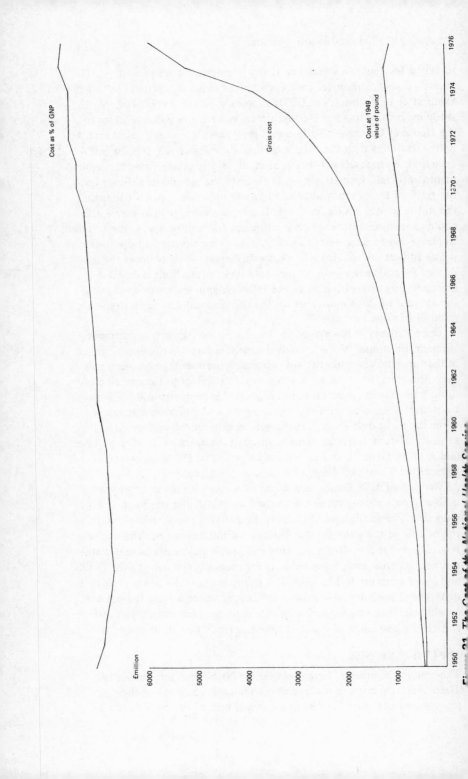

£million

6000

5000

4000

3000

2000

1000

1950   1952   1954   1956   1958   1960   1962   1964   1966   1968   1970   1972   1974   1976

Cost as % of GNP

Gross cost

Cost at 1949
value of pound

Figure 31 The Cost of the National Health Service

the steepest curve, and it shows how much money the DHSS has spent on the health service from year to year. But this figure is affected by inflation, and the second curve shows the annual cost when the rise due to inflation alone is discounted. The second curve is not as steep as the first, but it shows all the same that the definite trend is for more money to be allocated to the DHSS each year. The last curve represents expenditure on the NHS as a percentage of gross national product (GNP). GNP is the total value of goods and services produced by the nation and is conventionally taken as an indication of the level of national resources. The proportion of GNP spent on the NHS is also increasing, but at a slower rate than the actual spending of the NHS.

All these trends make more sense when they are compared against others, and the proportion of GNP that different countries spend on their health services is one that can easily be made because its calculation is not complicated by currency exchange-rate considerations. A study of the health care systems of twenty countries in Western Europe, the Soviet Union and the USA[2] showed that most of the other countries increased their spending on health by about 1 per cent of GNP from 1950-60, and the trend continued in the next decade, amounting to 1½ per cent of GNP for some of them, to give an average level of about 6 per cent of GNP. The study also concluded that health expenditure in all countries is rising faster than GNP, no matter how fast GNP itself has risen. However, different countries' expenditure on health care is not recorded in strictly equivalent ways, so the comparisons have to be interpreted with some caution. The money spent does not necessarily buy a 'better' system of health care, and the question of whether the UK gets 'value for money' through the NHS, even though it spends proportionally less than other countries will be discussed at the end of the chapter.

Within the country, the resources allocated to the NHS can also be compared with other items of public expenditure. Some items are intrinsically more costly than others so any conclusions from the comparison need to be carefully made. Figure 22 shows that for all items of public expenditure, the NHS falls into fifth place, exceeded (in spending terms) by social security payments, education, defence and trade and industry. In 1975, all public expenditure amounted to £49,952 million, of which the NHS received 10.5 per cent. The total public expenditure amounted to 53 per cent of GNP for that year.

Looking more closely at the distribution of expenditure between the different elements of the health and personal social services, their relative positions as suggested by successive Public Expenditure White Papers is only gradually changing, even though the Personal Social Ser-

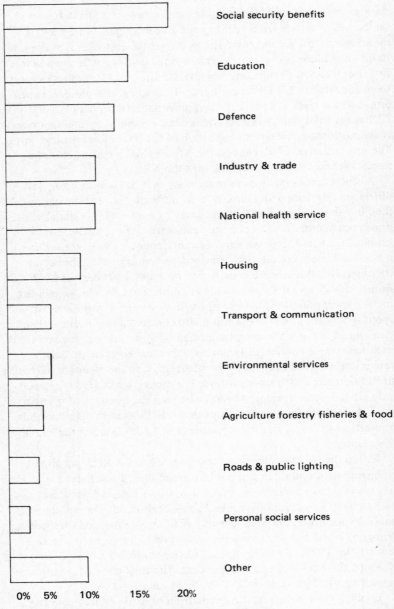

Figure 22 *Analysis of Public Expenditure 1975*
Source: Annual Abstract of Statistics, 1976

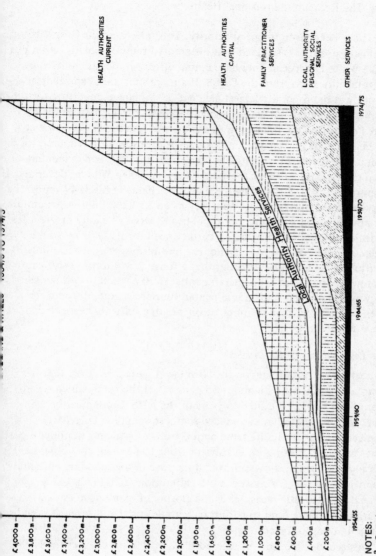

£4,000m
£3,800m
£3,600m
£3,400m
£3,200m
£3,000m
£2,800m
£2,600m
£2,400m
£2,200m
£2,000m
£1,800m
£1,600m
£1,400m
£1,200m
£1,000m
£800m
£600m
£400m
£200m

1954/55   1959/60   1964/65   1969/70   1974/75

HEALTH AUTHORITIES CURRENT

HEALTH AUTHORITIES CAPITAL

FAMILY PRACTITIONER SERVICES

LOCAL AUTHORITY PERSONAL SOCIAL SERVICES

OTHER SERVICES

Local Authority Health Services

NOTES:

a   Over the years, the content of the services has varied somewhat, and charges to patients will have affected the net expenditure. But the broad trend is as shown.

b   Separate accounts were kept for England and Wales from 1967/68. This chart keeps them together to present a consistent picture.

c   Health Authorities Current and Capital includes Local Health Authority Services from 1974/75.

Source: DHSS Annual Report 1975

Figure 23

vices have been given financial priority. This is because the hospitals' dominant position is so fixed that differential rates of expansion set out in the White Papers can only have a mild effect on the distribution of the total allocation from the DHSS. If a more substantial and radical change was required, the largest element of revenue expenditure for the hospitals — salaries and wages — would have to be switched to the preferred sector. As the discussion of capital and revenue expenditure at the beginning of the chapter indicated, the creation of new sources of revenue commitments through building new hospitals and expanding old ones has consequences for many years on. When William Beveridge proposed a comprehensive national health scheme in his 1944 report, he was convinced that its cost would stay at under £200 million per annum because the effects of its action on ill-health would steadily create a healthier population who had no further need for its services, so the scheme would not have to expand. His optimism was a serious miscalculation, since it is now apparent that a finite demand for health care does not exist. There is no guarantee that if 20 per cent or 50 per cent or even 100 per cent of funds allocated for public expenditure were given to the NHS, that the population would eventually cease to consume its services.

The Distribution of Resources

A breakdown of spending on the NHS (see Figure 23) shows that the hospitals started off with about 55 per cent of the total, which rose to over 65 per cent in the first 25 years of the NHS. Consequently the other sectors had to have a reduced share, so spending on general medical services fell in the same period from 11 per cent to under 8 per cent, and general dental services went from 10 per cent to 4.5 per cent, although the graph shows an overall increase in the spending on family practitioner services. Any substantial alterations could only come through such drastic measures as the closure of many hospitals or the creation of a large fund to permit increased capital and revenue spending in the non-hospital sectors.

This account has not yet tackled the question of whether the NHS spends its money in the most effective way, and whether the reorganisation could have any influence in this respect. The White Paper on the reorganisation (1972) announced that, . . . the allocations of available funds to health authorities will be designed progressively to reduce the disparities between the resources available to different regions, and to achieve standards and improvements in services with due regard to national, regional and area priorities'.[3]

The figures for staff working in the NHS (see Figure 24) show that in

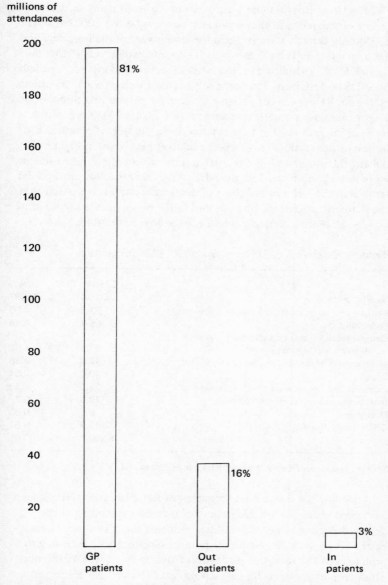

Figure 24 *Patients Receiving Hospital and General Practitioner Care
        1975 (Great Britain)*

Source: Review Body on Doctors' and Dentists' Remuneration 7th Report 1977

1974 in Great Britain there were over nine times as many in the hospital service compared with the community services (about 800,000 and 85,000 respectively). Wages form the largest part of the hospitals' revenue spending as Table 7 shows. It is also interesting to note that although total expenditure on the hospital sector accounts for over half the NHS budget, only 3 per cent of patients are cared for as inpatients each year. 81 per cent of patients are seen by general practitioners, and 16 per cent have outpatient treatment (see Figure 24). Some of the regional inequalities that have resulted from the lack of planned distribution of financial and manpower resources are shown in Figure 25. Solving the problems this has created does not simply require more and more money to be spent on the NHS. Available funds for most public services in the UK now fall short of demand because it is not felt that the share of national income devoted to the public sector should grow rapidly while the country's overall economic growth rate is so low.

Table 7 *Revenue Expenditure: Hospitals 1974 (England)*

	£ million	%
Salaries and wages	1,033.4	68.87
Medical and surgical appliances and equipment	73.1	4.80
Provisions	65.7	4.38
General services (power, light, heat, water, cleaning and laundry)	57.4	3.82
Maintenance of buildings, plant and grounds	42.9	2.85
Drugs	42.6	2.84
Domestic repairs, renewals and replacements	23.3	1.55
Staff uniforms and patients' clothing	10.8	0.72
Dressings	9.5	0.63
Other expenditure	142.7	9.51
	1,500.4	100.00

Source: Health and Personal Social Services Statistics, 1975

Achieving the equitable distribution of those funds the NHS does have depends on a workable policy for increasing spending in the deprived regions by correspondingly reducing the allocations to the better-off regions. The NHS is beginning this process by adopting the principles of the Resource Allocation Working Party (RAWP) Report. This provides a scheme for calculating future 'target' allocations for each region according to a formula which takes into account the differential needs of various groups within the population for a range of hospital and community health services. Under the RAWP scheme the total NHS resources should be allocated to the regions in such a way that

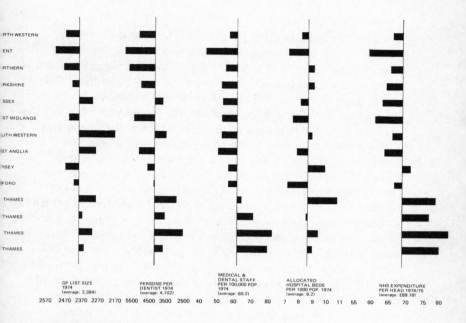

Figure 25 *Regional Variations*

Better than average provision is indicated by a block to the right of the vertical lines and poorer than average by a block to the left. The regions are shown in order of relative under-provision as given by the RAWP formula.

Source: DHSS

they can reach their 'targets' within a specified number of years.[4] The principles of the RAWP report could, over time, enable the NHS to provide services more fairly in relation to need, although successful implementation will depend amongst other things on the health authorities' ability to construct appropriate strategic plans that can be realised within their cash limits.[5] The reorganised structure should be able to assist in this through its control mechanisms which are intended to co-ordinate the sum of individual local activity into a more logical whole. The medium of control is money and the method is based on the ~~scrutin~~ scrutiny of budgets and expenditure by each level over the next. The result is hopefully a more effective pattern of care, especially since the hospital and community services are now considered together as complementary and interdependent elements.

Control Through Budgets

The control system works in parallel with the planning cycle, and focuses on capital and revenue expenditure. It is exercised through the injunction that each level of authority *monitors* the planned and actual spending of the one below it. In practice this means that the DHSS sets down guidelines for the regions to observe, and keeps an eye on them to see that this happens. Similarly, the regions watch the way that the areas keep within the limits they have set them, the areas watch the districts and the districts watch the managers of sectors and departments. Obviously, the more detail each level builds into its guidelines for the one below it, the less freedom the lower one will have for variations, so the official view is that the degree of detail should be '. . . kept to the minimum necessary to preserve accountability'.

Budgets serve three main functions in commercial organisations — planning, controlling and costing. In the NHS these functions have until recently had low priority, but with the reorganisation there are now closer parallels between commercial organisations and the operation of the NHS. The role that budgets play in the planning cycle has already been discussed; it is clear that without making estimates of future spending and assessing their relative importance in this systematic way, it would be extremely difficult to build a realistic model of the way the NHS should develop, or to influence planning decisions so that this is facilitated. Since budgeting and planning were generally so poorly used in the pre-1974 NHS, they failed to provide the comprehensive and efficient scheme of care that was originally envisaged. The planning cycle itself is a model that was unlikely to be put into practice as precisely as its designers would have liked. Two factors, the ever-rising bill for public expenditure to be met by a Government with a huge balance of payments deficit, and the relative newness of many NHS staff to the discipline of forward planning, meant that the cycle had to start in difficult 'operating conditions' that were not guaranteed to improve in the near future. It does however represent the DHSS's commitment to the view that unless a more systematic control was exercised over the NHS, they would not be able to have confidence in its future.

Control is the second function of budgets mentioned above, and it refers to the fact that by comparing the use of his allocated resources regularly during the year with his budget, a manager (e.g. of a service or a department) has a reliable way of assessing his work, and of altering certain elements in the light of this. The budget is not simply about how fast the allocated money is being spent, since it can provide details of such factors as the productivity of staff, the efficiency of machines, and the changing cost of supplies. In commercial organisations the budget also serves as a control against total overspending, but in the NHS, although this is true, unanticipated spending caused by factors outside the manager's control, e.g. increased salaries and wages bills resulting from nationally negotiated pay awards, or increased spending on raw materials caused by rising prices in an inflationary situation, is to some extent compensated for by supplementary allocations on top of the cash limit which are negotiated by the DHSS. It was shown earlier that the Treasury builds into its plans for public expenditure certain amounts which are provided to departmentments when this sort of overspending is unavoidably incurred.

The budget also indicates the amount of money to be spent on individual items (as well as the total amount) and these sums can be analysed to show the costing of the service that they produce. In other words, the value of resources used up in providing different types of service can be identified from information contained in the budget. This use of costing in a commercial organisation, even if it is a service enterprise (as opposed to a manufacturing one) is straightforward to apply, and essential for the calculation of profit margins. The NHS, on the other hand, has no concept of profit, nor does it have a reliable definition of its objectives against which performance can be assessed. The useful information contained in the budgets has not, as a consequence, been fully exploited, and many ineffective and wasteful practices (both clinical and administrative) have persisted. However, this situation has not gone unnoticed and a steady stream of papers and reports have been appearing since the 1960s, confirming the problems of the costing system and suggesting various reforms. In a sense, the whole reorganisation is a reaction to the problem since its stated objectives are to unify the administration of health care in the interests of achieving a better quality of service from the existing expenditure. The attitudes of doctors are relevant here because by maintaining the medical profession's freedom to direct the use of such a large part of the available resources without stringent controls, the task of management to obtain better value for money in the NHS is made harder. Doctors are allowed to treat individual patients as they think best, yet DMTs and health authorities have to have policies which will control doctors' activities without interfering in them.

Value for Money?

With regard to the objectives of the NHS, the kind of statements that are generally acceptable refer to obtaining the maximum benefit from the resources that are used, or maximising the health of the community for a given expenditure. But since there is no way of *measuring* health or of recognising *maximum* benefits, the choice between alternative types of care becomes very arbitrary. The trend is towards finding some way of measuring outputs of the NHS which will be useful indicators for management decisions, even if they are not absolutely unbiased definitions. Certain output statistics have been recorded for the hospital service since 1948. From the accounts, departments' spending is costed in relation to inpatients, outpatients and day patients in each hospital. This provides figures for the unit costs of departments and for the average costs per inpatient week, and the average cost per 100 outpatient attendances. Inpatients and outpatients are divided according to clinical specialty, and total outpatient attendances and inpatient admissions are counted under these headings. The data that result from these analyses, although of some use to the hospitals concerned, are unreliable as a record of national activity since there are many sources of error built into them. In 1965 a new system, called Hospital Activity Analysis (HAA) was introduced; for each inpatient date of birth, sex, marital status, area of residence, length of stay, hospital, consultant and specialty are recorded. This gives information about rates of discharges and deaths and differential lengths of stay between specialties and hospitals and consultants, that can be used for comparisons between hospitals and regions. Maternity and mental illness admissions are not always recorded in this scheme, but if *all* admissions were included and the system could link individual records (to allow for more than one admission per person) HAA would be able to compare performance in different areas more reliably, and would also show details of the way patients are referred for inpatient care, both within and between areas. Without accurate information of this kind, NHS planners cannot make proper decisions about adjustments to services, since they cannot be fully aware of the current situation. HAA is also used to provide information for the Hospital Inpatient Enquiry (HIPE); this is a 10 per cent sample of the discharges recorded through HAA returns, and it is published annually. As far as statistics about the output of general practice are concerned, the only available information comes from two national studies of morbidity carried out by the Office of Population Censuses and Surveys (the second in conjunction with the Royal College of General Practitioners) in 1955-56 and 1970-71. All these assessments of workload do not match in strength the analyses of NHS costs, so by relating the two to each other, information of consistent reliability cannot be ensured. Only by comparing measures of performance within one unit or institution can managers develop sound yardsticks that will guide them in working towards their objectives.

Four successive systems of cost accounting have been introduced in the NHS, the most recent being in 1973. This latest one does permit some functional outputs to be assessed and compared according to specialty, but as with its predecessors, it gives no way of judging how well resources are being used, and this is the item that is so urgently needed. Advances in techniques of treatment and the invention of new drugs contribute to the quality of care as do the screening programmes, but the problem is in deciding whether these are more desirable outputs — i.e. whether they are preferentially increasing the health of the population. One economic technique that was regarded in the 1960s as the new breakthrough in evaluating alternative choices of public expenditure policy is 'cost-benefit analysis'. It was first applied to the case for building a new underground train line in London (the Victoria Line). The time saved by road travellers due to the reduced congestion on the streets was included in the calculations. Although the value of this time saving does not contribute to the actual income of London Transport (the authority which owns and runs the underground), it is a benefit resulting from the building of the line, which would not otherwise have been created. Cost-benefit analysis is therefore a way of analysing the spending of public money so that the resulting advantage is as large as possible, regardless of who receives the benefit and who pays the costs.

The technique has been applied to a range of other projects, including forms of treatment used in the NHS. One example is the introduction of cervical smears in the hope of detecting cancer of the cervix in its early stages and treating it before it becomes intractable. About 2,500 women in Britain die from this disease each year and a nationwide sceening service for it is available and costs about £3 millions each year. However, the number of lives, if any, that the screening saves is unknown. The assumptions on which it is based (e.g. that the early 'pre-cancerous' stage always progresses to clinical cancer, and that the 'pre-cancerous' stage lasts long enough to be detected by the smear programme) have still to be proved. The cost of treating 'pre-cancerous' cases in hospital, combined with the greater demand for smears from women in the higher social classes mean that it is almost impossible to evaluate the results of the screening programme. The decision to introduce it was taken in response to quite widespread public demand rather than on any clear economic assessment of the implications of the programme. Although it cannot be demonstrated that more lives are being saved, the fact that a number of women *feel* better protected from death by cancer of the cervix is undeniably a benefit. This example shows that there is no absolute way of calculating whether a given proposal is worth what it will cost. So, although cost-benefit analysis does not provide unequivocal guidance for health service planning decisions, it does clarify the areas where value judgements have inevitably to be made. As one official from the DHSS has said, ' . . . if decisions do go against the logic of economic argument, it seems to me to be still right that the economic costs of making the decision should be established'.[8]

This points to the conclusion that medical care, at this stage in its history, provides tangible benefits in terms of the quality of health that an individual and his family can enjoy, but these are not necessarily convertible into quantifiable economic benefits that can justify consistently increasing public expenditure on the NHS. Consequently, some critics have proposed an alternative system of finance for the health service, in which the user pays for the cost of his treatment. The arguments are based on the view that the consumption of medical care is excessive when consumers do not pay for what they receive. Given that some form of rationing does exist, individual users should make the decisions about what to consume on the basis of price, instead of departmental officials doing this through their administrative decisions. Furthermore, it is said that a better standard of care would develop if treatment was available in a free market, because unnecessary 'frivolous' demand would be eliminated, true priorities for health expenditure would become clear and doctors and hospitals would raise the quality of their services in order to maintain their incomes.

10 THE PUBLIC AND THE NATIONAL HEALTH SERVICE

This chapter is concerned with a range of issues that illustrate the relationship between ordinary people and the health services that are provided for them by the State. In the first section, statutory and other arrangements that relate directly to the public rather than to people who have become patients are discussed. The next section goes on to consider selected health care issues on which sections of the public have expressed their view, particularly in criticism of prevailing NHS policy. Finally there is a discussion on the present rationed distribution of NHS services and the option of private health care.

The NHS in the Community

Community Health Councils

Community Health Councils (CHCs), an innovation of the NHS reorganisation, are bodies whose broad task is to represent the views of local users of the health services to the health authorities. The idea of setting them up arose principally because it was felt that health service users had exerted too little influence on the provision and planning of services in an organisation that had become dominated by professionals. In the past, the tasks of managing the provision of services and monitoring their quality had been combined. Some members of the old hospital authorities and the former local authority health committees were specifically meant to represent the lay view, but their influence is felt to have been limited. On the new authorities the lay members are appointed to shoulder managerial responsibilities, and the emphasis is to separate this from the responsibility for representing consumers' views. There are 207 CHCs in England — one in each of the 205 districts plus one each for the Isles of Scilly and South East Cumbria. In Wales there are 22 CHCs corresponding to the 17 districts. Scotland has 48 similar bodies called Local Health Councils while Northern Ireland has 17 District Committees. These together provide for over 6,000 people to play an active part within the health service as members of statutory bodies for expressing consumer opinion, quite separate from the health authorities which take care of the day-to-day running of the services.

CHC membership has been worked out principally on the basis of the resident district population, and ranges from 18 in the smallest to

36 in the largest. Half the members are nominated by the local authorities, one third by voluntary organisations and the remaining one sixth by the regional health authorities. RHAs have the job of officially appointing all the nominees, normally for a period of four years, and half the members retire every two years (although they are eligible for re-appointment). A limited number of people can also be coopted. Generally, each CHC has two full-time staff — the Secretary and his or her assistant — who work from offices chosen by the CHC. In some cases CHCs have obtained shop front accommodation while others work from offices which may be rented from the health or local authorities. The money to pay staff salaries, office costs and all other expenses is made available by the Regional Health Authorities on the basis of agreed budgets, and amounts to between £10,000-20,000 per annum. The CHCs' staff are employees of the Regional Health Authorities and training opportunities for them and the members are arranged by the RHAs.

Circular HRC(74)4 issued by the DHSS outlined the organisation of CHCs and some of the subjects they might direct their attention towards, but it did not specify exactly what their role should be. Interpretations of this differ, but CHCs have certainly initially had to concentrate on becoming informed about the health care needs of the population and the degree to which local provision meets this. They have also had to develop working relationships with District Management Teams (Area Management Teams in single-district areas) and other officers and staff of the Area Health Authority, and to devise ways of putting their own views across. Community Health Councils face a considerable difficulty in making their existence known to local people. To the majority of the population, questions of administration and planning in an organisation as extensive as the NHS are not interesting. Individuals tend to have views about 'illness' rather than 'health', and they tend to find it difficult to consider questions which extend beyond their own personal experience. This is not a criticism but a reflection of the very low priority which governments and authorities have given to explaining issues of policy and administration in a clear and honest way. Newspapers, radio and television are the principal sources of information about all aspects of national life for most people, and these are quite inadequate on the whole to enable people to develop a considered view of complex problems. So CHCs are faced with the task of providing a certain amount of information to interest the public and activate its awareness. Public meetings, advertisements, exhibitions as well as contact with many local groups and press briefings are some of the ways to do this. Through members' own contacts with voluntary organisations and the local authorities, the work of the CHC can be further explained and developed, but this all requires time and effort which may be in short supply. CHC members give their time voluntarily in addition to their other commitments, so the degree to which CHCs can become known and hence reflect the needs of local people is very dependent on the determination of the members and the staff.

The meetings of CHCs are open for members of the public to attend (as are those of the RHAs and AHAs) who may be given the opportunity to speak. People can also call at the CHC office for help and advice. If they have complaints about the NHS the CHC can explain how to make best use of the official channels and procedures. Although it is not the responsibility of CHCs to judge or investigate individual complaints, by playing an active part they can support people through what may be complex and bewildering encounters with the NHS administration and they can comment constructively on areas of complaint to the health authorities. In terms of their overall influence in the NHS it may appear that CHCs are relatively powerless — they certainly have no managerial responsibility for the provision of any services. But they do have the right to ask for and receive information from the administration; they have the right to send one of their members to AHA meetings; they have the right to visit NHS premises; they have the right to be consulted about development plans and to play a part in the annual planning cycle; consultation with them on hospital closures and substantial changes of use is obligatory; they can give evidence to official committees; they can enlist the support of MPs and above all, they can use the press to articulate their views forcibly.

Most CHCs have divided into working groups which each concentrate on a defined sector of health care by meeting regularly to consider information, conduct investigations, make visits and reports. CHCs also have to prepare an annual report to the RHA and there is a statutory annual public meeting with the AHA. In relation to the family practitioner services, CHCs have more limited official powers. They only have observers at the meetings of FPCs which permit this and they do not have automatic access to GPs' surgeries. As a result, many councils have found it advantageous to make their own informal contacts with doctors and the Local Medical Committee in order to establish an atmosphere of mutual respect and to improve the exchange of information. In contrast, a growing number of CHCs is being invited to send observers to the meetings of joint consultative committees; observer status or full membership of health care planning teams is also gradually increasing.

In May 1974 the Secretary of State issued a consultative paper called *Democracy in the NHS*[1] which put forward ways in which the Govern-

ment was prepared to strengthen the principle of delegated authority in
the NHS. With reference to CHCs, the two main suggestions were that
two members should be appointed to the AHA, and that a representative body should be created, with a budget drawn from central funds, to
advise and assist CHCs. The paper announced firm decisions to allow
the posts of CHC secretaries to be filled by open competition (instead
of being restricted to within the NHS); to oblige DMTs to send a spokesman to CHC meetings when invited, to answer questions in open session;
to include CHCs among the bodies consulted by RHAs before making
appointments to the AHAs; to make NHS employees and family practitioners eligible for CHC membership and to give CHCs a key role concerning hospital closures. CHCs, health authorities and other interested
bodies were asked to submit their views on the paper's tentative proposals to the DHSS. In July 1975 the Secretary of State announced that
in the light of these representations she had decided to allow each CHC
to send one member to attend AHA meetings with the right to speak
but not to vote. In 1976, circular HC(76)25 was issued by the DHSS
amending the advice about appointing CHC members. It indicated that
RHAs should include a trades council representative and a disabled
person amongst its own nominees, and pointed out that all members of
CHCs should be ' . . . prepared to devote a considerable amount of time
and energy to their Council's work. It is important that appointing
bodies should take account of this, and confirm with prospective
members that they can undertake the necessary duties before putting
forward nominations.'

The idea of a national body for CHCs was discussed for some time
until a meeting of CHC representatives decided in November 1976 to
proceed with its establishment. The first Annual General Meeting of the
Association of Community Health Councils for England and Wales was
held in June 1977, attended by representatives of more than 70 per cent
of CHCs who had decided to join. At the request of the DHSS
in 1975 a national information service for CHCs, including a regular
publication called *CHC NEWS,* was set up and sponsored by the King's
Fund. This proved to be successful and in 1976 the DHSS assumed
responsibility for its costs. Later it was run by the Association of CHCs
on the understanding that it would continue to be available to all CHCs.

The reorganisation of the NHS and hence the creation of CHCs
occurred at a turning point in the history of health service provision.
Continued growth and expansion was for the first time seriously in
doubt, and the public expenditure cuts of successive Governments in
the 1970s had a significant effect on the NHS. CHCs were therefore not
in a position to expect demands for increased overall spending to be

met, but they were in a position to pioneer attempts to encourage shifts in spending, particularly away from the hospital services towards the community services. They are, through their knowledge of the way the NHS works, and through their involvement in the planning cycle, uniquely able to promote the more effective use of limited resources. particularly in relation to the needs of the local community.

Complaints Procedures

CHCs are also in a position to help the public to make effective use of the official complaints procedures, which can seem bewildering to many people. Formal complaints about hospital services are handled by the district administrator responsible for the hospital in question. According to DHSS circular HM(66)15, informal complaints are usually dealt with on the spot by the head of the department, while any action following investigation of the complaint has to be agreed by the head of the hospital department involved. In both cases the complainant has to be informed of the outcome and told that he can pursue his complaint with higher authorities if he remains dissatisfied. The Davies report on hospital complaints procedure, which was published in 1973,[2] recommended several innovations including a detailed code of practice and the establishment of investigating panels. These panels would be quasi-legal bodies which would deal with serious complaints that could otherwise be taken to court. The report also prescribed a strong role for CHCs both in helping and advising people on how to make the best use of the procedure, and in commenting directly to the health authorities on issues that the CHCs considered potential areas of complaint. The Government welcomed the report, but lengthy consultations lasted until 1976 when it was announced that a uniform code of practice would be implemented for hospital and community (but not family practitioner) services. Opposition to the proposed investigating panels delayed a positive decision so this point was referred to the Select Committee on the Parliamentary Commissioner for Administration, for further consideration. Decisions on some other proposals of the Davies report were not specifically announced.

In the case of complaints made against GPs, general dental practitioners, opticians and pharmacists providing NHS services, the complaint has to be made in writing normally within eight weeks of the event which gave rise to it, to the family practitioner services administrator. It has to allege a breach in the practitioner's terms of service (i.e. his contract with the FPC). The administrator initially tries to settle informally all those complaints that are relatively minor with the complainant, but if it is a more serious matter, he refers it to one of the

Service Committees of the FPC. These are small bodies appointed by the FPC with professional and lay members, who hear the complaint and give the complainant and the practitioner the opportunity to present their cases and call witnesses. The Service Committee's decision can be appealed against by either party if it is adverse to them, in which case the Secretary of State can arrange for a small committee to consider the case again, sometimes with an oral hearing, both parties having the right to be legally represented. Various penalties can be imposed on a practitioner who is found to have breached his terms of service, and can involve a warning or a withholding of remuneration. In exceptional cases a practitioner can be referred by the FPC to the National Health Service Tribunal. This body has the power to remove a person from the FPC's list if continued inclusion would 'be prejudicial to the efficiency of the services'. The practitioner then has the right of appeal to the Secretary of State who may confirm or revoke the Tribunal's decision. This procedure is distinct from the professions' own disciplinary powers to erase the name of a practitioner from the professional register and hence to disqualify that person from practising at all. A practitioner who has had his name removed from an FPC list by a decision of the NHS Tribunal is still free to practise privately or as a salaried employee of the NHS.

All these arrangements for investigating complaints are governed by the *Service Committees and Tribunals Regulations 1974* (as amended by Statutory Instrument 1974 No. 907) and the Council on Tribunals has suggested a number of improvements to them. In 1976 the DHSS initiated a review and invited interested parties to submit views on those suggestions and on any other improvements. In particular, the Council on Tribunals said that the Service Committee procedure could be criticised for being insufficiently independent since the FPC is responsible both for providing services and for deciding whether a complaint about them is justified. The machinery for hearing complaints rests entirely with the administering authorities and the professions which are the parties to the contractual arrangements. Furthermore, at Service Committee hearings, both parties can be assisted by a person of their choice provided that person is not a 'paid advocate'. The position of CHC secretaries as active helpers to patients under the regulations has led to some controversy, and the Council on Tribunals suggested that the term 'paid advocate' should be clarified in order to resolve the position of MPs, paid officials of trade unions and professional associations and CHCs.

A further channel for the consideration of complaints was created by the appointment of the Health Service Commissioner under the

1973 Act. The Commissioner took up office on 1 October 1973 and is empowered to investigate complaints received directly from members of the public concerning failures in provision of services or incidents of maladministration by the health authorities in England, Wales and Scotland. These mainly concern grievances about the treatment and care of patients and the failures in communication between patients and the hospital staff. Specific examples quoted in the Commission's reports include complaints about the length of time patients have had to wait for hospital treatment, the repeated postponement of a major operation, and the performing of an operation without a patient's consent. The Health Service Commissioner is specifically excluded from investigating actions taken solely in consequence of the exercise of

Table 8 *Service Committee Cases* (England, 1975)

	Medical	Dental	Pharma-ceutical	Ophthalmic
Cases investigated	545	272	40	6
No breach found	453	147	13	5
Breach found	92	125	27	1
Decision to withhold remuneration	23	91	6	—
under £25	1	22	—	—
£25-£99	8	38	5	—
£100 and over	14	31	1	—
Representation made against witholding	2(1)	17(6)	1	
No.of reductions following representations	—	4(1)	—	—
Appeals against FPC decisions	85(40)	29(6)	1	—
Appeals by complainant	65(21)	19(4)	—	—
Appeals by practitioner	20(19)	10(2)	1	—
Appeals allowed to complainant	3(2)	—	—	—
Appeals allowed to practitioner	4(4)	2(1)	1	—

(Figures in brackets indicate the number of appeals where there was an oral inquiry)
Source: Health and Personal Social Services Statistics, 1976

clinical judgement, personnel matters or any action taken by a person providing general medical, dental, pharmaceutical or ophthalmic services for which the FPC is responsible. Health authorities may also refer matters to him if they have been unable to resolve them satisfactorily. The Commissioner is based in London and has a small staff of civil servants and staff seconded from NHS work. There are also investigating units in Cardiff and Edinburgh, and thirteen members of the medical profession are available to give him advice in deciding whether a particular complaint from a patient involves clinical judgement. During his first eighteen month's work, the Commissioner received 973 complaints, 57 per cent of which had to be rejected as outside his jurisdiction (mainly because the body complained against had not been given the opportunity to consider the complaint first — this step being required by the Act before the Commissioner can take up the complaint). More recently, the Commissioner has had to reject as many as 72 per cent of the complaints received, but of the remainder, over half have been justified, in his opinion.

The Work of Voluntary Organisations

As the historical summaries in earlier chapters have shown, many of the existing health services have their origins in the work of volunteers and voluntary organisations — outstanding examples are the voluntary hospitals themselves, district nursing and health visiting, the blood transfusion service, occupational therapy and family planning services, although there are many others. The term 'voluntary organisation' covers those non-profit-making associations of individuals (or organisations) which are not created by statute. Depending on their constitution or statement of objects, they may be registered charities, registered companies, chartered bodies or have some other legal status. The contribution of voluntary organisations alongside the statutory provision of health and social services is considerable. Governments continue to recognise that this cooperation is mutually beneficial since in some cases the work of the voluntary organisations supplements that provided by the State (or vice versa), while in other cases the voluntary organisations fill in the gaps of State provision. There is, however, an important distinction between voluntary and statutory services. Voluntary organisations often identify particular areas of need and specialise in educating public opinion on the deficiencies and potential improvements in statutory services, and they can often do this more flexibly and experimentally than a statutorily prescribed organisation.

Those organisations registered under the Charities Act 1960 (probably the majority in the health and welfare area) enjoy a number of financial benefits. Much of their income is derived from donations, legacies, government grants and fund-raising activities. They are entitled to direct relief of tax payable on this as well as being able to reclaim the tax paid by individuals on donations given

as a covenant, and being allowed considerable relief on the rates
payable on their premises. Some of the larger charities also derive
a part of their income from their capital assets. Money is required
to cover staff wages and administrative costs, advertising campaigns,
research support and direct grants. The increasing inflation of
recent years has put considerable financial pressure on many
charities, particularly those whose income from year to year is less
predictable.

Health Education

There are few who doubt that effective health education would
transform the NHS from a scheme tied to illness to one that could
be truly protective and preventive. Health education could be
judged to be effective if most people confidently understood what
constitutes health, if they were able to assess which of their
ailments were avoidable, which could be self-treated and which should
be taken to a doctor. It is, however, difficult to say how successful
health education has been. The development of proper sewerage
systems and drug therapy, improvements in diet and in housing
conditions have altered the patterns of illness substantially so that
the health problems of the present are closely related to the
comparative sophistication and freedom of current life-styles.
Until 1974, local authorities were responsible for teaching certain
sectors of the community about the promotion of health, and there
is evidence that some authorities achieved great improvements.
In Aberdeen, for example, careful social and clinical studies
of pregnancies enabled 'at risk' mothers to be identified early in their
pregnancies, and the perinatal mortality figures have as a result fallen
to well below the national average.[3] With the reorganisation of the
NHS, health education (except in schools) became the responsibility
of the Area Health Authorities, and Area Health Education Officers
were appointed to coordinate these activities and to promote improvements locally.

Circular HRC(74)27 was issued by the Department in 1974, giving
guidance to AHAs on the employment of health education staff, but
there was a delay of eighteen months before salary scales for health
education officers were agreed. In 1976, 29 AHAs in England and
Wales still had not appointed Area Health Education Officers, and 13 of
these had no other health education staff either. A further problem was
created when the Department's review of management costs (see p. 161)
included a freeze on health education staff recruitment by categorising
these jobs as 'management' posts. Protests about this to the DHSS were

successful and in 1977 health education staff were excluded from these recruitment constraints. A further complaint from health education officers has concerned their lack of supporting staff. They have claimed that small budgets and the lack of resources allocated to health education limit their contribution severely, but the DHSS has not so far thought it appropriate to direct AHAs to spend more on this aspect of services. The Department's approach has been more indirect.

However, general practitioners, health visitors, dentists and pharmacists are all implicitly health educators since their work hinges on giving explanation, advice and support to people who have identified themselves or who have been identified as needing this contact. The success of all illness-avoiding measures such as the immunisation of children, cervical cytology examinations, hygienic preparation of food and contact tracing in cases of venereal diseases all depend on individuals choosing to participate in them. The role of the health educator is therefore one of persuasion as much as instruction.

In 1968 the Health Education Council was established as an independent but government-funded body and until 1973, its Medical Research Division conducted several constructive studies on such issues as the incidence of gonnorrhea, participation in measles immunisation programmes and the causes of accidents in the home. The division has since been closed down and research is now done by a variety of other bodies, but the Health Education Council has been criticised by some for failing to be effective. It has, through commercial advertising agencies, conducted national campaigns against smoking, venereal diseases, alcoholism and drug abuse to name a few subjects, but the evidence of the success of these campaigns is not conclusive. The problem rests with the fact that health education really means changing people's behaviour and attitudes by providing them with comprehensible information and support that they can accept. In 1976 the DHSS announced a new series of publications through which it intended to stimulate greater awareness of the possible contribution of preventive measures. The first one was called *Prevention and Health: Everybody's Business* and it presented information derived from research in clinical epidemiology which could be used in the efforts to solve some major health problems. A committee of MPs was also exploring these questions at that time and their report published in 1977[4] summarised very clearly the major areas of concern. These are numerous, and each merits further discussion, but one example will serve to illustrate some of the difficulties of introducing preventive measures.

Studies of the effect on teeth of the fluoridation of water supplies have demonstrated that protection from decay is significantly increased, particularly in children. Often-quoted evidence suggests that adjusting the fluoride level to one part per million in drinking water can reduce the incidence of dental caries by half. The DHSS has adopted fluoridation as its policy and made available a total of £0.5 million per annum to assist health authorities with the capital cost of introducing schemes. The responsibilty for water supplies rests with the water authorities whose agreement has to be obtained, and progress has been slow. In 1976 only 24 AHAs were partly or wholly supplied with fluoridated water. This issue arouses strong feelings, and the anti-fluoridation lobby is very vociferous. They hold that it is ineffective, it can have harmful side-effects, and that it amounts to compulsory medical treatment. Yet dental disease is a major problem in the population. One third of the population has no natural teeth and several hundred thousand working days are lost each year as a result of dental disease. Although the evidence in favour of fluoridation as a preventive measure is strong, it is apparently not strong enough: the committee of MPs was unable to recommend it. The problem lies in assessing the benefits of fluoridation compared with the price of a continued high incidence of dental disease, unless alternative preventive measures are found.

Occupational Health Services

A separate but linked example of health promotion exists in the occupational health services. Unless recently there were enormous gaps in the provision of safe and healthy working environments and responsibility rested outside the NHS, being shared between a number of government departments which organised inspectorates (alkali, clean air, explosives, factories, mines and quarries and nuclear installations). These were not uniformly effective and the legislation did not require employers to inform their employees of the risks entailed in working under exposure to various dusts, fumes and chemical substances, nor to inform those who were not their employees of the risks entailed in entering such working environments. Occupational health services were set up independently by a number of firms and industries, but it was estimated that only 65 per cent of factories with 100 or fewer employees had the services of a full-time or part-time doctor. Yet for every working day lost by strikes, about ten days are lost by industrial injury or disease; most occupational accidents and diseases are preventable.

In 1948 occupational health services were not included in the remit of the NHS, and many feel this has led to their neglect and a poor understanding of their relevance to patterns of illness and health. An appointed factory doctor service was run by the Ministry of Labour, but it was only in 1973 that the Employment Medical Advisory Service came into being. This was designed to work through the Department of Employment in providing advice to ministers, employers, trade unions and other interested parties on occupational health and hygiene, and medical aspects of training and rehabilitation. Only about 120 doctors were involved in this service all over the country, the Department of Employment taking the view that engineers, chemists and other specialists rather than doctors had the expertise to assess and change the working environment. In 1972 the Robens Committee on Safety and Health at Work published its report,[5] and three years later, its full proposals were embodied in the Health and Safety at Work Act 1974, which unified responsibility for coordinating services with the Health and Safety Commission — an independent body with representatives from employers' and employees' organisations and the local authorities. The Commission has taken over the work of the Employment Medical Advisory Service and the former inspectorates and operates through the Health and Safety Executive, which employs inspectors, engineers and doctors necessary to enforce the application of the Act's provisions. Under these, all employers, employees and self-employed people (except domestic workers in private employment) are protected in the work situation and risks to the health and safety of the general public arising from work situations must be prevented. This includes control of noise, the emission of fumes, the handling of toxic materials and the risks of specific working environments. The Act operates through a series of codes of practice and requires employers to maintain safe plant and equipment, safe systems of work and premises, to arrange for adequate training, instruction and supervision, to provide facilities and arrange-ments for employees' welfare at work and to lay down a health and safety policy in writing and to inform employees about it. The legis-lation covers all staff and practitioners in the NHS for the first time, and guidance will shortly be issued by the Health and Safety Executive relating to the particular hazards of work in health services.

Obviously existing occupational health services vary with different types of work setting so that the requirements of heavy manufacturing industries will differ from those of non-mechanised service enterprises. Some firms have provided services far beyond the pre-1975 legal requirements and have delegated responsibilities to special fire and safety officers and appointed medical advisers. Nevertheless, the health and safety legislation will improve conditions overall in time, and create a better awareness of avoidable hazards. In October 1978 regulations are scheduled to come into force enabling safety representatives and committees to be appointed by employees. These will have the power to make regular inspections and reports on conditions in the workplace and to take the advice of health and safety inspectors and make representations to the management.

Selected Issues of Public Concern

Mental Illness and Mental Handicap

It is estimated that there are patients with mental illnesses or handicaps in 44 per cent of all occupied hospital beds. As the discussion in Chapter 4 showed, the policy of isolating such 'deviants' well away from their homes and families flourished in Victorian times and earlier, and although current attitudes may be changing, there is so far no comparable alternative, in terms of the extent of provision to the care of these patients as in hospitals. The Hospital Plan of 1962 aimed to decrease the intake of the old psychiatric and subnormality institutions as the provision of care in units within district general hospitals and in the community developed, and estimates of 10,000 mentally ill and 22,000 mentally handicapped people who could be discharged into the community have been made. However, health and local authorities have not been able to provide these alternative facilities at the desired rate — the DHSS recommended targets of 12,000 residential and 30,000 day care places for the mentally ill, but so far less than 20 per cent of these have been made available.[6]

The Mental Health Act 1959 obliged local authorities to provide a full range of community services for the mentally handicapped, including residential homes and hostels, special schools and training centres, sheltered workshops and social support. The 1946 National Health Service Act had already required them to provide health and social services for the mentally disordered people in the community as a complement to the hospital services, but the Mental Health Act aimed to revolutionise attitudes in this sector by emphasising the need for treatment and support rather than for custodianship. It changed the legal basis for admitting people to psychiatric hospitals, enabling about 90 per cent to enter voluntarily while the remaining 10 per cent could be admitted and detained compulsorily. Under Section 26 of the Act, a person suffering from mental illness or subnormality so severe that he is a danger to himself or others can be admitted for treatment for an initial period of up to one year. The application has to be made by a relative or social worker, and supported by a consultant psychiatrist and by a GP who knows the patient's background. By the same process a person can be compulsorily admitted for observation for up to twenty-eight days under Section 25, if his own safety or the safety of others is threatened. Section 29 covers the same matter as Section 25 but allows the application to be made with only one recommendation, and the order lasts for three days, this section being used where an emergency admission is required but where detention for twenty-eight days might be injurious to the patient's health. A policeman may, under Section 136, send a person appearing to be suffering from a mental disorder in a public place to a police station or a psychiatric hospital for detention of up to three days, to allow a doctor and a social worker to examine him. Another related section of the Act is Section 65 which allows a court to send an offender to a psychiatric hospital rather than to prison if he is suffering from a mental disorder which led to his crime. This 'restriction order' allows only the Home Secretary and not the hospital authorities to order their discharge. Rampton and Moss Side are the mental subnormality hospitals and Broadmoor the mental illness hospital used for restriction orders, and they are run with maximum security provision.

These sections of the Act prevent a person from leaving the hospital legally, and it is unlikely that such patients can refuse the treatment given them — they are not allowed to sue for assault if treatment is given against their will (although voluntary patients do have this right). The Mental Health Act created bodies in each region to allow 'sectioned' patients (i.e. those under compulsory detention orders) to put forward their cases for consideration. These Mental Health Review Tribunals are independent bodies consisting of a lawyer, a consultant psychiatrist and a layman experienced in social administration, and Section 26 patients can apply to them for a hearing within six months after admission or within a renewed period of detention. After receiving evidence from the hospital, the patient and witnesses, the tribunal doctor examines the patient and the Tribunal can then recommend discharge or continued detention. Patients on restriction orders cannot apply directly to the Tribunal but have to apply to the Home Secretary who can decide whether to refer the case, and if a Tribunal does hold a hearing, the Home Secretary may still exercise his power to confirm or reject the Tribunal's recommendations.

Although Mental Health Review Tribunals clearly represent a safeguard to monitor wrongful detention of patients, critics point to several deficiencies in the system. First, many detained patients do not know that Tribunals exist and secondly there are only certain times when an application may be made. Thirdly the patient has to be articulate and well-versed in the workings of the system to make a good case for himself, and fourthly he may not know how to arrange to be represented. But perhaps the most important restriction on the powers of the Tribunals is that they are unable to recommend delayed discharge although this would enable patients to be detained only until adequate accommodation could be found for them in the community.

In 1975 a White Paper was issued, proposing an integration of existing policies on aspects of care for the mentally ill. The capital cost of its full implementation by health and local authorities was estimated at £38 million annually over 20 to 30 years. The document however recognised the slender chance of achieving this order of improvement. Earlier, in 1971, the DHSS had also issued a White Paper (i.e. a statement of government commitment) on mental handicap services.[7] It described the causes and effects of mental handicaps, different assessment methods and some statistical information. It laid down the principles for care of mental handicap patients and support for their families, covering similar headings as those mentioned above for the services for the mentally ill. It emphasised the need for more space, more equipment, more staff and support services and both documents may be regarded as programmes for radical improvements in provision and for a more humane approach to the care of all mentally disordered people. Unfortunately implementation has been slow and uneven across the country, and in 1975 the Secretary of State said she was disappointed that there had not been a dramatic change in attitudes. Hospitals' policies on discharging patients had not been matched by local authorities' plans for building hostels. She announced the setting up of a development group to advise on the planning of a small number of projects in areas where both health and local authorities had a duty to provide some services and where funds could be specially allocated. She maintained that despite economic difficulties, this sector of care was protected, so targets for community services in this sector should be achieved.

Although clear evidence of government policy helps, there is no doubt that the 'dramatic changes' that were hoped for will not arrive quickly. The fact remains that while governments find it necessary to restrict public expenditure on health and social services, it will be hard to divert strictly limited amounts of money from the more attractive short-term acute services to the more demanding and difficult areas of mental disorder. As the reports of committees of

inquiry at hospitals such as Ely, Farleigh, Wittingham and South
Ockenden show, staff are too often seriously overworked in substandard
and overcrowded environments, and the stresses that develop can
push them beyond their personal limits of tolerance. The Hospital
Advisory Service was mentioned earlier as an attempt to spot difficult
situations and remedy problems before they reached flash point, and
its work has clearly achieved some improvements. However, the need
is for these complex problems to be avoided in the first place, and only
by determined implementation of the programmes of reform is this
likely to happen.

Medical Research and Intervention

Research into new and more effective forms of treatment is a necessary
and expected activity, and the benefits of its results are well known.
However, a strong body of opinion is opposed to certain techniques
and experiments both on animal and human subjects. The State finances
research directly through the Medical Research Council and through
grants to individuals, and indirectly through its funding of academic
institutions which carry out research, and most of this work is carefully
done. Concern has arisen over cases where the rights of the subjects
may appear to have been disregarded. In 1967 Dr M.H. Pappworth
published a book called *Human Guinea Pigs*[8] in which he documented
over seventy experiments using human subjects in Britain which were
dangerous, unethical and sometimes, illegal. The response of some
members of the medical profession was embarrassed and defensive, but
a direct result was the establishment of committees of doctors in
hospitals to vet all new proposals for clinical research. This acknowledged
that the responsibility for deciding on the ethics of an experiment
should not rest with the investigator alone, and by 1975 the DHSS had
issued a circular advising that lay members, possibly from community
health councils, should join these ethical committees.[9]

In the case of developing new drugs, the Medicines Commission
scrutinises methods of testing, but it still remains true that animal
and human subjects have to be used at an early stage, before a
medicine can be known to be safe and effective or not. The case of
thalidomide illustrates a possible outcome of insufficient preparatory
research. The drug thalidomide was first synthesised in Germany in 1956
and marketed as a sedative and hypnotic. In 1958 it became
manufactured and marketed in Britain under licence to Distillers
Company Biochemicals Ltd, under several brand names including
'Distaval'. It was found to be a particularly effective sedative which

did not have some disadvantages of the barbiturates, and was prescribed for pregnant women to reduce feelings of tension. In November 1961 a German paediatrician reported the suspected connection between congenital deformities in babies and the use of thalidomide in early pregnancy. On 2 December 1961 Distillers announced withdrawal of the drug. About 8,000 deformed children were born as a result of the use of thalidomide, over 400 of them in Britain.[10] Legal actions against Distillers have been pursued by a number of the children and the settlements are not yet finally resolved, because of the technical complexities of the issues in law.

This affair was one of the factors contributing to the revised legislation on the testing of new drugs and the advertising of their properties (discussed in Chapter 6). Even when drugs have been thoroughly developed, the doubts about their safety can remain, as for example with certain steroid preparations and the contraceptive pill.

Another related problem which concerns the ethics of medical intervention is that of keeping people alive by artificial means. When heart transplants were first performed in the 1960s they captured the interest of the press, but the success rate was relatively disappointing. The high cost of the procedure and the problems of finding suitable donors at the right time have tended to work against much development in this area. Kidney transplantation however is being much more actively pursued. Many people with chronic renal failure are kept alive by being attached to a kidney machine for intermittent dialysis, but the demand for their use far exceeds the availability of the machines. However, the transplant operation is technically less difficult than for the heart, and if a suitable donor can be found, and the considerable problems of tissue rejection managed, a patient with a transplant can recover to lead a fully active and normal life. The untreated disease is fatal, and life with a kidney machine is full of difficulties, so transplantation can offer the best solution for many sufferers. In 1972 the DHSS launched a public campaign to encourage people to decide to allow their kidneys to be used for transplantation if they died. Response to the campaign was disappointing, and although many hospitals were fully equipped to perform the operation (except for shortages of technical staff in some places) people with the disease are dying because there are insufficient donors and machines.

However, the decision on whether to prolong a patient's life or not can be extremely difficult to make, especially when facilities for their continuing care are in short supply. The increasing incidence of degenerative and terminal illnesses in old people bears witness to considerable mastery over the infectious and damaging diseases, and the poor social conditions that limited the life expectancy of earlier generations, but this brings problems with it. One observer has written: 'It is clearly pointless to keep a patient with an inoperable brain tumour breathing when a fatal outcome is certain, and in the case of recurrent chest infections in the elderly respiratory cripple there may come a time when it is unkind to rescue the patient yet again from an acute episode only to restore him to distressing permanent disablement. The decision to submit a patient to resuscitation or intensive therapy must be informed, deliberate and responsible.'[11] Cases of serious and possibly irreversible brain damage following road accidents or the birth of babies with congenital abnormalities such as spina bifida exercise the judgement of doctors and families to the extreme, and the definition of meaningful survival and the cost of intervention, both financial and emotional, have to be made somehow.

The Rationing of Health Care

Two points which have arisen several times in earlier chapters are (1) that the NHS has seriously limited resources with which to provide health care and (2) that this provision varies considerably in quality and quantity from region to region. It was genuinely believed in the 1940s that a comprehensive and free health service would reduce the level of illness (and hence the level of services required) to the point where a stable annual expenditure in the region of £200 million would be required. However, the NHS has claimed a steadily rising share of public money and resources, thus falsifying the earlier assumptions, and creating a situation where rationing is unavoidable. The reasons for this are complex, and result from the inter-relationship of people's requirements for help from the health services, insufficient evaluation of the effects of clinical intervention, technical advances in prevention and treatment, the research drive, social attitudes to sickness and several other factors. The result quite simply is that demand — however it is defined — greatly exceeds supply.

Rationing affects the providers as well as the consumers, but the points relevant to this chapter concern the constraints acting on the consumer. (The rationing that confronts the providers of health services has already been mentioned, as for example in the differential competition for consultant posts in clinical specialties, or the budgetary constraints that health authorities face in the planning system). For the consumers, rationing means the inability freely to obtain the quality and quantity of treatment of their choice. Certain categories of health care consumers are better off than others; thus people with mental disorders or with chronic or degenerative conditions or with non-urgent surgical conditions are the most disadvantaged, while those with acute emergency conditions probably do much better. As a further generalisation, people in the north and west (of England and Wales) are more at risk and receive less health services than people in the south and east.

One aspect of the evidence of rationing can be seen through the phenomenon of waiting. Depending on their condition (and excluding emergency situations) people may have to wait (1) to see their GPs, (2) to obtain an appointment for outpatient consultation or treatment, (3) to be admitted for inpatient care and (4) for discharge back into the community. Periods of six to eight weeks between a surgery visit and an appointment for hospital consultation are quite common, as are waits of eighteen months for subsequent admission to hospital for non-urgent surgery, even though the patient may have to suffer considerable discomfort and anxiety. Patients in psychiatric hospitals can wait for the rest of their lives without being discharged, even though hospital care is no longer suitable for them. In the primary care sector people may have to wait several days for an appointment with their GP, they may be unable to obtain NHS dental treatment in their locality, or they may have to accept less than sufficient help from community nurses and social workers.

These examples of shortcomings are only a selection, and comparisons between regions serve to emphasise the disparities that exist. Nevertheless, two important factors which influence this situation must be acknowledged. First, the coupling of potentially unlimited demand with clearly limited resources is not confined to the health service alone. The shortages that result are a normal economic phenomenon when rationing does not work through the price mechanism. Secondly, despite the 'market' mechanism of rationing through waiting rather than through price, effective demand can nevertheless be channelled in specific ways. Well established procedures such as the surgical repair of hernias, tonsillectomy, and hospital bed rest for heart disease and TB are among those that are of at least questionable benefit. Referrals to hospital for diagnostic investigations can be reduced by providing easy access for GPs to pathology and diagnostic facilities, and the need for major episodes of hospital treatment can be reduced by more effective analysis of morbidity trends in practice populations to identify those at risk at an early stage.

Private Health Care

In August 1975 the DHSS published a consultative document called *The Separation of Private Practice from National Health Service Hospitals* which set out proposals to reduce the number of pay beds in NHS hospitals and to control developments in alternative private practice, in line with the Government's stated commitment to this policy. The proposals met with fierce opposition in a number of quarters, and some hospital doctors were particularly hostile to them. The issue of private practice had been an element in the consultants' dispute with the Government in 1974-5 (see p. 107). Nevertheless, the *Health Services Bill* was published in April 1976 taking some of the objections into account, and after Parliamentary debate the *Health Services Act* received Royal Assent on 22 November 1976. It enables the Secretary of State to promote the separation of facilities available for private practice from NHS premises, while protecting consultants' right to engage in private practice. 1,000 of the 4,444 private beds in NHS hospitals were withdrawn by May 1977 and made available, wherever possible, for the use of NHS patients. The Act created the Health Services Board which had to recommend which 1,000 beds should go within the first six months and has to propose further withdrawals of private beds and private outpatient facilities from NHS hospitals, taking into account representations from any interested parties. In addition, the Board had to make proposals within the first six months for the introduction of common waiting lists for private and NHS patients. It also has to control the authorisation of private hospitals and nursing homes so that the interests of the NHS and its patients will not be disadvantaged.

From the patient's point of view, private health care ensures that treatment will be obtained from a chosen consultant, a private single room will be available in hospital, the date of an outpatient consultation can be fixed quickly, the date of admission can be planned with a significantly shorter wait than would be involved for an NHS bed, and the sheer amount of attention from the private doctor is likely to be far greater than in an NHS setting. But the choice of private care is costly in that the patient has to pay for the hospital's 'hotel' services (which currently involve several hundred pounds per week) together with the fees of the doctor, anaesthetist, and other specialist staff, and the costs of any tests, dressings and drugs. Insurance to cover some of this expenditure is available, and a survey carried out for the DHSS in 1974[12] showed that over 2¼ million people were covered by insurance schemes, although over 90 per cent of them were registered with NHS general practitioners. The great majority of people are covered through group

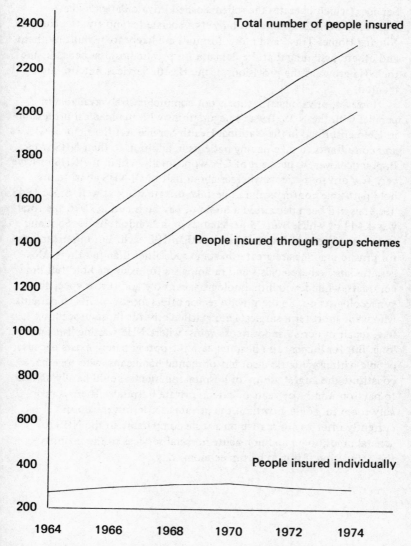

Figure 26 *Insurance for Private Medical Care Through the Major Agencies*
Source: UK Private Medical Care, Lee Donaldson Associates, 1975

subscriptions arranged by their employers (see Figure 26). The three major private medical insurance agencies are BUPA (the British United Provident Association founded in 1947), the Western Provident Association (based in Bristol) and the London Association for Hospital Services (which operates the scheme called Private Patients Plan). BUPA has over 20 hospitals run by its associated company, the Nuffield Nursing Homes Trust, and more hospitals are likely to be built by them and others, assuming that the demand for private hospital beds outside the NHS grows as the provisions of the Health Services Act are implemented.

However, private health care is not comprehensively available in parallel with the NHS. Bevan's negotiations with the medical profession in 1946 enshrined in the National Health Service Act the right of GPs and consultants to take paying patients in addition to their NHS work. In practice over 90 per cent of GPs work totally within the NHS or have very few private patients whereas about half of all NHS consultants hold part-time contracts and undertake private work as well. Since 1948 hospitals had been permitted a quota of pay beds and in 1976 the total was 4,444 of which over 25 per cent were in London; Wales, Scotland and some regions of England had less than 100 each. But opportunities for private practice are greater in some specialties than in others. Most geriatricians, venereologists and radiologists for example hold full-time contracts, while few ophthalmologists, ear nose and throat specialists or gynaecologists do. So the private sector offers most benefits to patients who want short-term surgical care, particularly for those procedures (e.g. repair of hernia and varicose veins) where NHS waiting lists are long. But for longer-term hospital care the option barely exists because people with psychiatric disorders or mental handicaps, who together constitute the largest group of hospital inpatients, could hardly afford to pay for months or years of care in private hospitals. There is probably room for some growth in the private sector, but it cannot currently offer an alternative on a scale comparable to the NHS for general practitioner and non-acute hospital services to the majority of the population if it is to be run economically.

11 THE FUTURE

This final chapter is concerned with a discussion of some problems that still remain unresolved after the reorganisation. Some of the social and economic issues that influence the way the NHS can serve the community both now and in the future are also discussed. The Preface to this volume referred to the Royal Commission on the NHS and previous chapters have covered some of the ground that should be the concern of the Royal Commission. It may be that the Commission's report (expected by 1979) will be able to show a way through some of the dilemmas that are now raised.

Unresolved Problems

One major fault of the NHS during its first twenty-three years has been identified as its inability to organise the integrated provision of care through a range of resources. The reorganisation theoretically represents an attempt to create a structure that will not be hampered in this way. Certainly the span of control of the new health authorities encompasses several elements that were previously separated by the tripartite structure, and the new emphasis on decision-making through multi-disciplinary teams acknowledges the need to broaden individual attitudes in respect of integrated health care. But two areas in particular, where these attempts to improve planning and cooperation can be seen to have an uncertain future are (1) collaboration of the NHS with personal social services and (2) family practitioner services.

Collaboration

Although the First Green Paper proposed joint administration of health and social services under unitary local authorities, and although the Royal Commission on Local Government firmly supported this move, this option proved to be totally unacceptable. Joint administration under elected local authorities was seen as a fundamental threat to the status of the medical profession in the NHS, and as an undesirable introduction of political forces into a 'non-political' sphere of activity. The result of the reorganisations of local government and the NHS was therefore to create quite separate administrations which had to find ways of collaborating with each other. However, the new structure makes this a difficult task. First, the AHAs are meant to be coterminous with the non-metropolitan counties and metropolitan districts for the specific purpose of facilitating joint planning of their respective services, yet the day-to-day work of the health and social services occurs in the health districts, non-metropolitan districts and the boroughs. Planning cannot be separated from provision if it is to be successful, yet this is the situation that has been created. In addition, the coterminosity is imperfect, particularly in the conurbations, and many AHAs and DMTs are faced with complex problems arising from overlap of boundaries, extra-territorial management and agency arrangements. Joint Consultative Committees are the statutory mechanism through which collaboration is to be achieved, but how effectively they can do this is uncertain. They meet infrequently and in most cases have not yet been able to be sufficiently receptive to the problems and priorities of each side so that true collaboration over planning and provision of services can become a reality. The joint financing arrangements certainly offer small-scale assistance to encourage this, but a greater commitment at local level to collaboration over major developments will be required to overcome the difficulties caused by separate administration of health and local authority services.

Family Practitioner Services

The question of the integration of family practitioner services with the rest of the NHS is rather different. Originally, the cooperation of general practitioners could only be obtained by respecting their status as independent contractors instead of making them salaried employees. The Family Practitioner Services Administrator is essentially concerned with clerical and paymaster functions and his involvement in AHA planning has usually only extended to discussions on health centre developments. Indeed there is little overall planning of GP services at all since, apart from financial inducements to practise in under-doctored areas, the investigation of complaints and the monitoring of excessive prescribing, GPs are relatively independent of the NHS administration. The inclusion of the Family Practitioner Services Administrator and the FPC under the wing of the AHAs has not, in practical terms, altered the position in comparison with the separation of the former Executive Councils from the hospital boards and local health authorities. However, some more tangible moves towards greater integration could do much to help create a priority for primary health care.

For dental, ophthalmic and pharmaceutical services, a clear distinguishing feature is the fact that money changes hands between the practitioners and their clients. The relatively independent financial position of these contractors from the NHS and the buoyancy of the private sector works against further integration. For ophthalmic services, partial integration still enables an adequate comprehensive provision to be arranged that benefits the NHS and the private sector alike. Although there is not a great shortage of dentists, NHS work still does not attract sufficient practitioners to provide a comprehensive service, and the independent status of the dental profession prevents the NHS from resolving the problem, short of increasing the financial rewards for general dental practice. The NHS is, however, entirely dependent on the pharmaceutical industry, so the ever rising cost of pharmaceutical products can only be contained through cooperation between the manufacturing companies and governments. There seems to be no easy way of ensuring that the interests of the companies and the NHS are protected simultaneously.

Planning

Apart from moving towards greater integration, the reorganisation has also pinned its hopes for success on a formal planning system that will enable the NHS to achieve positive advances in the provision of health care. The timetable for introducing this system turned out to be over optimistic, and for the first two years (1974/75 and 1975/76) it could not be applied in the form described in the Grey Book and the Guide to Planning. The success of the system's design cannot therefore be assessed, either in terms of its operating details or its achievements, until it has been working properly for a few years. However, if it is to work, the managerial relationships between the officers of the health authorities need to be in good order. The model of these relationships drawn up before 1974 did not anticipate the strong control that is now, apparently, being exerted by some RHAs and their officers over AHAs and their officers, nor between area and district officers within area health authorities. The success of 'delegated authority downwards matched by accountability upwards' requires those most in touch with the day-to-day problems to take responsibility for their own management decisions while being held finally accountable for the result by a higher authority. There is evidence that some district officers have been placed in a line management position by their Area Team of Officers and this has undermined their ability to be properly responsible for their allotted spheres of decision-making. It is not possible to chart the exact extent of these complications nor to assess their long-term effects objectively, but they have raised the question of the appropriate number of tiers of authority for managing the reorganised NHS.

Too Many Tiers?

While the concern to allow NHS staff to settle down after the upheavals of 1974 has been dominant, this question has been kept outside public debate. But as the new arrangements become established, there may be pressure from some quarters to remedy the situation before the structure becomes irretrievably entrenched. The reorganisation itself has been a very costly exercise (the official figure for central expenditure on it to 1976 has been given as £9 million) and it is not yet clear in any detail how the service would be administered if either the RHAs or the AHAs were abolished. The position of the health service in Northern Ireland is beyond the scope of this book, but it is interesting to note that there, health and social services are jointly administered both centrally and locally. The position in Scotland may also provide clues for alternative schemes in England and Wales, particularly in relation to the work of the Common Services Agency (Appendix 1 describes the administration and provision of the health services in Scotland). Another factor to be considered in relation to any further reorganisation in England and Wales is the willingness of Ministers and local authorities to be party to any moves which might weaken their electoral support, despite the needs of the National Health Service. The problem is nevertheless a critical one, and one on which the Royal Commission on the National Health Service has received some strong views. Although Ministers have stated that they would not tackle any fundamental reorganisation again at least until the Commission had reported, it is interesting to note that the boundaries of districts in multi-district areas are being reviewed to see whether more single-district areas can be created. The need to control administrative costs has been the main reason for this review, together with evidence that some single-district areas are managing quite well. However, whether the original concept of a 'district-based' service has been sufficiently tested and whether it is wise to amalgamate districts into larger administrative units without first assessing the most effective structure for rational local planning of services is not clear.

Social Issues

Other significant questions arise, not solely because the NHS has been reorganised, but because the NHS is an instrument for involving the State in the lives of individual people. The basic assumption behind the legislation for the NHS is that the State has a duty to provide a comprehensive range of health care services and that individuals have the right to consume these services as they require them. Earlier chapters have, however, shown that there are several reasons why the services are not fully comprehensive and why individual choice has been restricted. The implication is that these limitations can give the State certain powers over the individual. A study published by the Consumer's Association in 1975 found that although the NHS seemed to give good value for money, patients still had an unequal chance of obtaining treatment, depending on where they lived and on what was wrong with them.

Patients' Rights

Individual patients who are personally aggrieved are only able to express their views through the mechanism of the formal complaints procedure, and there is no doubt that the volume of unexpressed complaints, both major and minor, is very large. Part of the explanation for this reluctance to make complaints may lie in the fact that people are generally frightened of illness and are very grateful for the help that they do receive. If things go wrong, complaining about them appears ungrateful, and so doing nothing about grievances can often be the simpler way to cope with the problems. Errors and deficiencies do occur inevitably, some patients suffer unnecessarily and some staff are unable to relate sensitively to people who are anxious and unwell.

The reports of the Health Service Commissioner contain many examples of this, and emphasise the continuing need to preserve the rights and dignity of individual patients. Clearly Community Health Councils can play a constructive part by expressing consumers' views generally and by helping individual complainants. But in addition, professional attitudes need to become more tolerant of consumers' views. There are a number of instances where consumers may not have access to the type of health services they require, e.g. for the termination of pregnancy, for treatment of emotional problems or for euthanasia. In such cases because acceptable alternatives may be inaccessible or unavailable elsewhere, the individual has either to put up with unacceptable practices or to abandon the requirement for these services. One further point is that although the NHS exists to improve the health of the community, over 100,000 people are admitted to hospital each year for treatment for adverse reactions to drugs or complications of medical or surgical care. This 'iatrogenic' or doctor-induced disease is now a major problem.

Professionalism

The explicit support that the NHS gives to doctors to exercise their 'clinical judgement' freely is relevant to this point. The medical profession consistently maintains that only qualified doctors can decide what is right for the care of people needing medical treatment, and the NHS is organised around this principle. But the independence of GPs and the status of consultants in hospitals has extended further than clinical freedom alone requires. Although it acts as an important and positive force, it can also obscure problems which require more open and cooperative action, such as the management of waiting lists and admissions procedures in hospitals, and the control of prescribing costs. In other words, where professional ethics are the pivot of a complex system that subjects them to comparatively few controls, the system stands or falls on the quality of its professionals' participation.

The term 'professional' bestows a higher status on certain occupations, and it is clear that apart from medicine, a number of others, such as nursing, the paramedical, scientific and administrative spheres all aspire to this designation. Through the internal control of educational programmes and standards, registration and discipline, a position of highly valued independence can be achieved. The result is that the professionals regard themselves as the arbiters in deciding which of their services are properly needed by consumers and how these should be provided. Professionalism obviously brings advantages to the health service because, for example, standards of behaviour are laid down in order to protect the public (e.g. the disciplinary code of a body like the GMC). There can also be disadvantages because by removing control from the public forum, the professionals become ultimately responsible only to themselves. In the lifetime of the NHS the arrangement has, on the whole, worked in favour of the consumers' interests. Problems have arisen, rather, through the disagreements within and between professions which have hindered the fullest cooperation and progress. In the hospital sector, for example, nurses, doctors and administrators need close and trusting working relationships to provide the services effectively, and many of the organisational problems that have prevented some hospitals from functioning efficiently can be traced to this source.

Economic Issues

The Choice of Priorities

Moving on now to economic issues, a critical question concerns the kind of health service that governments can afford to provide through public expenditure. The evidence shows that if there were no financial restrictions, the NHS could rapidly grow by consuming an increasing share of public money. The economic climate is however one in which there are restrictions which force the provision of health services to be rationed. So long as the nation's rate of economic growth is slow, the NHS will be unlikely to have much money for overall expansion. Most resources for development will have to be found within its existing allowance. The Government has made this message very clear and its two major policies: to achieve more equitable distribution of health service resources geographically, and to give a greater priority to long-term and primary care, have to be seen in this light. The implication is that developments in acute hospital services will be much slower than previously, and that existing resources will have to be used more intensively and efficiently. As the historical pattern of financing the NHS has shown, hospitals intrinsically cost and demand more money over a period of time than community services. Not surprisingly therefore, people working in the acute hospital sector resent any cut in their share of funds, but unless the consequences of unrestrained finance for acute care are recognised, the new policies will not be implemented. Their success depends on active choices being made at all levels to support the changes. Not only the health authorities are involved in making these priority decisions. Taxpayers and ratepayers also have to indicate, through the ballot box, what sort of health and social services they wish to have and are willing to pay for. It is a matter of choosing between alternatives — if the NHS had a much reduced coverage, if it was only available in its present form to specified sections of the population, if it involved higher or more extensive charges to patients, if waiting lists were even longer — would this be acceptable? It is hazardous to forecast both the short-term and longer-term developments in the economic climate, but it seems reasonable to expect that governments will not support the full extent of expansion that the NHS could easily absorb in achieving its objective of integrated health care. It seems that the position requires choices of priorities to be made so that health, social services, education, defence, housing and other items requiring public expenditure will have to go through a sustained period of restriction, competing for what they each regard as a minimum share of the limited public funds that are available.

Evaluating Services

Another factor relating to the rapidly rising costs of the NHS is the degree to which attempts are made to do away with costly and uneconomic practices. The conventional wisdom of providing certain treatments has not always been examined critically, and there is growing evidence from studies in all sectors of health care that cheaper and more effective practices may not be being used to the fullest advantage. Without trespassing the domain of doctors' clinical freedom, it seems

that a more concerted effort to apply objective assessments of benefits to different kinds of intervention, and comparing them with
similarly assessed alternatives would be of great value. Matters such as
screening programmes, intensive care units, certain drug therapies, day
surgery, planned care and discharge programmes, community hospitals
can all be studied to see whether the benefits they provide are unique,
less expensive than equally effective alternatives, or of unproven value.
Medicine has resisted this kind of pressure to measure outcome, but it
is clear that unless such studies are applied to all sectors of the NHS
as well as to methods of preventive care, the huge spending on health
care will be difficult to justify. Real savings can be achieved by
agreeing on desired targets and refining organisational procedures in the
light of them.

Social Income

The view that more money would solve all the problems of the NHS
is widely held but not really proven. Other countries spend a greater
proportion of their GNP on health care than the UK, but the NHS is
thought to achieve a wider and more equitable cover than most others.
The crucial point is that the NHS, apart from providing health care, acts
as an instrument for redistributing national income. All the services
that are provided through public expenditure and which are not
controlled by the price mechanism represent 'social income' for each
individual consumer. People consume different amounts of these services
according to their needs but they only contribute through taxation
what they are required to, from an assessment of their income. In this
way, for example, families needing more support from social services,
housing and the NHS are not financially penalised in comparison with
families who need relatively less of this support. In other words, by
removing the barrier of 'market forces' from health and other public
services, people are freer to consume these services according to their
needs. The public money that finances these services therefore needs
to be seen as an instrument acting to equalise the availability of these
resources to individuals, irrespective of their incomes. This contribution
to the social wage is a significant feature of the NHS, yet it is one that
does not appear on the balance sheet.

APPENDIX 1 THE SCOTTISH NATIONAL HEALTH SERVICE

Introduction

1 April 1974 was the appointed day for the reorganisation of the NHS in Scotland as it was in England and Wales. The legislation that originally created the Scottish Health Service was the National Health Service (Scotland) Act, 1947, passed on 21 May 1947, and it established an organisation based on the same tripartite principle as in England and Wales. The hospital and specialist services were administered by five Regional Hospital Boards: Northern, North-Eastern, Eastern, South-Eastern and Western with sixty-five Boards of Management between them, analagous to the Hospital Management Committees in England and Wales. Family practitioner services were administered by twenty-five Executive Councils, and there were fifty-five local health authorities providing community and environmental health services. The Secretary of State for Scotland was responsible for the whole of the NHS in Scotland, with support from civil servants in the Scottish Home and Health Department.

In December 1968, after extensive consultations with a wide range of interested parties both within and outside the NHS, the Secretary of State for Scotland published a Green Paper containing suggestions for reorganising the service called *Administrative Reorganisation of the Scottish Health Services*.[1] It met with a wide measure of support which enabled the Secretary of State to proceed with the publication of a White Paper in July 1971 entitled *Reorganisation of the Scottish Services*[2] containing the Government's proposals for legislation to institute the reorganisation. The *National Health Service (Scotland) Bill* was introduced in Parliament in January 1972 and received Royal Assent on 9 August 1972. There remained just under two years for preparations to be made to implement the new arrangements. No specific study was commissioned to analyse the management arrangements in the new structure, although the Grey Book (published by the DHSS) did not apply to Scotland. However, the Scottish Home and Health Department started a new series of circulars giving guidance to the health authorities (HSR Series — Health Service Reorganisation Scotland) and the Information Office of the Scottish Office was also very active in disseminating information to bodies within and outside the NHS.

Under the National Health Service (Scotland) Act, 1972, health boards were created for each area of Scotland to act as the single authority for administering the three branches of the former tripartite

Table 9 *Scottish Health Boards*

AREA	AREA POPULATION	NO. OF DISTRICTS PER AREA					TEACHING DISTRICTS	DISTRICT POPULATIONS (000s)			
		1	2	3	4	5		<50	50-149	150-249	250+
Argyll & Clyde	456000				*		—		3	1	
Ayrshire & Arran	367000		*				—			2	
Borders	99000	*					—		1		
Dumfries & Galloway	144000	*					—		1		
Fife	328000		*				—		1	1	
Forth Valley	263000		*				—		2		
Grampian	436000			*			1		2	1	
Greater Glasgow	1126000					*	5			2	3
Highlands	175000		*				—	1	1		
Lanarkshire	610000			*			—			3	
Lothian	742000			*			2	1	1		2
Orkney	17000	*					—	1			
Shetland	18000	*					—	1			
Tayside	397000			*			1		2	1	
Western Isles	31000	*					—	1			
	5229000	5	4	4	1	1	9	4	14	11	5

Source: SHHD Circular HSR(73)C31

structure. The Scottish National Health Service Staff Commission was consulted in the handling of the recruiting, transferring and appointing of staff before and during the period of reorganisation, and the reviewing of the arrangements so that the interests of the 100,000 affected staff would be safeguarded. Two new bodies without precedents in the pre-1974 structure were created at national level — the Scottish Health Service Planning Council and the Common Services Agency. These are not precisely mirrored in England, their functions being shared by the DHSS and the Regional Health Authorities, although in Wales, the Welsh Health Technical Services Organisation shares some features of the Scottish Common Services Agency. Provision was made for professional advice to be available both nationally and locally through consultative committees, but no specific bodies were established to pursue collaboration between the local and health authorities in the same way

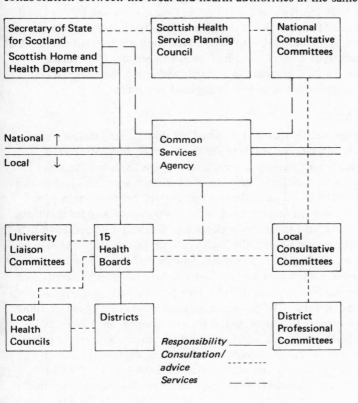

Figure 27 *Organisation of the Scottish National Health Service*
Source: Scottish Information Office

as the Joint Consultative Committees in England and Wales. There was, however, provision for health boards with higher populations to set up administrative organisations in districts to handle some of their functions locally (see Table 9). There are bodies for representing the views of users of the health services in each district or undivided area called Local Health Councils (see Figure 27). The 1972 Act also established the Health Service Commissioner for Scotland who started work on 1 October 1973, and is currently the same individual as the Commissioner for England and Wales, and the Parliamentary Commissioner (the Ombudsman).

The reorganisation of local government created new local authorities in Scotland which came into being on 15 May 1975 – that is, just over a year after the NHS reorganisation and the new local authorities in England and Wales. There are now nine Regional authorities divided into fifty-six Districts, and three Island Councils created by the Local Government (Scotland) Act, 1973, and their boundaries are closely followed by the health board boundaries, the main difference being that the Strathclyde Region contains four health boards. This Act also provided for local community councils within the Districts – a feature absent from the arrangements in England and Wales.

Health Boards

The fifteen health boards in Scotland are directly responsible to the Secretary of State for Scotland for the planning and provision of integrated health services in their areas. Figure 28 shows the area boundaries, and indicates how ten of the fifteen areas are divided into districts. Each board has a chairman appointed by the Secretary of State and between fourteen and twenty-two members appointed from nominations put forward by regional and district local government authorities, trades unions, the health care professions, the universities and a variety of other organisations. In July 1974 the Secretary of State issued a discussion paper called *The National Health Service and the Community in Scotland*[3] which proposed a pattern of membership illustrated in Table 10. This was largely achieved during the last round of appointments for the period of service commencing 1 April 1975.

The health boards as such are concerned mainly with major policy matters and the broad allocation of resources, delegating authority to manage the service to four senior officers of the board – the Chief Administrative Medical Officer, the Chief Area Nursing Officer, the Treasurer and the Secretary – who together constitute the Area Executive Group. These officers have both individual professional and team responsibilities in a similar way to the Area Team of Officers of

Figure 28 *National Health Service, Scotland: Health Board Boundaries*
Source: Scottish Office Brief on the National Health Service in Scotland, 1974

Table 10 *Possible Pattern of Health Board Membership* (Scotland)

HEALTH BOARD	MAX. NO. OF MEMBERS	LOCAL GOVERNMENT NOMINEES	TRADE UNION NOMINEES	HEALTH CARE PROFESSIONS NOMINEES	UNIVERSITY NOMINEES	OTHER NOMINEES
Agyll & Clyde	20	5	3	5	1	6
Ayrshire & Arran	20	5	3	5	1	6
Borders	14	3	2	5	1	3
Dumfries & Galloway	18	5	2	5	1	5
Fife	20	4	3	5	1	7
Forth Valley	18	4	2	5	1	6
Grampian	20	6	3	5	2	4
Greater Glasgow	22	6	3	5	2	6
Highland	18	5	2	5	1	5
Lanarkshire	22	7	3	5	1	6
Lothian	22	5	3	5	2	7
Orkney	14	3	2	5	—	4
Shetland	14	3	2	5	—	4
Tayside	20	4	3	5	2	6
Western Isles	14	3	2	5	—	4
	276	68 (24.6%)	38 (13.7%)	75 (27.1%)	16 (5.5%)	79 (28.6%)

Source: The National Health Service and the Community in Scotland, HMSO, 1974

the AHAs in England and Wales. The Chief Administrative Dental Officer and the Chief Pharmacist join the Area Executive Group for the discussion of items relevant to their responsibilities. The team has to present advice and information to the board to help it to establish policy and priorities. Day-to-day management in the larger Boards which have been divided into districts is referred to below. Health boards were encouraged to set up area programme planning committees, similar to the English district health care planning teams. Most boards have created such commitees for the main groups of users, but it is too soon to say how effective they are at advising the boards on policy options. The joint care planning teams and joint financing arrangements in England do not yet apply in Scotland although they are now being discussed.

Family Practitioner Services

There is no separate administration of family practitioners' contracts in Scotland to compare with the FPCs in England and Wales. General medical and dental practitioners, pharmacists and opticians hold contracts directly with the health boards, who also arrange for all the necessary paymaster, registration and service committee functions. This is a notable step towards integration which has not evidently been achieved in England and Wales.

University Liaison

Collaboration in varying degrees between the universities with medical schools and the health boards is formalised through the establishment of four University Liaison Committees one for each of the Universities with medical and dental schools. At least one third of the membership is nominated by the universities having an interest in the health services in the Area, an equal number are nominated by the Health Board (or Boards) and there are some other members. The University Liaison Committees are the descendants of the Medical Education Committees set up under the 1947 Act which advised the Regional Hospital Boards on clinical teaching and research provision.

District Organisation

In each of the districts, there are four officers directly responsible to their counterparts on the Area Executive Group, but they have a considerable degree of independence. The District Administrator, District Nursing Officer, District Medical Officer and the District Finance Officer constitute the District Executive Group, and they are, as such, jointly accountable to the Area Executive Group for a number of functions. An important difference between the district organisations in Scotland and in England and Wales is therefore that the Scottish district officers are directly subordinate to their area officers although both are officers of the health board. The relationship in England and Wales was described in terms of monitoring and coordinating rather than as direct line responsibility, with a view to ensuring that the district organisation was not placed in a subordinate position. Another important difference is that in Scotland there are no GP or hospital consultant representatives directly involved in the district management arrangements.[4]

Local Health Councils

It is the responsibility of each health board to establish the local health councils (similar to community health councils in England and Wales) normally for each district. Their membership, which ranges from totals of eighteen to thirty, is drawn from the local authorities, voluntary organisations, trade unions and other local bodies, the normal term of appointment being for four years, half the membership retiring every two years. Each local health council produces an annual report which is submitted to the health board, and copies go to the Secretary of State.

Initially, the process of establishment was delayed, and the first of the forty-eight local health councils did not meet until March 1975. The discussion paper published in July 1974 suggested that the formation of a National Association of Local Health Councils, could, among other functions, provide nominations to the Scottish Health Service Planning Council, and it raised the possibility of giving LHCs the right to nominate two of their members to their Health Board.

Central Organisation

The Secretary of State for Scotland is, through the form of the NHS legislation, personally accountable to Parliament for the Scottish health services in the same way as the Secretary of State for Social Services and the Secretary of State for Wales are for the NHS in England and Wales. In Scotland, the supreme government department is the Scottish Office, and the figure shows how the Ministers' responsibilities are arranged. The senior civil servant in the Scottish Office is the Permanent Under-Secretary of State, and he presides over the Management Group which includes the senior civil servants from the five other major government departments in Scotland (see Figure 29).

Scottish Home and Health Department

The department responsible to the Secretary of State for the central administration of the Scottish NHS is the Scottish Home and Health Department (SHHD). This department is also responsible for the central administration relating to the police service, criminal justice, legal aid, the

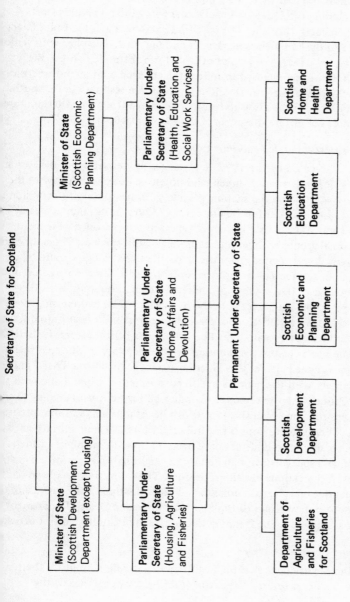

Figure 29 *Scottish Government Departments*

administration of prisons, the administration and legislation relating to superannuation of public service employees, the organisation of the fire service, home defence and emergency services, the legislation relating to shops, theatres and cinemas, licensed premises and land tenure matters.

Within the SHHD there are a number of officers of the health professions including the Chief Medical Officer for Scotland and his staff of Medical Officers, the Chief Dental Officer and his staff, the Chief Pharmacist, and the Chief Nursing Officer and her staff. Together with senior departmental officials, the chief officers form the policy group. the SHHD has been reorganised to reflect the changed administrative structure of the NHS, and four Divisions within it are responsible for central plans and policy in relation to health care, while five other Divisions are responsible for different aspects of the use of resources.

Scottish Health Service Planning Council

This body, created by the 1972 Act, was partly derived from the former Scottish Health Services Council, an influential body which advises the Secretary of State on the shaping of policy for health service provision i Scotland. Like the Central Health Services Council, its counterpart in England and Wales, it is made up of representatives from all the major professional groups with an interest in the health services. The new Planning Council was created to ensure that effective strategies could be devised and implemented to improve Scottish health service provision on a integrated basis, in a context of limited available resources, with the fullest participation from the health authorities. The membership therefore specifically includes one representative from each health board, on from each university with a medical school, six officers from the SHHD and some other members appointed by the Secretary of State, as is the independent chairman of this Planning Council. Just as the DHSS has to work closely with the regional health authorities in England and with th Welsh Office to secure effective planning, so the Scottish Planning Cour has to ensure comprehensive targets can be established, and that progre towards their achievement is carefully monitored. A number of programme planning committees have been set up with members of the Council and specialists nominated by the eight national consultative co mittees of the various health professions. The Council gives advice on th implementation of agreed policies and on evaluation of the success of th policies. A policy group of top Scottish Home and Health Department officials is linked to the Planning Council by the Planning Unit of officia

Common Services Agency

With the requirement that the health boards should administer their services on an integrated basis, and with the disappearance of the

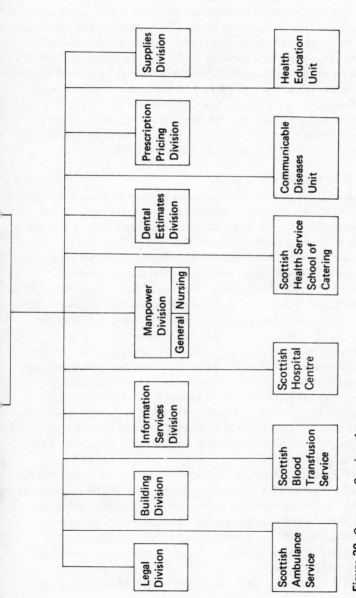

Figure 30 *Common Services Agency*

Regional Hospital Boards, a central mechanism was sought for
providing supporting services so that health boards would not have
to duplicate these functions unnecessarily and uneconomically. The
Common Services Agency (CSA) was therefore established to run
those services that could be organised centrally in this way. Figure
30 sets out the main functions of the CSA – many of the 6,000 staff
involved in providing them were previously doing similar work, but
were either directly employed by the SHHD, the Regional Hospital
Boards or Executive Councils. The CSA is therefore a loose federation
of agencies each providing different services, under the supervision
of a Management Committee. The Chairman is a health board
chairman, and three members are health board members, three
members are health board officers and five members are SHHD
officers, all being appointed by the Secretary of State.

Medical Services

Scotland has for centuries maintained a strong tradition of medical
education to very high standards, and its four university medical
schools (Edinburgh, Glasgow, Aberdeen and Dundee) produce one
fifth of all medical graduates in the United Kingdom. The
professional bodies have grown up independently of those in England
and have achieved notable prominence. The Royal College of
Physicians (Edinburgh), the Royal College of Surgeons (Edinburgh)
and the Royal College of Physicians and Surgeons (Glasgow) are the
oldest; the Scottish Radiological Society, the Scottish Committee
for Community Medicine and Scottish members of the Royal
Colleges of General Practitioners, Obstetricians and Gynaecologists
and Pathologists, the Faculties of Anaesthetists and of Community
Medicine join them in being recognised professional groups
contributing advice through the National Medical Consultative
Committee to the Planning Council. The BMA is also active in
Scotland and its Scottish General Medical Services Committee
contributes to the National Medical Consultative Committee. The
Scottish Junior Staffs Group Council is a similar body to the
Hospital Junior Staffs Group Council for England and Wales, while
hospital consultants are represented through the Scottish Committee
for Hospital Medical Services. In the field of postgraduate medicine,
the Scottish Council for Postgraduate Medical Education was
founded in May 1970 to promote the ongoing development of
medical practitioners through extensive programmes of teaching
and refresher courses.

Health centres are a more prominent feature of health care in

Scotland than in England and Wales, and the SHHD has been pursuing a policy which is designed to provide health care for 50 per cent of the total population (about 5.3 million) from health centres by 1980, and for 80 per cent by 1985. Table 11 shows the state of existing and planned health centres at April 1975. Over 400 GPs are involved with them, and two particularly interesting schemes, in Woodside (Glasgow) and Clydebank, each involve up to thirty GPs in providing care for populations as large as 70,000. Two further large health centres are planned for Dumbarton and East Kilbride. Over 50 per cent of GPs practise in groups of two or three, and the average list size is 2,000 patients. Links with the hospital service are strong, and 400 GPs hold hospital specialist appointments, while 300 GPs have access to beds in community hospitals.

Hospital service developments in Scotland were influenced by major reviews of policy in 1966, 1970 and 1972 which identified priority areas and patient groups. In 1974 the first new custom built teaching hospital since the war was opened at Ninewells. It cost £22½ million, and, in a 230 acre site, it provides 800 beds and about 3,500 staff.

Table 11 *Health Centre Development at April 1975* (Scotland)

In operation	64
Under construction	24
At rental/tendering stage	5
At rental stage/FCL	6
Plans approved	11
Plans under consideration	15
Functions defined and range of accommodation under consideration or sketch plans not yet prepared	37
Approved in principle	12
Others under consideration	32
	206

Source: SHHD

Finance

Table 12 illustrates the financing of the NHS in Scotland.

Other Health Services

There are a number of other professional and administrative bodies with important duties in the Scottish National Health Service which are similar in constitutions and objectives to those bodies described in the chapters relating to England and Wales. These include the Scottish Hospital Advisory Service, the Scottish Medical Practices Committee, the Scottish Tribunal, the Mental Welfare Commission and the General Nursing Council for Scotland. In addition, the mental health services are governed by the provisions of the Mental Health (Scotland) Act, 1966, and social work probation and after care services are covered by the Social Work (Scotland) Act, 1968.

Table 12 *Finance of the Scottish NHS*

(a)	Costs of Services 1974/75	£ thousands
	Hospital Services	305,734
	Community Health Services	24,611
	Family Practitioner Services	80,321
	Common Services Agency	13,552
	Planning Council	18
	Other Central Services & Administration	4,275
	Health Board Administration	16,035
	Research	1,894
	Other	6,790
		453,230
(b)	Sources of Finance 1974/75	
	Exchequer	425,534
	NHS Contributions	20,772
	Payments by patients	6,924
		453,230

Source: Scottish Health Statistics, 1975

APPENDIX 2

Ministers of Health

1919-21	Dr Christopher Addison
1921-22	Sir Alfred Mond
1922-23	Sir Arthur Griffith-Boscawen
1923	Neville Chamberlain
1923-24	Sir William Joynson-Hicks
1924	John Wheatley
1924-29	Neville Chamberlain
1929-31	Arthur Greenwood
1931	Neville Chamberlain
1931-35	Sir E. Hilton-Young
1935-38	Sir Kingsley Wood
1938-40	Walter Elliot
1940-41	Malcolm MacDonald
1941-43	Ernest Brown
1943-45	Henry Willink
1945-51	Aneurin Bevan
1951	Hilary Marquand
1951-52	Harry Crookshank
1952-55	Iain MacLeod
1955-57	Robin Turton
1957	Dennis Vosper
1957-60	Derek Walker-Smith
1960-63	Enoch Powell
1963-64	Anthony Barber
1964-68	Kenneth Robinson

Secretaries of State for Social Services

1968-70	Richard Crossman
1970-74	Sir Keith Joseph
1974-76	Barbara Castle
1976-	David Ennals

NOTES

CHAPTER 1

1. Great Britain. Ministry of Health. Consultative Council on Medical and Allied Services, *Interim Report of the Future Provision of Medical and Allied Services* (Chairman, Lord Dawson), HMSO, London, 1920.
2. Great Britain. Ministry of Health. *Hospital Survey*, HMSO, London, 1945 & 1946. (Separate reports on the ten areas of England and Wales.)
3. Great Britain. Parliament. *Social Insurance and Allied Services*, Report by Sir William Beveridge. HMSO, London, 1942 (Cmd. 6404).
4. Great Britain. Ministry of Health and Department of Health for Scotland. *A National Health Service*, HMSO, London, 1944 (Cmd. 6502).
5. Great Britain. Parliament. *National Health Service Bill*, HMSO, London, 1946 (Cmd. 6761).
6. Great Britain, Parliament. *The National Health Service Act, 1946*, HMSO, London, 1946 (9 & 10 Geo. 6 Chapter 81 Part I Section 1. (1)).
7. Great Britain. Ministry of Health. *Report of the Committee of Enquiry into the Cost of the National Health Service* (Chairman, C.W. Guillebaud), HMSO, London, 1956 (Cmd. 9663).
8. Medical Services Review Committee. *A Review of the Medical Services in Great Britain* (Chairman, Sir A. Porritt), Social Assay, London, 1962.
9. Great Britain. Ministry of Health. Central Health Services Council. Standing Medical Advisory Committee. *The Field Work of the Family Doctor* (Chairman, Dr Annis Gillie), HMSO, London, 1963.
10. Great Britain. Ministry of Health. *Report of the Maternity Services Committee* (Chairman, Earl of Cranbrook), HMSO, London, 1959.
11. Great Britain. Ministry of Health. *A Hospital Plan for England and Wales*, HMSO, London, 1962 (Cmnd. 1604).
12. Great Britain. Department of Health and Social Security and Welsh Office. Central Health Services Council. *The Functions of the District General Hospital*, Report of the Committee (Chairman, Sir Desmond Bonham-Carter), HMSO, London, 1969.
13. Great Britain. Ministry of Health and Scottish Home and Health Department. *Report of the Committee on Senior Nursing Staff Structure* (Chairman, B. Salmon), HMSO, London, 1966.
14. Great Britain. Ministry of Health. *First Report of the Joint Working Party on the Organisation of Medical Work in Hospitals* (Chairman, Sir G. Godber), HMSO, London, 1967.
15. Great Britain. Ministry of Health. *The Administrative Structure of Medical and Related Services in England and Wales*, HMSO, London, 1968.
16. Great Britain. Parliament. *Report of the Committee on Local Authority and Allied Personal Social Services* (Chairman, F. Seebohm), HMSO, London, 1968 (Cmnd. 3703).
17. Great Britain. Parliament. *Report of the Royal Commission on Local Government in England, 1966-1969* (Chairman, Lord Redcliffe-Maud), HMSO, London, 1969 (Cmnd. 4040).
18. Great Britain. Department of Health and Social Security. *The Future Structure of the National Health Service*, HMSO, London, 1970.
In Wales there was a separate publication: Great Britain. Welsh Office. *The Reorganisation of the Health Service in Wales*, HMSO, Cardiff, 1970.
19. Great Britain. Parliament. *Reform of Local Government in England*. HMSO, London, 1970 (Cmnd. 4276).

238 The Reorganised National Health Service

20. Great Britain. Department of Health and Social Security. *National Health Service Reorganisation; Consultative Document,* DHSS, London, 1971. In Wales, there was a separate publication: Great Britain. Welsh Office. *Consultative Document; National Health Service Reorganisation in Wales,* Welsh Office, Cardiff, 1971.
21. Great Britain. Parliament. *Local Government in England,* Government Proposals for Reorganisation, HMSO, London, 1971 (Cmnd. 4584).
22. Great Britain. Parliament. *National Health Service Reorganisation: England,* HMSO, London, 1972 (Cmnd. 5055). In Wales there was a separate publication: Great Britain. Parliament. *National Health Service Reorganisation in Wales,* HMSO, Cardiff, 1972 (Cmnd. 5057).
23. Great Britain. Parliament. *The National Health Service Reorganisation Act, 1973,* HMSO, London, 1973 (Eliz. II Chapter 32).
24. Great Britain. Department of Health and Social Security. *Management Arrangements for the Reorganised National Health Service,* HMSO, London, 1972. In Wales there was a separate publication: Great Britain. Welsh Office. *Management Arrangements for the Reorganised National Health Service in Wales,* HMSO, Cardiff, 1972.
25. Great Britain. Department of Health and Social Security. *Democracy in the National Health Service,* HMSO, London, 1974. In Wales there was a separate paper: Great Britain. Welsh Office. *Making Welsh Health Authorities More Democratic,* HMSO, Cardiff, 1974.

CHAPTER 2

1. Great Britain. Department of Health and Social Security. *The DHSS in Relation to the Health and Personal Social Services,* Review Team Report, Volume I, HMSO, London, 1972.
2. Great Britain. Ministry of Health. Central Health Services Council. *Report of the Committee on the Internal Administration of Hospitals* (Chairman, A.F. Bradbeer), HMSO, London, 1954.
3. Great Britain. Ministry of Health. Central Health Services Council. *The Welfare of Children in Hospital,* Report of the Committee (Chairman, Sir Harry Platt), HMSO, London, 1959.
4. Great Britain. Department of Health and Social Security and Welsh Office. Central Health Services Council. *The Functions of the District General Hospital,* Report of the Committee (Chairman, Sir Desmond Bonham-Carter), HMSO, London, 1969.
5. Great Britain. Department of Health and Social Security. *Report of the Committee of Inquiry into allegations of Ill-Treatment of Patients and Other Irregularities at the Ely Hospital, Cardiff,* HMSO, London, 1969 (Cmnd. 3975).
6. Great Britain. Ministry of Health. *The Administrative Structure of Medical and Related Services in England and Wales,* HMSO, London, 1968, p.9-10, para.12.
7. Great Britain. Parliament. *National Health Service Reorganisation: England,* HMSO, London, 1972 (Cmnd. 5055), p.8, paras. 32-5.
8. This figure is an approximation but because of the high rate of inflation the amounts alter substantially from year to year.
9. Great Britain, Department of Health and Social Security. *Management Arrangements for the Reorganised National Health Service,* HMSO, London, 1972, p.10, para 1.5, b.- e., and p. 11, para 1.7, (4) and (5).

CHAPTER 3

1. Medical Services Review Committee, *A Review of the Medical Services in Great Britain* (Chairman, Sir A. Porritt), Social Assay, London, 1962.
2. Great Britain. Ministry of Health. *The Administrative Structure of Medical and Related Services in England and Wales,* HMSO, London, 1968.
   Great Britain. Department of Health and Social Security. *The Future Structure of the National Health Service,* HMSO, London, 1970.
3. Op. cit., *A Review of the Medical Services in Great Britain,* p.10, para. 77.
4. Ibid., p.23, para. 88.
5. For example, through the publication of the 'Grey Book' which became known, in some circles, as 'the bible'.
6. Great Britain. Parliament. *National Health Service Reorganisation: England,* HMSO, London, 1972 (Cmnd. 5055), p.v.
7. The Report of the Royal Commission on Local Government emphasised that *all* the needs of a locality should be considered when deciding on boundaries. The difficultires that have resulted, since 1974, because in reality the boundaries of AHAs and districts are not coterminous with local authority boundaries in several places, cannot be ignored.
8. Op. cit., *A Review of the Medical Services in Great Britain,* p.99, para. 367.
9. *The NHS Reorganisation,* Office of Health Economics, London, 1974.
10. Department of Health and Social Security Press Release. *Democracy in the NHS; Greater Local Participation Proposed,* Department of Health and Social Security, London, 1974, No.74/60, p.1.
11. These figures are approximate for 1977/8, but because of the high rate of inflation, there would be substantial changes from year to year.
12. Great Britain. Department of Health and Social Security. *Democracy in the National Health Service,* HMSO, London, 1974, p.9, para. 16.
13. Some observers, particularly within the NHS, question the basic premise of the consultative paper that more local authority members can, by their presence, make health authorities more democratic.
14. However, the fears (or hopes) that some observers held before the reorganisation came into effect, that the ATO-DMT relationship would become a manager-subordinate relationship, were being substantiated in several instances within months of April 1974.
15. However in 1976 and 1977 it became apparent that the merging of districts in multi-district areas would be allowed, and that single-district areas were coming to be regarded as a more successful arrangement in many places.
16. Op. cit., *A Review of the Medical Services in Great Britain,* p.18, para. 70.
17. Nevertheless, some authorities have managed to combine the two JCCs' functions into one.
18. Some authorities have encountered difficulties with this system because the efforts of such working groups can conflict with those of the Health Care Planning Teams set up by individual District Management Teams (these teams will be discussed fully in Chapter 4).
19. The Working Party published three reports covering its work from 1972-74: Great Britain. Department of Health and Social Security and Welsh Office. *A Report from the Working Party on Collaboration between the NHS and Local Government on its Activities to the end of 1972,* HMSO, London, 1972; *. . . on its Activities from January to July 1973,* HMSO, London 1973; *. . .on its Activities from July 1973 to April 1974,* HMSO, London, 1974.
20. Great Britain. Parliament. *Local Government Act, 1972,* Chapter 70, HMSO, London, 1972.
21. Great Britain. Department of Health and Social Security. Health Service Reorganisation Circular, *Collaboration Between Health and Local Authorities:*

Reports of the Working Party: Establishment of Joint Consultative Committees, DHSS, London, March 1974, HRC(74)19.

22. See the more detailed discussion in Chapter 10.

23. However, many observers feel that Family Practitioner Committees are merely Executive Councils under another name. In Scotland, FPCs do not exist, and practitioners hold their contracts directly with the area authorities (see Appendix 1).

24. Great Britain. Parliament. *Mental Health Act, 1959,* 7 & 8 Eliz.2., Ch.72.

CHAPTER 4

1. Great Britain. Department of Health and Social Security. *Management Arrangements for the Reorganised National Health Service,* HMSO, London, 1972, p.13, para. 1.16.
2. The recommendations of some Joint Liaison Committees are thought to have given low priority to purely health care factors in the face of strong pressure from the political demands of some pre-reorganisation health and local authority interest groups.
3. The effect of this is to retain the responsibility for integrating the services with the DMT, who are that much further removed from face-to-face contact with health care clients than those actually working in the sectors.
4. This is either handled by a member of the DNO's staff or delegated to the District Personnel Officer.
5. At the time of writing, the DHSS was still continuing to select the schemes for completion in each year, thus preventing the AHAs and DMTs from exercising their own discretion in this sphere.
6. See, for instance, the analysis in: R. Rowbottom and others, *Hospital Organisation: A Progress Report on the Brunel Health Service Organisation Project,* Heinemann, London, 1973.
7. Gordon Forsyth in: I. Douglas-Wilson and Gordon McLachlan (eds.), *Health Service Prospects: an International Survey,* The Lancet and Nuffield Provincial Hospitals Trust, London, 1973.
8. Great Britain. Department of Health and Social Security. *Guide to Planning in the National Health Service,* DHSS, London, 1975.

CHAPTER 5

1. Further Medical Acts, passed in 1956 and 1969, consolidated amendments to the membership and powers of the Council.
2. Great Britain. Parliament. *Report of the Committee of Enquiry into the Regulations of the Medical Profession* (Chairman, Dr A.W. Merrison), HMSO, London, 1975 (Cmnd. 6018). The GMC had decided to change the registration system to require doctors to pay an annual fee instead of the existing once-only payment. Doctors refused to comply with this so if the GMC had proceeded with the new system, the NHS would have been forced to employ non-registered doctors — an illegal arrangement. The inquiry into the GMC was announced to forestall the problem, and the committee itself decided to widen its brief to look at medical education and training as well as the membership and activities of the GMC.
3. Great Britain. Ministry of Health. *Report of the Interdepartmental Committee on Medical Schools* (Chairman, Sir William Goodenough), HMSO, London, 1944.
4. Great Britain. Parliament. *Royal Commission on Medical Education*

(Chairman, Lord Todd), HMSO, London, 1968 (Cmnd. 3569).

5. Equivalent qualifications were also issued by the Conjoint Board of the Royal Colleges of Physicians and Surgeons (MRCS, LRCP) and by the Society of Apothecaries (LMSSA).

6. A further point for consideration is that comparison with figures published in the 1955/56 National Morbidity Survey shows an increase of 36 per cent in morbidity between the two surveys, which would imply an increased work load for doctors.

7. Great Britain. Ministry of Health. Central Health Services Council. *The Field of Work of The Family Doctor,* HMSO, London, 1963.

8. Great Britain, Department of Health and Social Security and Welsh Office. Central Health Services Council. *The Organisation of Group Practice* (Chairman, Dr R. Harvard Davis), HMSO, London, 1971.

9. Great Britain. Ministry of Health and Department of Health for Scotland. *Report of the Inter-Departmental Committee on the Remuneration of Consultants and Specialists* (Chairman, Sir Will Spens), HMSO, London, 1948 (Cmd. 7420).

10. Great Britain. Ministry of Health and Department of Health for Scotland. *Medical Staffing Structure in the Hospital Service; Report of the Joint Working Party* (Chairman, Sir Robert Platt), HMSO, London, 1961.

11. Great Britain. Ministry of Health. *Report of the Committee to Consider the Future Numbers of Medical Practitioners and the Appropriate Intake of Medical Students* (Chairman, Sir Henry Willink), HMSO, London, 1957.

12. Elizabeth Shore, *Medical Manpower Planning,* Health Trends, 1974, Vol. 6, p.32.

13. Great Britain. Ministry of Health. *First Report of the Joint Working Party on the Organisation of Medical Work in Hospitals,* HMSO, London, 1967.

14. Great Britain. Department of Health and Social Security. *Second Report of the Joint Working Party on the Organisation of Medical Work in Hospitals,* HMSO, London, 1972.

15. Great Britain. Department of Health and Social Security. *Third Report of the Joint Working Party on the Organisation of Medical Work in Hospitals,* HMSO, London, 1974.

16. Quoted from the introduction to the Standing Orders, in Wilfrid H. Parry, 'Community Medicine', *Community Health* (1972), 4, p.23.

17. Great Britain. Department of Health and Social Security. *Report of the Working Party on Medical Administrators* (Chairman, Dr R.B. Hunter), HMSO, London, 1972.

18. Great Britain. Ministry of Health and Department of Health for Scotland. *Report of the Inter-Departmental Committee on the Remuneration of General Practitioners* (Chairman, Sir Will Spens), HMSO, London, 1946, (Cmd. 6810).

19. Ibid., p.10, para. 12.

20. Great Britain. Parliament. *Royal Commission on Doctors' and Dentists' Remuneration* (Chairman, Sir Harry Pilkington), HMSO, London, 1960 (Cmnd. 939).

21. Ibid., p.145, para. 428.

22. In fact a total of 17,800 forms were eventually returned.

23. British Medical Association, 'A Charter for the Family Doctor Service', *British Medical Journal,* 18 March 1965, No. 3138, p.89.

24. Great Britain. Parliament. Review Body on Doctors' and Dentists' Remuneration. *Twelfth Report* (Chairman, Lord Kindersley), HMSO, London, 1970 (Cmnd. 4352).

25. Great Britain. Parliament. Review Body on Doctors' and Dentists' Remuneration (Chairman, Lord Halsbury), *Fourth Report,* HMSO, London, 1974 (Cmnd. 5644).

26. Great Britain. Parliament. Review Body on Doctors' and Dentists' Remuneration. *Supplement to the Fourth Report*, HMSO, London, 1974 (Cmnd. 5849).

27. Great Britain. Parliament. Review Body on Doctors' and Dentists' Remuneration (Chairman, Sir Ernest Woodroofe), *Fifth Report*, HMSO, London, 1975 (Cmnd. 6032).

CHAPTER 6

1. Great Britain. Parliament. *Royal Commission on Doctors' and Dentists' Remuneration* (Chairman, Sir Harry Pilkington), HMSO, London, 1960 (Cmnd. 939).

2. Great Britain. Ministry of Health and Department of Health for Scotland. *Report of the Inter-Departmental Committee on the Remuneration of General Dental Practitioners* (Chairman, Sir Will Spens), HMSO, London, 1948 (Cmd. 7402).

3. Great Britain. Parliament. *National Health Service Act, 1946,* HMSO, London, 1946, 9 & 10 Geo. 6. Ch 81, Section 41(4).

4. Great Britain. Parliament. *Health Services and Public Health Act, 1968,* HMSO, London, 1968, Chapter 46.

5. Great Britain. Ministry of Health and Department of Health for Scotland. *Statutory Registration of Opticians;* Interdepartmental Report (Chairman, Lord Crook), HMSO, London, 1952 (Cmd. 8531).

6. Great Britain. Department of Health and Social Security. *Statement Specifying Fees and Charges for the Testing of Sight and the Supply or Repair of Glasses,* HMSO, London.

7. Great Britain. Department of Health and Social Security. *Report of the Inquiry into the Prescription Pricing Authority* by R.I. Tricker, HMSO, London, 1977.

8. Great Britain. Department of Health and Social Security. Scottish Office and Welsh Office, *Report of the Working Party on the Hospital Pharmaceutical Service* (Chairman, Sir Noel Hall), HMSO, London 1970.

9. Great Britain. Ministry of Health, *Final Report of the Committee on the Cost of Prescribing* (Chairman, Sir Henry Hinchliffe), HMSO, London, 1959.

10. The reference to overseas prices actually favoured the UK industry since its prices in the home market were comparatively lower.

11. In at least one case, the supplies were found to fall short of expected standards.

12. Great Britain. Parliament. *Report of the Committee of Enquiry into the Relationship of the Pharmaceutical Industry with the National Health Service 1965-1967* (Chairman, Lord Sainsbury), HMSO, London, 1967 (Cmnd. 3410).

13. It is the view of some observers (and notably those connected with the pharmaceutical industry) that the setting up of the Sainsbury Committee was a politically motivated act, and that the Report itself reflected political rather than economic arguments.

14. See, for example: Runnymede Research Limited, *Competition, Risk and Profit in the Pharmaceutical Industry*. The Association of the British Pharmaceutical Industry, London, 1975.

CHAPTER 7

1. Quoted in: A.M. Carr-Saunders and P.A. Wilson, *The Professions*, Cass, London, 1933. p.118 (from Elizabeth Haldane, 'The British Nurse in Peace and War', 1923).
2. Great Britain. Parliament. *Local Government Act, 1929*, 19 Geo. 5, Ch. 17, HMSO, London, 1929.
3. Great Britain. Ministry of Health and Scottish Home and Health Department. *Report of the Committee on Senior Nursing Staff Structure* (Chairman, B. Salmon), HMSO, London, 1966.
4. Quoted in: A.M. Carr-Saunders and P.A. Wilson, op. cit., p.122 (from Emma Brierly, 'In The Beginning', 1924).
5. Great Britain. National Board for Prices and Incomes. *Pay of Nurses and Midwives in the National Health Service*, Report No. 60, HMSO, London, 1968 (Cmnd. 3585).
6. Great Britain. Department of Health and Social Security. Scottish Home and Health Department. Welsh Office. *Report of the Working Party on Management Structures in the Local Authority Nursing Services* (Chairman, E.L. Mayston), 1969.
7. Great Britain. Department of Health and Social Security. *Report of the Committee of Inquiry into Pay and Related Conditions of Service of Nurses and Midwives* (Chairman, Lord Halsbury), HMSO, London, 1974 (Supplement to the Report published in 1975).
8. T.W. Matthews, 'The Panel of Assessors for District Nurse Training', *Queen's Nursing Journal*, Vol. 17, No. 12, March 1975, p.256.
9. Great Britain. Parliament. *Report of the Committee on Nursing* (Chairman, Professor Asa Briggs), HMSO, London, 1972 (Cmnd. 5115).

CHAPTER 8

1. Great Britain. Ministry of Health. Department of Health for Scotland. *Medical Auxiliaries*, Reports of the committees (Chairman, Dr V. Zachary Cope), HMSO, London, 1950 (Cmd. 8188).
2. The effect of making state registration a requirement of employment in the NHS is a valuable asset to these professions. It protects their name and educational standards, and also safeguards patients' interests.
3. Great Britain. Department of Health and Social Security. *Management Arrangements for the Reorganised National Health Service*, HMSO, London, 1972, p.84.
4. Great Britain. Department of Health and Social Security. *The Organisation of the Dietetic Service within the National Health Service*. Health Service Circular (Interim Series) HSC(IS)56, DHSS, London, July 1974.
5. Great Britain. Department of Health and Social Security. *Report of the Committee of Inquiry into the Pay and Related Conditions of Service of the Professions Supplementary to Medicine and Speech Therapists* (Chairman, Lord Halsbury), HMSO, London, 1975.
6. Great Britain. Department of Health and Social Security, Scottish Home and Health Department, Welsh Office. *Statement by the Committee on the Remedial Professions* (Chairman, Professor Sir Ronald Tunbridge), HMSO, London, 1972.
7. The Council for Prefessions Supplementary to Medicine, *Report and Recommendations of Remedial Professions Committee*, CSPM, London, 1970.
8. Great Britain. Department of Health and Social Security. *The Remedial Professions*, a report by a working party (Chairman, E.L. McMillan), HMSO,

London, 1973.
9. Great Britain. Department of Health and Social Security. *The Remedial Professions and Linked Therapies,* Health Service Circular (Interim Series) HSC(IS)101, DHSS, London, December 1974; and Great Britain. Department of Health and Social Security. *Occupational Therapists: Joint Review by Area Health Authorities and Local Authorities,* Health Service Circular (Interim Series) HSC(IS)102, DHSS, London, December 1974.
10. Great Britain. Department of Education and Science. *Speech Therapy Services,* Report of the Committee appointed by the Secretaries of State (Chairman, Professor Randolph Quirk), HMSO, London, 1972.
11. Great Britain. Department of Health and Social Security. *Speech Therapy Services: Interim Guidance* Health Service Circular (Interim Series) HSC(IS)22, DHSS, London, April 1974.
12. See Note 5.
13. Great Britain. Department of Health and Social Security, Scottish Home and Health Department. *Hospital Scientific and Technical Services.* Report of the Committee 1967-68 (Chairman, Sir Solly Zuckerman), HMSO, London, 1968.
14. Great Britain. Department of Health and Social Security, Welsh Office, *Hospital Laboratory Services,* Hospital Memorandum HM(70)50, DHSS, London, August 1970.
15. Great Britain. Department of Health and Social Security. *Organisation of Scientific and Technical Services,* Health Service Circular (Interim Series) HSC(IS)16, DHSS, London, April 1974.
16. Great Britain. National Board For Prices and Incomes. *The Pay and Conditions of Manual Workers in Local Authorities, the National Health Service, Gas and Water Supply,* Report No. 29, HMSO, London, 1967 (Cmnd. 3230).
17. Great Britain. National Board For Prices and Incomes. *The Pay and Conditions of Service of Ancillary Workers in the National Health Service,* Report No. 166, HMSO, London, 1971 (Cmnd. 4644).
18. Great Britain. Parliament. *A Hospital Plan for England and Wales,* HMSO, London, 1962 (Cmnd. 1604).
19. Great Britain. Ministry of Health, Scottish Home and Health Department. *Report of the Study Group on the Grading, Training and Qualifications of Hospital Engineers* (Chairman, Major-General Sir Leslie Tyler), HMSO, London, 1962.
20. Great Britain. Department of Health and Social Security. Scottish Home and Health Department. Welsh Office. *Hospital Building Maintenance;* Report of the Committee 1968-70 (Chairman, D. Woodbine Parish), HMSO, London, 1970.
21. Great Britain. Department of Health and Social Security. *Management Arrangements; Works Staff Organisation and Preparation of Substantive Schemes,* NHS Reorganisation Circular HRC(74)37, DHSS, London, October 1974.
22. *Hospital Building Notes, Hospital Technical Memoranda, Estmancode, Capricode, Data Sheets, Cost Allowance Guidance* and *Adapted Needleman Formula* are some of the titles. They are prepared and revised by the DHSS which distributes most of them; others are available through HMSO.
23. Great Britain. Ministry of Health, *Report on the Grading Structure of Administrative and Clerical Staff,* Sir Noel Hall, HMSO, London, 1957.
24. Great Britain. Parliament. *Report of the Committee of Inquiry into the Recruitment, Training and Promotion of Administrative and Clerical Staff in the Hospital Service* (Chairman, Sir Stephen Lycett Green), HMSO, London, 1963.
25. Great Britain. Nurses' Salaries Committee. First Report. *Salaries and*

Emoluments of Female Nurses in Hospitals (Chairman, Lord Rushcliffe), HMSO, London, 1943 (Cmd. 6424).

26. Great Britain. Scottish Nurses' Salaries Committee. *Interim Report* (Chairman, Professor T.M. Taylor, later, Lord Guthrie), HMSO, London, 1943 (Cmd. 6425).

27. National Joint Council for Staffs of Hospitals and Allied Institutions in England and Wales (Chairman, Sir George Mowbray).

28. Great Britain. Ministry of Health. Hospital Memoranda: RHB(51)80; HMC(51)73; BG(51)77, Ministry of Health, London, 1951.

29. Great Britain. Whitley Councils for the Health Service (Great Britain). General Council, Circular No. 118, DHSS, London, 1975.

30. Great Britain. Department of Health and Social Security. *Making Whitley Work,* by Lord McCarthy, DHSS, London, 1976.

CHAPTER 9

1. Great Britain. Department of Health and Social Security. Health Services Development. *Cash Limits and the Health Capital Programme: Revised Definittion of Capital Spending.* Health Circular HC(77)6, DHSS, London, March 1977.

2. Robert Maxwell, *Health Care, the Growing Dilemma,* McKinsey and Company, Inc., London, 1974.

3. Great Britain. Parliament. *National Health Service Reorganisation: England,* HMSO, London, 1972 (Cmnd. 5055), p.40, para. 160.

4. RAWP was set up by the DHSS in 1975. It produced an Interim Report later that year and a further report in Autumn 1976 called *Sharing Resources for Health in England* (HMSO). The 1976 report contained the formula for redistributing both capital and revenue resources, and it also included a basis for calculating the extra allocations for clinical teaching and research. The report stressed that RHAs should in turn adopt the overall principles when calculating their allocations to the areas and districts, so that relative need for health services within the populations concerned was kept as the guiding theme.

5. The detail of the RAWP formula has however met with some criticism that it fails to measure 'need' for health services accurately enough, particularly if it is to be used exactly as set out in the report for calculating area and district allocations. In addition, distribution of GP services (the responsibility of the Medical Practices Committee) is not covered by RAWP or the planning system, although it is known to be a key to the level of use of hospital and community resources. Until the MPC becomes more effective or GPs are brought into the planning system, the assumptions of the RAWP formula may be inadequate, even though they are currently the best available.

6. Great Britain. Department of Health and Social Security. *Management Arrangements for the Reorganised National Health Service,* HMSO, London, 1972, p. 57, para. 3.42a.

7. Great Britain. General Register Office. Studies on Medical and Population Subjects No. 14. *Morbidity Statistics from General Practice,* HMSO, London 195. Great Britain. Office of Population Censuses and Surveys. *Morbidity Statistics from General Practice; Second National Study 1970-71,* Studies on Medical and Population Subjects No. 26, HMSO, London, 1974.

8. H.C. Salter in: M.M. Hauser (ed.), *The Economics of Medical Care,* Allen and Unwin, London, 1972.

CHAPTER 10

1. Great Britain. Department of Health and Social Security. *Democracy in the National Health Service,* HMSO, London, 1974.
2. Great Britain. Department of Health and Social Security. Welsh Office. *Report of the Committee on Hospital Complaints Procedure* (Chairman, Sir Michael Davies), HMSO, London, 1973.
3. A. Yarrow, 'Health Education in the Re-Organised Health Service', *Health Trends,* Vol. 6, 1974, p.12.
4. Great Britain. Parliament. *Preventive Medicine.* First Report from the Expenditure Committee, Session 1976-77. HMSO, London, 1977 (H.C. 196-i).
5. Great Britain. Parliament. *Safety and Health at Work,* Report of the Committee 1970-72, HMSO, London, 1972 (Cmnd. 5034).
6. *With Us in Mind,* MIND and Community Service Volunteers, London, 1975.
7. Great Britain. Department of Health and Social Security. Welsh Office. *Better Services for the Mentally Handicapped,* HMSO, London, 1971 (Cmnd. 4683) and Great Britain. Department of Health and Social Security. *Better Services for the Mentally Ill,* HMSO, London, 1975 (Cmnd. 6233).
8. M.H. Pappworth, *Human Guinea Pigs; Experimentation on Man,* Routledge and Kegan Paul, London, 1967.
9. Great Britain. Department of Health and Social Security. Welsh Office. Health Service Circular (Interim Series) HSC(IS)153. *Supervision of the Ethics of Clinical Research Investigations and Fetal Research,* DHSS, London, 1975.
10. Great Britain. Ministry of Health. Reports on Public Health and Medical Subjects No. 112. *Deformities caused by Thalidomide,* HMSO, London, 1964.
11. Henry Miller, *Medicine and Society,* Oxford University Press, London, 1973, p. 62.
12. Lee Donaldson Associates, *UK Private Medical Care; Provident Schemes Statistics 1974,* Lee Donaldson Associates, London, 1975.

APPENDIX 1

1. Great Britain. Scottish Home and Health Department. *Administrative Reorganisation of the Scottish Health Services,* HMSO, Edinburgh, 1968.
2. Great Britain. Scottish Home and Health Department. *Reorganisation of the Scottish Health Services,* HMSO, Edinburgh, 1971 (Cmnd.4734).
3. Great Britain. Scottish Home and Health Department. *The National Health Service and the Community in Scotland,* HMSO, Edinburgh, 1974.
4. In most areas, the Chairman and Vice-Chairman of the medical advisory committee do attend Area and District Executive Group meetings. The difference, however, is that they have no responsibility to represent their professional view since they are not actually part of the decision-making process.

INDEX

Accounting system (NHS), 185-6
Addison, Dr Christopher, 231
Administrative staff, **142**, 157-60,
 180, 212
Ambulance service, 41, 62, 144
Ancillary staff, **142**, 153-5, **154**, **180**
Apothecaries Act (1815), 88, 115
Appointment system, 95-7, 98
Area Administrator, 60, **61**, 61-2, 66,
 73
Area Boards, 20, 22, 49
Area Chemist Contractors Committee,
 119
Area Dental Committee, 110, *see also*
 Professional Advisory Committee
Area Dental Officer, 64, 110
Area Executive Group, 219-22
Area Health Authority, **25**, 26, 27
 41, 47, Ch.3 passim, 68, 72, 73,
 83, 84, 94, 110, 115, 116, 131,
 135, 150, 163, 174, 191, 192,
 193, 197, 208-9, 210-11
Area Health Authority Chairman, 57,
 59, 73
Area Health Authority members, 57-60
Area Health Authority (Teaching),
 55-6, 57, 110
Area Health Board (Scotland),
 Appendix 1 passim.
Area Health Education Officer, 65, 197
Area Management Team, 68, *see also*
 Single district areas
Area Medical Officer, 60-1, **61**, 65,
 74, 102, 197
Area Nursing Officer, 60-1, **61**, 64,
 133, 136
Area Optical Committee, 115, *see
 also* Professional Advisory
 Committees
Area Pharmaceutical Committee, 119,
 see also Professional Advisory
 Committees
Area Pharmaceutical Officer, 62, 77,
 116, 118, 119
Area Scientific Committee, 153
Area Specialists in Community
 Medicine, 63, 64, 74, 82, 102-3
Area Speech Therapist, 150
Area Team of Officers, 57, 60-2, **61**,
 68, 73, 84, 133, 210, 219-22
Area Treasurer, 60-1, **61**
Area Works Officer, 62, 76
Armed forces, 19

Association of Dispensing Opticians,
 114
Association of Scientific, Technical
 and Managerial Staffs, **158-9**
Association of the British
 Pharmaceutical Industry, 121-2
Audiology technicians, 144, **152**

Barber, Anthony, 231
Bevan, Aneurin, 16, 17, 187, 231
Beveridge report, 15, **179**
Blood transfusion service, 14, 17, 41,
 180
Board of Governors, 16, **18**, 19, 21,
 54, 59, 163
Board of Guardians, 11, 14
Board of Management, 216
Board of Registration of Medical
 Auxiliaries, 143, 144, 145, 149
Boer War, 12
Bonham-Carter report, 21, 38
Boundaries, 23, 41, **42**, 50, **52**, 68,
 69, 86, **220**, 235n
Bradbeer report, 38
Briggs report, 137-41
British Association of Occupational
 Therapists, 147
British Dental Association, 108,
 110-11
British Dietetic Association, 146
British Medical Association, 13, 15,
 16, 17, 49, 89, 90, 94, 97, 103-6,
 113, 143, 144, 227
British Optical Association, 113, 114
British Orthoptic Council, 149
British United Provident Association,
 207
Broadmoor, 200
Brown, Ernest, 15, 231
Budgets, *see* Planning cycle
Building, *see* Works

Cabinet, 29, 30, 172-3
Capital expenditure, 167-70, **169**,
 171, 176-9, **178**
Castle, Barbara, 26, 57-8, 140, 231
Central Committee for Hospital
 Medical Services, 90
Central Council for Nurses, Midwives
 and Health Visitors, 138, 140
Central Council for the Education
 and Training of Social Workers,
 128

247